Promises

Drifters, Book Two

SUSAN RODGERS

*F*or my parents, Thomas and Rosaleen Mahoney
And for Joe, Shawna and Kathy
Growing up was fun with you as my companions.

*A*lso for Prince Edward Island, Canada,
a magical place where many wonderful stories are born each day.

Contents

"*L*ove is a promise, love is a souvenir,
once given never forgotten, never let it disappear."
—JOHN LENNON

Chapter One

What's really marvelous about the Orpheum Theater in Vancouver is the grand old theater's history. Its lush interior of ivory, moss green, gold and burgundy trim, grand columns and meandering staircases all lend it a sincere and delicate beauty. The time in which the theater was built, what it was originally intended for—1927, Vaudeville—still holds its audiences under a spell, audiences who are happy to partake of shows in the grand old dame's belly but who don't care to look for her cracks.

Artists relish the opportunity to perform at the Orpheum—Jessie Wheeler included. The spectacular vintage theater is a survivor, just like Jessie. In 1973, the old place that had housed a multitude of artists and shows and even films for a time was scheduled for a gutting in favor of a cinema multiplex. But a public protest saved the aged girl. Jessie and her audiences have become a part of her tapestry, new threads in the storied history of a true and noble fighter.

This fall Jessie's mini-tour, comprised of eight knock 'em dead high-energy shows, was kicking off at the stately timeworn Orpheum. Besides giving audiences a taste of fresh music from the new album, the primary purpose was to raise funds for the shelters Jessie and Deirdre were building in North American cities in memory of Jessie's young friend Terri. At least, that's what the public believed. Dee had ulterior motives as well. She was working on a damage control mission with the Keating publicist, Janet, a dynamic git 'er done dyed blonde in her early fifties.

No doubt about it, cracks had been peeking through the singer's façade. But most of Jessie's fans, like the audiences at the Orpheum, didn't bother to

1

look very deeply. Any image damage likely inflicted by calling off her engagement to the suave and popular Charlie Deacon was skin deep, at most. The people loved Jessie Wheeler, and were aware of Charlie's indiscretions. The break-up was credited equally to both parties, cited as mutual irreconcilable differences, so the blame was parceled out to both. Canada and the world did not get to experience the Canadian version of the long awaited "royal wedding". Charlie did not publicly blame Jessie for their break-up, and Jessie didn't point fingers at Charlie and his philandering. So the fans expecting a glamorous break in their routines were left somewhat wanting, but with no one in particular to blame. The deepest crack was there, hidden, yet to be revealed, and Dee was on a tear to prevent its opening or, at the very least, to soothe it with the sweetest balm she could find.

She put Jessie on the stage.

Late on a sultry Friday afternoon, the last week of August, the dance company, musicians, technicians and Jessie were slogging it out at the Orpheum, rehearsing the show. At the end of a fast paced dance number, sweaty and tired from the long day's demanding schedule, Jessie limped downstage and bent over to accept notes from Priya, her Canadian born Indian choreographer. Wiping beads of sweat off her brow with a small white towel that was already dripping wet, Jessie inclined her head and listened carefully to the lithe dancer whose refined black hair was tied back in braids, and who had approached from the empty seats where she was analyzing the show. As Jessie and Priya discussed the number, the rest of the dancers took a well-deserved break. Kayla Sawyer took the opportunity to grab her water bottle from the wings. She had refilled it numerous times over the day—dancing in Jessie Wheeler's troupe was greatly satisfying, but was arduous work.

At the same time Kayla raised her green bottle and reveled in a long drink, excess drops spilling from the corners of her thirsty lips, the slim pony-tailed twenty-five-year-old spotted a dark figure standing at the back of the house. Silhouetted by light shining into the darkened theater from the windows in the lobby behind, the vague shape was leaning against the doorframe, watching, hands thrust in the pockets of faded denims. Regardless of the fact that she couldn't see him well, Kayla knew instantly it was her brother Josh. There could be no doubt—he stood with his shoulders just a little bit forward, feet apart and toes turned slightly inward. Besides, he was supposed to pick her up right about now. They were going to dinner with Kayla's new boyfriend, Paul.

Exuberant, Kayla waved and smiled at the same moment Jessie wrapped up her chat with the choreographer who, clipboard in hand, wandered back to her seat to make some notes. As Jessie stood, Josh moved and the light at the top of the aisle shifted, catching her eye. She glanced up. There he was, as unmistakable to her as to his sister. Josh, the man she'd last seen two months ago at the *Drifters* wrap party in the arms of a teenage starlet—sloshed, wasted. Josh, the man she'd fallen in love with—the reason Charlie released her from their engagement.

After a week of heady high-spirited days in rehearsal, Jessie's arms felt like lead weights, but she managed to lift a silent hand in greeting. She couldn't bring herself to smile. It was enough of a shock just seeing him there, although running into him now that she was back in Vancouver was inevitable. Whether or not Jessie signed on to season two of *Drifters*, the film and artistic community was inextricably intertwined. There would be screenings, premieres, fundraisers and social events that both Jessie and Josh would be attending. He would be impossible to avoid.

Josh, with his typical vintage flair, had topped the jeans with a western style checked yellow 1970's long sleeved shirt with chest pockets and pearl snaps. Always the timeless guy Jessie found in Charlie's garbage, he sauntered carelessly down the aisle between rows of worn ageless red velvet seats. Undoubtedly the old theater had played host to a number of love affairs in her lifetime—if she could talk, oh, the stories she would tell of the folks who had sat in the womb of her cherished red velvet, or who had lit up the stage. This meeting too, between a simple man and woman, would go down in the storied annals of the theater's romantic past.

Jessie jumped off the stage and waited for Josh, one booted foot placed on the other, toes in, so that they formed an L. Her back was to the stage, and she was leaning on her elbows. She had twisted her light copper-accented brown hair up into a bun, but the heavy dancing had loosened some strands, which fell lazily around her blushing pink cheeks. Tight jeans were tucked into her favorite embroidered dusty brown cowboy boots; on top she wore an eighteenth century style white linen blouse with a drawstring neck, and overtop that a corresponding baby blue mid-thigh length brocade jacket with wide umbrella sleeves, a knock-off of the one John Lennon wore when he recorded *All You Need Is Love*. Jessie was a John Lennon fan from way back— she got a kick out of incorporating his wardrobe into her shows.

Josh couldn't help but grin as he got closer. He came to a halt four feet away and critically regarded her, head tilted to the side so the straggly lock of hair that always fell in front of his ear and graced his high cheekbone did just that, tantalizingly. Jessie's heart was pounding. She pressed her forearms more firmly onto the stage so he couldn't detect that his presence unnerved her.

"Is there a vampire number in the show?" he asked, gesturing towards Jessie's John Lennon jacket and white linen blouse with a mischievous glint in his eyes. Pink cheeks growing even rosier, she glanced at her toes before meeting Josh's soulful chocolate eyes.

"It's a Civil War number. I had to rehearse in this outfit today so I would know whether it gets in the way. The dancing, right?"

"Looks hot." Then it was his turn to blush as he realized what he'd said. He got a reprieve from his embarrassment when Kayla bounced over and treated her older brother to a generous hug.

"Josh! I never see you!" She whipped around to face Jessie. "Big brother is taking me and my new man to dinner. You should come!"

Jessie froze as Josh eyed her questioningly.

"I was actually thinking of asking you, even though I know you're busy with the new show and all that…but I figured you have to eat sometime, right?"

Smiling happily, Kayla seized the moment. "Come on, Jess. Paul would be beside himself if he got to meet you. And anyways he's a lawyer. We can talk about more than just motorcycles and cars and horses."

"You're sure?" Jessie asked, peeking up at Josh. It was common knowledge that over the summer her co-star had been seeing Leeza, the young actor who entertained him at the *Drifters* wrap party last June. Jessie wasn't sure how much more time she could spend in his company and not be his.

He shrugged his shoulders and nodded casually, hoping she couldn't detect his quickening heartbeat. "We're going somewhere in Kits. Somewhere quiet."

"Maybe somewhere Irish pub-bey," Kayla tossed in as she turned to go. "I'm off to shower. I've lost ten pounds in sweat since I started on this show. Meet you back out here? Assuming rehearsal's wrapped?" she asked Jessie, who nodded just as Priya called, "That's a wrap, everybody."

As Kayla skipped off to her dressing room she glanced back at Jessie, who was peering at Josh rather intently, she thought. The singer had crossed her arms in front of her body and seemed curious about something.

"I guess we do have some stuff to talk about," Jessie was saying to Josh.

Tilting one black-booted ankle over on its side, Josh shoved his hands back in his pockets. "Like what?" He grinned again—that lopsided half-smile that Jessie wanted to swallow up.

She stepped forward and grabbed his left elbow, placed his arm around her waist, then reached for his right arm and did the same. Jessie wrapped her own arms around his shoulders, then squeezed, held on tight, and sighed.

"Stuff," she said into the cozy hollow between Josh's shoulder and neck.

He closed his eyes and held her close, breathing in the musky damp scent of her sweat-soaked jacket. "Why, Miss Jessie Wheeler. If I didn't know better, I'd think you've been missing me."

Jessie lingered there for a moment without responding until finally she dared to peek up from underneath long eyelashes. Josh spied the ice-blue eyes that never failed to take his breath away.

"Josh," she said. And that was it, just his name, although it was so much more than that—it was hope and reconciliation and love and friendship, all wrapped into one.

He brushed wet strands of hair out of her eyes and kissed her forehead. "Okay little one," he said. "I've missed you too." Then, tenderly, "Go have your shower. I'll see you back here in a bit."

Pulling away, she smiled mischievously up at him. "Who says I need a shower?" She waved her arms out to the sides as she backed up, so that the sleeves of the rich brocade jacket fell open. Jessie looked like a human cross standing there like that. A sacrificial totem.

Josh put a thumb and finger on his nose, teasing. Then he grabbed her one more time and squeezed tight.

"Jessie Wheeler," he whispered into her ear, "you will be the death of me."

Josh felt a shiver course through Jessie's body. He released her, shocked at the sudden extreme fear that zigzagged across her face. He touched her cheek with his fingertips and then let his palm rest there.

"Hey," he said. "It's just an expression. That's all." She tried to smile but couldn't. Was that a sign that she needed to keep her distance from him? Was the universe trying to tell her something?

Nervously Jessie swallowed, turned on her heel, and then held five fingers up behind her as she walked towards the stairs on the side of the stage. "Five minutes," she said.

He watched her walk away. *What the hell was that about?*

Jessie Wheeler was indeed a mystery. Josh knew there were obscure aspects about her past that she never seemed willing to discuss. He understood they were dark—sinister perhaps—and that they pertained to life as a teen runaway in South Carolina. He could imagine what kind of things might happen to a sweet young girl on her own in a large city, although he generally pushed those thoughts away when contemplating Jessie's past misfortunes, mainly because they were too painful to bear thinking about. He would do anything to protect Jessie, and the thought that she'd been hurt so badly she could never speak of it except in the most vague terms—well that was too much. Maybe someday she would open up—if he could keep her in his life.

That was the thing—Josh was pushed to come here tonight. He had asked Kayla out to dinner on the pretense of meeting her boyfriend, but the real reason was that his cast mates on *Drifters*, Jessie's friends as well, were tired of waiting for her decision on whether she'd be shooting season two with them when the show started up again. She was the last holdout. Everyone else had signed. What was she waiting for, more money she didn't need? Knowing Jessie, they doubted it. A good portion of her earned income went to charity. Money—its inequality and the toils it expended on many because of its lack—took a back seat in Jessie's life.

Easing comfortably into a ghost-worn velvet viewpoint in the historic theater, Josh watched as a few of the dancers stayed late to review a part of the Civil War choreography. Intrigued, his eyebrows furrowed as the athletic dancers, four men and three women, mimicked raising a flag amidst gunfire. Little did he know that soon he, too, would be fighting a major battle.

Crossing an ankle over one knee, hands clasped contentedly on his lap, Josh settled in to wait for his girls.

～⌒ ⌒～

After maneuvering her cherry red 1966 Mustang into the underground parking lot beneath her downtown condo, Jessie jumped into Josh's brand spanking new dark grey metallic King Ranch pick-up.

"Comfy," she grinned, wiggling her butt deeper into the roomy saddle-leather seat.

Chuckling, Josh shook his head and steered towards a new place in trendy Kitsilano—Liam's, an Irish pub where he knew Kayla would order a pint of Guinness so she could finger-draw a smiley face in the foam. Josh's sister didn't need to worry about calories when she was dancing with Jessie's company; all of the dancers burned more than they could consume.

Kayla's newly minted hipster boyfriend Paul was not tall. Also rather thin, he had what he referred to as a *Mother, Mother* haircut—long on the top and shorter on the sides—the same fashion as the lead singer of the popular band. Styled in an old army jacket with a red checked shirt underneath, skinny jeans, and black ankle boots, he looked like anything but the suited lawyer Josh and Jessie expected at dinner, but he was smart and funny and not cowed by Jessie's fame. They liked his good humor immediately and were happy for Kayla, who had been dredging the singles market for more than a few years.

Dinner was comfortable in the dark tavern with its warm ginger cushioned bench seating. Although both Josh and Jessie refrained from ordering alcohol, they indulged in traditional meals with homey, old-style Irish flair. Josh had coddle stew with plenty of bacon and sausage; Jessie used Kayla's dancer calorie rationalization and delighted in a rare treat of bangers and mash. The Pogues were piped over the speakers; Jessie closed her eyes and soaked up the lead singer's mournful, political lyrics. Infused with a traditional combination of tin whistle, mandolin and accordion, the music added to the cozy feel of the place.

"Did you know The Pogues' original band name, in English, meant kiss my arse?" Jessie decidedly told the group as she forked up biting hot gravy and mashed potatoes.

"That's nothing," Kayla responded, a happy grin creasing her face. "How's this grab you? Tony Flow and the Miraculously Majestic Masters of Mayhem!" Furrowing her brow, she eyed Paul thoughtfully. "Is that right?"

"What? Who?" Jessie interjected, her curiosity aroused.

"Yeah, that's it," Paul said knowingly to Kayla before leaning back in the bench seat, draping an arm lazily around his girlfriend, and grinning at Jessie. "The Red Hot Chili Peppers."

"Tell me you're joking," Jessie moaned before bursting into whole-hearted laughter. "The creators of one of the best songs to come out of the nineties? Under the Bridge? It just wouldn't have been the same." She wrinkled her nose in consternation. "But then again, who would have thought Red Hot Chili Peppers would ever be a cool band name?"

"It's the songs that make the band, not the other way around," Paul decreed.

"Yeah, but Tony Whatever and the Majestic Miraculous Whatsit Crazy Masters of Musical Chaos? Really?" Jessie said, highly entertained by the music biz inspired topic of conversation.

Josh leaned forward and tapped the table. "Try this one. What band was originally Starfish?"

Jessie pursed her lips thoughtfully. "Umm…that American band…from the South…Georgia, maybe. They played a song about music videos after radio or something…"

Kayla threw in, "What era? Guessing it wasn't Canada's own Blue Rodeo… they were probably oh, I don't know, Hoofprints or something…"

Paul jabbed her in the ribs. "Isn't that an ice cream flavor?"

"Oh yeah!" Kayla threw back her head and laughed heartily. "It's up there with Puppy Paws, my fave! Chocolate fudge and caramel cups, gotta love it."

"You'd eat anything with chocolate in it," Paul teased.

"Who wouldn't? It's one of the blessings of being female. Thank God we have that, considering all the other crap we have to deal with," she pouted.

"Hey, most women I know are treated like princesses, Kayla. That should be enough to make up for the other crap, as you call it."

"Ha. Nice try, Casanova. You wouldn't believe the dregs I dated before I found you."

"What are you trying to tell me, girlfriend? That I'm one in a million?

8

I'll take it." Paul's lips curled up in a mischievous grin as Kayla snuggled closer under his arm.

Smiling quietly in amused wonder at his sister's newfound happiness, Josh sat back as Paul ordered Kayla another frosty pint of Guinness. Glancing sideways at Jessie, he found himself reflected in her eyes, which were dancing with delight in the sheer joy of hanging out in the comfy Irish pub with good friends. He leaned in to her so that his forehead touched hers.

"Coldplay," he whispered conspiratorially, a thrill running up his spine when he felt a warm hand rest itself casually on his thigh. "Once known as Starfish."

"A-ha," Jessie responded happily, her eyes locked into Josh's soulful gaze. It took every bit of willpower she had in her not to lean forward, touch Josh's stubbly cheek with her fingertips, and press her soft lips to his. She shivered as a supercharged blue current ran on an unseen wire back and forth between them.

Eventually Kayla's infectious good humor called them back to attention, but Jessie let her hand stay where it was, lightly relaxed on Josh's faded denims and, after a bit, she thrilled to his touch when his strong fingers wrapped themselves gently around hers.

It was a fun evening, and although Jessie was sorry to see Josh's effervescent sister and her new beau make their exit, she and Josh had some serious discussions ahead of them, and the sun was already long gone to bed.

Josh paid the bill at the front cash and they left Liam's with promises to the star struck wait staff that they'd be back with friends in tow.

As he opened the pick-up's passenger door for Jessie, Josh asked hopefully, "Interested in a drive? Or do you have to get to rehearsal early tomorrow?"

Jessie climbed into the truck and settled herself comfortably on the leather seat. "I'm not in any hurry to get home. We're just scheduled for the afternoon tomorrow, since it's been a heck of a week. Everybody's tired." She was considerably more relaxed than when they arrived at the restaurant, as Kayla's irresistible sparkling nature and gentle sparring with Paul and Josh had eroded, in a good way, Jessie's nerves and discomfort.

Unable to resist a small victory smile as he closed the door, Josh walked around the back of the truck and slid in behind the wheel. If even for a short time, he now had Jessie to himself. He felt a little guilty knowing Stephen, Maggie, Carter and Sue-Lyn were likely sitting by their cells waiting for news on Jessie's involvement in season two. Discreetly, he'd turned off his phone earlier, while he was in the men's room at Liam's. He didn't want to be hounded for info before he was ready to respond.

Josh pointed the truck south towards Benny's, the abandoned ice cream place where he and his co-star really got to know each other last winter as they sat wrapped in a blanket sharing body heat and holding hands under the stars. Tonight's weather was just the opposite—it was a hot, hazy late August evening. He parked backwards so they could enjoy a view of the inky starlit Pacific Ocean, then Josh snuck a closer glimpse at Jessie.

She was nothing less than exquisite in a loose racer-backed light blue silk top over a blue bra. She had taken off the cowboy boots in favor of a strappy pair of wedge sandals—she loved the boots, but there were limits to how long one can endure sweaty, hot feet. The sandals were refreshing and cool, and Josh took sneak peeks at Jessie's painted burnt-orange toenails as she girl-ishly swung her feet back and forth off the tailgate of his truck.

Josh, in the timeless faded jeans Jessie loved best on him, sat next to her as they shared their stories of last summer.

"You'd like Prince Edward Island in the summertime," Jessie was saying. "As you're flying in you see this tremendous long thin span of concrete in the water. It's the Confederation Bridge that links the Island to the mainland in New Brunswick, it looks like some kind of gigantic water snake from the sky; it's quite something. It's, like, the longest bridge ever built over ice-covered waters—well, it used to be, I don't know if it still is. Who knows what's been built in the world since that bridge was constructed? Anyways I got in just before sunset, and between the water glistening and the miniature sailboats and the sun popping golden and pink off the bridge, it was breathtaking."

Jessie glanced over at Josh to see if he was listening—he was, attentively, his brown eyes jovial and optimistic.

She continued, "The Island itself seen from the sky is like a checker-board of greens and reds. A pastoral patchwork quilt, the locals say. Besides white sand beaches bordering the sandstone cliffs, there's lots of picturesque farmland with quaint old barns and fancy new barns and these sentimental cedar shingled and clapboard Victorian farmhouses…salt marshes…ocean coves…did I tell you the dirt roads are red there?"

He laughed at her exuberance. "No, Jessie. But I've heard that somewhere before. How red?"

"Like…a rusty color, I guess. I don't know. Red. The dirt roads are fun in the rain. The mud is thick and the puddles are endless. I feel sorry for dog owners who live along those old country roads. I can imagine what their floors look like after little Max and Shadow have been out exploring in the rain!" She knew she was rambling, but her nerves were increasing again now that she found herself alone with this man under peeling Benny's watchful eyes on the neglected sign above them. "Seriously, the unpaved roads are all red dirt. So are the fields after they've been plowed, before they're planted with potatoes, wheat, canola, barley…fields of gold, you know, like in that song by Sting. It's so cool." She sighed. "I would have liked to have shown it to you, my Island." Jessie looked down at her hands, which were folded in her lap.

Josh reached over and took her hand. They were those kinds of friends, the type that can touch and hold and hug and love without fear of judgment. Jessie cherished his simple gesture and pondered the way his sturdy hand felt between her fingers. She brushed a thumb along his and, in her heart, felt the pleasure of his touch. There were times in her life when she'd had nobody with whom to share that exquisite and often taken for granted basic necessity of life—the simple unfettered touch of another.

"Mostly I wrote songs for the new album I told you about those few times that you actually called me," she punched him lightly in the ribs, "but other times I just put on my floppy artist's hat and wandered into the Saturday morning Farmers' Markets for fresh veggies, and got ice cream at the dairy bars that are thriving in P.E.I., unlike poor Benny's here," she waved her hand back at the vacant building and its giant flaking and peeling Benny on the sign behind them, "and then other times I went swimming, or kayaking. I got to go to some campfires on the beach, too, which was nice. The lady who owns the house where I stayed has a big family that was home on vacation for the summer, and they just lived down the road, so that was fun. They were friendly, and were careful about who they told that I was around, so it was pretty cool, actually."

He brought up a difficult question. "Did you get to see your mother?" Josh studied her.

Jessie felt herself melting. What was it about this guy that she felt so comfortable talking to him about parts of her life she'd rather forget? She wondered if she would ever tell him about Charleston, about what happened to her there, to Sandy.

"I found her." Jessie leaned into his shoulder. "She and my dad were older when they had me, you know. I suppose that's why I never had any brothers or sisters. I think Mom was maybe forty-two or something. So she's like… seventy now." She paused, remembering the seniors' home where she found her mother a month before. "I just went to a neighbor's place, from when I used to live in our old house, my mom and dad and me. Wore the floppy hat," she said and laughed. "She had no idea I was the same Jessie Wheeler who sings some of her favorite ballads on the radio. She even commented on the coincidence that I shared the same name as someone famous. Anyways she made me tea and told me my ugly step-monster father died of cancer three years ago, and that my mom had been put into a home suffering from some kind of dementia, maybe early Alzheimer's, I don't think anyone really knows. So I tracked her down and there she was, my old mom, sitting in a rocking chair by a window in this institutional kind of place with people ten and twenty years older."

"Did she know you at all?"

"Nah. She talked about her daughter, though. As if I were still twelve. I tried to tell her who I was but it was pointless." She looked up into Josh's eyes. "I'm not convinced that she has Alzheimer's. I think she's just disappeared into that place where people go when they can't take anymore."

He leaned forward and kissed Jessie on the forehead. They'd had their own experiences with that kind of pain when Jessie's friend Terri was killed last June. Only, fortunately enough, Jessie had come out of it.

"Maybe it's genetic," she whispered.

"Well," he responded. "If it is, we'll just have to make sure you get a nice room with a view of the ocean." She laughed sadly and wrapped her arms around his waist. Josh tilted his forehead down to touch hers. "I'll bring you chicken soup."

"And flat whites from Rebel on a Mountain Coffee, right?" she inquired expectantly.

"I don't know about that. Caffeine might not be the best thing for you. Might get you excited."

Chuckling, Jessie added a postscript to her summer story. "I moved my mom from that place. I know they do a good job there, but I found a private care home by the ocean for her. It perked her up a little. A view of the ocean and all. I brought my dad's Gibson and played some of his old songs." She paused as she remembered her mom closing her eyes as tears trickled slowly down her cheeks.

She sighed.

"Those were the best years of her life, the ones with my dad. Not so sure about when I came along...maybe I have just always assumed I came between them, I don't know. He died driving home for my twelfth birthday party, too, so...well..."

"Jessie. It wasn't your fault. You didn't kill your dad."

"I know that, Josh, but still..she went to pieces after she lost him. It was like I didn't exist anymore. The thing that I will never know, though, is whether my leaving impacted her. Like Jackie, Terri's mom—she was broken when Terri ran away. But I'm not really sure if my own mom even noticed."

"Of course she did," he said softly. "How could anyone not notice if *you* were suddenly gone?"

"But Josh," she added, urgently. "What if she did notice, and that's what destroyed her mind?"

He paused. "What do you think she thinks about all the time?"

"My dad. His music."

He smiled down at her. "Then likely she is in the world where she wants to be. A better place, in her mind."

Jessie thought hard for a few moments as she watched the reflection of the starry night sky flicker in Josh's eyes. Not much wonder she loved this man. At some point, she was going to have to tell him that. And she decided that with the pressure of the *Drifters* contract on her mind, it should likely be now.

But first, a whisper. "How did you get so smart?"

He brushed his lips against her, in that place in the corner of her eye just

13

above her cheek, where friends can kiss friends without question. But it was killing Jessie. It was time to air the elephants in the room—or, under the sky. She took a deep breath.

"Okay," she said. "Your turn. How was the feature?"

"It rocked. It was cool to work with Wes Anderson. He's brilliant, not afraid to be eccentric, a little wacky. Woody Allen-esque. This film was his usual fare—an unconventional romantic comedy...lots of pesky mosquitos in the woods...it was hot...great cast and crew. Not as great as *Drifters*, though," he added with a grin. "That's a given."

"Cool. So you, uh, had a fun summer, it seems? You had company on set, all that jazz." She looked down, uncomfortable. Then back up at him with a smile as her hands rubbed his more profoundly. "Josh," she intoned quietly. "You were all over the rag bags. With Leeza. You know that."

He frowned as he realized their feet were entwined, her swinging legs propelling his from behind. "Jess, I don't know, it's not like it seemed. She showed up a few times, that's all. She's there twice, and all of a sudden to the tabloids it's a relationship."

Jessie's heart suddenly felt like a stone. She was afraid to breathe. "Is it? A relationship?"

He glanced over at her, sitting there next to him on the tailgate of his truck, her blue eyes searching his. Josh pulled his hands away from hers and jumped off the truck, and then stared at the sky before turning back to Jessie, facing her. He ran his fingers through his layered chestnut hair, and Jessie longed to jump up and do the same, but she would have to wait. Slipping her fingers underneath her butt so as to force herself not to reach out to him, Jessie swallowed nervously, but her eyes locked into his and she didn't waver. Enough wishy-washying around. She loved Josh, she had to tell him, and it was now or never, regardless of the consequences.

He skirted the issue, and her heart-stone sank.

"Jessie," he said. "Everyone wants to know what the hell's going on with season two. Why haven't you signed?"

This wasn't the response she expected. So—maybe he *was* still seeing Leeza. The gossip rags certainly seemed to think so. Jessie could feel a wetness pricking at her eyes. She stared at her colorful toenails, and realized she'd stopped swinging her feet. Slipping off the tailgate, she leaned away from him, her fingers gripping the edge of the truck. She would look like an idiot if she told him now, if he was still seeing that little tart. But she had a responsibility to Jonathon, the show's executive producer. He was losing patience, and she knew it. The show had to be defined, written, conclusions faced and characters given new storylines. That was getting harder to do the longer they waited for Jessie to make up her mind.

"Lordy, this is hard," she muttered under her breath.

Then Jessie drew herself up tall and dove in.

"Okay, Josh," she said. "Enough is enough. No more dicking around. Okay? Time for some honesty, for once?"

He tensed. Was this the last time he'd be alone with her? Was she leaving the show? Josh found himself staring at her, studying the blazing blue eyes intently, unable to look away.

Jessie exhaled, and then, "This is the thing. You remember season one and although it was surreal and fantastic, it was also hell. I can't do that again. I can't go through that agony again of touching you and being with you and of not *really* being with you, you know? Not again." The last few words came out in a whisper, as if she was afraid of what saying them at full volume might mean.

He shifted his weight. "Okay." He was thinking. "So, what, you're just going to run away and forget about all of us? About the incredible work we did, and Maggie and Sue-Lyn and Carter and Stephen...Pier, Jonathon, everyone? Go work alone again? Leave us all behind?"

She stood there with her feet planted in the dried up ground gaping at him, knowing what she needed to say but having no idea how to say it. Jessie was hurt that he mentioned running away—she knew she did that; she ran away and left her problems behind on occasion but really, truly, in her life she felt that was occasionally the only choice. Once again she glimpsed a flicker of understanding into her own mother.

Josh filled in the gaps. She had to turn her head so she could more easily hear him over the hushed beck and call of the nearby incessant waves. "You don't think I suffered too, Jessie? You don't think it was hell for me, too, to have to be with you all those months, to be your shoulder to cry on, but that was all? Knowing you were marrying Charlie? Knowing what you—." He stopped; bit his tongue. Josh couldn't say anything more.

"What I what, Josh? What were you going to say? What I really felt all that time?"

He paused awkwardly, and then ducked his head and toed at the dirt beneath his boot, his layered hair a cascading waterfall hiding a somewhat confused expression.

"Josh," she murmured. "I'm sorry I yelled at you at the wrap party."

That's it, he caught himself thinking. *She is getting ready to say her good-byes.* He forced himself to meet Jessie's solemn gaze.

"I deserved it," he said quietly.

She paused.

"Ahh. So you remember everything that happened—what I said to you."

He hesitated. "Yes."

"You were pretty out of it."

"No more out of it than you were in Ashland."

Shit. Ashland. He'd brought up Terri's funeral in Oregon.

"That's right, Josh. And I remember everything I said in Ashland, in the hotel room, after you—retrieved me from the bathtub." She changed her stance, summoned up her courage, and faced him square on. "And Josh, just so you know...I meant what I said."

He stared at her, afraid to comprehend—what it would mean, how things could change, and what a risk that would be, with her.

"Jessie," he breathed, aching for her to tell him more. Suddenly he, too, was desperate to know exactly where they stood. The thought of not having Jessie in his life at all was far worse than the idea of working with her while she kept herself at arm's length on a personal level.

"So the thing is," she went on, holding up her hand to stop him as he tried to speak. "I wasn't really expecting to see you tonight but here you are, and here I am. And the thing is that I feel like there's this little window of time opened up to us right now, and that it's going to close soon. And when it does, that's going to be the last chance for us, Josh, cause I am not sure if that window will ever open up again. Cause you will be out there doing *your* thing and I will be out there doing *my* thing and geez I think that will be it for us and I, for one, don't want to live my life with any more regrets and so this is the thing…"

She took a deep breath, swallowed past the lump of cotton in her throat, and dove in further, as he ceased breathing altogether.

"I know what I said that night in Ashland, and I meant it, and just so you're clear on this, that was the night things ended with Charlie because he had finally figured it out as well, and that thing is that, well…"

She blinked, summoning up the courage, begging her heart to stop threatening to leap out of her chest.

"I have loved you since the day I met you, Josh Sawyer. I have always loved you, and I don't see that ever changing and I am just wondering if, maybe, there might be a chance that you maybe feel the same way about me. And that's why I can't sign on to *Drifters* just yet, because until I know how you feel about me, and whether we have a chance together, I can't go back to that show and be with you and yet not *be* with you. I have endured a sweet lot of hell in my lifetime, and that is not one hell I care to repeat. I want all of you. *All of you.* All that *is* you, Josh. Or nothing."

Josh forgot about the hole he was digging in the dirt with the toe of his boot. He raised his chin and stared at Jessie for a bit, thinking. Lifting his hands up to his hips, he planted them squarely, so that the vintage yellow shirt wrinkled underneath his fingers. In consternation he tilted his head, trying to discern exactly what she was saying. He was speechless, afraid to say anything for fear of saying the *wrong* thing.

She jumped in again. Heck, Jessie was already over her head. What was a little more water when you felt like you might already be drowning?

"And just so you know, if you choose it, life with me will be hell for you because the paparazzi and the media will be all over us and all over you and they have the power to destroy us. And there will be times when that will really suck."

Josh bit his bottom lip as he stood there watching her. Awash with an exquisite bluish-white moonlight, Jessie was petulant, defiant, terrified and sweet all at once as she crossed and uncrossed her arms. Her shoulder length hair with the big curls at the ends was blowing in the light breeze, covering her eyes, which was frustrating Jessie as she swiped at it, although she didn't really seem to notice it, so caught up was she in him and in their little window.

"Well," he said reasonably, softly. "We could always fly to your magical Island and hide away." The sweet anticipation of that—extended time alone with this girl who stood apprehensively before him, in love with her and she with him—was more than he could bear, and finally he grinned. Jessie could see that Josh was playing her a little, standing over there four feet away looking sexy and adorable, pretending he was contemplating an offer to buy chocolate covered peanuts instead of raisins.

He tipped his ankle over again, punctuating an ever-widening grin.

Finally, an exquisitely relieved victor, Jessie blushed back at him. Josh covered the few unsteady steps that would seal their deal. Extending an arm, he grasped her hand and pulled his girl close.

"Of course," he whispered into her curls. "Of course I love you back, silly girl. I have always loved you too."

Tears were threatening Jessie's brave countenance. She had waited so long for this moment, for him to tell her that what she'd always wondered—believed—was true.

"Always?"

"Always. And forever. For always."

"I kinda thought maybe you did."

"You knew I did. All along." He was murmuring in her soft hair, kissing her forehead and cheeks by her eyes and then the hollow of her neck and soon her pink lips. Jessie was heartened that their truths had now extinguished all borders. His feathery kisses were free to land wherever they wanted.

Josh stopped planting a plethora of chaste kisses and gazed at his girl. Radiant and over-the-moon happy, Jessie swiped away at leaky tears with the back of her hand. With her thumbs she erased the wetness his joyful acceptance of her had leaked onto his lightly grizzled cheeks; then they climbed into the back of the new pick-up and christened it by making love on the old comforter that had held them in its warm embrace so many months before. As the twinkling stars winked in pleasure and continued on their everlasting journeys overhead, and the echoing waves kept up their haunting lilt on the moonlit shore below, Jessie pulled Josh to her, and the magic was complete.

Chapter Two

"*A*hhhh!"

Jessie screamed and ducked as a small lime green cushion with teal and brown stripes flew through the air, almost hitting her on the head. Squealing, she snatched the cushion and threw it back at her adversary, but Josh caught it, firing before she could duck behind the soft leather couch in his media room. It landed in the middle of her back. Propelled forward, the singer threw herself on her belly atop the couch, then grabbed the matching pillow and covered her head with it.

They were both laughing uncontrollably—it felt so damn good just to let go. After months of uncertainty and confused feelings, plus a summer apart, Jessie and Josh were downright joyous. Ecstatic since finally making their feelings known to each other last night—with the results for which each silently hoped—the pressure was off.

Now it was time to play.

The pillow fight started after a surreal night in each other's arms. The lovers drove to Josh's house in the early dawn after a night reacquainting their bodies in the bed of the pick-up. It was the most blissful, serene feeling either had ever experienced, although Jessie had fond, faded memories of her abbreviated time with Sandy. Like her first love, she and Josh were similar in their past hurts; they were two scarred people who hid their true selves from the world for so long that now they'd found each other, somehow the world was right again. The stars were once more aligned, and there was a strength and power in their 'two-ness' that would make the world easier to face, despite the certainty that the media would surely trounce Josh and Jessie's newfound togetherness once they caught on.

They'd had a few hours sleep in Josh's big comfy bed, although not nearly enough considering the demands of Jessie's very physical show rehearsal scheduled for that afternoon, plus she was expected at Charles and Dee's for dinner at eight that evening. But it would have to do—she'd get by on the adrenaline rush of being in love.

The first pillow had been tossed as they argued over one of the numbers in Jessie's show, the upbeat tune Josh watched from the entrance to the theater upon his arrival at the Orpheum the day before.

Each of Jessie's numbers in the show had a staged theme that included props, set decoration, and a costumed dance number. The Civil War number was the finale. She wrote the song years ago during her time in Charleston, and had only recently dug it out and fine-tuned it. The lyrics were about the futility of war—the ruthless violence and the willingness to lay aside social mores. In essence, the song was a metaphor for her life and the darkness she experienced at the hands of Deuce McCall in Charleston. It was a buoyant fast paced tune, a call to passive arms, and she sang it with passion and gusto, jumping and stamping her feet and raising her hands in a call to decisive yet non-violent action. Behind her, a multi-media presentation illustrated and accentuated the lyrics; dancers carried flags and prop muskets, and pyrotechnics flashed bright lights akin to gunfire. The number would be a fantastic whimsical emotional display at the Orpheum the following weekend.

There was one catch—being a Canadian with a newly indoctrinated interest in history, Josh wasn't well versed in the American Civil War, despite the fact that on *Drifters* he played a war veteran. But he had somewhere along the way, perhaps in a high school history class, thought he'd heard that the North had fired the first shots, the catalyst to the physical blow-up elevating decades old tensions in the Union. In fact, he was quite adamant about that. Jessie, who lived in Charleston for three years, knew otherwise. Playfully annoyed at his stubborn insistence, she pushed his buttons as they perused the DVD collection in the media room.

"Josh, I lived there, and believe it or not I checked out all of Charleston's amazing museums. I even did the silly touristy carriage ride tours." She blinked as she caught herself remembering Sandy and Rachel cozied alongside her on a bumpy carriage, the three of them laughing heartily and swapping jokes with the driver, a twenty something dark-haired girl with an enchanting Southern accent. Clad in Confederate grey, the girl occasionally dropped a marker on the streets when her big horse, Earl, decided to relieve himself. She told the kids it was protocol. Drivers marked the streets in order to ensure staff came along later to hose down the waste to reduce the *eau de Charleston*, as she called it. Jessie smiled in memory at the guffaws that drew from Sandy. She could remember her first boyfriend as clearly as if it were yesterday, sitting there in stitches next to her on the old cracked leather seat, teasing Rachel as they swayed gently from side to side with the motion of the carriage. The three musketeers shared a lot of laughs in those heady days.

Josh noticed a darkness wash across Jessie's face at the mention of living in Charleston, so he grabbed his girl around the waist and swung her around, then planted a big kiss on her pink lips. "The North fired first because they were hungry and short of supplies; they needed their supply ships to land safely at Fort Sumter."

Giggling, Jessie felt a lightness quickly return within her soul. God, how good it felt just to hold Josh, and to nuzzle in his neck. She sighed with pleasure. But she still had a point to make. "Josh. Beauregard fired first, at 4:30 a.m., because the South had heard there was a supply ship on its way down to Fort Sumter. And they didn't want the Union Blue reinforced in any way, shape or form. The North didn't fight back until like 7:30 or something, then there was, like, this long bombardment that lasted more than a day. Finally, the commanding officer at the fort surrendered. Anderson, I think, was his name. Google it."

Josh beamed and brushed his lips behind Jessie's ear. He inhaled deeply. She smelled of the lavender he remembered from months before. "Jessie," he said, without conviction. "I'm telling you, the North fired the first shots." But he knew he was wrong now—he was just enjoying teasing her, getting a rise out of her.

She withdrew from his strong embrace and crossed her arms, pouting. "Are you always going to be this stubborn?"

He paused, tilting his head and grinning at her. Then, quicker than lightning, he reached behind Jessie and grabbed the offending cushion. He held it up with both arms above and in front of his face, and then let a threatening growl erupt slowly. Spying his menacing look, Jessie screeched, turned and ran behind the couch, and the fight was on. They chased each other around the media room, laughing and just having fun, until the moment when Jessie threw herself on the couch in surrender.

Breathing heavily from the exertion, Josh lay down on top of her, then Jessie rolled over onto her back and they cuddled for a while as their breathing returned to normal. Josh took the opportunity to ask a question that had been on his mind for the past few months.

"Jessie," he said with the reverence the query deserved. "Since we've been talking about Charleston…at the cabin when Terri died, you told me someday you'd talk to me. About what happened there that made you leave. And never go back, from what I understand. You never play there, right?"

Lying there in his arms, Jessie felt as safe as she thought it would ever be possible to feel. He was strong, muscular…but Sandy had been, as well. Her old boyfriend had worked as a landscaper, and was tanned and robust.

"I don't know, Josh," she responded faintly. "Maybe one of these days." She couldn't look at him, and her stomach clenched with the terror of remembrance. She stared at a small crack in her new man's ceiling, the laughter gone as if it were the sun, and the memory an intrusive dismal grey cloud.

He grasped her chin in his big hand and turned her face so that she looked at him. "Jess," he said. "It's me you're talking to. You can tell me."

She smiled sadly and rewarded his patience with a lingering kiss on the lips. "Josh," she offered carefully. "It was bad, but it's over now. I lost people I loved—two people—a good friend, and my boyfriend at the time. I only survived because…" she blanched, recalling a terrible time in her life. "I think because the person who caused all the trouble thought death was too easy for me. That remembering would be the worst way he could torture me. And he was right. It's been ten years of remembering. Every day and every night. Every second of every day. My past holds me hostage, Josh."

"I get that, Jessie. There are things about my past that I don't like to think about either. We all have skeletons. And I recognize that yours are more frightening than most. But…maybe this isn't a burden you should be carrying alone." He paused. "Have you told Charles and Dee? Or ever gone to any counseling?"

"No." A whisper. "I just want to keep it to myself. And not worry anyone else. Especially Dee. Or you," she said, hooking her finger in a belt loop on his jeans.

"I've got news for you, Jessie. I love you, and I want to know everything about you. What desserts you like, what films you like to watch, your favorite color…" he softened, and ran a thumb over her cheek, "…what hurts my girl the most."

"Someday," she said. "Not now though, okay? I don't want to ruin what we've finally found by talking about something…someone…I lost years ago."

"Two people," he said tenderly, thinking about the extraordinary amount of pain this twenty-eight-year-old girl had apparently experienced in her lifetime.

"Yes," she said. Then, "Blue."

"Hmmmm?" he asked absently, kissing her neck.

"My favorite color. It's blue. But not just any blue. That indigo color the sky turns in late afternoon on a sunny summer day."

She could feel him smile, his lips at her neck, and she turned to face him, marveling in this exceptional man she loved from the moment she bent down to talk to him in Charlie's garbage. As they lay there and kissed, wrapped up in new love founded sincerely over time on deep friendship, Josh thought of another question he wanted to ask—about the man in the blue overcoat Jessie had asked him to speak to Charles about. He was wondering if anything came of that, and reminded himself to ask Charles what he and Matt found out about that club owner they looked into when they flew to Charleston in June.

But now was not the time. He felt bad for bringing up nasty memories for Jessie on their first full day as a couple.

As Jessie surrendered to the intensity of Josh's kisses, and then to the exquisite pleasure of the hand he slipped under the old T-shirt of his she threw on that morning, she thought briefly about the Civil War number from the show, and hoped that her own battles relating to Charleston were as done and gone as those of the haunted boys who'd fought for North and South many years ago.

Then she was lost in the glorious abyss of desire, and the last cohesive thought she recalled until later was one of gratitude that the evils of life were balanced with such exquisite, extraordinary beauty.

Josh dropped Jessie off at the Orpheum with a coffee in hand. He kissed her tenderly with regret that she had to go to work on their first day together. He worried she'd be exhausted by the time they showed up at Dee's dinner that evening, but she was a fighter; their discussion about Charleston had proven that about Jessie. Something wicked had happened in the great historic city, but she had survived—at least, a part of her survived. There was still a great sadness in Jessie, despite the deep love and joy he saw in her sea-pearl eyes last night and today.

Someday she'll tell me, he thought, as he watched her wave *So long* to him from the backstage door. In the meantime, he was off to find some flowers for the great and imposing Deirdre Keating.

Jessie's manager would be popping into rehearsal today, and Jessie planned to request an extra seat at the dinner table for the evening. Jonathon, *Drifters'* executive producer and the Keatings' friend, was going to be there with his glamorous raven-haired wife, Giselle. Jessie knew it was a sort of ambush as he awaited her decision on season two, but she thought he would be pleased with her final decision, although she wondered how he would respond to the news that his two lead cast were dating.

There was another element to the mysterious Jonathon. Charles and Dee had told Jessie that Josh was cast in *Drifters* right out of rehab because he was Jonathon's son. As Jessie pulled on a pair of leggings for the first dance number, she wondered whether Josh had any idea his boss was also his biological father. It was a hell of a secret to keep from someone, especially given Josh's rocky relationship with the indomitable Wes Sawyer, the man he'd always thought of as his dad. She felt a surge of love for her new man and the difficulties he had experienced in his own life. Yeah, Charleston was bad for her, but there were others in the world with problems—not the least of whom, her Josh. Jessie didn't see any real resemblance between Josh and Jonathon, as Josh really favored his mother but, if one looked close, both men did have similar eyes and high cheekbones. Jonathon's hair, too, was long and layered, but wavy and snow white, whereas Josh had gorgeous chestnut hair that, thinking about how it fell over his eye, made Jessie shiver in adoration.

She found the elegant Deirdre Keating already at the Orpheum, standing on stage in a creamy-beige business suit with matching heels, in serious consultation with Priya. Jessie wandered over, stretching her biceps and triceps in preparation for a hard afternoon's work, as Dee looked up with a smile and awarded her a welcoming hug.

"Hi, honey," she said. Then her eyes narrowed at Jessie, who was already stifling a yawn with the sleeve of the yellow hoodie she stretched over her fingers. "You're exhausted. Did you not sleep well last night?"

Jessie colored instantly, staring down at the scuffed stage as she stretched first one calf and then the other. "No. Not much, actually." But she was beaming and, with the instinct of a mother who knew her child well, the corners of Dee's lips curved up into a tiny smile.

"I see. Did some of you go out last night?" She knew the dancers sometimes went for a drink after rehearsal. Jessie must have met someone. A tiny alarm bell started to ring in the back of Dee's mind. Any new man Jessie met would have to be "managed" through the media.

Bouncing by in black yoga pants, Kayla gave Jessie a little squeeze before starting some gentle side stretches. "What'd you and Josh do after Paul and I left last night? Did you stay at Liam's much longer? Ya gotta like the Irish. Comfort food and comfort tunes."

"Umm…," Jessie put both sleeves over her face, which turned crimson red. She toed a dust ball on the black stage and dared a peek up at Dee. Her manager was standing there in complete shock. She had hoped Jessie's affection for the troubled guy would have evaporated along with the dewy crystal prisms of many Prince Edward Island summer mornings.

"Oh, honey," she said, sympathetic but terribly unsure about the match.

Jessie removed her sleeves from her beet red face as Kayla stopped stretching and stared at her.

"Dee," Jessie asked innocently, her blue eyes wide, "could you set an extra place for dinner?"

Deirdre was almost run over by the dancers as Priya called, "Places, please!" and got the rehearsal under way.

The elegant rosewood dining table was set with Dee's finest tableware, antique red and white Royal Crown Derby inlaid with gold. Dim lighting was employed to allow the candles to flicker pleasingly. Crystal goblets encouraged the soft light as the tiny flames were reflected in the glass. A mild draft floated in the open window, cooling the high ceilinged room with its decorative medallion highlighting a twinkling crystal chandelier. In short, Dee wasn't helping to quash any romantic liaisons at her dinner table that evening.

Jonathon was especially surprised to have his two lead cast arrive at dinner together. Mystified, he wondered whether something was once again going on between the two, or whether Josh was simply offering moral support to Jessie regarding the season two question. After all, the two had become good friends. That was not a secret.

After they were seated, Carlotta served a selection of warm cheeses with cranberry and phyllo pastry. Jessie smiled warmly up at her and, in return, Carlotta gave her a little hug. The maid detected something different about Jessie—it seemed a weight had been lifted off the girl's shoulders. She was relieved—Carlotta had overheard many conversations about the season two decision and figured Jessie would be on the hotspot tonight.

Charles shook Josh's hand firmly to counteract the somewhat cold shoulder Jessie's new boyfriend was receiving from Dee. Charles liked Josh, but he planned to have a serious chat with him about Jessie. Matt, the Keating head of security, would be present. The riot act would be read. Nobody would hurt Jessie Wheeler.

Dinner was exquisite, a colorful harvest season mélange of new vegetables, served with roast goose. The conversation was safe, mostly referencing politics and the tragic loss of government programs with the Conservative administration, including cuts to the public broadcaster and the National Film Board. As they were finishing strawberry shortcake, Jonathon couldn't stand the suspense for another second. He pushed back his chair, which scraped threateningly on Dee's hardwood, succeeding in drawing attention to his mission.

He eyeballed Jessie.

"You're killing me," he declared.

Glancing nervously over at Dee, Jessie laid her silver spoon next to the empty dessert plate and wiped sweaty hands on the linen napkin on her lap. Next to her, Josh couldn't suppress a grin. He picked a spot on the hardwood floor and focused on it.

"Jessie," Jonathon said, three glasses of wine slurring his voice just slightly. Giselle reached over and laid a manicured hand on his thigh. "Please, no more suspense."

In response, Jessie cleared her throat. "Jonathon, I'm sorry. I planned to let you know in June but things didn't quite pan out then." A sideways peek at Josh revealed that he was smirking now, so Jessie swatted him under the table. He was enjoying this far too much.

She exhaled, trying hard—for Dee's sake—not to break out into a full-fledged grin of her own. "Jonathon, I'm happy to do season two." Jessie ran a forefinger over her bottom lip, then she grabbed Josh's knee and squeezed. Hard. He yelped loud enough for only Jessie to hear, and then dropped his hand over hers.

Their executive producer perked up immediately, but then hesitated from raising a glass of wine in a toast when he saw that Jessie had more to say. He paused, the delicate crystal a few inches off the table.

"But there's a condition," she added hesitantly.

For courage she looked squarely at Josh, who met her searching eyes and then lifted their hands up onto the table. Dee groaned inwardly, Charles chuckled, and Jon buried his head in his hands and moaned.

"Why do I put myself through this shit?"

But silently, secretly, he gloated. What father wouldn't want Jessie Wheeler as a potential daughter-in-law? He had been so worried for Josh over the last several years. Jessie was a remarkable woman. Jonathon was thrilled that the chemistry he saw on set that first day was now being shared in real life between the two. He felt a glow that came from more than just the expensive wine, despite the new worry that his set could become an emotional battleground should things not work out.

Charles raised a toast to Jessie and Josh, and then there were hugs all around. Although she finally gave in and timidly embraced Josh, overall Dee could not lay aside her worry for Jessie. She watched discreetly as Josh pulled his co-star close and tenderly kissed her. He whispered something softly in her ear that garnered a sweet blush. Deirdre was an intuitive lady with a gut feeling this was not going to end well. She prayed for Jessie's sake that she was dead wrong.

A sudden gust of wind blew the white gauzy dining room curtains inward; ghostly apparitions, they stood sentinel over the table as the candles flickered out and the crystal was left wanting in the dim light.

Chapter Three

The following week was long and arduous for Jessie as she and her team rehearsed all day every day for the premiere of her new show, which was sneaking up quickly. Vancouver was as beautiful as ever, with crisp late summer days inviting residents to spend their evenings in artsy outdoor cafes before the arrival of cooler weather and the all-Canadian preference to hibernate or fly south to warmer locales.

Around eight each evening Josh waited until Jessie texted, and then he scooted downtown and picked her up. Mentally and physically wiped out from the day's exertions, she climbed exhausted into his new truck before he drove them to a restaurant for a late dinner, or to his home where a robust homemade meal awaited his tired girl.

On the Thursday before the cue-to-cue tech rehearsal, when light and sound cues would be finalized, Jessie was almost too tired to eat. Josh tucked her under the expansive auburn duvet on his comfy Queen-sized bed, kissed her softly, and then went downstairs to clean up the remains of the dinner he'd picked up from his favorite sushi bar in Dunbar. He was eagerly anticipating the show that Saturday, and was also quite nervous about being seen with Jessie at the reception in the grand Orpheum lobby afterwards. They had eaten publicly a few times over the week, and eyebrows were raised, but so far nothing had been published about their blossoming romance. Saturday would be a night when Jessie would be in the spotlight. The media was invited in spades, and the paparazzi would be parked outside the theater with their long lenses, hoping for glimpses of Vancouver's celebrities and wealthy patrons. This would be Josh and Jessie's first real test as a public couple.

Since they'd finally gotten together on the previous Friday, the new couple hadn't had a lot of time to spend together, apart from the nights when Jessie was really too beat to face much more than some nourishment. There were issues they would have to discuss at some point. Dee wanted some time to sit with the two along with Josh's manager—his brother Zach's wife Hilary—and their publicists. She knew from experience that the new relationship would have to be spun to the press in a manner that brought the media and the public alongside favorably right from the start. It wouldn't do to allow misguided writers to misinterpret the situation, given Jessie's abrupt break-up with Charlie less than a week before their scheduled wedding last June.

Opening the lid of his green compost bin, Josh dropped the sushi containers inside. One of the reasons he liked that particular sushi restaurant, besides the tasty spicy rolls, was that it used entirely compostable cornstarch based take-out containers. There was a time when Josh didn't care about such things as the environment. But now it seemed his conscience had kicked into high gear, and he cared about everything. It was nice to care again.

He wondered how Jessie felt about their impending "coming out" to the press as a couple. She had been pretty quiet the last few evenings. He knew she was tired and, even though she wasn't new to performance, it was likely she would be dealing with nerves. The show was receiving a great deal of publicity and, with all the dancing, was technically difficult for its star. Add to that the presence of Josh in her life a short time after the breakup with Charlie...

Absently, Josh wiped a yellow dishcloth over the counter and then ran it under warm water, wrung it out, and hung it over the faucet to dry. He opened the dishwasher and dumped some glasses in upside down, closed it up and left it to gather dishes another day before running it. He turned off the light and trudged upstairs to cuddle Jessie and grab some winks. Tomorrow he would be expected early on the set of his new film for some wardrobe camera tests. He and Jessie had a big weekend coming up. He figured he should rest up as well.

Jessie was having trouble shutting off her brain and easing into sleep— the adrenalin of the day was still coursing through her veins. In her head she kept reviewing the difficult numbers again and again. She thrived on such performances; dance-heavy numbers were a rush, a physical workout the gym could not equal. It was fun to experiment with and then master new choreography. Priya was professional and reasonable, but she expected perfection from all of her dancers, Jessie included. The result was a sensational spectacle of color and sound, bodies moving in synchronicity; a fluidity of motion that, when highlighted by programmed computerized lighting designed specifically for the show, and a dynamic multi-media backdrop, was a masterful, magical blend of performing arts. Jessie was psyched but she, too, anticipated a flawless performance, mostly from herself. So sleep was somewhat elusive.

As she heard Josh quietly poking around in the en suite bathroom rummaging through a drawer in search of his toothbrush, Jessie had something else on her mind as well. She knew Dee attributed her quiet nature prior to shows as nerves, but over the last ten years, since Charleston, Jessie had never gotten over the fear of Deuce McCall reappearing in her life. Sometimes she thought she could feel him—his evil presence out there in the dark, in the shadows, threatening, creating a dusky void around him into which she hoped she would never again fall prey. Deuce was a black hole. The sturdy man's misguided, malevolent ministrations had turned her into a ghost, a shell of her former self.

Jessie had spent a lot of time thinking she could care less if Deuce ever showed up at a performance. But that was before she met Josh, before the external wall around her soul started to break down. Now, since she'd found Josh, and because of what had happened to Sandy—and perhaps Terri—she was suddenly terrified of McCall again. But she was bound to Josh, drawn to him. She felt powerless to walk away from her new relationship and wondered, for the umpteenth time, if there would ever be a way to eradicate from her life this gnawing fear of such a horrific adversary as Deuce McCall. She was Jessie Wheeler. She had power now that she didn't have in Charleston years ago. She had private security. She had Charles and Matt. Surely something could be done to make Deuce pay for his crimes, to destroy him. To stomp him out like a bug on a steamy hot Charleston sidewalk. Surely Jessie—and Josh—could live in peace.

Josh slipped into bed behind her and carefully placed his hand on her hip as he settled into his pillow. Jessie was too tired to respond but she was glad of his presence. She finally drifted off to sleep with a reminder to herself that she must focus on the present day, not fret over the past, and not worry too much about the future. And right now—with the warm hand of the man she loved on her hip, his quiet breath whispering and caressing her neck—was a moment she planned to cherish forever.

The concert was every bit as mind-blowing as Jessie hoped and as Josh figured it would be. Jessie had planned the show with an effective fusion of fast and slow numbers and, as expected, her audience couldn't get enough. The ballads were melodious, gracious and lovely, highlighted by Christian's sparkle at the piano and a simple orchestra in the pit, accentuating Jessie's spellbinding lyrics with the rise and fall of strings in ode to Beethoven and Mozart. The fast numbers were pop-ish tunes, still with meaningful lyrics but designed for a trendy fast moving demographic. The Civil War number was one of these, and it didn't disappoint.

Josh was spellbound, as was everyone else nestled in the marvelous old theater. He sat next to Stephen, who had been updated on the new relationship status of Josh and Jessie. Occasionally the boys looked at each other and just laughed with sheer joy at the adrenalin rush and pure magic of the show; of being close to such a talented woman; and at the delightful secret knowledge that Josh and Jessie were, finally, Josh and Jessie.

In the lobby afterwards, Jessie received her third standing ovation of the night—the first two were after the finale and encore—when she appeared above her audience on one of the Orpheum's grand meandering staircases in a short, backless red dress with halter straps, sequined Manolo Blahniks, and her hair in a graceful updo. One would never suspect she was the same girl who punctuated the Civil War number onstage with a John Lennon brocade jacket and embroidered leather boots. She was breathless from excitement but—unknown to most—not due to the show's resounding success, but because she could see Josh waiting for her below. Her eyes were only for him, and it took his breath away as well, to see her there on the stairs, a vision in red, smiling down at him.

A quick scan, and Jessie did not see or sense the presence of McCall. She pushed him out of her mind as some kind of phobia that didn't make sense—besides, her security team was everywhere—and she focused on making her public debut with Josh by her side as special and magnificent as they both deserved.

"Hey," she said, instantly raising eyebrows as she kissed Josh lovingly after reaching him at the circular stand-up bar.

"Hey yourself," he said, pleased. She was a vision. He was blessed. Finally.

He handed her a glass of champagne. Although Josh was drinking ginger ale, he felt righteously that Jessie deserved champagne after her spectacular performance. She raised her eyebrows at him, and he tenderly brushed his lips against her forehead.

"You deserve it," he whispered. "That was some show."

Jessie glanced at his glass and he mouthed *Ginger ale*. She smiled lop-sidedly up at him, chagrined that she'd even wondered. She trusted him.

Maggie and Sue-Lyn, with their partners nearby, were hanging onto the bar, gossiping and getting caught up on each other's weeks, and so there were hugs and congratulations all around.

"So what's this all about?" Maggie asked, waving at Josh but eyeballing Jessie.

"Uh, yeah, about that," Jessie breathed. "Um, remember that talk we were supposed to have after the fundraiser at Annika last winter?"

Maggie narrowed her eyebrows. "Girl, you're a little late. But I suspected all along. This is not exactly a surprise—although why him? What could you possibly see in Josh?" She winked at the object of her derision that, one elbow leaning on the bar, was shaking his head, his cheeks an interesting shade of pink.

Sue-Lyn laughed and gave Jessie a second hug. "It's definitely not because of the black jacket or the tight jeans or the sexy belt or the black cowboy boots, no, I don't guess it's any of those things, huh?" She stood back, crossed her arms and appraised Josh favorably, receiving a swat from her own man for the misplaced attention.

Jessie chuckled, and her eyes met Josh's. "Nah," she said. "It's the way his hair falls over his eyes, like this." She reached out and moved the favorite lock of hair over and in front of his ear. Blushing hotly from the attention, Josh grasped her hand and pulled it down by his side.

The image of Jessie moving Josh's hair was the image gracing the cover of the Vancouver Sun the next day, then eventually People magazine, and a myriad of other celebrity magazines worldwide. It became one of the most famous photographs of the year, just before *Drifters* premiered and Josh and Jessie became household names as a couple.

Discreetly watching the new couple that night was Charlie. He had sincerely wished Jessie's infatuation with Josh wouldn't evolve into anything. For his own sake he was saddened to see them together, but he was still gracious enough to shake Josh's hand and give Jessie a delicate kiss on the cheek as a congratulatory nod to her performance. He donated $ 50 000 that evening to her fundraising campaign for the new shelters. Although it made headline news, from that moment on he was largely forgotten in Jessie's media world.

Josh was not accepted readily, but his acting on *Drifters* and Jessie's obvious love for him helped smooth over his somewhat bumpy transition into her life as boyfriend.

In a certain smoky office in Charleston, though, he would never be accepted except as, perhaps, a certain and desired target.

Chapter Four

$\mathcal{D}$euce McCall slammed the office door after his assistant Cindy sidled in, her head down as she focused on filing a broken fingernail, the Charleston Post and Courier dangling from the hand with the broken nail. A skinny little waif in her mid-twenties with mousy brown hair hastily scrunched up into a loose bun, a virginal puffed-sleeve white and peach floral blouse, and a russet corduroy mini-skirt so short it angered her boss for its distracting qualities, she was the glue that kept the Charleston club running when he was away. Unafraid of her often intimidating boss—and that was saying something, because most of the Renegade staff were indeed cowed by him—and happy to indulge his physical needs as they arose, she was a gal who took life with a grain of salt and a shrug-your-shoulders *C'est la vie* attitude.

She yawned during Deuce's tirade.

Her boss was literally growling, his balding head blooming with an interesting vague purple tinge. "I am not interested in hearing about how well Jessie Wheeler's fundraising campaign for teen addicts is going, and no, I am definitely NOT donating to the cause."

Grabbing the Post and Courier out of Cindy's manicured fingers, Deuce threw it on the floor by her teetering high-heeled sandals. It landed right side up, the headline glaring *Charleston's Girl Does It Again.*

"This city has a short memory. Jessie lived here for what, three years, if that? And what did she do here—she played in my club and prostituted herself the same as the rest of you sluts. In my mind, she doesn't bear remembering, much less celebrating."

Inside, he was churning, but it wouldn't do to let cocky Cindy know how he really felt, that Jessie was his and would always be his. That he was in the thick of planning how to coerce her into becoming his for eternity. That he, Deuce McCall, had big plans for the former lounge singer who so unceremoniously quit his employ just over a decade ago, almost single-handedly destroying his business. Never mind that things had picked up in the last few years of Jessie's fame, when word got out that she once worked at the Renegade.

Trying to keep the place afloat had been hell for a while. Deuce was humiliated in the business community and amongst his own family, including a father who loved to smoke a pipe on his front porch in nearby Mount Pleasant and declare Deuce a failure—not just in business, but also in life. Deuce had been biding his time, choosing the right moment to strike. Especially after that yuppie kid's death, the boyfriend, he felt he ought to lay low. But the time was coming. Jessie might think he was out of her life, but after his test run with that Terri kid, he was growing more and more hungry to speak face to face with her again, to see the fear in Jessie's eyes at the moment she realized he was still in control.

Deuce glanced down at the newspaper as Cindy lounged coquettishly in the corner and prepared a soothing glass of brandy for her boss. He blinked, and then peered closer. *What is this?* With a pointed velvety white snakeskin boot, he toed the paper closer. *Huh. She is dating her co-star. What's his name? Josh?*

Grinning spitefully as he lowered his tight butt into the red leather office chair, Deuce anchored his feet on the expansive glass desk with its neat piles of papers and notes, and lit a cigar. *Well. That explains the new sparkle in Jessie's eyes*—a look he hadn't seen in her photos with Charlie. She had a new man in her life, one that made her feel the way she felt with that Sandy kid a decade ago. Suddenly Deuce knew exactly what he needed to do in order to get access to Jessie once again. The timing was perfect. He had ammunition. And its name was Josh.

He would need to go shopping. *Ah, well,* he thought as he roughly grabbed the brandy from Cindy, spilling a few drops on some unimportant business-related note, and then clicked on the Google search bar on his computer. *That'll give her a little time with the new boyfriend before I make my appearance. I suppose I can at least do her that kindness.*

Deuce's brain functioned in what he alone thought was a weird and wonderful way. He had a strange method of reasoning. He typed *surveillance gear* into the search engine and hit the return button. As he pondered the suggested sites, he complimented himself on the kindness of letting Jessie enjoy her newfound love. Then he clicked on a site that featured wireless bugs and bumper beepers, and out of his wallet he yanked the credit card he used for his more covert operations.

Deuce McCall had work to do.

Jessie leaned her belly against the grill and front hood of Josh's truck, her arms partly crossed, one hand holding Josh's as he leaned kitty corner across from her. Fondly, she brushed his knuckles with her thumb.

"I don't want to live this way, Josh," she said faintly, peering earnestly up at him from beneath long eyelashes. "Us being apart. Leaving each other all the time."

"We won't have to," he responded convincingly. "This is just temporary. In a month or so we'll start on *Drifters* again. You'll get sick of me."

His answer earned a sweet smile and a blush. Jessie shifted her balance. She loved the idea of spending so much time with Josh that she'd get tired of him. Picturing them as an old grey-haired couple still head over heels in love dancing in the moonlight, she retorted assuredly, "Never. You're stuck with me."

He touched her cheek and leaned in for a kiss. "Better be."

"Like bubble gum under a chair."

"Yuck."

"Strawberry flavored."

"Okay, I rescind my yuck. But only if it's strawberry."

She laughed. They were parked on the tarmac of the airfield where the Keating jet was accepting passengers from Jessie's show for the trip to their next engagement—Toronto. From there the cast, choreographer, Dee, assorted stage crew and others would fly to Montreal. After that, they would complete their eight-show run in the States—in New York, Washington, Boston, Chicago and San Francisco. Each show would highlight and benefit a shelter Dee and Jessie were building, and each was only available to exclusive audiences with a promise that a longer, more intense tour available to larger audiences was in the works. Jessie was tired just thinking about it. But for now...

A loud holler from Dee, who was protecting her modesty from a brisk wind by hanging onto her skirt at the steps' entrance to the plane, beckoned her. "Time to go, Jessie!"

Grudgingly, Dee waved bye to Josh and then observed none too discreetly as Jessie sidled around the pick-up and folded herself into her new boyfriend's arms. Dee felt a little pang of guilt as she spied on them. Maybe she wasn't being fair to Josh—Jessie certainly adored him.

Josh buried his nose in Jessie's lavender infused hair. It was going to hurt to be physically separated from this girl, even though the tour would only take about two and a half weeks. At least he would be busy on his film shoot. The time would fly. He hoped.

One last melodious lingering kiss and a quick squeeze, then Jessie willed herself to turn and stroll towards the plane. At the top of the stairs, she looked back once and then disappeared inside. Landing in a beige winged chair next to Kayla, who giggled and gave her an excited hug, Jessie made a vow to plan her future schedule as much as possible with Josh in it. This *leaving* thing was excruciating.

The tour went well and time did, indeed, fly. Between press conferences and trying to get adequate rest, then travelling and the shows themselves, there wasn't much time to think, apart from the flights between cities. Jessie called and texted Josh as much as possible, but she still longed to be home with him, and counted the hours until they could be together again. Her shows were all a resounding success, and both she and Deirdre were thrilled with the donations pouring in to their foundation. Dee was a charismatic, charming envoy for the small troupe, impossible to ignore; she was the kind of gracious lady people easily wanted to please.

One day after an agreeable lingering brunch at their hotel in Chicago, Kayla approached Jessie with glee. She slid into the comfy floral-cushioned high-backed wicker chair just vacated by Dee, and briskly rubbed her palms together in front of her face, as if she was about to disclose the secrets of the universe or, at the very least, some titillating gossip.

Jessie crossed her arms over her chest. With a curious twinkle in her eyes, she took the bait. Kayla was such a happy-go-lucky likeable girl.

"Okay, girlfriend. Spill it."

Bursting, the dancer erupted. "You and Josh made the cover of *People*."

Teeming with pride, Kayla reached behind her and yanked the popular entertainment magazine out of her jeans' back pocket. One hand on each side, the bubbly dancer held the cover in front of Jessie like a trophy. Initially a butterfly fluttered in Jessie's heart when she spotted the large image featuring Josh by her side at the Vancouver show, an expression of utter happiness caressing his face as she brushed the lock of hair behind his ear. But then a black door closed over her heart, locking the butterfly carefully away, and Jessie felt her hopes for a peaceful future with her man sink. Inevitable as she knew it would be, this in-your-face cover would be fuel for the fire.

There was no doubt in her mind that Josh would be the victim of much scrutiny and derision. She ached to keep him from the pain the media had the power to cause, as a parent would protect a child from a horde of bullies. The only recourse they had as a couple was to avoid the Internet, the gossip rags and radio and television stations. There had recently been another school shooting in the States. More than twenty-five teens, plus three teachers and a school janitor, were killed suddenly and heartlessly for some unknown reason that spiraled to the bottom of the grave with the shooter. Gun control in the States—homelessness, wars on foreign soil—those were news. The fact that Jessie had fallen in love with a misunderstood man whose troubled past haunted him should not factor into people's minds. Never would Jessie understand the compelling need for others to dive into celebrity gossip, to want to harm her and Josh with barbs and ridicule. To her, it was cut and dry. They were just another couple in love, two people who by God's grace had found each other in an unsettled world amidst confusion and heartache, and who desired nothing more than the gift of time spent in each other's arms.

"Kayla," she said distantly, as her mind shrank against the even deeper menace of Deuce McCall and the ever-present fear of his return, "your brother's life is about to get really crazy. You know that, right?"

Softening, witness to the alarming cloud instantly sinking her boss' mood, Kayla set the magazine on her lap. "I know, Jessie," she replied, somewhat chastened. "I guess I'm a little naïve when it comes to all this madness. I mean, I'm getting a taste of it by virtue of dancing in your company, and my dad's work on TV meant that our lives were never really our own as kids, but somehow our parents managed to shelter us from most of the crap they must have endured. It's just that—well," she wriggled in her wicker nest as the excitement was too much to bear alone, "I'm as crazy about you as my big brother is, and I've never seen him so happy. I guess I just want to celebrate the two of you."

Her face fell then, as another train of thought crossed Kayla's mind. "Unless...well, everything's okay, isn't it?"

Forcing herself to smile, Jessie reached out, grabbed Kayla's wrist and gave it a squeeze. "Of course it is, kiddo," she said. "It's just that unfortunately not all of the world is as happy about Josh and me as you are." She blinked. "Speaking of which, I hope Zach and Hilary are okay with us. I know Hilary's got her hands full with the kids and now she has to help Dee manage our crazy lives..."

"They're over the moon, Jess." Somberly, Kayla added, "We all know what you did for him, Jessie. Just by calling Zach and Hil that night...thank God they were in the city...whatever you said to Josh...and then that card you sent him..."

Raising her eyebrows, Jessie's cheeks turned faintly pink. As her lips eased upwards, just slightly, her gaze dropped to her toes.

"Come on, Jessie, we all saw the card in his room at rehab. He left it on the windowsill. And being the opinionated people we Sawyers are, well we all had our say in who we thought it came from. And the thing is...well... in those days there wasn't a soul on the planet who cared a shit about Josh, except for us. Not even our dad. And we had a hard time caring then, too, Jessie. I mean—we always cared, but it was like the Josh we knew had died. Substance abuse...it's just another kind of death, right? The *Black Death*, that's what Josh still calls those days. So the card had to have come from you, the person who called Zach outside Charlie's Club. Zach said you called him a week or so later, just to see if Josh was okay, if he was getting help. We were all surprised you cared enough to call the first time, much less the second."

A nonchalant shrug was Jessie's response.

"And the song," Kayla added knowingly.

Looking up, Jessie smiled openly at her new good friend. "The song was for everyone who needed a dose of hope in their lives. Not just for Josh. Although I admit he was my inspiration."

"What was it, Jess? What was it you saw in him that night? Why did you follow him outside, and what made you believe in him when nobody else did?"

Holding Kayla's gaze, the singer loved the light she saw there, shining from the depths of the deep brown eyes somewhat similar to those of an endearing man waiting back in Vancouver.

"What was it I saw in him that night? Me, I think," was Jessie's simple response. "I saw myself. Lonely. Sad. And maybe there's something to the universe matching people up with each other, Kayla, because I knew instantly that I loved your brother. Maybe from the second he walked into the club, or maybe from the moment I looked into his eyes, but it was like that old cliché—hit by a lightning bolt—and I know I will love him forever. I just know."

"With Paul it was more like a friendship that grew. And it grows stronger every day."

"I guess there are all kinds of ways to fall in love, kiddo. The hard part is keeping it, with all the crap we have to deal with in our everyday lives. Therein lies the challenge."

She seized the magazine from Kayla's lap and held it up, an Olympic torch for all to see.

"And this kind of stuff—I mean, I know people are curious, but—it doesn't help. People read this crap and they believe it, and my guess is that it paints Charlie as the one who got hurt. Which on some level I guess is true, but he and I have made our peace with our break-up. Mostly," she added wryly, knowing Charlie still wished for a second chance to make things right. But at least they had salvaged some sort of genial friendship out of the dregs of their ill-fated romance.

"I know," Kayla said. "You're right." As she got up to go, she bent down and gave Jessie a gentle embrace. "Jessie, my family will always be indebted to you. Whether or not you and Josh stay together, it doesn't matter. Although of course I hope you will. You gave him a second chance at life. None of us will ever forget that."

"Thanks, Kayla," Jessie whispered, hugging her back. "But I only got him started. The rest of you stood by and helped him through it."

As Kayla left the dining room, a bounce in her step and a twinkle in her eyes, Jessie felt a wave of ennui wash over her. She wished she were back in Vancouver with Josh, holding him close and teasing him, playing with his hair, keeping him in her sights, as if her presence alone could protect him from all of the negative elements hidden under rugs and buried under low-land swamps. She caught herself wondering what the Sawyer clan would think of her if they knew what happened to Sandy in Charleston, and the fact that Jessie was still very much afraid of the man who caused the harm.

She shook her head as if to chase the bad thoughts away, and she felt her heart swell with love for Kayla, and for Zach's little clan as well. Loving somebody like Josh was such a gift—he brought a whole sweet family into Jessie's life. Including the little ones, Zach and Hilary's rambunctious, adorable youngsters.

Placing a linen napkin almost tenderly on her empty plate, Jessie rose from her comfortable wicker sanctuary. Absently, as she moseyed across the navy blue carpet, she couldn't help but wonder what she brought into Josh's life—public assaults, a circus lifestyle, endless late hours and extensive travel? Perhaps even...but *no*. She refused to entertain any more thoughts of McCall, and wondered why his sadistic presence always seemed to be on her mind of late. Was there such a thing as channeling? Was she on McCall's mind? She shuddered.

There would be time to worry later. For now, as if she were entertaining visual slides in her head, Jessie slid McCall away and replaced him with Josh. And on that happy thought, she punched in the elevator's *Up* button and, while waiting for the upstairs shuttle to arrive on her floor, she signed an autograph for a petite Asian lady who didn't at all seem to mind that Jessie was now with Josh. And then Jessie slipped into the forgiving abyss and let it carry her up, up and away.

She had a show to do.

Chapter Five

*B*y the end of the two and a half weeks, Deirdre's goals had been reached and surpassed. A tired, happy group landed at Vancouver International late one rainy night. They were welcomed with open arms by family and friends. Waiting by the King Ranch pick-up under the moon's haphazard cloudy glow on a slick glistening tarmac, the fresh scent of new rain tickling his senses, Josh gathered Jessie into a big bear hug, wondering how he'd survived for so many years without her in his life.

"Missed you," he breathed into the hollow of her neck.

"You better have," she murmured back.

"Or else what?"

She giggled and buried her nose deeper into his musky Josh smell, squeezing him tightly. "Or else no presents. I'll keep them to myself."

He grinned and leaned back so he could see her face. "I knew there was a reason I should hook up with you. What'd you get me? Chocolate?"

Mischievously, Jessie pressed her forehead against his, and then kissed him softly on the now-familiar lips she'd dreamed about for the past few weeks. She sighed. "Chocolate wouldn't have survived the airplane trip home. Not in my bag, anyway. No, I got you something much, much better than chocolate." She peeked up at him playfully. "But you'll have to wait until we get home." Winking, she slipped both arms under his denim jacket and around his waist.

He kissed her back then, and swung her around. One of the male dancers, a chiseled Filipino coffee-skinned twenty-three-year-old, sauntered by and made a face at them. "Jessie, you're breaking my heart. What's he got that I haven't got?"

"Um…heated seats?" She chuckled as her dancer swung a leg over an environmentally friendly electric scooter he pulled out from underneath a low building by the metal security fence. Without taking her eyes off Josh, Jessie asked, "Sure you don't want a ride, Benjie?"

"With you two? Think you'll actually make it home? Or will you be taking a room in some sleazy hotel?" Benjie twisted around in the scooter's cushioned seat and fastened his duffle securely on behind. Grinning at Jessie, he gestured loosely somewhere off beyond the airport where the neon lights of a number of hotels beckoned weary travellers. "Take your pick."

"A room works for me," Josh whispered solemnly to Jessie, provoking another giggle.

"Bye, Benjie," she called. "Drive safe! I'll try not to miss you!" Jessie waved to her friend as he puttered contentedly away in the light mist on a small, quietly purring engine. Benjie, grinning roguishly, waved an arm in farewell while manipulating shallow puddles as he steered towards the gate.

More goodbyes were said and hugs shared, and then home and privacy awaited, where Jessie could give Josh his gifts in peace in the comfort of his media room. Amongst various types of chocolate (she had lied, although she had indeed eaten some during the flight, as evidenced by the missing Y in a giant chocolate NY for New York) was a simple photograph of the now famous Orpheum shot. Mounted in a plain silver frame, it was the best example Jessie had at the time to let Josh know she had been thinking of him—pretty much always—during the trip. At Jessie's request, Dee had contacted the original photographer and obtained a copy of the photograph image file. So to both Jessie and Josh, it was also Dee's way of saying she was trying to accept the new man in Jessie's life. *Trying.*

To the photographer, there was no greater accolade than having Jessie covet one of his photographs of her. To Josh it was a Karsh inspired image—the moment before he had lowered Jessie's hand, embarrassed, was forever theirs to cherish. A simple touch between lovers, a truth, a glimpse into their souls—that's what it represented. And it held the future, absolute and complete, a pregnant moment filled with a multitude of promises, of many graceful touches to come. Josh treasured it, and planned to carefully place it on his nightstand next to the *Drifters* photograph from season one.

After the gifts were shared and Josh filled Jessie in on the feature film he was shooting, which was going well—the dynamics on most shows were highly dependent on the director and crew involved, and this was proving to be a smooth, well-run shoot—Josh pulled Jessie upright into a slow dance. He had his iPhone on the shuffle setting, and Adele had just come on. A slow ballad caressed the room and swept into the corners, setting a tender tone. Loving that her man was the snuggling type, Jessie eagerly took him up on the offer to reconnect through music. She wrapped her arms around Josh's neck and, with a contented exhale, let her head fall to rest on his shoulder. His navy blue T-shirt hung appealingly just over the belt buckle on his jeans and, after only a few moments holding him under the enchanting tune, Jessie was completely under his spell.

The music was captivating, enduring, an old traditional romantic piece that brushed around and underneath them like a fresh breeze in an ancient city, lifting the lovers to greater heights and towards the possibilities of dreams and happy-ever-afters. It was the prelude to their lovemaking, and theirs to rejoice within, as Adele carried them to the secret place inside her own soul from whence the music was borne. The restlessness that suffused both Josh and Jessie for so long was gone now, buried underneath a mutual and sincere trust, respect and devotion, elevated by passion and song and a longing borne of distance that now, in their reunited state, the two lovers took the time to cherish.

Touch was the sense both underestimated until the day they first found each other. Now, imbuing themselves into the slow waltz tempo of the music that led and orchestrated their dance, they allowed themselves the exquisite pleasure of time to experiment and reacquaint and feel the simple gracious gifts of their bodies and souls. Jessie let her fingers wander over Josh's broad athletic shoulders and then pass down his back. She applied a gentle pressure that brought his body closer to her, and she could feel his breath on her cheek, warm and inviting, as his face was turned slightly towards her. Josh leaned forward and let his right hand frolic playfully in Jessie's hair, twisting ringlets as he had seen her do so many times when she was nervous about something. She felt his smile when he buried his nose in the auburn locks— it was in his body, that happiness, emanating from his heartbeat deep within, from that long ago innocent place where children haven't yet experienced the heartache of lost pets and other grown-up worries.

He was here, in front of her—Josh—and the music they moved slowly to was a pedestal on which to stand as they declared their love with the divine magic of touch and breath; of soft sighs borne of the sweetest knowing, of pleasure savored and anticipated, of realizing you have found the one you will love until the day your life on earth is done, and perhaps even afterwards when the mysteries of the universe are revealed.

Her head still on his shoulder, Jessie slipped a finger under the T-shirt and then, slowly, allowed the palm of her hand to lie flat on the warm skin underneath. Josh helped her out by lifting his shirt up so she could place her second hand there as well. He rested his hands over hers, just to feel the closeness of her and, by osmosis, to bring her inside him. If they could have melded together as one that way, they would have, but there were other ways to feel as a complete whole, and so they took steps to head in that direction instead.

After slipping up her top, Josh allowed Jessie the freedom to pull the T-shirt up over his head, too, and then he urged her close so their bellies could rub up against each other. He smiled down at her and tipped her face up to meet his so he could taste her lips and tease her with his tongue in sweet anticipation of the intimate coupling to come.

Laughing, she lifted her arms, wrapped him loosely around the neck, and they danced magically together in the moonlight's embrace, two people living life to the fullest in the way God intended—together, joyous—enjoying a simple tenderness in a way that negated such artifice as fame and success and money.

When the song ended and their kisses intensified to the point of no return, Josh let Jessie take the lead. She fumbled with his belt buckle, her body already trembling, and when she looked up she saw not just an electric desire in his gaze, but love too—and it brought back memories that brought tears to her eyes. Memories of other men, other times...some good, some bad...and she wondered what she had done to deserve this man in front of her, and a trust in his devotion to her that left no room for doubt.

Josh helped her with the buckle, and then he took her by the hand and led her towards his cozy bedroom, a comfortable place in which to relish each other fully and completely. Their lovemaking had settled into a known and meaningful exploration with a tempo and a rhythm all its own, but this night—after being apart for two and a half weeks—was more urgent and intense.

When Josh climaxed, Jessie's thumb was in his mouth and he felt her final satisfied cry before he could hear her. He lay on top of her panting while her body squeezed him again and again in the serene afterglow of their coupling, and then he broke the splashes of the enchanting moonlit beams by leaning to the left and blocking their light as he slowly pulled away. He reached up and grasped the back of her head, focused her mouth on his and secured another kiss, this one gentle, long and lingering, testament to the way he intended to love her—forever.

They lay that way—together, for quite some time—lost in each other's eyes and only speaking through touch and soft whispers, humbled, until nature called and bathroom breaks were a necessity, and then Josh retrieved some chocolate chip cookie dough ice cream from the freezer and they teased each other mercilessly while they shared a spoon and ate it in bed.

In the weeks and months to come, Jessie and Josh settled into as normal an existence as possible in the heady world of entertainment. As Josh acted in his feature film up the hill at Simon Fraser University in nearby Burnaby, Jessie recorded the last of the fresh songs for her new album. She also spent time on the SFU set watching her man and hanging out with him during lighting set-ups. He had come a long way as an actor over that first season of *Drifters* and then on the Wes Anderson film. He was a joy to watch. His career was exploding.

Visits to Jessie in the recording studio on Robson were Josh's priority when he had the time. Josh was enamored with her music. Secretly, he was tickled to be the motivation and source of some of her new material, a fact Jessie didn't hide. She was in love, although she had been hurting over the past year as her relationship with Charlie was grinding to a halt. Her life was the perfect inspiration for songwriting—her music, surreal.

Late one afternoon in the Keating building on Robson an auburn orange sun painted the studio lobby with long brushstrokes of optimism as Josh touched Jessie's lips with a soft kiss and said good-bye. He ran his tongue lightly over the underside of her top lip before he left, leaving her with woozy legs and a burning anticipation for the evening's activities. He was needed back on set. Even after a few months, it was still a challenge to turn and walk away from her. Inclined against the reception desk as she watched him go, Jessie threw a wistful glance towards Charles, who wandered up with a steaming earthenware coffee mug in his hand. He threw his other arm loosely over his recording artist's shoulders.

"Okay, you win," he said with a mischievous smile. "Even Dee is falling prey to his powers. Slowly."

Jessie wrapped an arm around her producer's waist. "He's amazing, Charles. He cooks and does dishes. I've even witnessed him vacuuming. What more could a girl want?"

"Ouch," Charles replied. He rarely touched a dish and he preferred French restaurants or Carlotta's cooking to trying his hand at any kind of cuisine. "Touché. He doesn't wear ties. So there." He fingered his cranberry silk tie, which he wore with class and elegance over a perfectly cut expensive grey button down shirt.

"Give him a chance. He's good to me. We're happy."

"You know," he said, his voice suddenly lowered a few notches as they walked back towards the studio arm in arm, "last June Josh came to me and asked me to do some nosing around for you. Checking into the man who supposedly dropped Terri at the drug house."

Jessie's heart skipped a beat. "Yeah." She was afraid to look at him.

He continued. "There wasn't much to go on. Nobody's been able to find out anything. All we really have is a vague description, and even that's muddled. Matt and his crew did a lot of asking around too, at Revolver, at the shelter..."

Hopeful, questioning, she looked up at him. Charles answered her with a shake of his head.

"Sorry, Jessie." A pause, and she watched the older man crinkle his brow as he summoned up the courage to tell her a little more.

"Jess," he started, hesitantly. "After we hit a road block with that—asshole, whoever he was—Matt and I deduced that the man you thought might have dropped Terri off had something to do with the—the things—that happened in Charleston when you lived there."

Deduced. De-Deuced. Jessie couldn't help but blanch at his choice of words. *Where is Charles going with this?*

"Honey, the thing is... don't be mad," he beseeched her, "but after we dropped you off at the airport the day you flew to P.E.I., Matt and I took the jet to Charleston. We checked out a few things. It's common knowledge, for instance, that you worked at that club, the Renegade. Owned by some highbrow Southern gentleman named McCall. The place has become quite famous because you played there."

Instantly, Jessie stopped and swooned over a couple of white Ikea chairs placed in the hallway for Charles' clients. *Charles and Matt, two people I love, were in Deuce's club? Oh, God, I'm going to faint. Or throw up. Or both.*

Charles froze. Jessie's physiological reaction to his and Matt's trip to Charleston was immediate and disturbing. Suddenly her face was piqued, the blood precipitously gone and her expression white and pained. He wasn't prepared for this response, even though Charles knew things were bad for her in that great city. He set down his coffee cup and turned her face up towards him so Jessie had no choice but to look him in the eye.

Quietly he entreated, "Jessie, honey, what happened when you lived in Charleston? Did this man hurt you?"

"Not now, Charles," she whispered. "I mean, I can't talk about this, okay?"

Charles decided he had waited long enough to hear about Charleston. Damn it, Jessie was like his daughter. She was terrified—at what, the mention of McCall's name? Charleston? The Renegade? He dove in further as he watched Jessie stumble onto the first chair and drop her head between her knees. She was staring at the smiley faces on the yellow plaid Converse Chucks.

She crossed one toe over the other.

"We asked this McCall guy if he had ever been to Vancouver."

Jessie's heart was pounding so hard she thought it was going to leap out of her chest. The ringing in her ears was so loud she could barely hear Charles. She wondered if he could hear her heart racing around her chest, or whether he could physically see it pounding, trying to escape in fear.

"He said yes, many times." Charles knelt down in front of Jessie and tried to gauge her terrorized expression.

It was everything Jessie could do to keep herself from passing out. "Charles," she managed to breathe despite the dizziness threatening her vision. "Did you ask…if…" She couldn't finish.

"If he was here the weekend Terri died? Yes, we did. We asked him that. He said yes."

This time, she couldn't hold back. Her hands over her ears, rocking back and forth, Jessie moaned.

"Honey," Charles continued, lightly reaching his fingertips towards her hair as if he weren't sure how she would respond to his touch. "He had a solid alibi for that weekend here. And if he *is* the man you are concerned about, then why would he admit to being here? He would know we were asking for a reason…anyway, Matt had him thoroughly checked out by his contacts at the Royal Canadian Mounted Police and Interpol. He's clean, Jessie. At least in their eyes, he is."

Jessie just kept rocking. The memories conjured up by any mention of Deuce McCall were not thoughts she wanted to remember. *Alibi, shmalibi. Deuce could talk his way out of anything, pay his way out of anything. Of course he had arranged some kind of alibi, likely with payment of a BMW or Porsche. My God. There's a good chance it was him who drugged Terri, likely with promises of expensive dresses and jewelry. And he's been here many times? In Van? Oh God.*

"If you're worried about this man, Jessie, about him hurting you, we can step up security. But then you have to listen to Matt—you have to play by the rules. No more sneaking off for long drives on your own. We can put a tail on McCall, see what he's up to for a while."

"You can't tail Deuce McCall," she whispered, still looking down. "And you can't fully protect me or anyone else, Charles," she said. "It's impossible. But thank you for wanting to try."

And then Jessie did something unusual. She leaned forward and kissed the top of Charles' balding head. Shaking, she got up, retreated into the studio, and left him wondering.

Jessie's mood spiraled downward for the rest of the day, and Charles later commented to Dee that they hadn't been able to get anything else out of her in the recording session. She had withdrawn into herself again.

"I don't know," he said later that evening as he yanked an already buttoned striped pajama top over his head. "There's something about this McCall asshole. Obviously some bad shit went down in Charleston. Maybe we *should* just put a tail on him for a while."

In bed, leaning back against the headboard with a pen in one hand, scribbling notes on a script she intended to pass on to Jessie, Dee spoke cautiously. "Charles," she said, "whatever happened, it was a long time ago. If this Deuce McCall character has been in Vancouver, well it doesn't seem like he's tried to contact Jessie. But keep an eye on him anyway, okay?" She closed the script and pondered the situation. "Maybe we should talk to Josh. Maybe she's told him more. In the meantime, I can't see that it would hurt to just watch him for a while, this McCall guy. See what his days are like. Especially if he comes back to Vancouver."

Charles sank down onto the couple's mammoth king-sized bed and snuggled up against Dee, his head on a favorite ultra-soft goose down pillow. "It's so strange though, he seems clean. Matt's system of checks is pretty thorough, especially given his contacts with his old policing buddies."

"Charles," Dee said, running her fingers through the last vestiges of her husband's thinning hair. "There are a lot of folks out there who are supposedly clean. Then they get caught after years of sexually abusing their daughters, and we wonder how they fooled us for all that time."

Raising his head off the pillow, Charles stared at his graceful wise wife. It killed him to think anybody might have hurt Jessie that way. His eyes were steel ribbons of angst. "Dee. Do you think that's what it was? That someone abused her—like that?"

"Yes," she replied delicately. "I do. But we knew something was terribly wrong when we first met Jessie, Charles. It seems logical that it might have had something to do with sexual abuse. This isn't news to you," she added, chiding him.

"I know, but now that I've met that man, I could kill him. I could. I could slit his throat." He stared hard at her and then suddenly sat up in bed, rising blood pressure inciting a spreading flush across his angry face.

Dee sighed, and set her script on the bedside table. "Charles, as I said, it was a long time ago. Our haunted girl is less tortured now. She is beyond happy with Josh, in fact this is the happiest she has been since we've known her. She's looking forward to going back to *Drifters*; she has friends, finally. Let's just get Matt to keep an eye on this McCall for a while and, in the meantime, celebrate this time with her."

Charles frowned. "In that case, you'll have to try harder to accept Josh. She's crazy about him."

"I'm trying! It's just that, well, you talk about this McCall guy…what about Josh? He has a reputation for fighting, for substance abuse; even though he's Jonathon's son, he's still coming from a troubled background thanks to Wes Sawyer. He's not exactly my number one choice for Jessie. No mother wants her daughter hooking up with a guy like that."

"No mother, huh?" Charles allowed himself a small smile and attempted to tickle his wife's waist, but she pushed him away. "Jessie is a big girl. Josh is trying hard. He deserves the benefit of the doubt, Dee." He sobered. "Innocent until proven guilty, my love."

She acquiesced. "One day at a time, Charles." But she lifted the covers and urged her husband closer. They snuggled in together and enjoyed some nice lovemaking of their own before drifting off to sleep with the knowledge that their Jessie was currently safe in the arms of the man she loved, and not with some pedophile that preyed on young women. Charles and Dee were reasonably certain that, should Deuce McCall or any other sick predator enter Jessie's life, they could protect her. But they didn't know the power this particular psychopath had over Jessie. They were unaware of his plans to control her. They had no idea that the sexual predator they feared was in fact capable of much, much worse.

The next day, Charles instructed Matt to put a tail on the Charleston man, which he did, and whom Deuce became aware of almost right away. After a few months, with Deuce playing to the miniature cameras and to the supposedly invisible security team, they relaxed their surveillance and eventually let it go altogether.

But Jessie didn't forget, and she lay awake at night watching Josh sleep and sometimes, at least at first, she went into the bathroom and closed the door and cried, because the memories of Sandy and Rachel and now Terri were so damn strong, and she knew in her gut that Deuce killed Terri too, maybe not directly, but with drugs, and for God's sake now there was Josh, not to mention Charles and Dee and Maggie and Sue-Lyn and Stephen and Carter...it was just too much to take. Loving people meant that suddenly she *cared* again.

She prayed that Deuce McCall would leave her and the people she loved alone, but since Terri's death—and then the love she had found with Josh—Jessie continuously looked over her shoulder. She wondered constantly whether her old boss would attempt another move, and if his twisted game would begin anew.

For in Jessie Wheeler's experience, nothing good in life ever came without a price.

Chapter Six

*P*rior to the *Drifters* premiere in North America, Jonathon set up a press junket followed by a small tour for his lead cast. Although they were on a tight schedule, Jessie and her friends had a great time hanging out together. The show was already the most anticipated drama premiere of the season so the interviewers were, for the most part, on their best behavior. Jonathon stressed to his own marketing team that the interviewers needed to adhere to a certain code or he'd pull his cast. He was, of course, referring to questions about the newly public relationship between Jessie and Josh. He wanted to ensure that his two lead cast—his son, in particular—were treated with respect. The media hadn't been kind when they initially got wind of the romance. The usual questions were posed—when had the relationship burgeoned, and what impact did it have on the break-up between Jessie and Charlie? Was it fly-by-night, as in the case of many lead cast whose characters were hooked up, or was it deep enough to survive the challenges life could throw towards new couples? Jessie and Josh knew the answer—they knew their feelings were genuine. Jonathon trusted them, and hoped they would survive. But he, like Charles and Dee, also understood the pitfalls of celebrity romance. As well, Jonathon wanted *Drifters* to succeed on its own merit, not on the curiosity and gossip of news-hungry interviewers.

The most exciting interview of the press tour was with an enduring afternoon daily talk show host, Shawna Coupland. She was also the most daunting. Jessie had met the sophisticated Asian lady before, and they connected instantly. Both survived difficult childhoods, and both were dealing with fame and success on the highest level. They had a lot in common and often enjoyed dinner, usually with Deirdre in tow, when Jessie was in New York. Shawna was gutsy enough to ask the difficult questions on camera and this discussion with the cast of *Drifters* was not likely to escape her prodding.

The dialogue commenced with Carter, Sue-Lyn, Maggie and Stephen. *Drifters'* two leads were then introduced fifteen minutes in, after some introductory footage courted them on the video screen at the back of the stage. Jessie and Josh entered together and sank down into Shawna's velvety peach furniture. Initially, Shawna adhered to her script and inquired politely about Jessie's involvement in the period show, and how she maintained her busy schedule, etc. Then Jessie stepped to the right of the stage and performed a song written for *Drifters*, a dreamlike ballad that would soon become the drama's secondary theme song as well as a popular hit in its own right. After her performance, Jessie took her seat again next to Josh.

As always, entranced by her music, Josh found her breathtaking. As Jessie casually laid a hand on his thigh—her cheeks blazing cherry red in response to the standing ovation and voracious cheering of the audience, which she always found surreal and even intimidating—Josh adjusted the black cowboy hat he wore for the occasion, and then he slipped an arm protectively around her shoulders. He turned his head slightly, nervously, and leaned in to his girl. *So beautiful,* he whispered in her ear, eliciting a sweet smile from Jessie just for him.

Shawna didn't miss a trick as the rest of the cast, cheering loudly along with the audience in genuine admiration for Jessie's surreal songwriting and singing, hunkered down on stools set up behind the peach chaise.

"So there's not much point in beating around the bush here," Shawna started roguishly, as she glanced down at cue cards in her lap. "You two are obviously a couple."

Blushing to a new level of crimson, Jessie looked down to where her long fingers rested comfortably against Josh's thigh. She pulled away a little, as if she hadn't even realized where she'd placed her hand. Josh glanced over at Jessie and wondered whether he should respond to their hostess, or just take his cue from Jessie herself. She met his eyes and he could see fear there, which surprised him.

Shawna filled in the pause. "It hasn't been easy for you. Josh, you've got to admit, you've had a bad rap in the past. Jessie was supposed to marry Charlie Deacon; a lot of people think she made a bad choice by ending that relationship. How are you dealing with the negativity from the press? That must be difficult."

Behind Josh and Jessie, Stephen wriggled on his stool and bit his tongue.

Jessie shifted her position on the comfy chaise. "There are a lot of reasons why my relationship with Charlie ended the way it did. At the same time, I'm crazy about this guy," she gestured to Josh, "and soon, when *Drifters* has its run, the rest of the world will be as well. He's a tremendous actor and one of the kindest, most genuine people I've ever met. I don't see the need to explain my relationship with him to the world. They'll just have to accept that we're together and leave it at that."

Not unkindly, Shawna scrutinized Josh as if she was trying to get a stronger sense of him as a person—as a man, perhaps—and then she glanced back at Jessie. She narrowed her eyes and leaned forward. "Last week someone spit on him at a coffee shop in Detroit. Why do you think that is? And how is any new couple supposed to survive that kind of bullshit?"

Eyes narrowing at Shawna's audacity to bring up the recent personal attack, Jessie reached over Josh's lap and wrapped her fingers over his right hand. She knew how much that very public assault diminished Josh's sense of comfort in their relationship. She was aware that he desperately needed her reassurance.

As she squeezed his hand, Josh marveled at the fact that he was able to sit there next to Jessie in this very public arena and not get up and run away. Embarrassed though he was, he trusted her. Yet he could not bring himself to look up and meet the eyes of their famous interviewer.

Jessie shifted in her seat and dove in. "We knew when we got together that the image of Josh conveyed by the gossip rags would be misconstrued and misinterpreted. We have always known we would have to be strong, that there would be criticisms by the media and by the public of our choice to be together. But the thing is Shawna, and you guys, too," she waved her hand to include the audience, "I love this guy. He is sweet, and real, and it breaks my heart to look at him sometimes and realize how lucky I am to have found him. These guys," she twisted around to look up and behind at her fellow cast, "love him too. So does the crew of *Drifters*. There's a reason for that. You guys need to give him a chance."

She could sense Josh squirming beside her. He couldn't look up. It was killing him to have to sit there on international television and be defended by his girlfriend, who had been walking next to him when some disgruntled thirty-something in Detroit chose to convey his feelings about their relationship by spitting on him. Josh chanced a brief glance up at Shawna and could tell that she sensed his discomfort.

To her, Josh seemed to be pleading for this interrogation to stop. But Ms. Coupland had one thing left to say.

"Josh," she said, looking straight at him so he'd have to meet her eyes, just for a moment. "You have to admit. You've got a history of violence. Drug abuse. The world out there loves Jessie. They're not going to put up with any shenanigans from a guy who has been arrested for beating up his own father."

It was as if she were challenging him on behalf of the world. Josh felt his heart sink. It seemed that this battle to gain acceptance would never end. He had no idea how to respond. The chips were stacked against him, and it seemed all God's creatures would turn fully against him on a dime, should he ever have the misfortune of taking a wrong step where Jessie was concerned.

"Ma'am," he heard coming from behind him as he sat there stiffly, aching to disappear, unable to respond. "I beg your pardon, but I can't sit here and watch my friends sit on the hot seat like this. I have to have my say." Stephen put a hand on Jessie's shoulder as she sank a little in her seat. "If anything, the world should be celebrating. It's not often you see two people so closely connected as Jessie and Josh. No matter what life throws at them, they will survive. Whether or not the world approves. Whether any of *us* approve. Which, for the record, we do. Highly. I've never seen Jessie so happy. I've never heard such beautiful *music* from Jessie. Being in love agrees with her. Being in love agrees with Josh. And since I've already dived in, let me just add that I, too, don't know a better guy than Josh. You would be wise to get to know him," Stephen added, looking towards the audience. "Get to know him, watch *Drifters*, and your lives will be forever changed by the magic you see between these two."

"No bias there!" Shawna was amused.

"Well yeah, sure, I want all of you to watch the show, but I seriously love these guys!" Steve bent forward and wrapped one arm around Jessie and another around Josh, trying unsuccessfully to lighten the mood.

Maggie, Carter and Sue-Lyn started poking fun at Josh from behind. As he pulled his cowboy hat over his face, chagrined, Shawna had to raise her voice to bring the little group back under control. "Okay, okay, I get the picture," she said. "Bullying is not acceptable whether it's on behalf of the media or," she eyed Josh, "between family members."

Jessie cringed and resolved to skip her planned dinner with Shawna tomorrow.

"Josh," Shawna added as she steered her show towards a conclusion. "I will give you a chance, and I will ask the rest of world to do the same. You are obviously held in high esteem by your fellow cast and, if Jessie loves you, which it appears she certainly does, then you deserve some time to prove yourself, if nothing else. Because," she added, "like it or not, the two of you are in the public eye, and your relationship is about to become even more public since my understanding of *Drifters* is that you are also a couple on screen. So," she pointed a finger at Josh, "be beyond reproach and we will be on your side. But mess up, and you won't get a second chance."

It was rare for Shawna to voice her opinion so strongly that it came out as a threat. Jessie was mortified, Josh was embarrassed and, watching from his home in Vancouver, Jonathon was incensed. But Shawna was secretly pleased. She adored Jessie, she had no time for bullies, and she didn't know Josh. She gave the world a clear message—accept him if he behaves, condemn him if he doesn't.

And when Shawna Coupland spoke, the world listened.

⌒⌒ ⌒⌒

Josh slammed the Audi's passenger door behind Jessie and stormed behind the vehicle before dropping into the driver's seat. Despite the protestations of Charles and Matt, who were never fond of Jessie's unruly penchant for independence, the couple rented their own vehicle in New York so they could enjoy some freedom. The Big Apple was the last stop on the press tour, and Josh and Jessie had booked an extra couple of days for sightseeing.

After waving *So long* to their friends, Josh turned the key in the ignition, roughly thrust the car in gear, and hurriedly backed out of their spot in the parking garage. He skidded around the first corner but slowed after that when, out of the corner of his eye, he saw Jessie wince. Sheepish, he ran his left hand through his hair and slowly exhaled.

Pulling out of the dim parkade into the startling bright sunshine moments later, Josh leaned his left elbow on the door's armrest and stared straight ahead as he drove. Jessie decided now was as good as ever to jump in.

"Josh," she ventured encouragingly, "this is just entertainment to people like her, for her audience. We knew going in that this wasn't going to be an easy ride. Let it go."

"Let it go? What am I supposed to let go, Jessie? The humiliation of sitting in front of millions and being told I'm not good enough for you? The memory of that asshole's spit running down my arm? Or maybe the scorn of everyone on the Internet?"

"Look, this is new to them, to everyone out there. They don't know you the way I do."

"Jess, it doesn't matter whether they know me or not. Nobody but Charlie is ever going to be good enough for the great Jessie Wheeler. You broke more than just *his* heart when you ended that relationship."

"What does that tell you, Josh?" Jessie was raising her voice now, its pitch increasing like the climax in one of her songs, steady and sure. "Charlie was so good for me that he had to go screw a variety of big butted bimbos! *I'm* the only one who knows who's good enough for Jessie Wheeler."

Josh swerved to avoid a red Dodge Caravan pulling out of a Starbucks parking lot in front of them.

"Asshole," he muttered, and Jessie speculated for a moment whether he was referring to the van's driver or to Charlie. Perhaps both. As they regained equilibrium by pulling past the van in another lane, Jessie reached over and placed her small hand over Josh's big fingers on the gearshift.

"Josh," she entreated, "I'm in this for the long haul. It's you and me now, not me and Charlie, not me and the world. I want this to work for us. I want *us* to work. So don't go getting all dopey on me. After a while people out there will find someone else to pick on."

Switching to the fast lane, Josh cruised along for a while over the speed limit while Jessie held her breath and prayed that he wouldn't pull a Charlie either by yelling at her or by keeping up the silent treatment. She watched as the speedometer gradually slowed to a more reasonable pace, and then relaxed further as Josh twisted his fingers around hers.

"Hey," she said, and he took his eyes off the road for a second to peek over at her. "I love you, you dork." Her eyes glistened as she let the emotion of the afternoon's interview and the ache of other people's judgment overwhelm her. It would kill her if she lost Josh. She couldn't stand to see him hurting this way.

She was rewarded with a hesitant but genuine small grin. "I love you back." He lifted her fingers and kissed the backs of them, and then flashed her a mischievous smile. "Big butted bimbos? Take you long to think that one up or has it been on your mind for a while?"

She groaned and punched him in the bicep.

"Ow! Stop distracting the driver!" he pleaded.

"Or what?" she teased.

Josh winked at her as he switched lanes again in preparation for their upcoming exit. "Wouldn't you like to know?"

"Oh, so that's your game. Put the pedal to the medal, Josh Sawyer. I've had enough of placating the public for today. I'm in need of some privacy. I'm thinking maybe a hot bath and chocolate covered strawberries." Leaning back against the seat, Jessie sighed with the pleasure of anticipation.

"Well, Jessie Wheeler, I guess I don't know you at all, then." Josh pestered his girl. "I thought you were more the peanut butter chocolate kind."

She pouted. "Julia Roberts ate chocolate dipped strawberries in Pretty Woman. They're supposed to be romantic. Dork."

"Girls and romance. What is it with this romance thing? I'm in this for the sex."

Squealing, Jessie pounded her man in the rib cage this time. Chuckling, Josh pulled into their hotel where he surrendered the sedan to an excited towheaded valet parker. Life's sweetest pleasures awaited them upstairs, despite the overhanging bitterness of a disapproving world on their shoulders.

Sightseeing in New York could wait another day.

Chapter Seven

$\mathcal{D}$*rifters* premiered to great acclaim, well overcoming all estimation of expected audience numbers, and engendering surprise and praise from the critics. Life settled into a general cycle of work and pleasure as the cast and crew once again pulled together, this time for the lengthy shoot of season two. The mood on set was generally happy-go-lucky as the tension from season one morphed into the melodious delight of newly requited love. Everyone could feel the happiness in the air emanating from Josh and Jessie. There was no doubt the couple was not only in love, but that they were also plainly and simply well matched. They were quiet, easy-going, friendly and happy, and their moods were contagious. Even Jonathon, fresh from a round of positive reviews for his Vancouver gold rush western, was congenial and amiable most of the time, since the biggest pressure was now off and all that remained was essentially to just keep up the good work.

One Saturday, Josh and Stephen decided to dig out their off road motorbikes and practice some motocross. Enjoying the perks of work on a successful series, they had money to spend and a need to focus on something other than nineteenth century dialogue. Josh hadn't competed since his tragic accident years earlier during a race, when a teenager died after being hit by Josh's bike. The accident had happened in the blink of an eye, as those things often do; and had sent Josh spiraling into depression, despair and drug use, but his friends convinced him to get back on the horse and give it another go. Both Josh and Steve were motorcycle junkies, and so they tuned up their bikes and purchased some colorful new leathers. The next weekend they made some adjustments to their bikes to accommodate some freestyle riding, or FMX, which Jessie found hard to watch and of which she was fairly certain Jonathon would not approve—his two lead male cast members on their Honda CRF 450s going for big air over dirt jumps. But the sport was addictive, and the boys were hooked.

About a month into the new shooting season of *Drifters*, the gang drove east an hour and a half to the mountain-hugged town of Agassiz so the boys could practice on a local course. It was a gorgeous windless blue sky autumn day; the drive alone was worth the trip. Leaves of rusty reds and burnt orange lined the route, sentry to the small party of friends cruising casually along with their coffees and salty snacks of crunchy cashews and roasted almonds. The majestic snow-capped mountains were a more onerous guard. Like the leaves, they stood watch along the way as if they were protecting the boisterous group throughout their journey. Everyone was in good humor. The shooting of *Drifters* season two was off to a great start, and the reviews from season one were heartening. Besides, what could be better than a group of good friends hanging out together on a pleasant crisp fall Saturday?

The group convinced Jonathon to let them borrow one of the show's production vans so they could all travel together. Carter brought his new girl, Ashley, a quiet, pleasant addition to the gang. Stephen invited Sophie; Maggie and Sue-Lyn tagged along in the backseat, picking on the others and harassing Josh about his driving. As they approached the motocross track, the discussion turned to the sport. It was a dangerous activity even for guys like Josh and Stephen who, having raced in their younger days, were now out just for the fun of it. Josh was quiet as the discussion centered on known accidents, like Cam Sinclair's badly broken femur in Las Vegas, and Jim McNeil's death during a practice at the Texas Motor Speedway. It was a fact of life that injury followed riders of the sport, whether they were into racing or freestyle events. It wasn't lost on any of them that the Agassiz track was near a landmark called Cemetery Road, but they were all so happy on that particular day that the road's name became a joke and in no way a portent of things to come.

As the guys unloaded their heavy bikes from the trailer behind the van, the girls dropped their compostable coffee cups in nearby square covered wooden garbage bins and wandered around the site. Maggie elbowed Jessie and pointed towards a white sign with black lettering.

"*Black bear area—Beware.* I love British Columbia, but I can't get used to the bears." She edged a little closer to Sue-Lyn.

Jessie grinned. "You wouldn't have liked Charleston, then. We shared the city with alligators, four kinds of poisonous snakes, and black widow spiders."

Maggie whipped her head around to gawk at her friend, somewhat astonished. It was rare for Jessie ever to mention Charleston. Even Jessie looked slightly taken aback, surprised at how easily the reference to the historic city had left her lips, as Sue-Lyn hooked an arm in her co-star's elbow. Jessie glanced over at Maggie and shrugged. The slight admission was a good sign—maybe life in Charleston was indeed behind her.

The girls wandered over to the racetrack and watched some younger riders spray up dirt. They got a kick out of a little boy of maybe three or four, on a child's tricycle, circling the viewing area with a pronounced verbalized, "Rrrrrrrrrr".

"Just wait until *he* gets a motor," Sophie announced dryly.

Sue-Lyn piped up. "Boys and their toys. Starts in diapers, does it?"

Sophie giggled and added, "Hey, if it keeps my man happy to get out on the track once in a while then I'm all for it, since it usually means he's in a good mood afterwards and I can convince him to go listen to some jazz or take me out to a French restaurant."

They were attracting unsolicited stares. Although Jessie was on some level accustomed to it, it was new for the others. *Drifters* had become a big deal in the Fraser Valley, and there was a buzz around the track now that the show's stars were hanging around. Jessie inched a little closer to Maggie. She regularly fought Charles' and Matt's urging to keep some security close at hand, rarely taking advantage of any, and instead preferring to wander around on her own. At the same time, on the occasions that she did venture out in public alone, Jessie usually tried to disguise herself to some degree. And she was rarely in the company of others who would draw notice to her. So at Agassiz the attention was different, and so was somewhat of a revised experience for her, as well.

However, the people at the motocross complex were friendly and down-to-earth. Before they knew it, the girls were lined up at the freestyle track watching their boys practice, while Carter, his sleek black hair pulled back in an appealing ponytail, engaged the locals in a serious discussion to help him understand the rules and stunts of the sport. His sense of humor immediately dispersed any thoughts of tension or ego that the regulars might have perceived would attend Jessie and her cast mates, and soon he and all of the girls were enthusiastically engaged in learning about FMX. Soon they comprehended the benefits of two stroke engines versus four strokes, which bikes were the best and why, modifications made to bikes for freestyle and, lastly, the prestigious kiss-of-death stunt, and who on the competitive world circuit accomplished it best.

Soon Maggie stopped looking over her shoulder for bears, and Jessie took a personal inventory and discovered with pleasure that she was content and at peace. Life with her friends was almost the *normal* she continuously sought. They were caring, unassuming and nice to others, and she genuinely loved being in their company. She found herself relaxing more than she had in years and was almost surprised at the comfortable state to which her soul had arrived, finally, in the strange lifetime of turmoil and fame she'd been handed.

After a while, bruised and beat from the constant jarring his body was absorbing from the bike and the introduction to the demanding FMX skills, Josh took a break. He moseyed over to the girls and dropped down on a wooden bench beside Jessie as she watched Steve take a lesson with one of the sport's more notable riders. Jessie took Josh's dirty white leather gloves from him and for a pleasurable moment lingered over their softening newness. After a moment she laid her hand over his.

"Eww, you're all sweaty," she teased, squeezing his warm moist fingers.

Josh took that as a cue to lean over and brush his three-day whiskered face against her smooth cheeks. Then, as she giggly recoiled from the bristly pinpricks, he placed a big hand behind her head and forced her to hold still while he gave her an exaggerated smooch.

Jessie wrapped her arms around her man and held him tight. She loved the feel of his body against hers, and admitted to herself that the white leather padded motocross gear and boots were in fact tantalizingly sexy. *But then again*, she grinned to herself, *everything Josh wears is sexy*. She was crazy about him and was still amazed that they had finally found a way to be together. Life was good.

At day's end, with no injuries sustained with the exception of a few expected blue bruises, and a few crazy new tricks learned, the gang piled back into the van for the hour and a half ride west back to Vancouver, hauling the tired mud-splattered bikes behind them.

"I'm disappointed I didn't see a bear," Maggie threw in offhandedly, frowning, which stirred up a hornet's nest of retorts and responses.

"You're such a hypocrite!" Carter scolded her, his arm around the demure but smiling Ashley. "You didn't want to see a bear and now that you're safe you're wishing you'd seen one." Disparaging, he shook his head.

"Well, I know you guys wouldn't let it attack me, so it would have been okay to have seen one!"

Sue-Lyn threw in her two cents. "From a distance, you mean!"

"A safe distance of what, like a few hundred feet?" Carter kept up his playful banter.

Maggie pouted at their teasing while Josh pointed the van back to the city and Sophie called restaurants to try to find reservations for a late evening dinner.

They hadn't seen a bear, or any snakes, to boot—but a bear saw them. He'd hidden in the crowd of loyal observers and thrill seekers, watching as the group of friends shared one of the best days Jessie could recall in a very long time. Deuce McCall watched as the production van hauling the bikes pulled out of the parking lot, and he grimaced as he saw Josh reach over from the driver's seat, place a finger under Jessie's chin, and coax her towards him for a tender kiss. He was supremely annoyed when Josh gunned the motor, spewing dirt out behind the little troupe so that it arced into the air in Deuce's general direction.

Deuce would give her a little more time. Now was just for observing, to see if the relationship with Josh would stick. But he had no intention of forgiving her for quitting his employ and his life. His ancestors were wealthy plantation owners with many slaves and that cell memory passed on to Deuce. What was once his was always his. He would get her back when the time was right. And that time was imminent.

Climbing into his rented Ford Fusion, Deuce McCall kicked the dirt off his boots before slamming the driver's door behind him. He could see

Jessie and her friends singing in the van when he pulled ahead of them a few moments later. The Southern gentleman pulled his brown cowboy hat down over his balding head in the event Jessie decided to glance his way. She didn't see him but, oddly, she shivered when Deuce's vehicle passed. Josh rested his arm casually on Jessie's thigh after flicking up the van's heater in the cool late autumn evening. It wouldn't do to let her catch a chill.

The robust spectacled trees observed silently again as the two vehicles passed beneath their honor guard—the hunter and the hunted. Leaves, either hanging on until their last breath, or newly departed from the safety and relative obscurity of their hosts, sensed in their spines that a wicked, appalling game was just about to begin. If they could have, they would have cringed.

Chapter Eight

*O*n an inky star-kissed Christmas Eve, with an oppressive ceiling of grey snow clouds slowly moving in to shield the miniature sparkles glistening above Vancouver, Jessie sang *O Holy Night* at midnight mass. She hadn't been asked, it just kind of happened. She attended the service with Josh, Charles and Dee as a sort of conciliatory attempt to align the man she loved with her sort-of parents. The Keatings couldn't seem to find it in themselves to completely accept him, nor could many of Jessie's fans. Things had settled down a bit, as Jessie had expected; the gossip mags had no shortage of celebrity faux pas to pick on. Yet it seemed the climate surrounding their match was still—at least outside their main circle—not wholly friendly and receiving. Charles and Dee were social enough, partly because of their friendship with Jonathon, but they often enjoyed visits from Charlie when he was in town, and it was crystal clear where their hopes and allegiances truly lay.

At midnight mass a nervous twenty-year-old man with a warm timbre to his tenor voice stepped up to the altar to sing *O Holy Night* in the much esteemed Christian Christmas tradition. Watching as he made his way forward, Jessie—seated in a wooden pew, a short itchy sequined black scooped-neck dress distracting her from the service—was slightly cranky. She was brushing knees with a bristling Dee on one side of her, and twining her fingers amongst Josh's anxious hands on the other.

Although making valiant attempts at civility and social graces, Josh was edgy and obviously upset. It was awkward. Although kind to Jessie, Dee had a habit of couching her dislike of Josh through passive aggressive control tendencies. Throughout the entire Christmas Eve meal of broccoli crepes, mixed green salad and bacon wrapped scallops, which Deirdre and Charles hosted in the charming formal dining room at La Casa, the matriarch's unfavorable comments were less than subtle. She announced to the table, which included Jonathon and his wife Giselle, that Charlie had dropped by earlier and that he was recently cast in a new Clint Eastwood film. It seemed Charlie was making an effort to leave his light comedies behind, as this new film was touted as heavy drama. Jessie quietly wondered whether Charlie was trying to make a point, and whether Dee was completely hoodwinked by Jessie's ex-fiancé. Now, sitting in the uncomfortable wooden pew, she narrowed her eyebrows, remembering the quick rise of her blood pressure at Dee's insistence on heralding Charlie's victories in the presence of Josh.

So when in church the edgy young man started to sing the beloved Christmas Eve hymn and couldn't get past the first verse, Jessie had enough fight roused up in her to consider going to his aid. She didn't want to upstage him but she quickly realized he was in trouble and was likely unable to continue the beautiful carol. Jessie was also uncomfortable enough sandwiched between Dee and Josh to want an out and, for Jessie, music was always an out.

In front of the entire congregation, unconcerned with what anyone would think, she slipped past Josh, walked up the aisle and stepped lightly onto the altar, where the singer stood frozen and embarrassed. Feeling the boy's discomfort, the enthralled folks spellbound in the peaceful hum of their year's holiest night were starting to feel the yearned for Christmas magic bubble-of-tranquility dissipate. They were squirming in their seats, and a low shuffling and mumbling overtook the silence left by the organist, who removed her graceful hands from the faithfully restored Casavant organ's original ivory keys. The music director was also helpless. Immobilized in the choir loft above and at the back of the church, he was regretting his decision to take a chance and let the talented but obviously overwrought young man sing the treasured carol.

Mortified, the soloist was staring at the floor, overcome by stage fright, unable to move. Jessie paused four feet to his left, faced him side-on, and took up the verse. She reached out and gathered his hand in hers and, as he looked up, what he later recalled was seeing a presence like an angel, encircled—haloed—in the light. The entire congregation sighed in one collective breath, grateful entranced witnesses to the blessed magic that ensued.

The boy searched for his voice. When he found it, he and Jessie sang together, strong and true, imbued with the divine glow of Christmas Eve as the organist brought the historic Casavant back to life.

In the pew, Dee chanced a glance over to Josh. He seemed to have forgotten the earlier chides made by Jessie's manager. The *Drifters* star was sitting stock still, as mesmerized as anyone else who had the heavenly happenstance to be at the church on that ethereal evening. The hymn was mystical, lilting and lovely, and had the power to transport any non-believer. Watching Jessie help the young man on the altar find his voice was perhaps one of the most incredible glimpses into the girl's soul Dee ever witnessed as she had, over time, watched Jessie blossom and grow. And the rapture on Josh's face was equally revealing. There was no doubt that he loved her but, as the honeymoon period wore off, could he abstain from hurting her? He did have a temper, righteous or not, and had occasionally resorted to violence in the past.

In this brief twinkling on an evening when the glory and love of God and the Savior's birth transcended all of the minutiae and toil of life, Dee let a little window open ever so slightly. She, too, allowed herself to briefly become a momentary believer, but her new hopeful belief was in the love story of Josh and Jessie. Her love of God was already complete.

When the hymn found its last sweet note, and the mystical carol drew to its celestial close for one more blessed year, Jessie and the young tenor hugged each other, and the faithful exploded in an uncharacteristic standing ovation. Neither Dee nor Josh ever loved Jessie more, and Charles and his younger namesake Charlie, and everyone else present, were also completely captivated. Jessie's gifts were more than just music, songwriting, acting. Despite the troubles she'd faced in her lifetime, she was a giving, caring person. Not much wonder people throughout the world loved and admired her deeply.

Afterwards, in the church entrance, Charlie elbowed his way through the excited crowd over to Jessie and gave her a sweet, simple, tender kiss on the cheek.

"Jessie," he said, shaking his head in wonder, warm hands lingering in hers as he stared deeply into the much missed pearl eyes and thus into the girl's soul. "You never fail to amaze me."

Next to her—slightly uncomfortable, tense—Josh watched quietly, uncertain just how Jessie's ex would receive him.

Blushing, Jessie slid her hands up the sleeves of Charlie's Italian leather overcoat, grasped his elbows and leaned into a gentle embrace. She hadn't really contemplated what she'd done. It was just something that needed to happen. She couldn't sit there and watch the boy suffer.

"It was nothing, just a little helping hand," she murmured. "He was an accomplished tenor who needed a little nudge, that's all. It was scary for him, up there."

Charlie studied Josh, who was shifting his weight from one side to another. By glancing at the toes of his black boots, he was managing to avoid the eyes of the churchgoers lingering in the entry. A slow exhalation accompanied Charlie's extended hand. "Once again, I regret letting this girl go. You're a lucky man, Sawyer. Don't fuck it up. If you do, I'll be waiting in the wings. And I won't fuck it up next time."

All Josh could picture in his mind's eye when he faced his old friend was the debilitating humiliation from that horrifying long ago night in Wes Sawyer's black box studio. It was funny how those awkward old memories were seemingly impossible to let go. Josh accepted the handshake but he couldn't speak. The painful memories, and Charlie's history with Jessie, scared the shit out of him.

Thankfully, Jessie intervened. "Charlie," she chided gently, loving Josh even more for his vulnerability and slipping her fingers into his to offer comfort and reassurance, "this man is never leaving my side as long as I have something to say about it. Sorry. You know the old saying—you snooze, you lose."

She didn't see the need to rub salt in an open wound by adding *I love him desperately*, but she thought it, and the verity of the sentiment lit up her eyes like one of the stars above after the passing of a cottony grey cloud.

Wrapped in a fake fur mink stole thrown casually over the shoulders of a creamy white Donna Karan blazer, Deirdre weaved her way over to the little group. She embraced Charlie and wished him a Merry Christmas, feeling a pang of regret that he wouldn't be around the next day socializing with Charles and drinking bourbon in her lavish front room.

"Deirdre Keating," Charlie said with grace, finally letting go of Jessie to accept the imposing woman's heartfelt hug. "You are exquisite. Merry Christmas to you, too."

Josh was about as uncomfortable as the challenged singer earlier, so Jessie nudged him out of the door with a goodbye wave to Dee and her boys. Watching, Charles made a grand gesture. With an arm around his elegant wife, he commented on the couple.

"I've never seen her this happy, Dee," he admitted, a note of relaxed contentment stealing into his affirmative businessman's speech.

Charlie sighed and rested both hands on his hips as his solemn flecked eyes followed the exiting grey silhouettes of Josh and Jessie, who were framed in the entry of the church, front-lit by an eerie contrast between the semi-clouded white moon and the city's brighter night lights. "I'm the biggest ass on the planet."

Dee slipped her fingers into Charlie's and seized the opportunity to alleviate the ennui she knew the next day would bring. "We stocked up our bourbon. Stop by and have a drink tomorrow. Today, actually," she said, reminding herself that it was now after one in the morning. "Bring Jack and Lydia."

She breezed out the door and, despite a twinge for Charlie, even allowed herself a small smile as she watched Josh pull open the passenger door of his pick-up and then settle against it to kiss Jessie. Dee stopped just outside the church, on the top step, and saluted the couple silently as a few whimsical white flakes drifted lazily down from the snow clouds trying their hardest to obscure the starlit night above.

Josh was leaning into Jessie, and her face was turned up to his. Both pairs of eyes were shining as they shared some apparently secret joke. Dee had never seen a couple apparently more in love. She breathed in deeply, remembering a similar heady kind of love with Charles many years earlier. She prayed the sheer happiness and joy she saw before her would last; then her husband stole up behind her and wrapped his long arms around his wife's later middle-aged waist. He nuzzled her neck and all of the glory of the universe seemed suddenly revealed to Dee as she found herself encased in one of life's perfect moments.

Before them, in the parking lot across the road, Jessie and Josh stood illuminated underneath a frosty streetlight. They were no longer smiling, but were simply standing there nose to nose, hands held, eyes closed, reveling in the sweetest of life's gifts.

After a moment Jessie brushed her lips against Josh's again, and then she turned and eased her way up into the truck. Josh gently closed the door behind her, as if by slamming it he would break the spell, and then he walked noiselessly around behind the truck, his booted footsteps leaving wet imprints on the virgin snow. He hopped in on the driver's side, fired up the engine, and steered out of the parking lot, his hand in Jessie's.

When they got to his place Jessie poured them some Baileys and they opened their stockings against the backdrop of America's favorite Christmas film, Frank Capra's *It's a Wonderful Life* starring Jimmy Stewart. The lovers capped off a perfect day by snuggling and falling asleep on the couch in each other's arms.

As they slept, a number of cell phone videos forever chronicling Jessie's assistance with the fraught young male soloist were uploaded to YouTube. Immediately they went viral and Jessie's reputation, despite the fact that she had ended her relationship with the popular Charlie for the supposedly hot tempered Josh, was again set in stone as the beautiful, sweet, generous person everyone believed her to be.

At four-twenty in the morning, the city comfortably cocooned in a covering of fresh white snow that lay in "barely there" drifts outside their peaceful warm abode, Josh woke Jessie and groggily piloted her upstairs to his bedroom. Shyly, he reached into the closet and, from underneath a few folded navy blue and sage green hoodies, pulled out two small wrapped gifts. Jessie sat cross-legged on the comfortable bed; she had changed into red plaid cotton pajama pants and one of Josh's dove-grey long sleeved Henleys. Childlike, she pulled the sleeves down over her hands and tucked her fingers around them, then reached up and started twisting ringlets around a curl of hair.

Josh sat opposite her on the bed in faded jeans with the top button undone and a ubiquitous white T-shirt, loving how adorable she looked in his space all groggy and sleepy-eyed, twisting nervously at her hair. He set both boxes down in front of Jessie's crossed knees. She looked up, searching his eyes. He pointed to the silver one with the shiny green ribbon.

"This one first," he said.

Jessie let the ringlet fade into oblivion as she reached down for the box, which she held in her upright palms as if it were a fragile egg in danger of cracking. After a moment studying its pretty wrapping, she untied the ribbon and opened the box. Inside was a stunning silver heart-shaped locket engraved with their initials, two J's entwined around each other so you could barely see where one ended and the other began. She pried the locket open with a manicured fingernail. Inside was a tiny painting of the two of them, a replica of the *Drifters* photograph on Josh's nightstand. Crafted in the historic eighteenth century style of portrait miniatures, it was exquisite.

"Josh," she breathed, "it's beautiful! Who painted this for you?"

With trembling fingers Josh grasped the locket, then he carefully fastened it around his girlfriend's neck. "One of Kayla's roommates is a visual artist. Frank, the guy that teaches dance in that studio on Granville. He painted it." He sat back and admired the lovely silver against her smooth skin. "He did a nice job."

Jessie smiled up at him. She would wear the locket everywhere, and someday she would pass it on to their children. It was that kind of gift.

Timidly, Josh pointed to the second box. Giddy now, Jessie scooped it up and delicately tore open the wine and silver paper, setting the little bow carefully aside. Inside was a Tiffany & Co. box. Enchanted, Jessie lifted the lid. Nestled on a white silk cushion was an elegant silver diamond ring. Daringly, Josh lifted it and held it up, where its channel-set round brilliant diamonds, enhancing a classic six-prong 1.5 carat diamond setting, twinkled in the pallid moonlight dancing on the bed where they'd first made love so long ago.

"Jessie," Josh started, his voice cracking.

She was already crying, her hands clasped over her mouth, eyes wide.

Josh was struggling too. He wiped a thumb over a tear that leaked out of his right eye, then reached across the shallow divide between them and merged his tear with one of hers.

"Jessie," he said again, stronger this time, as she glimpsed downwards, found his left hand and enclosed it in hers. "I've loved you since the day we met. Your faith in me changed my life. I didn't even believe in me, yet somehow you did. I know we've only officially been together as a couple for four months, but I've never loved anyone more, and I never will. You are the only girl for me, Jessie Wheeler. I will love you always, Jessie. *Always.* You make me the happiest man on this crazy planet. Marry me. Say you will be mine— always and forever."

He slipped off the bed and knelt down on one knee. Jessie, turning to face him as she let her legs fall over the side, forced herself to remain composed but her left hand was shaking when she held it out to him. She nodded, silent tears betraying an outward calm, as the man she loved placed the magnificent ring on her second last finger.

"Yes," she heard herself whisper. "Yes, I'll marry you, Josh Sawyer. You and me. Always and forever."

Josh leapt up and swept her into his arms, and it was quite some time before either could speak. Neither had felt such peace and happiness, even when they'd finally admitted their true feelings for each other in late August. This was the real deal. This was love, perfection in an imperfect world, heightened by moonlit diamonds and the holy magic of Christmas. After tender kisses and sweet words of promise, Jessie slipped downstairs to the Christmas tree, returning with a small box of her own for Josh.

"It won't quite compare," she murmured softly. "But it carries the same sentiment."

They sat on the bed together as he opened it, and Josh gently reprimanded her for worrying about any comparison. It was a silver pendant engraved with a cursive J, hanging at the end of a tan leather string.

Jessie took it from him and fastened the leather around his neck, finishing with a long, slow kiss on his perfect lips. "There's only one J, but I figure you can decide whether it stands for Josh or Jessie. I figure it's for both of us. We are one."

"Definitely," he grinned, happy. "We are one." He pulled her onto his lap and then they lay on the bed and celebrated their first Christmas together, not only as a couple, but also now as an engaged couple. This would be a wedding Jessie could savor although she figured it would have to be a year away in order to give the world some time to support it as well.

As Jessie lay on her back and allowed Josh to slip the Henley shirt up over her head, his knees on either side of hers, she reveled in the memory that the day Charlie stammered through some kind of shaky proposal was also the day she met Josh. *My, how things can change in a short time*, she thought. Josh's proposal was a remembrance to be kept and cherished and shared with grandchildren. Joyously happy, she clasped the little bow she set aside earlier and almost squished it as Josh sexily slipped her pajama pants down, and then she surrendered her mind and body to the amazing man who had changed her life as well, and who was going to become her husband.

Afterwards, Jessie handed Josh a thumb drive and told him it contained the file of a new song she'd written for him. He played it on his Mac as they snuggled together under the covers. She'd written another classic soft dusky Jessie Wheeler ballad that proclaimed her deepening love for him. They drifted off to sleep for a few more hours, his hand resting on her hip and her fingers soaking up the warmth of his body under the sleeve of his T-shirt.

At ten they urged each other awake, showered, and toasted some cinnamon raisin bagels. Jessie sauntered off to a corner of the living room and called Charles and Dee to wish them a Happy Christmas. Deirdre, the grand lady herself, answered.

"Hi Dee," Jessie started, nervous. "Merry Christmas!"

"Merry Christmas to you, too," Dee replied coolly. She was sorry Jessie would not be spending the day with her, as had become their custom. They would have Jessie and Josh over for a fancy meal in a few days, instead.

"Did you guys sleep in?" Jessie was stalling for time.

"I did," Dee said. "Charles was up at the crack of dawn, as usual. He'll be asleep in his turkey before long."

"Charlie coming over?"

"Yes, he agreed to drop by today after the Deacon family dinner, and he's bringing Jack and Lydia. We'll have a few drinks and swap some stories. It's been quite a year."

Jessie winced. Yes, it had been quite a year. And now she was going to add a little more fuel to the fire for the evening's telling. It wouldn't be a bad thing for her to give Charles and Dee some time to settle into her news before she saw them in person again.

"What did the old man give you for Christmas this year?" she asked Dee, killing time as Josh watched from the kitchen where he was spreading a little butter on their bagels.

"Oh, a few good historic romances, some of that Cabernet Franc I like from Africa, what else, let me see…flannel pink pajamas…oh and he had that publicity shot of you framed, the one from the new album. I'll hang it in the music room."

Jessie blushed. "Aw, Dee," she said. "That's sweet. Not that you need any more pictures of me."

On her end, Dee smiled pensively as she settled onto the creamy chaise with an Irish coffee clasped between her delicate fingers. Charles was on his knees strategically placing wood on the fire in the hearth, as the Paul Peel above the mantel warmed the room. She loved the framed picture of Jessie best of all her gifts. They had no need of material things, the Keatings, and Charles always knew which buttons to push to help make Dee's Christmases and birthdays special. Anything to do with Jessie…they had missed out on having children of their own. Christmases were quiet around their large home. They would miss their girl, this day.

Biting back resentment because Jessie had chosen to celebrate with Josh's family instead of with her and Charles, Dee took a slow sip of her hot spiked coffee and casually asked Jessie what Josh gave her for Christmas.

"Um, well, a silver locket, for one. Heart-shaped."

Stab. *Of course*, Dee thought.

"With a miniature painting inside, of the two of us. Wait til you see it, Dee, it's really lovely." Jessie couldn't keep excitement from leaking into her voice.

"That's nice, dear." Dee was thinking of the gifts Charlie had given Jessie over the years. She couldn't remember a thing.

"Oh, and …um…well, Dee, a ring."

A ring, Dee thought. *How nice*. Then she sat up straight, almost spilling the coffee. She glanced over at Charles, who narrowed his eyes quizzically. "Oh? What kind of ring? Your birthstone, maybe?"

"Actually, it's a diamond ring, Dee. See, the thing is…Josh asked me to marry him, and I said yes." She squeezed her eyes shut and waited for the long pause to end.

At La Casa, Dee set her earthenware coffee mug down on the table without placing a coaster underneath. Her hand was starting to shake. Charles sat up straight, a length of wood poised in mid-air as if he were on the muddy field at Culloden, about to strike at an imposing foe.

"Honey," Dee stammered. "Oh, I don't know what to say, Jessie. Isn't it... isn't it a little soon? I mean, it's only been a few months..."

Interrupting, Jessie jumped in. "I know, Dee, and it won't be soon, I know we've got to give everyone some time to get used to the idea, but we're happy, Dee. Please be happy for us too. I love this guy like crazy. I really do."

Dee recalled the kiss from last night's midnight mass, under the streetlight in the fresh misty snow. *Yes,* she thought. *Love and its tenterhooks have Jessie by the heart.*

"Okay, honey," she sighed. "We'll talk about what this all means when we see you in a few days. In the meantime, of course I'm happy for you, and Charles will be as well." Then, "What about Charlie? Do you want to tell him, or shall we?" Her manager side kicked in. "Will you be wearing the ring in public right away? Should I be calling Janet to handle this?"

Inwardly, Jessie moaned. She just wanted to wear her ring and enjoy it, the whole she-bang; the being in love, the getting married, Christmas with Josh. She was so happy she thought she would burst. But in her surreal world, nothing was normal. Everything had a price, new corners had to be navigated.

"I want to wear the ring, Dee. But no one will see it for the next few days until we get a chance to talk to you and sort things out. I promise." She brightened. "Wait til you see it. It's from Tiffany & Co.! It has diamonds all around the band."

Well, at least the boy has taste, Dee thought, a little spitefully. She couldn't help herself. "And Charlie?"

"Uh, okay. Well. I guess you can tell him if you want to. It's not really something I want to talk about with him just yet."

"Okay."

She paused. "I just want to enjoy this for a little while, Dee. All of it."

Dee shrank back on the chaise. She felt like shit for raining on Jessie's parade. Of course the girl deserved happiness. She leaned forward and put her head in her hands.

"Okay, honey. Enjoy it. Congratulations. Give Josh a hug from us, and drive safe, okay?" She was less than enthusiastic, but she was trying.

"Thanks, Dee. We'll see you in a few days."

"Yes, we'll have a big dinner planned. We'll see you then. Love you."

"Love you too, Dee. Bye for now. Hugs to Charles and Carlotta. And hi to Jack and Lydia."

They rang off with Jessie feeling a little peculiar. She detected the sadness in Dee's voice, and thought a little sheepishly that she herself should have made time for Dee and Charles today. But this was her first Christmas with Josh and, despite her love for Charles and Dee, she felt almost obliged to give them some time to miss her, so when they were all together again perhaps Dee would treat Josh with respect and care.

She turned to Josh, who met her halfway across the living room and gathered her up in a big embrace. Jessie nestled sensuously into his warm neck and thought how wonderful it was to finally plan a future with this man, to have his hugs mean he was accessible to her in every way possible now as opposed to just in a painful and finite friendship.

"It's okay," he murmured with conviction. "I'll win them over."

"Yes, you will," she said, her voice sweet and caring. "I don't doubt it, Josh. It just may take a little time, that's all."

"Yep," he said. "Time. Well, we have lots of that, little one. A whole bright big future." *Little one.* Her father had called her that. Yet another reason to love this guy.

She nuzzled deeper into him, tucked her hands up under his T-shirt, hooked her fingers just inside the waistband of his jeans and then, too soon, it was time to go.

Time, that elusive, un-lasso-able entity, was urging them on. Always hurried, never patient to wait out the most precious moments of life, it had its own agenda, and that was to rush Josh and Jessie forward into a black void that would hold them hostage, until time itself decided they'd had enough, and released them from its hoary grasp.

After loading the truck to capacity with gaily-wrapped gifts, Josh and Jessie puttered happily off to pick up Kayla and Paul. The foursome hit the highway to Seattle singing Christmas carols almost the entire way, laughing at each other for missing most of the words. Jessie was the worst. Her defense was that she rarely sang carols and instead had to focus on her own songs, so she was subject to a merciless teasing.

Kayla was thrilled at their news. Jessie Wheeler as a sister-in-law was cool enough, but the fact she so obviously made Josh a contented man meant everything to Kayla.

In Seattle, life was simply divine with Hilary and Zach, who were ecstatic over the engagement. Their young children didn't have a clue who Jessie was other than a gentle soul who was patient and who loved to read stories and sing lullabies. Jessie was in her glory. She cherished the simple anonymity of being loved unconditionally by children who couldn't care less about her fame, and who also loved Josh for who he was, without prejudice.

The only glitch in the otherwise perfect day was the arrival of the Sawyer patriarch Wes and his new girlfriend, an attractive thirty-something brunette who wore her heels too high and her designer clothes a size too small, but Josh knew his dad was expected for Christmas dinner and so he mentally prepared himself. Surprisingly, his dad also seemed to be making an effort to keep the peace, so the little extended family worked their way through a pleasant Christmas turkey dinner with lots of chuckles and only superficial tension.

Jessie found herself speculating whether Zach and Kayla knew the truth about Josh's paternity. In fact, she wondered if Josh himself was somehow aware, but she didn't have the nerve to ask him and figured if he knew and wanted to tell her, he would. She guessed perhaps he was aware that the man he always thought was his dad was not, but not that his producer, Jonathon, was his real dad. Jessie understood instinctively that such news would not be welcome to Josh, despite the fact his acting was considered a critical success and he was now regularly courted for feature films, the first of which would soon be released.

After the dinner dishes were washed—during which Hilary and Jessie mercilessly teased Kayla over her hilarious stories of life with stylin' hipster lawyer Paul—everyone gathered in the homey living room and settled by a comfortable crackling red-ginger fire. Zach read *'Twas the Night Before Christmas* despite the protestations of his oldest son who proclaimed that it was Christmas Day and so the poem didn't fit.

Hunched on the floor across from the fire, Jessie rested her back against Josh's chest and wrapped his arms tightly around her, interlacing her fingers amongst his. Unable to keep a permanent grin from lighting up her face, she could feel his heartbeat, and it thrilled her. She relished the affectionate teasing and chiding between the very close Sawyer siblings, and she could sense Josh finally relaxing around the family headman. The littlest of Hilary and Zach's children, three-year-old Lana, crept sleepily over to them and burrowed into Jessie's arms. Josh's sparkling eyes, twinkling with a faint orange zest reflected from the fire, filled with wonder. He kissed the top of Jessie's head as she nestled and cuddled the little one, who was struggling to keep her small eyes open, a worn bedraggled pink bunny blanket snuggled dearly in her arms.

This was paradise, and both Jessie and Josh knew it. Remembrances of Jessie's childhood before her father died were dim, pushed underneath the surface of her working mind, too perfect and painful to recall. The glimpses Josh allowed himself into his own lonely past were filled with images of his parents fighting while he and Zachary removed Kayla to the basement. There, the Sawyer kids could turn the volume up on the television and drown out the prevalent anger threatening and permeating seemingly every family get together in the old days.

Later, after Zach gently lifted his small daughter into his arms and carried her up the stairs to bed, Jessie was begged to play the piano, and the Christmas carols started anew. The entire day and evening was a jolly time filled with laughter and love, the family bonding as tangible and welcome as soft swirls of ice cream dipped in chocolate. Overall, the season in its entirety was glorious as Josh and Jessie celebrated their first Christmas as a couple, and it was easy to see why they fell into a pattern of even deeper trust and love after the New Year when *Drifters* commenced shooting.

Together, with Dee's reluctant advice, they decided it would be best to set a wedding date after *Drifters* wrapped for the season, when they would know whether they'd be shooting a third season. Likely the big day would be sometime in May or June of the following year—a year and a half away. It was a bit of a wait but after the fiasco with Charlie, both Jessie and Josh felt it best to let people get used to them as a couple. Besides, Dee would need to recoup her energy before diving into another big wedding celebration, and she wouldn't have it any other way. With Deirdre Keating at the helm, it was always "go big or go home".

Then, one day in mid-spring, shortly after Agassiz cleared away the mud and the motocross track reopened, Deuce McCall decided the lovers had shared enough time together. He was sick of seeing them in the newspapers and rag bags, snuggled closely, engaged, and McCall was disgusted that Jessie's fans seemed to be easing up on Josh. It was time to make an entrance back into Jessie's life. It was time to shake up the perfect little world that left her eyes shining with happiness and her songs filled with love.

It was time for payback.

It was time to get her back.

Chapter Nine

*A*gassiz was clear and dry on the day of the exhibition event marking the new season of motocross racing and competition. Jessie and Josh decided to give Jessie's SUV a run, so they picked up Kayla and Paul. The upbeat couple reclined in the back seat and entertained the driver and his gal with stories and jokes. Jessie spent most of the drive turned around facing Kayla and chatting animatedly as Josh drove. She and Kayla had become quite close, and Kayla was now one of her permanent regular dancers. Their last big gig was a dynamic musical number for the Grammys, and the two women had lots to share about how they felt the evening had transpired, both for their own performances as well as in relation to many eccentric celebrities on the prowl that evening.

After pulling into the dirt parking lot off Cemetery Road they found a roomy spot near the fence for the SUV and then, linked arm in arm, Kayla and Jessie sidled off in search of their friends, who were expected to arrive in Stephen's brand spanking new Audi TT and Carter's new-to-him but ancient Beamer. Once the gang was all assembled, they hustled over to the wooden bleachers with buttery popcorn and garlic pretzels from the concession stand in hand, and enjoyed a cool, crisp spring day under slate grey skies and the caress of a gentle breeze.

The road on the drive up had showcased exactly the opposite palette of the fall trips. The ephemeral cherry blossoms were, this time around, in fleeting gorgeous candy cotton pink bloom, testaments to extreme beauty and quick death. The other native deciduous trees, maples and cottonwoods, mostly, sprouted delicious hope and enduring promise in their miniature green buds and enchanting earthy branches that extended optimistic assurances of renewal. To Jessie, the landscape was nature's art, God's covenant that beauty and hope are eternal and will come around again and again, even after the dark, bitter cold of a dreary, ashen winter.

After a day of earnest races and daring freestyle exhibitions, the small group of good friends was on an adrenalin-fuelled high. After they picked their way down from the bleachers, with Jessie's hand fitted snugly into Josh's to help navigate the depth between steps, mother hen Maggie rounded up the friends for a group photograph. Crowds moved around and behind them as they sorted out their poses, and lots of curious whispers were heard along with cheers for *Drifters* and for Jessie who, as usual, toed the dirt, embarrassed by the attention. They had to wait for her to sign a few autographs before Carter gently hastened her away and into the front center of their picture. Josh snuggled up behind her, his arms around her neck.

Later, the whole group met back in downtown Vancouver for dinner at the Cactus Club on Burrard. Exuberant chatter about the day's stunts and Josh and Stephen's goals for the new motocross season punctuated and illuminated their animated conversation. Maggie pulled out her iPhone, which she'd given to a thrilled baseball capped passerby to snap for the group photo, and passed around the day's pictures. Wrapped up in a heated discussion over how their favorite stunt, the "kiss of death", was executed, nobody noticed the color drain from Jessie's face when she scrolled to the group photo, although Josh did raise his eyebrows when she hastily climbed over him to make a quick retreat to the upstairs ladies' room.

Once there, Jessie had to force herself not to slam the cubicle's white shuttered door, and then she collapsed onto the lid of the toilet and put her head between her knees to steady her heart rate and keep herself from passing out on the cold, tiled floor.

No, no, no, no, no, no, noooooo, she heard herself moaning quietly as a slow terror permeated and overtook the quickly diminishing light in her newly blossomed soul. She rocked back and forth, squeezing her arms around her belly in an attempt to quell a rapidly rising panic. Then she stood and yanked open the toilet lid behind her, and threw up until she had nothing left but uncomfortable dry heaves. Wiping her mouth on tissue paper which she discarded into the basin, she gently replaced the toilet lid and sat down again, shaking, then placed her hands over her ears as she tried to block out a horrid sound that haunted her dreams, a memory of a very bad day in Charleston years before.

It was half an hour before she could bring herself to respond to Maggie knocking on the door, calling her.

"Jessie! Jessie, if you don't soon open that door I'm going out to get Josh and we're going to break it down. Are you sick, or what?"

On trembling legs, Jessie finally hoisted herself upright. Slowly, as if she'd aged fifty years, she opened the door. To Maggie, it was obvious her friend had come down with some bug, maybe food poisoning from the barbecued sausages which they'd drowned in onion and sauerkraut, purchased from a lunch truck at Agassiz, and so she led her straight to the restaurant entrance after texting Josh to tell him to meet them there straightaway with the SUV.

After enlisting Carter to drive Kayla and Paul home, Josh said his good-byes, paid the bill, and then retrieved Jessie's vehicle. Mystified and concerned, he steered the car carefully towards the restaurant's entrance, parked, then jumped out and buckled Jessie into the front passenger seat. Her expression frightened him; her face was a distorted white mask against the droplets of rain now trickling down the car window as the overbearing slate sky gave way to a sinking barometric pressure.

As he veered away from the curb, Josh reached over to wipe a wispy strand of hair off Jessie's cheek. She was staring at the sidewalks, and at the vehicles on Burrard, searching, her eyes darting back and forth as if she were looking for someone.

"Jessie, what the hell?" Josh demanded urgently. "I thought you'd passed out or something."

She was unresponsive and, in fact, only heard his voice somewhere off in the distance, as if it were disembodied, a hiker's cry from a distant mountain far, far away.

"Jessie!" he called, to no avail. "Jess!" Just as Josh was starting to panic, and as other drivers beeped frantically, urging him to focus on his driving, she turned and looked blankly at him and the questioning, haunted look he saw in the much-loved blue eyes immediately alarmed him. A cold chill crept up Josh's spine and his stomach tightened in fright. He hadn't seen terror like that in Jessie's velvety eyes since he'd asked about Charleston and, even then, it was only momentary, a glimpse into a horror he had yet to understand.

Now, for some intuitive reason unbeknownst to him, it seemed here to stay. Unrelenting. An evil snake that had suddenly crept into their lives unnoticed as they celebrated the joy of being together, the wonder of discovering each other, the passion and ache of love.

Afraid of what he did not yet comprehend, a sinking, portentous feeling mudding his brain, Josh drove Jessie to his place and led her inside. He ran her a warm bath and poured her a glass of Baileys, yet she still didn't offer him any verbal explanations. He sponged her back and, just as Josh was debating the placement of a call to Dee, a last resort as far as he was concerned, Jessie's eyes cleared a little and she took his hand and placed it on her breast. She looked up at him, tragically, and he could sense she was trying to tell him something. In answer, Josh grasped the waist of his T-shirt with both hands and yanked it up over his head, and then he slipped off his jeans and boxers. Climbing into the tub, he drew his girl back against his chest and wrapped safe loving arms around her shoulders. It was the best he knew to do at the time, to embrace her in their sheltered cocoon so she would feel protected, secure, and invulnerable.

As the water cooled Josh reached around Jessie and, with the backs of his fingers, tenderly wiped some bubbly stray suds off her warm pink cheek, and then they heaved themselves—exhausted from the day's efforts and its sudden strange turn—out of the soothing tub and he dried her off. As if she were a child, Josh steered Jessie to the bedroom, and then he kissed her and loved her and held her, terrified at how she trembled and shook.

"Jessie," he begged her, whispering, his forehead pressed against hers as they lay in bed. "Please, please tell me. What's got you so upset? Please!"

She took his face in her hands, one hand on each bristly one-day-old whiskered cheek, and peered into her beloved man's deep brown eyes. The age-old pain in Jessie's soul was eating away at the little joy she desperately held onto, a joy she could feel diminishing as quickly as the murky water from the tub they'd just drained. It was all she had in her to speak, yet she knew she had to give him something to hold on to, for she knew not what the future would bring, only that it would be filled with uncertainty and an ever darkening presence.

"Josh." She spoke his name with reverence and demand, and he stopped caressing her and listened, as he knew she was willing him to do. "You listen to me," she said, her voice low and commanding. "Whatever happens, you remember this, okay?" He saw a mist build up in her eyes and, once again, a feeling of dread overtook him.

She continued, pressing her palms to his cheeks, forcing him to meet her eyes. "You remember that I love you, that I have always loved you, and that I will always love you. Always and forever, okay? Promise me that?"

He stared at her, curious, confused, afraid.

"Josh!" she commanded, louder, insistent, drawing him away from the unspoken spider web of dark thoughts reeling like a rogue roller coaster through the caverns of his mind.

He responded by pressing a big warm hand over hers on his cheek, and then Josh twined his fingers through and around hers.

"Jessie."

She waited, but nothing else was forthcoming.

"Josh. Please."

He hesitated, sensing that whatever he could say to her on this mysterious black night likely wouldn't be enough.

But all she needed was a yes. A nod, even. An assurance that the unknown future was secure in his assent.

"Jessie. Of course. You and me. Always and forever."

"Just promise me," she whispered, and he knew that was all he would get from her that evening, and so Josh pulled Jessie close and comforted her as best he could. After a while he drifted off into a restless sleep while she shivered in his arms and forced herself to stay awake so she could memorize every depth and breadth and hair of his body—his touch, his breathing, his skin, his musky smell, that brazen hair falling over his ear that had secured her seduction in the first place. And then, when she could fight it no longer, Jessie let sleep take her and, mercifully, she dreamed of a boy named Sandy, and of playing guitar near the fishing pier at Folly Beach in Charleston. The dream was happy and good until the end, then as she moaned and cried out Josh woke her, and she had to face the truth. Deuce McCall was back.

There he was, in Maggie's group photograph, standing behind Josh amongst a few other stragglers who managed to get into their picture by walking behind them. Deuce was grinning sardonically at the camera, his hand poised just behind Josh's head as if he were waving. But Jessie knew otherwise, she knew he was not waving, she knew better. She recognized the demonic, crazed look in McCall's eyes and the threatening poise of that evil hand that was capable of so much hurt, and she knew that life with Josh, as she knew and loved it, had suddenly shuddered to a crashing halt. For as long as Deuce McCall walked this plane called earth, there could be no love called Josh in Jessie's life.

There could be no *life* in Jessie's life. Just a deepening pain, and confusion, and a numbness that would never go away.

But she was a survivor. She had made it this far. She would make a plan and, somehow, Jessie Wheeler would survive.

She wondered how much time she had.

After a solemn Josh Sawyer breakfast of fried eggs and salty bacon, Jessie apologized quietly for her dark mood and then she begged off from their planned Sunday afternoon excursion to Rebel on a Mountain Coffee with the others, on the pretense that she had some songwriting to do. Josh hated to let her go, but he understood that sometimes women needed their space, and so he watched her back out of his driveway in her SUV and he stood there for a few moments after she disappeared down the street, wondering what in the hell had come over her the night before.

He picked up Jessie's plate and scraped half an egg into the compost bin. Carefully, he lined her plate up behind his in the dishwasher and then he spent a few minutes scrubbing the frying pan free of fat and bacon residue. He went through the rituals, cleaning, tidying, Sunday morning stuff, but later couldn't remember whether or not he had brushed and flossed his teeth. With an empty space in his heart and a feeling of dismay he couldn't shake, Josh grabbed his tan leather riding jacket and the King Ranch keys and headed out the door to meet their friends at the nearby UBC campus coffee house. Maybe they could help him figure out what was up with Jessie. Maybe it was nothing, and would pass as quickly as it had come on.

He didn't see Deuce McCall's rented Ford Fusion parked down the street but, strangely enough, as Josh pulled out of his driveway, he shivered.

This time, Deuce didn't follow. He was a methodical man and, anyhow, he had the GPS surveillance bug he'd placed on Josh's bumper. He knew where Jessie's man was at any time; if he wanted to check up on him later, he could. But for now, it was enough to know that Jessie had clued in to his reappearance in her charmed life. It was enough to know that she was afraid.

Deuce had bugs placed strategically inside Josh's home, thanks to the substantial bribe he'd given that scraggly bearded guy from the fiber optic company. Deuce had eyes in the back of his head. Deuce had all the power he needed to start this age-old game he played with Jessie anew. One day, and already he had her on the run.

He sniggered, and then reached a hairy finger down and cranked up the radio. The station was playing one of Jessie's new ballads, a recent release she supposedly wrote in honor of Josh and gave to him as a Christmas gift. Deuce snorted, and listened to the lyrics. He didn't like the idea behind the song, but then again he had the power to pretend she had written it for him. He was Deuce McCall. He liked Jessie Wheeler's music. He closed his eyes and imagined their first new tryst together, which he decided must come soon. If he thought about it hard enough, he could feel her skin on his again. He tingled with desire.

Deuce slammed a fist down hard on the dashboard when his pleasurable thoughts were roughly interrupted at the end of Jessie's song by the loud blast of some inane commercial for a local hardware store. He relaxed when he remembered he'd have her soon, reminding himself he must be patient. Deuce started the sedan and easily manipulated his passage through the quiet Vancouver Sunday traffic back to his hotel, where he sat and schemed and planned the afternoon away.

At her downtown condo, Jessie did the same. She would not allow the horror of Deuce McCall to once again destroy her life. She would not lose Josh the way she lost Sandy. She was Jessie Wheeler, a celebrity with access to top-notch security and protection. She would prevail.

Josh was quiet at ROAM that day. He left early, relaxing a little only when Jessie responded to his texts.

That night was the first since they'd gotten together that Jessie spent a chilled night alone at her home, and Josh passed lonely dreams at his.

Despite her best efforts and her hopeful rallying, the world was already shifting once again from underneath Jessie's dusty brown cowboy boots. Unbeknownst to her at the time, except for maybe on some intuitive level, she was already losing. This was a battle she could not hope to win, at least not anytime soon. McCall was a wily bastard, and for all of his strangely conceived psychotic ideas, he was a master planner, a puppeteer, and thanks to his disgusting deplorable actions in a historic home on Tradd Street in Charleston years ago, he once again manipulated the strings that made Jessie's life go round.

For the next two weeks, Jessie lived in a fog of fear and betrayal. She found herself, on the more positive days, scheming and trying to find a solution to an evil problem she felt she could only solve on her own. She began to sink into the familiar despondency she'd lived with after that fateful day in Charleston more than a decade ago. It became a noose around her neck, a cloud that marred her view of the world around her, a world which should have continued on in that glorious rainbow Technicolor of new love and sincere and genuine friendships, of success and fame and freedom and music.

In the darkest of night, when she couldn't sleep for fear of horrific nightmares which had resumed their vicious and unremorseful haunting, Jessie sat on the balcony outside her condo or Josh's home, depending on where her mood let her lay her weary head. Wrapped up in a blanket to ward off the numbing cold that, in her state of shock and despair she barely felt tingle her skin anyway, she went over and over and over the possible scenarios that would release her from Deuce's deadly grip. She considered involving Charles and Matt, but there was so much at risk here. She knew this about Deuce. She knew his reach was far and wide, his tentacles deep and grasping. He got beneath your skin and clawed his way into your veins, and the only way to remove him would be by pulling him away with his teeth still intact in your soul, so that as he was removed, a good chunk of you would go with him, bloodied and forever destroyed. To involve Charles and his security team in Jessie's age-old agony at this stage would be like inviting the people she loved to wade into some foreign tribal war, where they'd potentially be bayoneted and speared and thrown into a bottomless pit.

But even more so, a loner for most years of her life, Jessie did not know how to let down her walls enough to ask for help.

True, realistically she knew they would want her to reach out. But there was still the tiniest part of her that believed she was alone, unlovable. A part of her died the day of her twelfth birthday, the day her father was wrenched mercilessly from her life, and her mother's mind along with him. Little bits were torn from her each night Jessie's stepfather climbed into her bed, and even more the day Deuce left her bleeding on the plush white rug in his office. Remaining parts of Jessie's own tired mind were lost when Rachel died. Tradd Street, where Sandy's life came to a crashing halt, ruthlessly claimed the largest chunk of all. What was left was fragile and unstable. What remained of Jessie was barely hanging on. Even though it seemed over the last many years of unconditional love and care from Charles and Dee, and even Charlie and his family, the *Drifters* family and, especially, Josh, that she was shedding her unstable past, growing anew…the growth was small and unstable, not yet deeply rooted.

Jessie was at risk, yet she still felt too small and vulnerable to involve her loved ones in the disaster she knew was Deuce McCall. She wanted to defeat the man, the bully, the poisonous snake from Charleston. The city she had loved so dearly—still loved, in fact, for its history, splendor, gracious Southern kindness and hospitality—felt inaccessible to her because of Deuce. So many beautiful things could be visualized beyond him, like Charleston, like family and friends and love. As if he were a thunder and lightning storm and, in the distance far beyond, enveloped in a serene gentle mist, was a rainbow.

So late at night she sat, paced, fretted and worried, and sometimes she gave in to the despair and cried heartily into the cold bathroom tiles where she hoped Josh could not hear her. But she decayed quickly in those two weeks. Barely able to stomach food, Jessie lost weight. Her friends at *Drifters* grew increasingly worried. Finally, with Dee's blessing, Jonathon called in Jessie's physician, who did a few tests and gave her some meds to decrease her stomach pain, believing her when she said the cause was gastro intestinal.

One day on set, after the others had mostly finished eating lunch and Jessie was with the doctor for the second time in two weeks, Stephen wandered over to Josh. He yanked out a chair beside his friend at the lunch table and sat backwards, his lanky arms wrapped around the backrest. Glancing down at Josh's plate, which was still half full, Steve watched his friend push broccoli and wild rice around with a fork.

He nodded towards the food. "Not hungry?"

Josh grumbled and set the fork down next to his plate. He shook his head. He appeared as despondent as during the season one shoot, when he and Jessie were trying to sort out where they fit in with each other.

"Something's up," he said. "And I can't put my finger on it."

Stephen shrugged. "Look, if she picked up some food poisoning, it can linger. Jessie's a fighter. She'll be fine."

Josh sat with his back to Stephen and stared down at the uneaten food. He reached out and, with one finger, pushed the plate away. A strand of loose hair fell from behind one ear and landed in front of a cheek, hiding his true emotions from his friend and separating him from the rest of the world.

"I don't think she's sick, Steve," he said, not looking at his cast mate. "Well, maybe, but not from food poisoning. From something else that's troubling her."

Steve was quiet as he waited for Josh to explain. He had the same gut feeling.

Josh turned then, and looked at him. "I think something happened that day, at Agassiz. Something that upset her, or pissed her off. I don't know exactly."

"She was fine all day," Steve considered. "She didn't get sick until she was at the restaurant. Suddenly. Like with food poisoning."

"That's what doesn't add up," Josh reflected thoughtfully. "If something happened at Agassiz, then she would have been pissed off earlier. But she was fine. She was the usual old Jessie—happy, fun, laughing...I don't get it." He paused. "Actually, I take that back. She was the new Jessie—happy, fun, laughing. Now she's the old Jessie again, sad, distant, maybe even scared, I think."

"She's not feeling well. That could account for how she's acting. How is she at home, away from here?"

Josh rested an elbow on the back of his chair, and then looked away.

He spoke as if he were talking to the wall, remembering, removing himself to someplace else. "Like she's two people. She barely functions. She goes through the motions, you know? It's as if she's locked in her mind somewhere and hardly knows I'm around. Scarcely talks, then when I speak to her and try to pull her out of it, she looks up suddenly, as if she doesn't know where she is, and then is surprised to see me there. Then at night, in bed," he blushed, embarrassed, "she hangs onto me as if she's terrified to let me go. We make love, and it's good, and I think okay, maybe everything is going to be all right…then I wake up in the middle of the night and she's in the bathroom with the door locked, or pacing the house, or outside sitting on the deck, shivering to death."

He looked intently up at Steve, then. "I've seen her crying, too, Steve. Something's tormenting her, only I have no idea what, except that it seems to be related to the day in Agassiz, and when I question her about it, she changes the subject or leaves the room, saying she just isn't feeling well."

Steve watched him, his brows knitted together in thought and contemplation. He inhaled deeply. "Any idea, Josh? What it is that's bugging her?" He said it in a way that revealed he had his own idea, and that he figured Josh knew what it was. But he wanted Josh to admit it, to say it out loud.

Josh shot him an icy stare. "Yeah, maybe," he said. "But I thought she was okay with all that."

He was referring to the negative attention he'd been getting from the media as a result of his relationship with Jessie. But things had settled down lately, for the most part. Yes, of course there were still the odd rumors and nasty comments on radio shows and in the rag bags, but Josh and Jessie usually avoided those. Only occasionally in public were people cruel. There had indeed still been the odd glares here and there at Agassiz, but he and Jessie just held each other tighter and tried to let them slide off. They had to have thick skin in order to be together. Crap had to slide off like water on a duck's back.

Josh sighed and rubbed a hand roughly over and over his face as if that might help exorcise the demons hanging over him and Jessie these days. "Maybe it's Dee," he said quietly. "Jess can let everything else go fairly easily, but she cares about Dee, and what she thinks."

"Dee's still being shitty?"

Josh laughed sardonically. "Like she's waiting for the proverbial shoe to drop. Hell, for all I know, she probably thinks I'm beating the shit out of Jessie or something."

"What's Charles been like?"

"He tries a little harder, but it's obviously a stretch for him to be all right with me. I think he knows if he doesn't reach out a bit, Jessie won't go around there as much anymore. But I feel like it will be a while before he trusts me. Dee, on the other hand…hah. Sucks. She's passive aggressive. Sweet as roses to Jessie, but either ignores me altogether or gets her digs in where she can. Drives Jess crazy."

"Maybe that's it, then," Steve offered, pondering. "Jessie's pretty close to Dee. Maybe she's starting to feel the distance growing between them. That would be hard on anyone, to feel like she's got to make a choice between two people she loves." Seeing the stricken look on Josh's face he quickly added, "Well, not a choice exactly, Jessie's head over heels in love with you. But even so, it must suck for her. Add the media crap and the insensitive assholes out there who treat you like shit, and that's enough to give anyone ulcers."

Josh nodded. "Well, if that's the case, then I hope to hell she opens up about it soon. Because I'm worried about her." His dark eyes peered painfully up at his good friend.

Steve was quiet, but he reached a hand out and gave Josh's shoulder a pat. Also distressingly obvious was the fact that Josh was worried about *them* as a couple. He was worried about Josh and Jessie.

Unable to disguise their anxiety, the boys shoved back the chairs and headed off towards the cast trailers to review lines before the long afternoon of shooting started. Jessie watched from her own trailer, which the doctor had just left. Josh's head was hanging low, the suspenders from his muddy 1860's pants drooping from his hips, the brown well-worn boots barely clearing the soft spring ground as he trudged along. For the thousandth time in two weeks she had to fight to keep the tears from flowing, because if she started to cry here Jessie doubted if she could stop, and she was afraid of what she might admit if someone with caring, kind eyes like Maggie tried to encourage her to spill the beans. She knew her shit was affecting the mood of the cast and crew, but she also knew there were powerful demons at play here that had to take precedence over *Drifters*.

Jessie shoved a fist into her mouth and sucked in a big breath, which made her tender belly hurt even more. She watched Josh disappear behind his trailer, and she reached out and placed a hand on the window as if, with a look or a touch, she could control him, and keep him in her life, safe and happy. Jessie shook her head in frustration. She had not been able to contrive a way to accomplish that task. All she could do now was wonder when the malevolent Deuce McCall would strike next, and how. She was being controlled like the puppet horses in the musical War Horse, beckoned towards a raging battle of which she wanted no part.

A soft moan captured her attention. Surprised and somewhat horrified to discover that it had come from between her own lips, Jessie crooked her elbows on the small cream-colored table and laid her tired head on her equally exhausted arms.

The next day, a Saturday, she had the answer she sought. And then the good was over and, at least for a time, the evil won.

Chapter Ten

Jessie spent the night at Josh's place, clinging to him and whimpering in what little sleep she managed to grab. He felt he had nothing left to give her that she would accept with the exception of love and affection, so he held her tight and brushed the sweaty wisps of auburn-tinted hair away from her flushed cheeks as Jessie cried in her sleep. He ached to know what abysmal dreams haunted the girl he loved.

In the early morning, with splashes of naive pale-white daylight tickling the duvet, Jessie held up the covers so Josh could climb in for a second cuddle after his shower and shave. She breathed in the spicy scent of his aftershave and laid cool hands on his warm smooth cheeks before heading out to rehearse with her dancers.

Later, while on break, she read a text from Stephen. It had been sent an hour earlier but she kept her phone in her dressing room while she was working. Now, she grabbed her bag and tore out of the rehearsal hall, the feeling of dread from the last two weeks escalating and sucking the life out of her as she ran towards the red Mustang.

Steve's text read *Josh tires slashed he ok call me.* Jessie didn't bother calling. She needed to see for herself that Josh was physically unhurt. She knew he'd be pissed, both at the pain in the ass of having to get the tires replaced, but also at the people out there in the world who insisted on bullying him. He was also likely to be somewhat embarrassed at the attention—she expected he'd called the police, yet part of her wished he hadn't. Because, if McCall had anything to do with this— and she figured there was a fifty-fifty chance that it was indeed his handiwork— then involving the police would only piss the Southern "gentleman" off further.

Crossing the Burrard Bridge, Jessie could see powerboats and sailboats taking advantage of the gorgeous sunny spring day. People were also out in droves cycling, running, strolling their babies, or walking the myriad of small and large dogs one could find in the city. Once again she found herself wishing to be one of those people, a simple resident of the west coast hippie city left alone by visions of the past, an ordinary mortal with no special cursed gifts attracting an unreasonable amount of attention from a man like McCall. Frowning, she swerved to avoid a boy on a bicycle who cut in front of her, and then she gunned the gas pedal for Josh's street.

The first thing she saw was a police car parked behind his truck in the driveway. The second thing she noticed was Matt's Audi. The third thing she spied was a small clump of people standing on the left side of Josh's truck. Jessie looked around for unknown vehicles, and then pulled up behind the Audi and steeled her nerves before opening the door. She was still wearing her dance leggings, over which she'd thrown her brown embroidered cowboy boots. She'd covered her white tank top with a soft pale yellow cashmere cardigan she hadn't taken the time to button. The loose hair escaping her bun was wispy around her face, encircling the fear and anger bubbling beneath the surface. She gently pushed her car door closed and then walked almost on tiptoes towards the little group of men, her heart pounding relentlessly.

Josh was giving an account to a youthful officer of what he discovered when he went out to his truck that morning. Pausing mid-sentence, he looked up at Jessie and curiously watched her narrow her eyes and glare at the nasty slits in his flat tires. This latest incident would not improve Jessie's mood from the last few weeks, of that he was certain.

Charles laid a hand on Jessie's shoulder and then continued a low-key discussion with Matt. Stephen, arms crossed, stood frowning behind Josh and watched Jessie.

Things had been changing over the last few weeks, but Jessie still held out hope that she could figure things out, that she could end this assault on her nerves and on her psyche. But now, her eyes searching Josh's truck for signs, any signs, her hope came crashing to a screeching halt, like some of the bikes she'd seen at Agassiz, dirt spraying everywhere as riders demanded the tires stop moving. Stephen, in a casual white button down shirt, long green checked shorts and a baseball hat on backwards to keep his blonde locks at bay, saw Jessie gasp in horror the moment she realized the wait was indeed over.

She spotted, lying conspicuously on the asphalt next to Josh's left back tire, a dagger.

The young Vancouver police officer later described it as a hunting knife; it was about six to eight inches in length overall. It had a steel blade with a wooden handle; one distinguishing feature was a steel guard separating the blade from the handle. The weapon also had a worn lanyard looped through a small hole. But what Jessie's eyes landed on, and what caused the bile to rise in her belly, was a symbol embossed in the top of the blade, just under the guard. It was a Celtic knot with a stylized B in its center. Jessie knew the name Deuce was a nickname, that McCall's real first name was Booth. She had also seen the knife before, sickeningly, stained red with Sandy's blood. This was not a supposed fan of Jessie or Charlie's sending Josh a message. This was clearly Deuce sending Jessie a sadistic memo. And it read *You are mine.*

Knuckling her hands into fists, Jessie forced her eyes upwards. She stared hard at Josh, her angry eyes frozen into icicle shards. He paused from giving his statement, chilling when his eyes met hers. He felt the world give way beneath his feet; for balance, he reached out a hand and grabbed the side mirror by the driver's door. Jessie stared at him, unblinking, curling and uncurling her fists, feet a shoulder's width apart, her heart racing and blood pressure pounding in her ears.

She could hear the sound of that knife even now, as it destroyed the first boy she'd ever loved. *Thwunk, thwunk, thwunk, thwunk, thwunk, thwunk.* Six times Deuce drove the wretched blade into gentle hazel-eyed Sandy's chest and belly as she watched, bound and helpless, less than six feet away. Deuce untied Jessie just in time for Sandy to die in her arms as Deuce stood over them laughing, before pointing her, crawling, sick, towards the door of his grand downtown Charleston home. He sent her away with the same message then, too. *You are mine.* And he told her he would always know where she was, and with whom, and that he would find her again someday. That she must never try to prosecute him and, anyways, no one would believe her if she did, because he was a respected businessman in the city, the state, in more than one state, in fact.

Jessie had been numb for so long that becoming famous hardly registered in her mind. She would not have cared if Deuce had found her and killed her. All those years with Charlie, she would have gladly accepted and welcomed death. But now, with Josh and her friends on *Drifters*, everything had changed. She cared about herself again. She loved people who loved her back. And Deuce had figured that out. That's why he was here, destroying her life again. Because he knew she had come back to life, finally, and he couldn't have her back in the land of the living because then he would not be the master who would own her. And he would not destroy her by killing her because then he wouldn't have what he desired most—Jessie herself. Instead, he would hurt the person she loved most in the world—Josh. He would kill him the same way he killed Sandy.

Later, Josh, backed up by Stephen, would confirm that on that dark sunny morning he was witness to the final light going out in Jessie's eyes. He watched as, like some robot whose power source was suddenly extinguished, Jessie's shoulders slumped and her fists uncurled and the soul-light in her eyes flickered and then—suddenly, hopelessly—was gone.

She pushed her way past Josh and then past Steve and ran up Josh's flagstone walk bordered by the breathtakingly beautiful pink and white Sakura—cherry blossoms—for which Vancouver was so famous. She vaguely remembered reading somewhere that these were blossoms that Japanese warriors once used as their motif, for a rare and present beauty with a certain seemingly heartless expiry date. She barely made it into the first floor bathroom before she threw up.

Outside, Stephen laid a quick hand on Josh's shoulder to let him know he would handle it so Josh could finish talking to the cop, and then he followed Jessie inside. He was bewildered, but Steve figured she was righteously upset over the appearance of the knife because it came so close to Josh himself. Plus Jessie herself was in the house overnight. It was light when she left, and she hadn't mentioned seeing anything unusual. She would not have been in such a rush to get to rehearsal that she would have missed seeing the damage to Josh's truck. The attack must have occurred in the daylight between the time she left and the time Josh went outside. *Risky*, he thought, as he slid the glass door behind him and entered the living room. *Fucking asshole*, he cursed at the idiot who left his dark message outside Josh's home. Muttering under his breath as he went looking for Jessie, Steve eased towards the first floor washroom. He could hear her being sick, and so he gave her a few seconds before he pushed open the bathroom door and went inside.

He smiled sadly down at Jessie, who was crouched before the toilet, white knuckles grasping each side of the bowl, her hair coming out of its bun and threatening to end up tainted. Steve bent down and pulled the loose hair back from her face, and then after a moment he eased the elastic out altogether and re-did the bun. After a moment, Jessie sat back and accepted the tissues he handed her, then she wiped her mouth and threw the dirty tissues in the bowl, where they soaked up the water and seemed to melt away. She leaned back against the pedestal sink and watched Steve settle on the tiled floor across from her. She wanted to memorize all of them, her friends, for she felt certain her precious time with them was coming to an end, one way or the other.

"I have sisters," Stephen said. At her curious look, he gestured to her hair. She nodded. There weren't too many men out there in the big wide world who knew how to manipulate female hair into delicate buns.

"So," he said. "Pretty scary, huh?"

She caught herself thinking *You have no idea*. Wrapping her arms around her belly, Jessie hunched over but didn't lose his solemn gaze.

Facing her there on the cold tiled floor of Josh's bathroom, he studied her. "Jessie," he said lightly. "It's just another one of those crazies. They're just trying to scare you, and it's obviously working. Nothing's going to happen to you or to Josh. That's why Charles and Matt are out there; they're scheming about how they need to improve the security here, by installing motion sensor lights, that kind of thing. Better alarms. Maybe even put a guy outside for a while, at least until things settle down."

She acquiesced because she didn't know how else to respond. Jessie was already turning back into the walking dead. Spotting Deuce's knife on the ground outside Josh's house—a knife she last saw soaked in Sandy's blood as she crawled out of McCall's charming home—was the last nail in her coffin. She ached to tell, but the truth of what the Southerner whose ancestors once owned one of the largest slave populations in South Carolina had done, was her undoing. Deuce's insurance that Jessie wouldn't tell was Jessie's secret terror that he would do the same to Josh.

She knew what she had to do. Steve took her hand and helped her up, wishing he could get more out of her, but it was clear she was still not talking. He put his arm around her as they started walking, but Jessie shrugged him away, and they walked single file out to the driveway where the cop was photographing the tires and the knife.

Josh walked up to meet them, recoiling at the clouded expression on Stephen's face. Usually his friend managed to get some truths out of Jessie, but if he had, what he'd learned wasn't good. More likely he hadn't been able to communicate with her at all.

Before wandering over to see what Charles and Matt were planning in terms of elevated security, Steve shot Josh a knowing look that didn't help boost his confidence.

Jessie stopped in front of Josh and said goodbye with her eyes, although, with the exception of maybe his gut, he didn't recognize that the finality of *them* was imminent. She leaned forward and placed one hand on his tense stomach and then laid her forehead on his shoulder. She closed her eyes and a subdued moan escaped from between her lips. Josh pulled Jessie's left arm around his body so he could draw her closer, and then he wrapped his arms comfortably around both shoulders and kissed the top of her head. He squeezed her tight.

"We'll get through this, little one," he murmured softly. "We promised each other. We knew it would be hard. We're survivors, you and me. We'll go on putting one foot in front of the other, breathing in and out, each day every day, so they'll know they won't win. That they *can't* win." He held her there against him, so he could feel that her heart was still beating, because he was afraid of what he saw earlier—the light fading from her eyes. Jessie couldn't speak if she wanted to, so great was her pain and the fear of what was to come.

After a while, Josh took hold of her shoulders and then turned her pinched face up towards his. He peered into the sea-pearl eyes he loved so dearly.

"Please Jessie," he whispered, his own eyes filled close to overflowing with tears of frustration. "Please don't be this way. Talk to me."

But she couldn't. She leaned forward and kissed him faintly, tenderly. Jessie held herself against those soft lips for just the littlest, lingering moment, and then she let go of him and walked away.

Jessie put up her hand when she walked by Charles and Matt as if to say *Leave me the fuck alone for now*, and they let her go. They knew their girl. They understood that this was a messed up morning, that she needed some time alone. When Jessie Wheeler needed space, she got it.

She climbed into her car, slammed the door shut, squealed out into the street, pulled a U-turn, and drove hell bent for the shelter of her beloved mountains in North Van, where she knew she could find a place to let go and scream. Somehow, she knew Deuce would hear her, or would find her, and she was ready.

She did, after all, have a few choices now that she knew the game was officially on. One, she could kill herself. That would teach Deuce a lesson. Then he would never have her. Two, she could go along with Deuce until she could figure out how to kill him, although that was not necessarily a reliable option. She thought he might have underlings that could still carry out his twisted desires. Therefore, no matter what happened to Deuce, Josh's life could still be threatened. Three—well, that remained to be seen. She could run away, but what would that solve? She and Josh could run away, for that matter. But then they would be forced to live with the constant fear of being found by Deuce or his henchmen. And what kind of life would that be? A life in exile. But what kind of a life was this, if it wasn't already some form of imprisonment?

His heart sinking, Josh watched Jessie speed away in the Mustang. He, like Charles, agreed that sometimes women needed their space, but this was one of those times when he needed Jessie, and when he felt she should want him. It hurt for her to shut him out. Toeing the ground with his boot, he watched a caterpillar squirm its way slowly across the pavement. Wishing it could talk, since it may have been the only witness to the unseen terror that stalked them this day, Josh kept his head down and forced his temper to stay in check. Mostly, he just wanted to be in the Mustang with Jessie. Maybe if he could get her alone—get angry at her—she would break.

He joined the others and they made some decisions about stepping up the security around the home, like trimming shrubs for increased visibility, adding motion sensor lights, allowing Matt to keep a hired security guard around the premises for a while, perhaps even gating the driveway and fencing in the property. Josh reluctantly agreed to the increased security, although he felt in his heart that Jessie wouldn't be thrilled. His mind wasn't on the task at hand, though; his mind was with Jessie in her little red Mustang, wherever she had gone.

The malevolent dagger was carefully bagged as evidence, and a tow truck was called to collect the pick-up and haul it off to have the tires replaced. Josh and Steve said *So long* to the others, then climbed into Steve's silver Audi TT and went for coffee before cruising the car lots to get their minds off the morning's sinister events.

It was late afternoon before Josh heard from Jessie, and even then, it was just a text.

Staying at my place tonight

It was the last straw. Josh pitched his phone across the room. It landed underneath his leather couch and bounced to a position against the wall behind it. He had to get down on his hands and knees and fish for the cell with a broom in order to retrieve it.

He called her repeatedly, to no avail. The beginning of the end was upon them, and Jessie was once again an impenetrable fortress.

Earlier, just after leaving Josh's place, Jessie wasn't surprised when she realized she'd been followed. Deuce was a smart old South Carolina snake. He was driving a black Ford Fusion, a rather conformist sedan for such a slithering monster, *All the better to blend in with*, she thought distractedly. She leaned against her car door, arms crossed, and glared at him as he pulled up behind the Mustang. They were on a remote road at the bottom of Grouse Mountain and, although it was a sunny day and lots of Vancouverites were out for weekend drives, she had led him to a stretch that was off the beaten track, and so they were alone.

She stepped away from the Mustang and planted her feet into the sand.

"Deuce the fuck McCall," she growled.

Grinning salaciously, he sidled towards her, stopping about fifteen feet away, his white snakeskin cowboy boots gathering dust from the dirt road, and a long canvas green riding coat flapping ever so slightly in the gentle breeze.

Just to let me know the creature in front of me is in fact a living thing, she figured, alluding to the movement of his coat. He was sucking on a piece of timothy grass he'd picked up somewhere. He hadn't shaved in a few days, and his whiskers were likely to be itchy, she thought, remembering and dreading the feel of him on her skin.

"Jessie Wheeler," he muttered agreeably in response, talking out of the side of his mouth so he could still chew on the timothy. His low voice with its slight Southern drawl, like liquid honey peppered with the carcasses of rotting houseflies, got under her skin, causing the miniscule hairs on the backs of her arms to rise up in defense. "You've done well for yourself. But then again that's no surprise. You filled my club night after night."

She frowned. Her memories of singing at the Renegade had, for the most part, been good ones. But then wasn't that the way with life—the good always infused with the bad? Sex with a stepfather—horribly wrong, yet on some deep, dark level felt good. Music, songs, melodies and lyrics—so lovely, yet almost always filled with pain. Acting—drama—always the ups and downs of life.

He continued in the deep slimy voice that still terrorized Jessie in her nightmares. "Then you quit my generous employ, and the club emptied. You almost destroyed me singlehandedly, Jessie Wheeler." He spat out the timothy and pulled a fresh piece of hay from his pocket. Laughed a low, angry guffaw that sent chills up her spine. "But then, by becoming famous, you filled it up again, and I opened more clubs, girl."

Deuce walked closer towards her, planted himself squarely in front, and touched the second timothy to her cheek. She recoiled but didn't resist as he let it crawl ever so slowly downwards.

"You filled it up, because people remembered that you played there. Word got out, and then everybody wanted to be in the club where Jessie Wheeler played. Tourism is huge in Charleston—idiots snapping pictures of every old house and cannon—did you know that this year our grand city was voted number one to visit in the world? In the world, Jessie Wheeler!" He stepped closer and she could smell the foul stench of whiskey emanating from his black soul. She blanched, and he grabbed her chin in his hand and forced her to look up at him, to breathe him in. To Jessie it seemed his steely eyes held foreboding echoes of crimson light.

He continued. "Every day I pose for their pictures, standing outside the club or inside on the stage where you played for me. Sometimes I stand for pictures on the carpet where I fucked you, Jessie Wheeler. And those imbeciles don't have a clue that the faint red stain in their photos isn't wine. They think life in Charleston is one big history party. They don't see that the plantations aren't what they used to be. The furniture's not even the same. It's all so fucking fake...!"

He turned on his heel and stomped a few paces away, his back to her, and Jessie absently wondered whether he was referring to the furniture or to the tourists. She remembered some visitors to Charleston who were afraid they'd see a snake while in the city. She wondered if any of those who took pictures of Deuce knew they had seen a snake, all right. The worst poisonous kind imaginable, in fact.

Suddenly, she found she was not afraid of him, for how could a girl who could summon no feelings be afraid of anything or anyone? She drew herself up to her full height and challenged her nemesis.

"What do you want, Deuce the fuck McCall?" she demanded in a voice so gravelly it seemed drawn from the surface of the dusty road beneath her boots. It was the voice of the dead.

"Ah, Jessie Wheeler," he said. "I think you know what the fuck I want."

Deuce sucked on the timothy and cocked his head. "You belong to me. You are my employee. You are my slave. Granted, you've had a taste of freedom these last few years, but then, I had to see where you'd take this career of yours. It's a lot more fun sucking the spirit out of a wild thing like you than out of a wussy little mouse like the slut who crawled out of my house that night years ago."

"I'll do whatever you want," she whispered.

"What?" he asked, leaning closer to her, even though he heard her clear as day. "What was that you said, Jessie Wheeler?"

Cocky fucking bastard, she thought, and then repeated herself. "I will do whatever you want. But on one condition."

"Ah! A condition! I knew you had some fire left in you, dear girl. What condition?" He reached out a hairy stovepipe wrist and yanked her head up by the bun, then ripped the elastic out so that her hair fell free around her shoulders. He almost moaned with delight.

She could barely whisper. "You don't touch my friends. Or Charles and Dee."

"Um hum," he whined, nodding exaggeratedly. "Okay. Deuce no-a tou-cha-Jessie-a Wheeler's-a friends-a. Or Charles and Dee-a."

He narrowed his eyes at her, waiting for her coup de grace. He loved the thrill of this game he knew he had already won. "And?"

"And if you lay a finger on Josh I will kill myself in front of you." It was a whisper, too. But the words were delivered steady and strong.

He paused. Pondered her. *Damn.* The girl did have some strength left, after all.

"All right, then," he responded in agreement as the sun faded behind a cloud and the fresh scent of the mountains was replaced with an eerie musty earthy scent that tickled his nose unpleasantly. Absently, he thought there must be a bear in the woods nearby, watching this earthly test of survival of the fittest.

"I will not touch your beloved Josh."

Jessie let a little breath escape as a tiny speck of relief washed over her. At least this would buy her some time.

"But," he added, grinning sardonically, as he channeled the bear in the woods. He had an uncanny ability of doing that, of becoming whatever creature he desired. *I am a good actor too*, he thought. "You don't touch Josh either."

She hesitated for only a moment, because Jessie already knew this would have to be the case. She was prepared. "Fine. But you have to give me a little time with him, to let him go. Otherwise no one will believe I left him because I wanted to. They'll think that something happened, and you don't want that, Deuce, or you'll have Charles Keating's whole fucking army after you."

She looked so small standing there beside her red Mustang, begging for Josh's life and offering her own, that her tormentor almost felt a pang of pity. Almost.

McCall stared at her for a bit, then reached out and grasped her hand. He nodded. "Two weeks," he said.

"Fine."

He pulled her close and pressed his lips to hers, and this time he did moan with desire and anticipation. He shoved her away, though, and strode back to his car.

"I'll be in touch, Jessie Wheeler."

Watching him drive away, Jessie rubbed a trembling hand over her face. The whiskers had indeed hurt. They felt like little porcupine pricks, hundreds of them all stabbing her at once. She stood there for a while and, finally, the watching bear ambled away, bored.

As the mountainous fresh scent reappeared and the sun came out from behind its cloud, Jessie was once again overwhelmed with a sense of despair. Then she climbed into the Mustang and pointed the car downtown. She had to look up an old friend.

She spun her tires again. Seemed she was spinning them a lot, today. *Oh hell*, she thought dismally. *Echoes the way I am feeling these days, going around and around with no solution in sight.*

She tried not to think of Josh, but she couldn't avoid seeing his troubled eyes in her mind. He was so confused and scared, and he had no idea how bad things were going to get before they could ever get better, if in fact they could ever get better. The damaged image of him broke her heart. She forced the tires to stop spinning as she slammed on the brakes and suddenly veered over to the side of the dirt road. Then she laid her head on the steering wheel and let great heaving sobs overtake her.

Was there still hope? Maybe. But right now, today, it was at the end of a long, dim tunnel and, even though she squinted hard, Jessie could barely make it out as it danced just beyond her sight in the summer breeze.

Chapter Eleven

The Downtown Eastside of Vancouver was a section of the city where Jessie was very comfortable, although most folks who knew the area were not. This was the poorest section of town, the area Jessie gravitated to when she first came to Vancouver. She lived there, mostly on the streets, for two years. Despite the fame and success that Jessie still found so strange and surreal, she kept up a lot of old acquaintances, often buying meals and clothes for the disenchanted. Now she needed a favor in return.

She parked the Mustang near the shelter she and Dee founded, where Terri lived before Deuce had likely gotten his mucky hands on her. Jessie was proud of the shelter and the number of young women it helped. Her autumn fundraising concert tour was a tremendous success, and as a result Dee was busy throughout the winter coordinating the building of new shelters in other cities. Jessie participated when she could, and she and Josh flew to the various cities on long weekends to see how things were coming along. They generally didn't travel with Dee, since the older woman was less than kind to Josh most times. Many of the shelters would be ready to open in the fall. This was something Jessie had been very much looking forward to, but as of today she was no longer looking forward to much of anything. She was caught in the moment, trying to simply move from one second to the next.

She ran a hand through her unruly hair and pulled the pale yellow cardigan tight around her belly. She became aware of some stares and noticed people pointing, and it was only then she realized she was still in her dance outfit, and that she'd skipped out on the rest of rehearsal. Priya would be livid, and Kayla would be curious, although perhaps by now Josh had texted his sister to let her know that Jessie was upset, which would explain her absence. Dee would also be aware, although she was in Chicago at the moment, checking up on the Windy City's new shelter.

Jessie laughed inwardly, sarcasm and anger grasping her insides, biting hard enough so that an ensuing cramp gutted her. She wouldn't be surprised if Dee suspected Josh of slashing his own tires. She couldn't put her finger on Dee's animosity towards Josh, who Jessie felt proved his worth again and again through kindness and generosity of spirit. But then again, Deirdre Keating was a confident, intelligent woman. She was also the kind of thinker who analyzed situations and then deduced a response from the data she'd gathered. She was not driven by emotion. Likely she just needed time to process Josh.

Opening the Mustang's trunk, Jessie grabbed a camouflage-green zippered hoodie and pulled it over the yellow sweater. She always kept a few extra clothing pieces in her trunk, since she was often away from home for hours on end and, in Vancouver, the weather could change in a flash. Besides, in this crazy life of hers, sometimes a girl just needed some smokescreen. She yanked the hood up over her head and waved dispiritedly to an old hobo guarding a shopping cart nearby.

"Hey, Frank," she mumbled in a cracked voice, but didn't stop to talk, leaving the dirty, grizzled old man without the fifty dollar bill she usually handed him. There were some folks down here today she didn't know, and Jessie didn't want to linger. Besides, she had other things on her mind.

She made her way a few blocks down Hastings to a derelict red brick apartment building. Some of its windows were cracked, and bricks were smashed and crumbling here and there, mostly within reach of a good strong pitcher's arm. The perimeter at street level was garishly graffitied with fire-breathing dragons and the odd expletive. She stepped up two concrete risers and pulled on the glass door.

Entering a little vestibule, she crinkled her nose in disgust. What was it about street people that they insisted on pissing wherever and whenever they wanted? In the old days she had occasionally needed to do the same, by times, but she usually at least found a treed park or shrub, and that was always a last resort. It was apparent someone had recently relieved himself here. It was revolting, and she could barely keep her already acidic stomach from emptying itself on top of the faded yellow urine patch in the corner. As the putrid acrid stench stung her nostrils, it wasn't lost on Jessie that even the smells today seemed to be a reflection of her current tormented state of being.

She reached a manicured fingernail up to the list of names next to their corresponding little rectangular black buttons. Finding *Sylvester, A,* she hesitated a moment and then pushed the button. It was just after 12:30. He'd likely be home, but would he be awake and responsive? Seconds later, a scraggly tired voice came over the crackling intercom.

"What? You better have a good fucking reason for waking me up."

"Arnie."

It was all she needed to say. She was one of the only people who called this guy Arnie. He had taken her under his wing when she first arrived on the streets in Van, and he was one of few men in her life who had not tried to get into her pants. She trusted him implicitly; he adored her, and was proud of her survival, much less her success.

A harsh buzz jarred her frazzled nerves. Jessie pushed open the inner glass door and ran up the six steps to number 201, on the left. Arnie was unlocking the apartment's grungy green door just as she arrived on his landing. Wrapped loosely in a threadbare plaid blue and green housecoat, he stepped out and leaned casually against the doorframe. Draped casually over a pair of pajama pants, the robe showed off a muscular chest and part of a worn red and black tattoo Jessie knew to be the letters of Arnie's mother's name, Eloise, a woman who taught her son to live a life of true value, not monetary worth. One of the world's genuine good Samaritans, she taught by her own caring example, and so Arnie learned to make choices based on what he believed necessary, drawn from his own past and current experience. He didn't always choose a lawful path, but he trusted his intuition and instincts to lead him down what he, in his heart, believed was the right path. He was a man of his word, a serious soul whose life was not always easy, but he was a survivor, and that counted for everything when those on the Downtown Eastside needed their own version of a cloaked hero, a confessor.

Jessie spied bare toes peeking out from below fraying hems. Arnie stood aside and, her gaze still focused on the floor, Jessie brushed by him. He watched her slide by, his all-seeing glance taking in Jessie's dance clothes and the fear he read on her pale face.

"Spill it," was all he said before gently resting an arm on her waist and urging Jessie into the comfort of his tiny living room. She lowered herself onto a camel-brown couch covered with a warm yellow and blue afghan that sported a few noticeable holes. One swoop of Arnie's arm and the tattered covering was unceremoniously shoved out of the way.

"Fight with the old lady," he muttered apologetically. "This ragged thing is pretty comfortable when you're drunk and tired."

"Is she…" Jessie straightened nervously and focused her eyes towards the small kitchen, then towards the narrow hallway to the bedroom.

"Nah, she's off to work. She's at a new Indian restaurant in the Tinseltown Mall food court. Been there a few months now. She's doing well, actually, Jess, which…" he studied her, "I'm not so sure I can say about you. What brings you down to my digs on a Saturday? I'm sure you have better things to do than share a smoke and a drink with an old friend."

It was a bit of a dig but at his friendly smile Jessie relaxed a little. Then she reached out and took a smoke out of the pack on the nearby glass coffee table, which was surprisingly clean. In fact, the whole place was in better shape than when she'd seen it last, when it was littered with chip bags and liquor bottles. Funny what pride did for people. Give Arnie's old girl a job and suddenly she cares about her environment again.

Curious, Arnie ran a hand over his chin whiskers, made a mental note to shave later, then picked up his lighter and helped hold Jessie's cigarette steady while he lit it for her. Something was wrong. Even in the old days, she rarely smoked.

"Okay girl," he said kindly, concerned. "Speak. Your new boyfriend hurt you or something? You need revenge?"

Jessie hauled deeply on the cigarette and then sat back and closed her puffy, tired eyes. Even Arnie had it in for Josh. After a moment she dared a peek and looked up at her old friend. He had the kindest eyes, a luminescent blue that just exuded gentleness. Those eyes were what convinced her to trust him in the first place, all those years ago. Despite his two-day whiskers, he had chiseled cheekbones and short, spiked dark hair that made him

110

seem younger than his fifty-six years. He was fairly fit for a guy who worked the streets; she knew him to box regularly at a local gym, where she'd often gone and watched, and sometimes even taken a few lessons, depending on his mood as well as hers.

"Arnie," she started, between deep pulls on the quaking cigarette. "I am only going to say this once, so listen carefully. Josh Sawyer is the nicest, sweetest man on this planet. He has not hurt me, he will not hurt me, he will never hurt me. Understand?"

Arnie sat back on the couch, and then reached out for his own cigarette and lit it.

"I'm sorry," he said apologetically. "If you're with him, then I know he must be a good guy, Jess. I didn't mean to fall into that crowd mentality."

"He's the best, Arnie. I mean it. And it's more like mob mentality, if you ask me."

They sat quietly and smoked for a moment, because Jessie still didn't have her emotions under control after her big cry on the mountain earlier. Plus the cigarette was giving her dizzying head-spins. Talking about Josh just brought it all home. She could feel her heart literally breaking.

She finished her smoke and ground out the butt in the glass ashtray her old friend provided for them.

"I need a gun," she suddenly told him, before looking up into those caring blue eyes. *He could be a star himself,* she caught herself thinking. For an older guy, he was strikingly handsome.

Arnie had lived on East Hastings for a lot of years. Nothing surprised him anymore. He finished his own smoke, and then nodded at her.

"Okay," he said. And then, uncharacteristically, a question. "Why? You have your own security."

"Arnie," was all she said. There was a code. No questions. That was why she came to him. That was why a lot of people came to him.

"All right." He pulled himself up slowly on sore knees, wincing, and crossed the room to a battered oak desk from which he retrieved a rather new MacBook Pro, which didn't surprise Jessie. Arnie liked his electronics—that was where most of his earnings went. There was also a 52-inch plasma television in the diminutive room, complete with a surround sound system.

He placed the computer on the coffee table in front of them and poked the power button. He left it to fire up and went into the tiny kitchen, returning with two glasses of water. When the Mac was ready, Arnie opened up Safari and typed in *NAA Guardian .380*. An image of a small short-barreled pistol popped up on screen. Arnie pushed the laptop towards Jessie so she could lean forward and have a better look.

"This would work for you. It's got enough wallop to kill somebody, but it's small enough to carry in an ankle wrap." After a moment he added, as if it mattered, "I might even be able to find one with a pearl handle."

He watched her study the gun. A chill ran down his hardened spine, then switched gears and peppered his belly with hard pricks, doubts. Arnie had procured a lot of illegal guns for people over the years, but those folks weren't like Jessie…sweet, kind, famous. They were generally hardened individuals who had no recourse but to resort to deadly weapons. Jessie should have no need of a gun. Straining his brain to think of what he'd heard on the news about her lately, he couldn't find a thing except a general public animosity towards her new boyfriend. Maybe she was researching a part for an upcoming film. Arnie shook his head as if he were clearing the cobwebs out of it. *Whatever. It's her business, not mine.*

"When can you have it?" Jessie inquired evenly, taking an anxious sip from the glass of water and marveling at the little wavelets her trembling fingers caused. "The gun?"

"Tomorrow," he said, lighting another smoke and offering her a second, which she accepted. "Be here at five p.m. No later, because the old woman gets off work at six, and she doesn't need to see Jessie Wheeler here buying a gun. And wear something a little less…noticeable, okay? You look too fucking good. You don't want to be seen, you want to blend in."

Arnie hoped Jessie would open up to him, but she didn't. Preoccupied, apparently lost in whatever secret fear that brought her to his door today, she simply stared at the geometric patterned rug Arnie picked up for his wife from Ikea last month. He wasn't surprised at her reticence to talk and he didn't push her.

The thing is, when Arnie first met Jessie, she was a shell. She was literally handed to him, one of the Downtown Eastside's unspoken leaders, by a striking blonde woman and her husband, who told him, "She rarely speaks, and she won't look you in the eye. But she sings and plays a soulful guitar like a fucking reincarnated John Lennon."

Arnie knew the couple had taken Jessie in after finding her huddled in a doorway struggling to breathe, lungs full of fluid. They got her the medical care she needed and then rewarded the girl with sketchy work in a black box studio Arnie didn't care to think about, although he knew damn well what kind of films they shot within its not so hallowed walls. He had asked them why they were giving her up. The woman, Caryn, a tall willowy blonde with pained green eyes and a heart laced with good intentions but weak when it required strength of character, had turned away. Her husband, Eric, literally handed Jessie to Arnie. "She can't stay with us anymore. Or work for Caryn. She's getting in the way."

Eric, like Arnie, was strong, fit, tanned; he was a dark-haired Italian man who moved with purpose. He was a good provider for Caryn although, with her own income from their first rate erotic movie biz, she could do okay without him, if she chose. Observing the couple's interactions—Caryn weepy, Eric adamant—Arnie understood that Jessie, with her hurting ice-blue eyes, had somehow come between the couple. He didn't know how or why; at the same time he didn't want to know how or why. But suddenly he had a homeless girl sleeping on his couch when the outside thermometer dipped below zero, and another of the Downtown Eastside's disillusioned to somehow help find the fight in herself to survive. He set her up to busk on East Hastings and then, one day, Jack Deacon started walking by. And Jack Deacon chose to listen.

Arnie never asked Caryn or Eric what Jessie meant to them, but he knew none of their other "talent" ever lived with them in their fixed-up spacious open concept apartment. Arnie chose not to query any of the other girls who worked in the erotic entertainment studio with Caryn either, but he overheard rumblings then, as well as after Jessie's success.

Caryn got too close to her.

Now, Arnie met Jessie's eyes, which was more than he was ever rewarded with early on in the old days. He wondered whether she ever told the Keatings, Charlie, Josh, or her *Drifters* friends about her life during that early Vancouver time. What Arnie failed to understand was that Jessie herself didn't know. She had only vague, hazy memories of life after Charleston until she started acting in the Deacon workshops. She wouldn't know Caryn or Eric if she stumbled across them in the street. Only in the dark of night were her dreams haunted by amorphous memories of a tall blonde, a dark haired man, or work in films she didn't, at the time, really understand.

They smoked in silence, and then Jessie got up to leave.

At the door, Arnie studied her troubled eyes.

"Jessie," he implored. "Whatever the hell this is about, I've got your back, okay?"

She nodded. Jessie couldn't speak because of the damn lump in her throat. How she wished she could tell him her latest troubles. But she didn't want to get Arnie mixed up with Deuce McCall any more than she wanted Josh or Charles or Matt involved. After all her success, the only thing she felt she had left to give any of the people she loved was total protection from the dangerous McCall. And that could only come by omission, by not telling anyone anything, at least until she had this terrorist under control. But still, on some level, it was good to know old standby Arnie was in her corner, even if it was just by finding her a gun.

Inadvertently, overcome by another onslaught of emotion, Jessie threw her arms around Arnie and held on tight.

"Thanks," was all she managed to whisper, and then she slipped away.

Arnie went back inside and watched her from his living room window as she made a hasty exit down Hastings, her head down, identity only partially covered by the hoodie.

"Jessie Wheeler," he muttered curiously. "Who the hell have you gotten yourself mixed up with this time?"

Then he set about showering and shaving. He'd better get to work if he wanted that gun ready for Jessie tomorrow. He nicked himself shaving and, as he fingered the blood, for the first time in many years of procuring weapons for people, he wondered whose blood would flow this time around.

Chapter Twelve

$\mathcal{D}$euce had promised her two weeks. She had fourteen days to convince people she and Josh were through. The timing wasn't bad because the shooting of *Drifters* season two would be ending at the same time as McCall's deadline. Jessie had already gotten Dee to start the paperwork on season three, which had just been announced. But she knew now that it wouldn't be an option. She had to maintain as much distance from Josh as possible, at least until she figured out how to control or destroy Deuce and any probable minions. And who knew when that might be? She would have to play McCall's wicked little game for a while first, until she could figure out the best time to strike, and how. She wasn't worried about Dee's reaction to her sudden change of mind regarding season three. Jessie's manager would be over the moon.

So. Two weeks. Every second would count, as painful as that might be. Jessie would have to reach deep inside herself to find a character she could play so as to remove herself from Josh and her friends with a modicum of planning and persistence. She did not want to give anything of her new horrid reality away. She went to her condo for the rest of the afternoon, ignoring everyone's texts and calls, and she Googled the new gun. She was pleasantly surprised to find it was the same ankle handgun Grace Hanadarko carried on the television series *Saving Grace*. Jessie had watched the series twice—three seasons of it. She could identify with Holly Hunter's character—sexually abused, belligerent, scared of attachment, a woman with her own walls. Jessie would channel her. That would help. Occasional drinking would help. Smoking. Maybe weed. She didn't need to think about it. Jessie would need at least some anesthetic to summon up the courage to get her through this challenge.

Later in the day she sent the text to Josh that resulted in him firing his phone across the room. A half hour later she got a summons from the concierge in the lobby of her building.

"Miss Wheeler, Josh Sawyer is here to see you. Shall I let him up?"

Jessie groaned. She had picked up cigarettes and Baileys on the way home from East Hastings, and as a result she was feeling spinny and sick, but she would have to face him at some point.

"Okay," she responded despondently.

A few minutes later, a quiet knock energized her to get up from her comfy place on the outside chaise. Still wearing her dance leggings and tank top, Jessie pulled open the interior door to the condo. Josh was standing there, as divine and sexy as ever in faded jeans, black boots, a black t-shirt, and a rust colored western style fringed hip length suede jacket. Around his neck, soaking up his warmth, was the stylized J pendant she gave him for Christmas. Leaning back against the elevator door in true Josh fashion, one ankle turned over, he was a picture of confusion and fear. He didn't speak.

Jessie moved out of the way and let him in. Josh edged into her living space and then turned to her in bewilderment when the harsh cigarette smoke accosted his nostrils.

"What the hell, Jessie?" he asked, baffled.

She looked at the man she had to hurt to love, and then pulled up her inner irascible Grace Hanadarko.

"What?" she asked. "A girl can smoke if she wants to."

His dark questioning eyes spotted the Baileys bottle on the counter.

"Look, Jess," he said, following her outside and sitting on the loveseat on her balcony as she teetered against the railing, facing away from him, yet another cigarette in her nicotine stained fingers. "I know you're freaked out from all this. But we agreed. We said we'd get through it. Together."

She glanced down at the people wandering the sidewalks many stories below. So many ants, so little purpose. Little did they know the only thing that really mattered in life was love.

Turning to face Josh, Jessie put her best Hanadarko out there. She even had Grace's boots on, dusty brown with pointed toes. "I don't know if I can do it, Josh," she said, a hopeless cast pervading her voice. "Maybe all this is putting me over the edge."

He felt as if the knife from the tire slashing was suddenly and ruthlessly slicing open his heart. This was the real deal. She was afraid. There was a chance he was losing Jessie. What could he say to fight back, to give her a reason to hang on, to convince her they were survivors?

"Jesus," was all he mustered as he dropped his head into his hands. He thought he was going to be sick. "Don't do this, Jessie."

Hanadarko dove in further. "Look, I'm not saying it's over, we still have to work together for a few more weeks. Let's just chill out and see what happens, okay? No pressure."

He looked miserably up at those sad eyes with their absence of light. Who was she, and what the hell had she done with his Jessie? *The pitfalls of loving an actor*, he thought. He wasn't stupid. Josh *knew* Jessie. In his breaking heart he understood that she was playing some kind of game in order to protect herself. What he failed to understand was that she was playing some kind of game in order to protect *him*.

This sucked, but it was real. Something heinous was happening, something he couldn't grasp. He had about two weeks until they were done shooting *Drifters*, until she could easily get wrapped up in her shelters and concerts, and he in the feature he was shooting that summer in Arizona. But he wasn't as stubborn as Jessie. Josh would go for help. But to whom? Charles and Dee would be thrilled to get him off their radar. Jonathon was a great producer, but he was all business, even though sometimes Josh felt a closeness he couldn't explain towards the great man. Steve and Carter and the girls...they were the ones he needed to talk to about this, and...maybe...Charlie. Charlie, who had stayed in touch with Jessie, and who would likely be thrilled about a potential break-up between the two. Charlie, who knew her and loved her and would be concerned about a new Jessie who smoked and drank and removed herself from her friends.

Charlie. Josh's old friend.

Somehow, Josh and Jessie managed to stay together that night at Jessie's place. They made dinner together and she stopped smoking and drinking, and then they snuggled up and watched an old Nora Ephron movie starring Tom Hanks and Meg Ryan. They hardly spoke. She avoided his eyes as much as possible, but he felt her watching him more than the film, and he responded when she traced his chin and played with his hair and kissed his neck so tenderly that he wondered if he'd only wished it, and not really felt her soft lips nuzzling his skin.

Three quarters of the way through the film, his arm around her and a blanket over their laps, he felt her even breathing and was glad she finally slept, although he doubted it would be for long, if her patterns over the last few weeks were any indication.

"Jessie," he whispered. "Little one. Come back to me."

An hour later he drifted off as well. They slept on the couch until five a.m. when another horrific nightmare woke Jessie with a start. This time, instead of running away she stayed nestled in his arms and sobbed endlessly, to Josh's utter terror and confusion. He whispered to her and rubbed her back, touched her cheek and kissed her tenderly. Their intimate touches escalated, igniting a deep burning within, and they made love, which calmed her for a time. Together they slept a little more there on the couch, because they were too afraid of impending endings to change the dynamic. Later, she forced herself to get up and pull away from him, although they showered together before going off in separate vehicles to join the others for brunch at Jethro's in Dunbar.

Jessie excused herself early in order to get caught up before dance rehearsal since she'd skipped out the day before, but it was everything she had in her to leave Josh's side. He walked her to the door of the popular diner, and then they wrapped their arms around each other and held on for dear life before she steeled herself and left him there, hands in his pockets, watching as she drove away.

He went back inside the busy dining room and dropped into his chair.

"Okay," he said to the others, interrupting a hearty conversation about the potential storyline for season three. He looked at Steve. "Call Charlie. We need to talk. My place. Now."

The table fell into complete silence.

Then Steve pulled out his phone and texted Charlie, who happened to be in town and so responded right away. They paid their brunch bills, drove to Josh's where the shrubs were shorter and new motion sensor lights were already in place, and they held their first meeting of many where the main subject of conversation was Jessie Wheeler.

～～～

Charlie showed up with a big box of Tim Horton donuts, curious as to why the close group of friends had beckoned him. He set the box unceremoniously down on the coffee table and plopped down beside Maggie on the leather sofa in Josh's media room. He looked around—the *Drifters* gang was all there, even petite blonde Sophie, around whose shoulders Steve's arm was draped possessively.

Usually in control but this time giving away his nerves by pocketing and un-pocketing his hands, Charlie opened the conversation.

"What's the deal, then? I know from Charles and Dee that Jessie's sick. You guys are freaking me out by calling me here. Is she okay?"

"You tell us," Steve said in response. Josh remained quiet as Steve filled Charlie in on Jessie's strange behavior the night of the Agassiz season opener, and her downward spiral and withdrawal from everyone since.

Charlie wrinkled his forehead and leaned forward. "So the only thing that doesn't fit here is how sudden this came about. Otherwise you think— Josh—that she's upset about the public's response to you?"

Carter growled. "No need to gloat, Charlie."

Charlie threw his hands up in surrender. "I'm not gloating. I'm worried. The only time I ever knew Jessie withdrawn like that was when I met her. It took her a few years to chill out, period."

"It took her a while to warm up to us, too," Maggie added helpfully. Charlie smiled gratefully at her. The last thing he wanted was to be ambushed by Jessie's new pals.

Josh finally spoke up. He looked questioningly at Charlie. "Did she ever tell you what happened in Charleston?"

Charlie reached out and seized a filled donut from the box. He licked the white sugar off his fingers before he spoke. *I'm an ass*, he told himself. He hadn't really tried to find out what happened in Jessie's life before he met her. He looked up at Josh.

"No," he said. "But Josh, I just accepted her without question. I knew bad shit had come her way, but we were all about just hanging out from day to day, from film to film or show to show. It was party land, you know? I didn't want to bring up bad memories and change our dynamic. It was stupid of me. I expect it's also part of why I lost her—we weren't really connected."

He took a bite of the donut, licked a few more fingers, and then risked asking a big question. It would hurt if Jessie had opened up to Josh. He swallowed. "What about you? Has she ever told you anything?"

"No," Josh said. "But she cries in her sleep."

Charlie nodded, humbled. "She's cried in her sleep as long as I've known her, Sawyer."

"Sucks," Josh mumbled, squeezing his bottom lip worriedly with his thumb and forefinger. "It had been getting better until these last few weeks, though." He looked down at his feet. "Maybe it *is* just all this crap that's going down."

Sue-Lyn, sitting on the opposite couch with her legs crossed under her, one arm leaning on a crooked elbow, tossed in tenderly, "Honey, Jessie is crazy about you. She couldn't keep herself from touching you at brunch."

"She couldn't take her eyes off you, either," Sophie threw in helpfully. Steve grinned and rewarded his girlfriend with a hug.

"She's not going to give up on you because of a few assholes," Carter added, his shoulder length raven hair framing his high cheekbones attractively. But he, like the others, was surprised to hear about Jessie's night terrors. It broke his heart.

"A lot of assholes," Josh muttered, eyes downcast.

Charlie jumped in, his donut consumed in three big bites. "Josh, Jessie is a big girl. She doesn't concern herself with fame the way some of us do. Okay, me. The way I do. Carter's right. She's a fighter. She won't let them get to her." He added, "Is that why you called me here? To get an opinion on whether Jessie will crack under all this pressure? That almost does make me want to gloat, but…"

Maggie elbowed him.

He leaned forward, his eyes morphing from their usual playful shade to one with decidedly darker flecks. "Seriously, though, I miss the hell out of her, but it's obvious she's in love with you. I know I've lost. So what is it you really want to ask me?"

The room was quiet with the exception of the odd muffled movement.

Meeting Charlie's eyes for the first time, Josh spoke. "Charlie," he said. "It's like a light went out in her eyes when she saw the knife by the truck yesterday. All four tires were slashed, and it must have happened just after she left for rehearsal because I left, like, fifteen minutes after she did. So whatever asshole did that, he was likely watching her. It scares the shit out of me to think what he could have done. Maybe that's what's going through her head today. She wouldn't take my calls or answer my texts yesterday. Then when she finally let me into her place, she had a fucking ashtray full of cigarettes and had been drinking all afternoon."

Josh couldn't sit still. His anxiety was increasing as he spoke. He jumped up and paced the room. "Then she told me she didn't know whether she could do this—us. I *get* the fear, but I guess what I want to know from you is whether this has happened before. Like—I'm thinking maybe there's more to this than just assholes who like you better than me. I'm thinking she recognized that fucking dagger, and that we need to get Matt on this. He's got the tools to really investigate this. Maybe he can figure shit out before something really nasty happens."

"Like what?" Charlie asked, not unkindly. "Like she dumps your stupid ass?"

"Charlie," Maggie chided.

"No," Josh said. "Like someone hurts her."

They were quiet as they took in the implications of that simple phrase.

He continued. "Maybe that knife was a message."

"It was obviously a fucking message," Steve said, removing his arm from Sophie's shoulders and taking her hand instead.

"The thing is, Josh," Charlie spoke up tentatively, leaning further forward, placing his elbows on his thighs. "If you're asking me to go to Charles and Dee on your behalf, then you'd likely better be prepared for the third degree yourself. You know what Dee thinks."

"Yes, I fucking know what Dee thinks. But I wouldn't hurt Jessie. I would never lay a finger on her! But I'm afraid that *someone* is planning to."

Slowly, Charlie stood and faced Josh. Steve shot a look of warning to Carter, silently asking him to be prepared to jump up and break up a fight should the need arise.

"You ass," Charlie grumbled. "What makes you think any of us really believe you wouldn't hurt her? Maybe you slashed your own damn tires. Maybe you're just covering your own fucking tracks."

They stared icily at each other for a few moments before Josh responded.

"She's everything to me, Charlie. And that's why I called you here. Because I know that despite all the shit that went down, she's still everything to you, too."

And that was the moment when Charlie realized Josh would indeed never hurt Jessie. Because he cared about her so much—and was so scared for her, for them—that he called in her ex-fiancé. He was admitting that he needed help, that he was seriously worried about Jessie, and that he would have to rely on people who were not necessarily on his side to help him. He was almost begging, and Charlie would have enjoyed that, had he not seen the deep fear in Josh's eyes.

Charlie nodded and picked up the box of donuts. He held it out to the others. "Want some more?" he asked. At their negative responses, he tucked the box under his arm. "Alright then. I'm off to North Van. Dee invited me for dinner."

He let that sink in, and Josh almost bent over as a sharp pain assaulted his stomach. Would Charles and Dee ever fully accept him? Then his cell beeped, and he instinctively looked down to see if it was Jessie. It wasn't. It was Kayla, texting from rehearsal.

Jessie with you? one hour late for rehearsal get out of the bedroom and get her here Priya having a fit

As the impact of the text sank in, the color drained from his face. He offered the phone to Charlie, who took it and stared hard at the message. When Charlie gave the phone back to Josh, he was also pale.

"Okay," he said. "Something's fucked up. In eight years, I've never known Jessie to miss rehearsal."

He stepped over Carter's long legs and waved goodbye as he made a hasty exit, calling behind him, "I'll talk to Charles. We'll get Matt on it."

The matriarch of the bunch, Maggie, stood up and hugged Josh. "Hey," she encouraged him, a calming voice of hope in the wilderness. "She's got every right to be scared. Maybe Dee can wave her magic wand and get some positive PR going, now that she knows how much this bullying you is hurting Jessie."

"And if it's more than just some psycho fan who can't stand me?" Josh implored her, the luster in his eyes fading from their usual liquid brown.

Maggie rested a cool palm on his cheek. "One day at a time, honey. Go find Jessie and hold her close and tell her you love her; maybe she'll open up to you. Then we can all solve this together."

They chatted a while longer about the fears they all shared. What if this psycho found his—or her—way onto the *Drifters* set? Steve assured them that Charles had ordered increased security on the set, which relaxed them a little. But it was sobering, the idea that any of them could be at risk.

At home, where she'd gone in order to do some Internet research, thinking she'd just be a little late for rehearsal, Jessie would have been mortified to know how scared her friends were. This was what she was trying to avoid. This was why she was dealing with Deuce on her own. This was the reason she was on the Internet.

She had typed in *stalkers* and, in doing so, sufficiently scared the crap out of herself even more. She read stories of the damage done by celebrity stalkers, including the deaths of famous stars like her hero John Lennon, who was ruthlessly gunned down outside his home in New York. She read about the different kinds of stalkers, such as rejected stalkers, who pursue their victims in order to reverse, correct, or avenge a rejection. She figured rightly that this was a good definition of Deuce McCall, a man who thought he had been wronged because she'd left his employ and thus initially caused him financial damage. The other types of stalkers—resentful, those who pursue a vendetta because of a sense of grievance against the victim; intimacy seekers, who seek to establish an intimate, loving relationship with the victim whom they consider a long sought after soul mate; incompetent suitors with a fixation or sense of entitlement to an intimate relationship with those who have attracted their amorous interest; and predatory stalkers who spy on the victim and plan a sexual attack on the victim; were all horrifying. And perhaps Deuce had some qualities of each. But over and above all, the stalkers were all described as delusional, on some level. Psychotic. And Deuce was, indeed, that.

Jessie took down notes about how to deal with her stalker. In some way, she found this empowering. It gave her a better understanding of the man she was dealing with, although it terrorized her even more about wanting to protect Josh from McCall, a man who was likely beyond capable of any sort of reasoning. The most important thing that came out of the research was the advice to keep detailed notes on any communications about what Jessie experienced in relation to Deuce, and in relation to what he did to her and when. A diary, of sorts. Jessie started one that afternoon. She had a quaint old leather notebook Charlie's mother Lydia once gave her as part of a Christmas gift. Jessie hated to tarnish it with such a terrifying, methodical journal, but it was all she had at hand. She wrote down the date McCall showed up at Agassiz and then she described where he was standing in the photograph, as well as his gesture. She then described exactly how close he was to Josh. She continued her entries with yesterday's date and the meeting with McCall on the dirt road, and she described the knife used to slash Josh's tires. She noted that she was familiar with the knife, as she had seen it up close in Charleston.

Finally, Jessie tucked the notebook between her mattress and box spring, and then she did a web search for handling instructions on the gun she was scheduled to pick up from Arnie today at five. After all, what was the point in having a gun if she didn't know how to use it?

By the time she was done it was three o'clock and her phone was buzzing incessantly. But she was driven. She had to deal with this shit.

She pulled on a pair of black Lululemon dance pants and ran for the door. At least she would get about an hour in at rehearsal, unless Priya decided to growl at her for the whole hour, in which case she'd tell her to fuck off and she'd leave. Jessie wasn't fooling around anymore. No more nice Jessie Wheeler. She was on a mission called survival, and it would be the difference between sharing this planet and her life with the man she loved, or giving up and calling it a day, period.

She texted Josh from the elevator.

Yeah I am running late going now

She didn't offer any excuses.

Jessie jumped in the Mustang and shoved the gas pedal down.

A black Ford Fusion pulled out behind the vintage car and followed her to rehearsal. But its driver wouldn't touch Jessie, for now. He knew she would be more agreeable if he gave her the two weeks he'd promised. But Deuce was still ascertaining Jessie's patterns, so he did a lot of watching these days.

He kept a respectful distance. Deuce McCall was a reasonable man, after all.

Chapter Thirteen

The next two weeks found Jessie busy trying to finish off her obligations to *Drifters* as well as rehearse on weekends. She was also swamped working with Dee and the rest of the team on her music and on the various events she was scheduled to perform locally, nationally and internationally. Jessie's one-on-one time with Josh was limited, which made it easier to pull away from him. She continued to smoke—although she did it with the *Drifters* technical crew, away from her friends—for no other reason than just to create another version of herself, to separate herself further. In the evenings she either went to Dee's to plan and hide, or to an out of town gun range, where Arnie gave her a few basic lessons on the NAA Guardian pistol she'd picked up from him.

She spent select nights with Josh at his place and allowed herself to just *be* with him, to make love and to cherish him and to miss him. She prayed she could some day salvage their relationship, that he would accept her explanations. But right now the priority was to simply save his life.

On Wednesday of that first week, Charlie sat down at the meeting he'd planned with Charles at their dinner the previous Sunday. Matt was also present.

As the head of Keating Security, Matt would be key to figuring out what was going on with Jessie. He had been with her from the beginning, and knew her as well as she'd let anyone get to know her. Matt was often frustrated with Jessie's disregard for his policies and protocols; he called her his wild child when his pretty wife Julie asked about his day job. A fitness fanatic, forty-five-year-old Matt was trim and fit, although he made a point of hiding his rather perfect physique under blazers and long sleeved button down shirts. His short black hair was spiked with gel, and his wife often teased him about needing to have each strand in perfect order before he'd leave the house. Matt was a man of order and discipline. An ex-RCMP officer, he was well versed in Canadian Criminal Law, and dedicated his life to stability and orderliness.

Matt fit well in Charles' employ. He had enough challenges day to day to make life interesting, and he enjoyed the prestige of working with one of the more successful husband and wife teams in the entertainment biz in Canada (and in the world, for that matter). He had come to adore Jessie and her music about as much as any of the rest of her fans, more so even, because he knew her and admired all but her tendency to disregard the protocols he felt would ensure her safety. She was not a princess, she shared her wealth with the less fortunate, and she was always pleasant, albeit shy and quiet. An observer, Matt had enjoyed watching Jessie blossom with Josh at her side. She was clearly madly in love with him. It irked Matt to watch how Dee pushed her away by not accepting Josh. He had always thought of Charlie as the playboy he finally proved to be, and had always thought Jessie was sad and lonely in that doomed relationship. Josh opened up a bright spot of sunshine in the girl's heart, and it radiated to those around her, including Matt.

As a security professional, Matt's ability to spot trouble was expected. There were those in the field, however, who settled into a sort of laissez-faire routine of hanging out with their celebrities and sharing in the joys of wealth and fame. Matt was the opposite, he removed himself enough from his employer so as to remain utterly professional and assured in the services he and his team were providing. This way, he could be supremely confident that all was well in the Keating camp at all times. He sometimes felt close to Jessie because he could see that she, too, kept a certain distance between herself and others. Maybe it made him even more protective of her. At any rate, he'd seen enough pain in his career as an RCMP officer to want to avoid that in this, what he considered his second career. And as much as his and his wife's families teased him about his "cushy" job, he took it seriously and ached to protect Jessie and the Keatings to the best of his ability.

When Charles asked Matt to attend this meeting with him and Charlie,

Matt's intuition kicked in. Something was up, something out of the ordinary. He'd chauffeured Jessie a few times over the past few weeks and, like the others close to her, noticed a startling change in her behavior and personality. After the tire incident last Saturday Matt had watched, disturbed, as Jessie tore off in her Mustang, belligerent and obviously terrified. So today's meeting wasn't necessarily a surprise. However, it did seem odd that Charlie was to be involved.

It was one of those soft, misty, early June Vancouver days. Matt pulled the black Audi up to the butter yellow house in North Van and flipped off the windshield wipers, noting that Charlie had already arrived, as evidenced by the mud-splattered 911 in the driveway ahead of him. He hopped out and inserted his own key, kept for instant access if need be, into La Casa's lock. Charles had told Matt to come right in. Dee was now in New York, and Carlotta would be out grocery shopping.

At the entrance to Charles' study, Matt knocked twice and then pushed open the door. The two Charleses (or Charles squared, as Jessie used to tease) looked up at once and nodded their greetings, and it wasn't lost on Matt that they seemed very much like father and son, as each had hoped and planned for not all that long ago. Charlie accepted Matt's outstretched hand and shook firmly. Judging by the grim look on the younger man's face, and his own inclusion in this meeting, Matt knew they weren't there to discuss how to "off" Josh so Charlie could have Jessie back, as he'd joked with himself on the drive from his home in nearby Burnaby.

Matt fortified himself for whatever was to come, pulled out a chair at Charles' boardroom table, and settled in.

As Charles established himself at one end, Charlie jumped in before Matt had even poured himself a glass of water from the decanter in the center of the rectangular dark glass table.

"Something's going on with Jessie."

Matt took a sip of his water and eyed the playboy. He would have rather held this meeting with Josh, who seemed to him to be more responsible and less flighty than Charlie. He shrugged. "I agree. She's not herself. Have you been talking to her lately?" It was a dig, but Matt chanced it anyway. Charlie didn't even flinch.

Charlie's voice was urgent. "Josh and his buds from the television show called me over to Josh's place on Sunday. They see her every day. They're worried sick. She's been skipping show rehearsals, too."

Straightening, Matt suddenly took Charlie a little more seriously. He glanced over at the pale and worried Charles, suddenly noticing that the lines in his employer's face were a little darker and more pronounced than normal. If Josh and Charlie were meeting to discuss Jessie and, truly out of character she was missing rehearsals, then the shit was really hitting the fan.

"Where should we start, Matt?" It was Charles, interjecting from his end of the table, his usual authoritative timbre rasping like a cello being played with a handsaw, uneven, low and tired.

Matt looked over at Charlie. As much as he wanted to dislike him, there was a bleak desperation in Charlie's eyes. Jessie had that kind of power over men, the power to undo them.

"Charlie," he started, leaning back in his chair. It creaked with his movement. "Do you think she's just having second thoughts about Josh? People get sick when it comes to affairs of the heart. Then add in all this bullshit with people slicing Josh's tires and spitting on him, for God's sake…"

He was testing Charlie. But Charlie Deacon was too worried about Jessie to go for it. And he'd been witness to the affection Jessie and Josh had for each other, as much as he hated to admit it. It took him a few seconds, during which he didn't break Matt's steady hazel gaze, and then he picked a spot on the hardwood to focus on, and shook his head.

"No," he said fervently. "Personally, I don't. It kills me to say so, but she loves the heck out of that guy. But she's pulling away from him, and he's scared shitless. He doesn't know how to help her. None of us do, and she's not talking."

Charlie glanced over at Charles. The older man was staring at his fingertips, despondent.

With a hard look back to Matt, Charlie spoke earnestly. "Matt. Josh and Steve think Jessie recognized the knife left by Josh's car."

"Hmm." Matt leaned an elbow on the glass table and rested his chin in his knuckles, then brushed his cheek with his thumb as if feeling for the whiskers he'd fastidiously shaved away that morning. "That would explain why she got sick." Steve had told them Jessie was puking before she spun off in her car, tires squealing on the pavement.

"And why she removed herself from the rest of us for the remainder of the day," Charles added. "In classic Jessie style, she needed to process this crap on her own."

"But enough is enough," Charlie said. "Matt, if she recognized the knife, then she knows who slashed Josh's tires, and she's running scared."

"And we need to find out who was sending her a message," Charles said, his stomach doing somersaults of its own as he pictured the damage that insidious dagger had the power to inflict.

Matt added the inevitable thought on everyone's minds. "And what that message was." He pulled his cell phone out from a chest pocket on his blazer and scrolled to a picture he'd taken of the knife. With his thumb and forefinger, he touched the screen and widened the image so he could more clearly see the blade and handle. He stared at the embossed image just below the handle on the blade but, wide like this, it was too pixilated to make out. He would have to pay a visit to the local authorities and question the young officer who catalogued the knife. Maybe the kid had already identified ownership.

He stayed and discussed Jessie and the knife incident with Charles and Charlie for another half hour. They talked about the increased security presence around Josh's place and at the *Drifters* set, and Matt promised to check in regularly with the team he'd posted at both locales. They'd be looking for any strange vehicles or suspicious walkers. This time of year that would be difficult, as the weather was generally so inviting and warm in Van these days that many folks were out and about.

Matt left the two Charleses with words of hope and optimism. "Look, Jessie's not the first celebrity who has been stalked, if that's what's happening here. Or Josh, if he's the target. The wisest thing we can do for Jessie at this point is keep a close eye on her, try to encourage her to follow the rules for her own protection, and get her to open up to us." He regarded Charles and then gazed pointedly at Charlie. Matt felt a surge of anger that this man who had been supposed to marry Jessie hadn't gotten to know her well enough that she'd feel comfortable telling him what the hell kind of chaos was going on in her life, a chaos that was making her obviously ill from worry.

Charlie felt the death ray glare. He shrugged his shoulders. "Look. I know I fucked up, man, but I still love her. We're friends, on some weird level, at least. Maybe she'll talk to me."

Shoving his phone back into his inside blazer pocket, Matt replaced his determined glare with a grudging dismissal. As he left the room he instructed Charlie to let him know what he found out, if anything.

Charles stayed seated glumly at the head of the table. Eight and a half years with Jessie and he and Dee seemed no closer to sharing confidences with her. In fact, with Josh now in the picture, their girl seemed to be drifting further away.

He and Charlie sat there together, unspeaking, for fifteen minutes before Charlie grabbed his cell and texted Jessie.

Coffee soon?

He didn't expect an answer right away, for Jessie was shooting on *Drifters* today and it wasn't likely she had her cell with her on set.

As Matt pulled away from La Casa he couldn't help but wonder if Jessie would ever open up to him. Sometimes scared people just needed a third party to talk to, someone a little removed from their closer circles, someone who wouldn't judge them or rock the proverbial boat in some unforeseen manner. He pondered that as he headed towards the downtown police headquarters. The visit would likely be futile, as the police were always understaffed and swamped; a mere celebrity tire slashing incident didn't likely rate high on the Richter scale of the busy Vancouver Metro Police. But at the very least maybe he could talk the young officer into giving him better copies of the knife photographs. Matt could do his own research. For sure that insignia on the dagger blade would turn up in a database somewhere.

At the same time as Matt crossed the Lions Gate Bridge, Jessie was sitting with her back against her favorite *Drifters* cottonwood tree being gently caressed by tufts of lovely white snowy fluffs. She had her dad's old Gibson propped by her side and Josh's head resting on his left arm in her lap. His other arm was loosely laid across her knees. He was watching steady rivulets of water trickle over the smooth rocks in the creek as she tenderly ran long fingers again and again through his tousled hair.

Jessie bent down and murmured in his ear.

"Josh Sawyer."

He could hear a tremor in her soft voice.

"You remember what I said that night after Agassiz, right?"

He tensed. This was more than she'd given him in a long time, in terms of verbal communications. "Yeah." It was a hopeful whisper. He waited for more. Josh could feel, in that moment, the pounding of his heart as somewhere the universe spoke to him and commanded that he pay close attention, that this was one of those key moments that really, truly mattered.

He was rewarded for his attention.

"What did I tell you, Josh?"

Pause.

Then, in a low gravelly voice—hesitant, unsure—he said, "You told me that no matter what happened, you would always love me. Always and forever."

The fingers stopped moving in his hair and, behind him, he could hear Jessie's breathing quicken. He turned himself around so that he faced her, just in time for his thumb to trace a tear on her cheek. His heart ached for what she wouldn't say to him.

"Jess," he implored, a last futile attempt. "Please."

She shook her head. He sat up a little, leaned his head in towards her, closed his eyes and felt her eyelashes tickle his cheek as he rested his forehead against hers.

"Wait for me, okay?" she begged him, her voice suffused with emotion. Then she lifted his whiskery chin and delicately brushed her lips against his. "Josh, please." She let the tip of her tongue run itself over his lips. She needed to taste him.

He quivered as his body responded to her faint overture, then held her, ran a hand through her curls and begged her again to talk. She was silent.

Finally, he lost it. He leaned back and firmly placed a hand underneath her chin. "Jessie, enough is enough. You need to tell me what the hell is going on." He was sitting straight up now, facing her, and he could see that his rising blood pressure was having the desired effect on his fiancée. Her face flushed, and she looked away, but he'd seen something flicker there, a yearning to talk, maybe? He would push her a little further…

"Jessie, everyone's freaked out by this secret you're keeping from us. We're your friends, we deserve more. Dee deserves more. She's out there running from city to city trying to help others, but I'm hearing she can't stay focused because she's so worried about you. Hell Jess, *I* deserve more. When are we going to set our wedding date? Please, just tell me what's going on! Talk to me."

She was lost on the fact that Josh apparently had some insight into Charles and Dee these days, which was more than she'd had with either of the Keatings in the last few weeks.

"Josh, it's just a lot these days. Okay? Balancing everything. Maybe I just need some free time. Some time to breathe."

He contemplated that, because in truth she hardly ever seemed to have free time, but Jessie could see his mouth twitching. He wasn't buying it.

"Bullshit. Something happened after Agassiz, and you're not talking. What was it, a text or something? What set you off?"

Staring at him and biting into her bottom lip, Jessie ached to talk. But the sight of Sandy—the bloodied knife—holding him while his gentle flecked hazel eyes begged her to help him as his soul flickered away...*no*. She could not involve Josh in this. She was totally, utterly, alone.

"I was wrong, Josh." It was a squeak, and he could see her fighting to stay in control of her emotions. But it was something, a rare glimpse. He took it.

"About what, Jessie? Tell me. Please."

But he wasn't rewarded with the answer he hoped for.

"About us. I'm not ready. I can't do this. It's too soon—after Charlie."

Silence. Then, "No. I'm not buying that. You just told me you would always love me."

Quickly, she interjected, cutting him off. "And I asked you to wait for me. Things need to settle down a bit. But I guess that's your choice."

This time when he peered into her soul Josh could sense that what she said wasn't entirely an untruth. But it still didn't sit right.

"I won't let you go, Jessie," he said, devastated but determined. "Not like this. There's more to this that you're not telling. I *know* it."

"All you fucking *know*, Josh, is that something's messed up right now. But maybe what you need to accept is that it's plainly and simply *us*."

Then a mask washed over her face and Jessie brusquely pushed him aside, grabbed the guitar, and headed back to her trailer without a backwards glance.

He sat immobile under the cottonwood and watched his girl light up a smoke as she stormed away, shoulders hunched over, a lacy white 1860's petticoat swaying just over the ankles of her dusty brown leather lace up boots, the tip of the cigarette testament to the last flickering vestige of light their relationship seemed to have left.

"Jesus, Jess," he whispered. She was sending him a message, as clearly as that knife must have been relaying one to her. It seemed all he would have to do is never give up. Wait, and never give up.

But for how long? And was that just her way of letting him down easy?

The futility of the situation was killing him. But he would be there for her, no matter what.

He was Josh, and she was Jessie, and their romance had just begun.

Chapter Fourteen

*J*essie didn't meet Charlie for coffee, and she refused to attend the *Drifters* wrap party the next Friday. Then, to everyone's dismay, she refused to sign for a third season. The way she saw it, they would likely take her back if she decided to sign later on anyway, although she hated doing that to Jonathon two seasons in a row. But there were some perks to being Jessie Wheeler. At this point, instead she figured she'd take on one of the many feature film projects Dee had lined up. Something that would take her far away from Josh, that would ensure his safety. Maybe, if she were lucky, Deuce would back off. Or she would be rid of McCall by then, one way or the other.

The night of the wrap party, Jessie dressed in a hot red skimpy dress and over-the-knee high black boots, into the right of which she stuffed a pack of cigarettes. Then, totally out of character, she texted Matt for a ride. She'd wrapped earlier than Josh from their last day at *Drifters*, gone straight to her condo, and immediately started drinking Jim Beam. She sent a second text, this one to Josh—*something came up catch up with you tomorrow*. By the time he wrapped and got the text she'd be passed out drunk and mercifully not feel the pain of leaving him, which had to happen this weekend.

Hell, Arnie had generously given her a solid start on handling the Guardian pistol. The remote shooting range where she found herself firing ruthlessly at tin cans—shuddering at the image of an actual human being in her sights— was also a source of inspiration and empowerment. *Hope.* Maybe she would have the nerve to destroy Deuce sometime in the next two days. Or, if she just had something to bargain with him…maybe he could be convinced to leave her and Josh alone.

Jessie shook her head in frustration, and angrily punched the button for the elevator. Matt would be waiting downstairs to give her a ride.

~ ~

Spying the concierge opening the glass door of Jessie's building, Matt tensed. He looked closely. Was that *Jessie* in the slinky little red dress? She seemed uncertain of her footing, and when she got closer to the car he realized why. Mizz Wheeler was already somewhat drunk.

Matt raised his eyebrows at Jessie as he pulled open the passenger door to the back seat, where she usually sat on escorted trips. He was surprised at her audacity when she grasped the front door handle and kind of fell in there instead. Peeking up from underneath long eyelashes, she smiled her best Hanadarko. Matt closed the door behind her, walked around behind the car and, annoyed, waved at the hawk-like concierge who was watching them with his intrusive beady little eyes. Matt settled carefully, hopefully, into the driver's seat beside his charge. Perhaps Jessie's presence in the front was a sign that she was ready to open up to him.

They were barely out of the parking lot when she spoke.

"Matt. You're going the wrong way."

He had turned left. He glanced at her, surprised. "Jonathon McCloud's house?"

Ouch, it hurt to hear her producer's name. Jonathon was hosting the wrap party this season. "No," Jessie answered carefully. "I'm not going to the *Drifters* party. I'm going to North Van."

Stiffening, Matt steered the car into a small crowded Starbucks parking lot, then turned around and headed in the opposite direction. He pictured Josh's face when Jessie didn't show up, and wondered if the couple had officially broken up. He peeked down at Jessie's left hand. She was not wearing her exquisite engagement ring.

"Jessie," he asked in his *I'm not in the mood for bullshit* low-volume throaty work voice, "would you mind telling me where I'm headed?"

She gave him directions to a home on the outskirts of the city. It wasn't an address he recognized, but he knew it to be in a swanky part of town.

Jessie pulled out her cigarettes and lit one. Matt wrinkled his nose at her.

"I would prefer you don't smoke in my car," he said, a hint of anger and confusion coloring his usually matter-of-fact voice. He knew she'd picked up smoking but was surprised she'd light up inside the vehicle. Suddenly she was a stranger to him and he caught himself thinking the same thing as everyone else—who was this girl, and where had she hidden Jessie?

"By any chance, are you rehearsing for a part, Jessie? Researching? Because I have to tell you, I sure as hell hope you are." He exhaled. She had callously ignored his wishes about the cigarette and was puffing rudely next to him, legs crossed at the knees so her short skirt rode just below what he referred to as the danger zone. At least she had the decency to roll the window halfway down so the smoke could partially escape.

Jessie leaned back in the leather seat and looked longingly over at the man responsible for her security. "Matt," she pleaded. "Tell me why everyone's so freaked out. I don't see why it's such a surprise that things aren't working out with Josh and me. I was with Charlie for eight years, for God's sake. Then I'm with Josh for a few months and it's clear the whole world hates him. Why would I want to stay in a relationship where people spit on my boyfriend and leave knives lying around in his driveway?" She took a deep pull on the cigarette, then turned and stared straight ahead. "Life is short. I just want to have fun. Charlie was a drag, and being with Josh is proving to be difficult. I just want to live the single life for a while. Party. See what all the fuss is about."

Watching her as he carefully navigated the car over the bridge, Matt wasn't fooled by her cool demeanor. Actor, shmactor. He knew Jessie Wheeler. And she was lying. Forensics had assessed the dagger, and it was now verified amongst him and the young officer working the case that it came from the Low Country in the U.S., perhaps even from Charleston itself. Miniscule particles of dirt native to that area were found on the blade; found, too, was another substance—human blood. The stylized B had not turned up anywhere yet. Matt and Charles were looking into Deuce McCall, the nightclub owner Jessie obviously feared, but so far there were no connections. The person who left the knife had cleansed it of his (or perhaps her?) fingerprints, and the B didn't appear to be an initial related to McCall who, unknown to Matt, had legally used the name Deuce instead of Booth from a very young age.

Diving in, Matt took a deep smoke-filled breath before he spoke sharply. The cigarette was annoying him, it stunk, and he was tired of all the drama surrounding Jessie these last few weeks. He was also a man who had seen and experienced a lot of the seedy side of life, the truly disgusting and horrific, and he believed in facing one's fear head on.

"You're full of shit, Jessie." He stared straight ahead as the car filled with silence. From his peripheral vision he watched as Jessie took a final drag and then flipped the butt out of the window, which also pissed him off. He loved and respected the environment, and couldn't understand why anyone, least of all kindhearted Jessie, would litter the ground with such waste.

Jessie didn't respond. She ached to tell Matt everything, but there was far too much at risk. Besides, in the side mirror she could see a black Ford Fusion not far behind them, and she didn't doubt that it was Deuce the fuck McCall. She'd seen him following her a lot these last few weeks. She figured he had placed GPS units on their bumpers. Called bumper beepers, she discovered their existence through her research on the net. They were the only explanation for why he always seemed to find her, regardless in which car she was travelling.

Softening, Matt said, "Don't think you're fooling anybody, Jessie. There are things going on around you that you're not aware of. Everyone's concerned, and there's not much doubt that whoever's got you cornered has scared you pretty good. But you should know you're not alone. You should also know you need to tell someone what's going on."

Jessie straightened, and sent Matt a beseeching look. "Matt," she implored him, a warning in her expression, and he could see the old Jessie in her face, the one that was indeed afraid. He also took note of the fact that she was asking him, with her eyes, to glance around the interior of the car. He was quick to realize she was concerned about the car being bugged. They'd have to shake down the cars as well as their homes.

Tentatively, she touched his elbow. "I'm sorry for smoking in your car," she mumbled. With his left hand, Matt reached over his stomach and grasped her fingers tightly. His lips were pursed in a straight line, and she knew he'd gotten the message that the car might be bugged.

At least if it isn't, she thought, *he won't try to get anything out of me.* Whereas he was thinking *At least she knows she's not alone.*

Matt was very good at his job, yes indeed, but not so good that he caught on to the Fusion a few car lengths behind the Audi. He dropped Jessie off at the front gate of the party as Deuce pulled in behind a Mercedes parked on the street.

"Jessie," Matt said, after offering a hand to help her exit the vehicle. "Should I stay?"

She paused before shaking her head *No.* "I'll be late, Matt. Go home to your wife and little daughter." Yet more reasons not to involve Matt in her sordid life.

"You'll call me for a ride?"

Another shake of the head. "I'll find a ride."

He watched her step lightly up to the front entrance of the pretentious, ornate grey brick house. She didn't look back and, as he drove away, Matt caught himself speculating that she didn't seem drunk anymore. Her footsteps were as sure as those of a tightrope walker gliding across a thin wire two hundred feet above a rocky ravine.

In the Fusion, Deuce McCall stayed put for twenty minutes before he pulled a U-turn and headed back to his Vancouver apartment. The hourglass of time was running out. He had her on the run, away from Josh and, for tonight, that was all that mattered.

The *Drifters* wrap party was indeed at Jonathon's house this year. Not far from Josh's home near the UBC campus, the party was a grand affair that celebrated the outstanding success of the series, which was largely in part due to the chemistry between Jessie and Josh (aka Kate and Billy). However, the festive occasion was marred by the dismal mood of the partygoers. By now it was obvious that Jessie had distanced herself from all of them, including Josh, although what seemed likely to be an impending breakup had not yet become official. But despite the few tender moments both held onto over the past month or so, Jessie's message was clear. She had been gradually pulling away, and her decision not to attend the *Drifters* wrap party was heard loud and clear. The cast and crew collectively agreed she had just been hanging on to Josh long enough to get through the last few weeks of shooting. He knew different. Their good friends on the show held out grim hope that she might not abandon them as well as Josh, whose heart could be heard breaking all the way to L.A.

Late that night as the friends sat around Jonathon's cavernous living room and listened to the crew swap stories of the shoot that season, Jonathon watched his biological son's agony gradually consume him to the point where he couldn't sit still. The older man followed Josh outside to the pool where a live band at the far end was treating the *Drifters* bunch to a rousing set of jazz and blues, a hopeless attempt at injecting life into the subdued revelers. The producer knew all about heartbreak in love, and not getting to share in his only son's life as a child was about as painful as it got. Still, Jonathon would have to be careful. Josh was not aware of his parentage or of the love Jonathon still held for the young man's mother, dead these past many years.

"Josh," he said, laying a hand on his shoulder. "I'm sorry about Jessie. I know how much you care about her."

Josh thrust his hands in his pockets and stared out at the pool, where a few crew were taking advantage of the warm air, indulging in a midnight swim.

"I don't know," Josh said. "I could maybe accept it if it made sense, but it doesn't make sense, Jon."

"I doubt if love ever makes sense, bud," Jonathon replied. He chuckled quietly. "Didn't the storyline from *Drifters* teach you anything?"

The storyline of the drama left an open ending. After a myriad of ups and downs, Billy and Kate rode away from each other. How could the writers keep them together if their female lead wasn't likely returning the next season?

Josh shrugged helplessly. "What I would like right about now is a big fucking whiskey." He hadn't indulged in alcohol since the season one wrap party a year ago.

"Nah," Jonathon countered. "That won't solve anything, son." He bit his lip. He hadn't meant to say that—son—the word just leaked out. Thankfully, Josh seemed to take it as affection, plain and simple. "Maybe Jessie will sort herself out. Or maybe you'll find someone else, even if she's always the one that got away. The thing to do, kid, is to hold on to the good times. And find a reason to go on living even when you feel like you're ready to cash it all in."

Subdued, Josh glanced up at his producer and friend. "You sound like you've been there."

Jonathon smiled at the antics of his cheery crew in the pool, a grip and a woman from wardrobe, racing each other from one end to the other on inflatable chairs. He liked that his show created the opportunity for intimate friendships. He loved watching Josh and his pals succeed in such close proximity.

"Yeah," he said. "I've been there. I've had to let go." He turned and looked at the boy who shared his eyes. "It damn near killed me, kid. Why do you think I became a writer? Because I like my fake world better than my real one." He swung around to leave because, even all these years later, almost thirty, to be exact, it still hurt like hell to look into the face of the boy he created with the love of his life.

The great loves never go away. They don't fade. They stick in hearts like arrows from a time gone by, or daggers given a twist now and again just to ensure the ungodly agony of defeat and loss is still felt.

There was a catch in Jonathon's voice when he spoke again, just before he walked back into the warm orange light of his gilded home. "It gets easier with time."

Not only was he a famous writer and producer, but Jonathon was also one of the world's greatest liars. It was all he could do not to turn back and hug Josh, who he left standing there in the blue moonlight being serenaded by sad love songs while miserably aching for a drink to soften the blow.

But the hardest life lessons to endure must be suffered alone. And Jonathon and Josh, surrounded by good friends and loyal co-workers, never felt so equally alone.

Steve's phone rang exactly fifteen minutes later. He answered it and then somberly forced himself to walk out to the pool deck, where he found Josh balanced on a striped chaise lounge pondering a drink he held between his fingers. He was holding it up to the light, fingering it, cherishing and admiring its amber clarity. Unwrapping Josh's stony fingers from around the glass, Steve took the drink and set it with a light thud on the nearby bar.

He held up his keys. He hadn't been drinking. That year, none of them were giving Josh an excuse to go under. Maggie, Carter, Sue-Lyn and he— as well as their partners—were all stone cold sober, and wishing they were drunk as hell.

Steve's voice shook. "Let's go," he demanded.

Josh looked up at him, and the fear in his eyes made Steve's knees go weak. This was going to suck. Bad endings always did.

"I got a call from Leeza. She's at a party in North Van. Jessie's there. We need to go pick her up."

Wrinkling his brow, Josh felt a momentary glimpse of hope. Jessie needed him. He squinted at his phone but there were no texts or calls. Leeza, of all people, had called Steve to come get Jessie. *What the hell?* He eased himself up off the chaise lounge and followed Steve out the gate to the side and then to the front of Jonathon's imposing brick house. The jagged flagstones seemed to go on forever underneath their feet. Then they were in Steve's car flying up the road towards North Van.

They found the party with no trouble. Luxury cars were double parked up the long driveway, leaching their entitlement into the street. At the wrought iron gate, the waiting Leeza gave Josh's hand a squeeze. She was sober, which surprised him. Seemed the young starlet was growing up.

Leeza led the way inside and up a gracious curved mahogany staircase. She pulled open a heavy door. As his eyes adjusted to the light, Josh spied Jessie naked in bed with Ryan Forester, a chisel chinned blonde twenty-something second-rate actor he recognized from one of her old films. His heart in his throat, Josh forced himself to carry on with some semblance of awkward forward motion. Steve had the decency to back out of the room while Josh grabbed Jessie's red dress, which Leeza helped wrench over the singer's head. Jessie groaned. The alcohol had achieved its desired effect. She was unsteady, uncooperative, drunkenly defiant, her face a curious olive green in the harsh bluish-white light swathing the room from the sizeable window.

Josh wrapped Jessie in a light beige cotton coverlet and then scooped her up in his arms. He carried her close to his hurting heart all the way down those interminable stairs, with the eyes of everyone at the damn party witness to his failure to love and protect her. He yearned to destroy something, that lamp in the corner, perhaps, for its inability to light Jessie's way. Or perhaps he should hurl, through the immense bay window, that damn Jim Beam bottle, the one lying tipped over on the round marble-topped table, its last droplets a dizzying maze of shallow puddles. Or maybe he should run back up the stairs and wield the heavy bottle angrily at the actor who still dozed in a drunken stupor on the cursed bed, oblivious to the sudden arrival of Jessie's fiancé. Josh wanted to brain him, to scream obscenities and leave him on the Persian rug in a puddle of his own urine and blood, but somewhere underneath the incessant low hum of decay there was another voice. It was calming. And it was Jessie's.

There is always hope.

Somewhere underneath this rotten mess Josh could still hear that long ago voice of reason. And it was because of her tender intonation and unwavering belief in him that he was able to stagger away, one horrendous step at a time, from the stinging desire for violence and retribution. Enough was destroyed that day. His heart, for instance, which was crumbling and disintegrating with each burdened footprint.

After opening the overbearing carved front door so Josh could leave the site of Jessie's treachery behind, Steve walked in the shadow of his good friend as Josh carried Jessie to the small sports car. Jarred to life as the fresh air hit her, Jessie moaned in protest. Josh positioned her illegally in between his knees in the front seat so she had no choice but to lean back against his pounding chest. He wrapped his arms tightly around her. After buckling them in together, he shot Leeza a hard look, thanking her in the only way he could manage. The younger woman was the picture of sorrow, standing there sober amongst all those lost souls and drunken idiots.

They drove towards Jessie's building with her head against Josh's chest, and only made it about halfway before she drunkenly begged Steve to stop. She grabbed the wheel and almost caused them to spin off the road, but Steve skidded to a halt just in time. Josh barely got the door open before Jessie gripped his thigh with both hands, leaned over, and retched on the ground. Whimpering, she tried to climb over him but he managed to stumble out first and help her, holding her hair back as Steve had done a few weeks—a lifetime—earlier. There was no need for words. The few words she'd needed to say to him had been spoken in whispers and intrigue and mystery over the last month. In the end she was speaking loud and clear.

Josh pulled her close and held her, but he could smell Forester's revolting sweaty scent instead of lavender on Jessie's skin, and that drove the dagger ever deeper. Silently, the boys steered Jessie to her place and Josh tucked her in for the last time.

Somewhere in her scattered nightmare Jessie heard Josh's husky tender voice off in the distance, whispering to her, entreating her. "I get it, Jessie. I get it. You don't need to do that anymore, okay?"

She nodded almost imperceptibly, then around her fragile body Josh tucked a duvet delicately imprinted with the sweet innocence of fresh pink Sakura blossoms, and he left the room.

Steve was waiting for him in Jessie's living room. He was sitting at the grand piano staring limply through the floor-to-ceiling glass wall out at endless stars and a vivid pale moon. Somewhere beneath them, Greg Keelor's painful lyrics echoed from an open window—*I've always been lost in this dream.*

"Do you think she'll be okay?" Steve asked soberly.

Josh thought for a moment. "No."

"Will you be okay?" Steve turned his head and looked at his best friend, a man who only a few years earlier was found in a garbage dump by a girl who instantly loved him.

Pause. "No."

Steve got up then. The piano bench emitted a sharp squeal on the cherry stained wooden floor. The ungodly sound yanked Jessie back to a brief consciousness.

"Well, okay then. Now that we've got that figured out." Steve moved forward and threw an arm around Josh, and then led him towards the front entry of Jessie's condo.

After the door slammed shut behind them—the man she loved and, by his side, her very good friend—Jessie pulled the sweet pink duvet up around her ears, the way her father used to when she was a child. She grasped Tedsy, the teddy bear as damaged as she, and she sobbed violently into the soft pillow for her daddy and for Sandy. She had been prey to such pain before, and did not want to know it again, but there it was, like some dark monster at the bottom of a quicksand pool, bottomless and hopeless and blacker than black, pulling her below a place of light and sun and sky towards an abyss that claimed her without remorse.

Just in to whose dream did who walk…? mourned Greg Keelor, a disembodied voice carried on the wind, as Jessie burrowed deeper into her pillow and cried her insides dry.

Chapter Fifteen

essie did not go back to Josh's house after that. He gathered up her things and put them in a box and then gave them to the concierge in her building. If she wanted space that badly, then so be it. He had thought they were stronger. He thought they could survive whatever life threw at them.

He kept a small stuffed tiger he'd bought for her one lazy Saturday when they were wandering a farmer's market in nearby New Westminster. The tiger had made the journey from Africa. She had commented on its stripes. Jessie thought they were remarkable, and the tiger, enduring. She had a thing for tigers, Josh discovered that day. There were a few on a small table at her place—wooden, jade, stuffed. Jessie told him they were supposedly these ferocious creatures, but were really just seeking love the same as the rest of God's animal kingdom. Josh thought Jessie was a tiger, someone the world saw as larger than life, but who was really just a girl who wanted to be loved. He kept the tiger. He put it on his bed, where it sat on the pillow on her side and threatened to snarl at anyone who came near.

Deuce kept his word. He waited for Jessie to leave rehearsal later that Saturday. Hung over as hell, she was a lousy failure as a singer and dancer that day, but Priya had heard the stories from the party Jessie attended the night before. She knew about the breakup with Josh. The demanding choreographer was forgiving.

Kayla, on the other hand, was pissed. She plunked down in a velvet seat beside Jessie in the empty theater as they watched Priya instruct a smaller group of dancers on stage. Kayla had thrown angry looks at Jessie all through rehearsal, looks that would mean instant dismissal for any other dancer, male or female. Now she would have her say, regardless of the consequences.

"Jessie, I realize everyone's worried about you, but I have to tell you, I'm not. I'm just fucking pissed. Can you please tell me what my brother did to deserve this shitty treatment?"

Sinking lower in her seat, Jessie closed her eyes and fingered her water bottle. Her skull hurt. She let Kayla rattle on as she pushed dark sunglasses onto her head to help corral stray wisps of hair. The glasses would be welcome later under the relentless beating of a hot, wayward sun.

"I mean, he loves you, goddammit! And you go off and get drunk and sleep with Ryan Forester? Geez, girlfriend, what the hell?!" Kayla was close to tears but Jessie had nothing to give her. She was almost too sick and tired to care. Almost.

"Jessie! Speak to me! Help me understand. Please." Kayla's voice was rising in pitch. People were starting to notice.

Jessie looked up at the dancers on stage who were staring at them. Petite red-headed Erin with the lovely Irish lilt, expressive spiky-haired Keira, even friendly Benjie…they were all super pissed at her. She told herself she didn't give a damn what people thought. But here was Kayla, Josh's sister, close to tears, aching for her brother. *So many people hurting,* Jessie thought absently. *I've left a trail of destruction. Like a minefield. Everyone's blowing up around me.*

"Kayla," she said numbly. "I'm really sorry. I am. Truly." She got up and pushed past the belligerent Kayla and started up the aisle. She wanted to go outside. She needed a smoke. She needed space.

"Jessie! Damn it!" Standing, planting both feet securely in the aisle, Kayla cried out to her. Josh's little sister was a picture of dismay, her shoulders sinking as she watched her boss walk away.

The aisles at the Orpheum were ramped so theatergoers in the back could see over the heads of those in the front. Jessie reacted to Kayla's cry by turning and studying the frustrated girl below her. Kayla threw up her hands, unsure what to say, completely exasperated.

Then, "Jess. Am I fired, then?" Out of loyalty to her brother she was honestly thinking about quitting, but Kayla still held out hope for Jessie and Josh. She prayed that this breakup was just a bad bump on the tumultuous road of celebrity romance.

Jessie felt her own eyes grow misty. God, if she could just keep Kayla close then maybe she'd always have a little part of Josh around. But that might depend on Deuce. For now, he had all the power. He was calling the shots. God, what if Kayla quit? Jessie willed Kayla to hang on, not to leave her.

"Not yet," Jessie croaked. She tried to smile at Kayla but it came out crooked.

Kayla watched her boss trudging up the aisle, digging a smoke out of the pack in her legwarmers. She was devastated, but inside she was also secretly pleased that she could still dance in Jessie's troupe. She hoped relations would improve between these people she loved. Maybe Jessie and Josh could work things out. Kayla cursed the public nuisances that were eroding a sweet relationship with stupid pranks. Josh was an awesome brother, a lovable guy whom many of her girlfriends had idolized over the years. He didn't deserve this shit. She bounced back up to the stage and grabbed her water bottle, took a lengthy swig and then did some stretches. Kayla had work to do. She was one of Jessie Wheeler's dancers.

Outside, Jessie walked around the corner to the quieter Seymour Street, leaned against the timeless old Orpheum, and lit up a smoke. She saw Deuce now, parked outside the building. This time he swung open his door and wandered over, digging out a monogrammed silver lighter as he approached. Flicking it with a manicured nail, he touched it to the end of his own cigarette. They smoked there together, the stalker and his prey, their ribbons of ash testament to the angry one-sided ardor that smoldered between them.

"Meet me here at seven," he demanded after tossing his butt wickedly on the sidewalk and snuffing out its life with the toe of a snakeskin boot. He handed her a matchbook. She assumed rightly that there was an address printed inside the cover. She'd stick it in her stalking journal later. Jessie nodded, staring straight ahead, her stomach tightening.

He left her alone then. She puffed on a second cigarette that she hoped would quell her nerves before she took her shaking hands back inside. Jessie would stop at the lobby ladies' room before going back into the theater. She had the overwhelming need to puke again.

Matt drove up in the Audi just after Deuce pulled away. He was running late that day because he'd stopped into the local police station again in the hopes he would have a chance to talk to the officer on the slashing case. The week prior, an email with a pristine image of the dagger had arrived from the young cop. Matt researched the nasty weapon in more detail but hit a dead end right off the bat. The model and serial number were illegible—the numbers were filed off. Ownership couldn't be proven. There was still some expectation that light would be shed on the blade's insignia. Matt was hoping the youngster would have some answers today, but it turned out he was at home nursing a bad flu.

Shrinking low in the Audi, which he parked a few car lengths down the perpendicular-to-Seymour Smithe Street in the hope that Jessie wouldn't notice him, Matt surreptitiously watched his charge finish her second smoke before her despondent trek back into the storied old Orpheum's warm embrace. She hadn't noticed him arrive, so orchestrated were her thoughts on whatever was on her mind. She looked like shit. Matt knew how she had gotten home from the party the night before. One of his men took over the private security at nightfall, hoping for a call. But Steve and Josh showed up at the pretentious North Van home and, well, that was it. It had been a fucked up night, for sure.

Laying his head back against the seat, Matt closed his eyes. Sleep was evasive these days, particularly since the meeting with Charles and Charlie. Charles in particular was demanding answers Matt simply couldn't provide. Dee was desolate.

Before he knew it, the dashboard's digital display read six p.m. in rather bright blue numbers, and Jessie's rehearsal was long over. Matt cursed and drove a palm into the steering wheel. He wouldn't eyeball Jessie again until two days later, when she left her condo for the Keating building downtown, sporting a significant ugly bruise on her left cheek.

Jessie had long since learned that the secret to enduring sex with someone you didn't care for—in fact, with someone you detested with every ounce of your being—was to close yourself off and become someone else. Fortunately as an actor this came easily to her. Grace Hanadarko was still her woman of choice these days, but occasionally she resorted to a fictional character her mind created, a darker version of herself based on her mother's reclusive hardened actions after the sudden tragic loss of Jessie's father. Living inside her head was easy. She was not so much frightened of Deuce herself anymore as afraid of his power to hurt her loved ones. So she co-operated as best she could. Tonight was a test night. What would he expect, how would he treat her, what would his conditions be? Would they change? She was giving up Josh, temporarily, she told herself. Deuce would see that she was trying to please him, that she was afraid, that she would bow to his wishes, and that he was in control. Hopefully he would be pleased.

She left the Guardian home that night. Like a dog looking for a place to piss, she decided she would be wise to source out the territory before she dared dig out the pistol. If she made the wrong choice, if she played the Knight when she should have moved her Bishop, then she'd be fucked. And so would Josh.

Jessie was coolly surprised at the residence Deuce chose as his home away from home in Vancouver. He was a man of affluence but the apartment was grungy. As she looked around, she realized she was in a place with sub-par furnishings garnered likely from people's curbs—a droopy sofa, an archaic television with rabbit ears, a scratched pine school desk. If she looked underneath the desk she bet she would find decades old clumps of chewing gum. They were on the sixth floor of a building in the Commercial Drive area of the city, East Vancouver. There was an A & W bag on the floor and the faint smell of onion rings in the stale air. A lightning flash reverberated throughout her body as Jessie recalled the dismal evening Terri died, when she and Josh sat in his pick-up and shared a bag of onion rings. Deuce probably bought his from the exact same fast food restaurant. They were in the same neighborhood. The thought made her sick, for all kinds of horrid reasons, not the least of which that McCall may have been watching her, even then.

Sitting above her on the window ledge, Deuce watched Jessie take in her surroundings. He felt a thrill of satisfaction. There she was, the little shit disturber that emptied his lounge when she left. No matter that she filled it again with her fame. He hated her, he told himself. He hated her and he *loved* her. Deuce couldn't stand the fact that Jessie was living her life without him, that she loved someone else. Not even just anyone else, either—a druggie with a temper. A self-important sunuvabitch whom even the regular public heartily disliked. No matter. Josh was gone now, if Jessie knew what was good for her. She was obedient, he remembered from long ago. She only put up enough of a fight to make things interesting, to show that she wasn't broken—yet. In fact, in the interest of keeping up her wild side, he didn't plan to break her too soon, if at all. He would need to be careful because he knew Jessie was just spirited enough to end his game, if she so chose. Dealing with this fiery woman required careful thought and delicate balance.

He handed her a Reidel Vinum crystal wine glass half filled with an expensive blackberry and cocoa Merlot, which Jessie found bizarre, given the shabby environment. It seemed he was celebrating. Eyeing each other cautiously, they smoked and sipped their wine for a while without speaking. Deuce spied a tremor in Jessie's hand as she awkwardly arced the cigarette towards her lips. A quake of excitement tingled through his bones when he noted a simmering fire in the cool blue eyes. It was not apparent that afternoon outside the Orpheum, but it was obvious now—a steady anger was playing beneath the surface. Curious, he tilted his head and watched her. Then she spoke.

"Let's get on with this."

"What?" he asked, cocky.

She waved an arm around. "This. Whatever the hell you brought me here for."

He laughed sardonically. "My dear, dear girl, what's your hurry? Do you have other plans?"

Jessie slouched and sipped on her wine. She took one last long pull on the cigarette and then extinguished the smoke.

"This isn't going to last forever, Deuce. You know that." She forced herself to meet his steely gaze.

He shrugged. "Your choice. You have all the power here, Jessie."

She drew in a breath. In one very final ultimate way, she could indeed have power.

"Yes," she said, just to piss him off. "I do. I can end this if I choose."

His eyes narrowed as he took that in, and his heart quickened as he realized that she was talking about suicide. "Don't be foolish, little girl," he warned. "There are a lot of great things about life that make it worth living."

Inside she felt tears threaten as she thought *not without friends. Not without Josh. Not without Sandy and Rachel and my dad and Terri. Not without Josh. Not without Josh.*

"You won't win, Deuce. I will. This time it's my turn to win."

"Oh, well, where'd you find that little bit of spunk in you, Jessie? Did it come with all that money you've made over the last ten years or so? With the two Oscars on your shelf? Or with some inflated sense of self-importance that came with all that fame?"

She stared at him and then generously poured herself more Merlot. She would need all the alcohol in the seedy little apartment to find the courage to get through this night. She changed tack.

"Nice place you have here, McCall." She glanced furtively away from him. Every time she looked at him she either saw him on top of her, grunting away like some hungry dog, or screaming like a mad man as he shoved his dagger into Sandy's chest and belly. She squeezed her eyes shut, hoping ridiculously that by doing so she would eradicate the nasty visions of that horrific evil day.

Deuce was a keen observer. With a stocky finger he reached out and touched her cheek, and she instantly recoiled. Rapidly, his demeanor changed. He hit her hard, so hard that the back of Jessie's head bounced off the wall behind her and the expensive wine glass flew across the room, its red beverage a bloody trail of rage littering the couch and carpet. She cried out and covered the hurt cheek with her hand, gasping as it quickly bloomed pink. Then she straightened and prepared herself for further battle. She might be numb, but she had experienced something sacred with Josh, and it was worth fighting for.

"Fucking bastard," she raged, spitting at Deuce.

He grabbed a handful of hair and furiously shoved Jessie's head back, then ripped open her top and forced her down on the maltreated couch that matched her battered spirits. As he heartlessly violated Jessie for the first time since Charleston, where he had abused her in front of Sandy, she disappeared to that safe insulated place deep inside where she could hide.

Somewhere off in the distance, though, she could hear him laughing. He was rough, and she fought back a little against him. What she would soon figure out was that he liked it that way.

When he finally let her leave with the promise that she'd be back in a few days, Jessie was sporting a great red welt on her cheek in accompaniment to a bruised lip.

Deuce was grinning cruelly from ear to ear as he watched her limp down the hall. He had his Jessie back and he had no intention of sharing her.

He lit up another smoke and poured himself the last of the wine. Adrenaline coursing through his veins, he paced the small room until all that remained of the smoke was a weedy butt, and until the wine settled his nerves. Then, with a satisfied arrogant pat on the back, Deuce lowered himself to the couch, toasted himself heartily on such sweet victory, and settled in for a nap.

For the entire duration of the next day, Jessie hid at home. She nursed her cheek with a bag of frozen peas and a daylong Netflix-a-thon. She viewed a whole season of *Saving Grace* again. She needed Grace to help give her the courage to see this through. And she needed Grace's redneck angel, Earl, to remind her that perhaps there was indeed a God and, if worse came to worse, there was a better place than earth to where she could retire.

Jessie was expected at the Keating building on Monday, and so her day of hiding was just that—one day. News of the break-up with Josh and her surprising behavior at the party Friday night was leaked to the media. On Robson, a boisterous and ruthless crowd of paparazzi welcomed her with expensive lenses and intrusive, curious stares.

Charles was on the phone to Matt the second he saw Jessie walk in his door. His second call was to Deirdre. Jessie heard him calling someone a *son of a bitch bastard*, but she didn't know to whom he was referring. She wished she could tell him it was Deuce the fuck McCall.

Magda, Charles' Assistant, leapt up abruptly and stared when Jessie walked by her desk. She reached out and grabbed Jessie's arm so the girl would stop.

"Honey," she said. And that was all. When Jessie started walking again, her head down, Magda simply added, "I'll get you some ice."

Jessie closed the door of her office and prepared herself for Charles' knock. It didn't come. Instead he burst in, unapologetic. He planted his expensive black dress shoes and glared at her, incensed.

"Enough," he hissed between clenched teeth. "Speak before I fire Matt."

Jessie sank down in her chair. "Don't fire Matt," she whispered. "This isn't his fault. I ordered him to leave me be."

"Whose fault is it, Jessie?" Then, "Oh, wait. I think I know."

One at a time, as if the effort were too great to bear, she leveraged her feet up on the desk. Jessie was wearing her comfort shoes, the favorite yellow chucks. She mobilized her feet and hands to roll the big leather chair in closer so she could wrap up inside herself. She pulled the sleeves of her grey hoodie down low over trembling hands, zipped it all the way up, and yanked the hood over her downcast face. Jessie was still in the mood to hide.

Moments later, Magda nipped in with some ice and a damp facecloth and then hastily removed herself. She wanted to kill Josh.

"So," Charles sizzled. "Am I to assume this is Josh's payback for your freedom Friday night?"

She looked up. It sucked that she had to hurt Charles, too. *Dee. Oh no.* Yeah, this sucked, all right.

What to say? She chose nothing. If they wanted to think it was Josh who hurt her, then fine. At least that way they'd stay off Deuce's trail until she could figure out how to destroy the evil bastard. At the same time, she wasn't going to lie and say the bruise was Josh's handiwork, either.

The papers did that for her.

The next day, the headlines in entertainment sections around the world read *it is assumed Josh Sawyer hit Jessie Wheeler after their break-up.*

Josh, nor Steve nor Carter nor Maggie nor Sue-Lyn even tried to contact Jessie when they spotted the headlines. On Sunday, Josh flew out to Arizona to shoot his latest feature. Not surprisingly mostly everybody treated him with hostility. The only exceptions were newbies to the entertainment business who wanted to impress the *Drifters* star. Josh and Jessie's friends rushed off to their summer projects and holidays, occasionally communicating between themselves and wondering if indeed Josh had hurt Jessie. After all, he had a temper and he had a right to be very, very angry with her. They were his friends but, at the same time, malevolent secrets were sometimes found behind the closed doors of many people's homes. Jessie had ended their relationship rather abruptly. Even though in their hearts their friends once truly believed Josh wouldn't lift a finger towards Jessie, there was now a shadow of doubt. To the *Drifters* group, there weren't any solid clues that someone else was to blame so, apart from Josh's own testimony, as far as they knew there was no reason to suspect anyone else. Josh himself felt too utterly defeated to dredge up any real fight to defend himself. For all he knew, Jessie's party night bed partner Ryan Forester was the bad seed in this awful play.

During the hot, sticky west coast days of July and August, Jessie continued to meet up with Deuce, and she was grateful for the times she had to travel to visit the new shelters or perform somewhere, for those occasions were her only grace away from the madman who stalked her. Deuce himself travelled home then as well. After all, he had businesses to run.

Matt reached a dead end, in more ways than one. He and his police officer friend came to no concrete conclusions about either the ownership of the knife or about the man they were investigating with the help of Interpol, in South Carolina. Also, Jessie made it perfectly clear that her life was her own, and that she was angry about being followed all the time. Charles, against Charlie's protestations, agreed to let Matt and his team stand down as long as Jessie didn't seem to be in any apparent danger. Josh was away, and Jessie wasn't sporting any new bruises. The men couldn't help wondering whether the stalking idea was Josh's own ruse. Perhaps he initiated the tire slashing himself. At any rate, he was away, Jessie was distant but functional, and they could find no dirt on McCall or anyone else who may have been stalking their girl. They sat back and let her be.

As the summer wore on, Jessie began to realize a few things about her aggressor. One, he was less abusive to her if she simply pretended she was in some kind of a mutual relationship with him. As long as she played his game, he was even somewhat congenial. As an actor, she began to find the power within herself to block out his real identity. She had to, for self-preservation, because otherwise she would have lost her mind entirely, if based only on what he did to Rachel, Sandy and likely Terri, and not based on what he was doing to her now. Two, although she tried to avoid the pitfalls of self-medication through alcohol and drugs, occasionally she found use of these substances did help numb the most acute pain. She tried to control her usage but as the summer went on she escaped more and more into Jim Beam and weed. She avoided hard drugs at all costs. That was another evil road, one she was not willing to go down. Three, the more she was around Deuce, the more she became aware of his own pain and torment. And Jessie being Jessie, as evil as she once thought him, she began to see Deuce in a different light.

One muggy weekend in early August, she met her tormentor at the East Van sixth floor apartment. Inside, she was surprised to find a rickety little table set with a snow-white linen tablecloth and a flickering candle. Deuce was grinning like a small boy on his mother's birthday. The stale musty smell of the dingy place was masked with the lingering aroma of Italian herbs and spices. Jessie inhaled deeply.

"You learn to cook, Deuce?"

"Haven't y'all ever heard of take-out, my dear girl?" The thickset man whisked open the oven door and, with a grimy potholder, grabbed two covered foil dishes and set them on the counter. He scooped their steamy contents onto plates and gestured for Jessie to sit herself down at the table. She leaned forward and eyed her pasta hungrily as he set it before her. After dancing all afternoon in preparation for a huge concert scheduled for the end of the month at the Rogers Arena, she was famished.

"Umm, ravioli," she said, almost agreeably. Then she looked up at him as he sat down opposite her, a bottle of Australian Shiraz in hand. Sometimes the man appeared almost human.

They toasted the survival of another day, and Jessie ate with gusto. She also drank most of the wine herself. Deuce got up and took the corkscrew to another bottle.

"Deuce," she asked warily, always on alert around him, her mouth full of the last of the ravioli. "Did your family always live in Charleston?"

"Hmm, yes," he said, thinking about his childhood home in the Mount Pleasant area of the great city. "My ancestors owned plantations. My mother's family had a tea plantation, and my father's owned a rice plantation."

"There were slaves in your family, then."

"Yes, sweet pea." He savored the wine. "Many."

"Are there any letters surviving, or any documentation that tells you about what life was like in those days?"

"Pre-War of Yankee Aggression or post?"

She shrugged. "Whatever. Either. Both."

He rocked tenuously on the back two chair legs, his burly frame urging a rhythmic creak as it moved. Jessie found the sound soothing, somehow. She felt a wave of ennui wash through her as she recalled the night Terri died, when Josh rocked her so lovingly in the little hospital room. She fortified herself against getting too friendly with Deuce the fuck McCall. Yet maybe that was the key to gaining an advantage over him someday.

Deuce spoke up. "The only clues we have to what life was like came down over the years through oral storytelling." He glanced over at Jessie, who was looking at him expectantly, her chin raised stubbornly. *She is always on her guard, that one*, he thought. "My father's family owned one of the largest plantations in the state," he said. "They lost everything after the war. It took a while, because they paid the slaves to stay put and work the rice fields. Most of them would have been homeless, they would have starved if they hadn't stayed. The only life they knew was on the plantation. The only work they knew was rice. But then they started to leave, one family at a time, and economics got tougher. By 1900, my ancestors were broke. They subdivided the plantation into smaller farms. Any papers were either destroyed or simply lost."

He eyed Jessie, but his mind was elsewhere. The creaking continued, and Jessie had to focus hard on what Deuce was saying so she could put the agony of missing Josh out of her head.

"The only thing that remained was the pride. The pride of having once been an economic and social power. Oh, the boats would be filled with rice and sailed down the Ashley River with the tides and the alligators in the old glory days, and they would come back laden with fine silks and glorious German cavalry sabers engraved with flowers and birds…there would be balls and lavish weddings, and my family would be invited to every party in Charleston during the social season. In the summers, the families usually travelled north to escape the humidity and pestilence of the Low Country." He chortled, thinking how grand life must have been before the Civil War split the country in two.

Jessie piped up, fueled by the heady Shiraz. "So your family somehow remained prosperous, though? You're obviously a wealthy man."

The front two chair legs fell back to the floor with a crash underneath his bulk as Deuce snorted disdainfully. "Ha. Only because I built up my wealth. No, my father and his father before him drank themselves into a stupor every day, lost in memories of who the old Irish McCalls were, once upon a time. In a time before the reckless emotions of a bunch of secessionists destroyed everything our family had. My father whipped it into me every day as a child. *You are a McCall, you are a McCall, you are a McCall*, he would say as he hit me." His voice was coming out tiny now, high-pitched, as if he were once again the little boy who got beaten because his country had separated more than a century earlier. Jessie couldn't help herself. She felt sorry for him as a child.

He continued. "It didn't matter that we were poor, that my father only worked off and on as a laborer between bouts of the drink. He still saw himself, and us, as mighty McCalls, as people who got invited to all the best parties and who everybody respected. Because it was drilled into him by his father. I gather that's how he won over my Momma, too, by telling her who our family *wasn't*. Boy, did she get fooled. He used to hit her, too." He recoiled then as he looked at Jessie, sitting there all small and curled up into herself across from him, tired and pale. The apple didn't fall far from the tree.

But Jessie comprehended then where Deuce was coming from. He was a man who lost everything long before he was ever born. He was a man of uncertain pride. He wanted to be proud, but he was never allowed that dignity. Only his ancestors truly deserved it. To him, any dignity and pride he possessed was fake, lost with the slaves who deserted the family plantation after 1865.

It was interesting being Jessie Wheeler then, because she played a character from the late 1860's in *Drifters*. Although it was television, Jonathon made sure his stories were well researched. Josh's character, Billy, was a Union soldier who made his way north after the Civil War in search of gold. He would have fought opposite Deuce McCall's people in the South. How apropos.

That raised another question. "Deuce, did any of your people fight in the war?"

"Sweet pea, we're still fightin' it," was his quick response. "Every single fuckin' day." He got up then, swayed once, and then roughly grabbed Jessie's arm and pulled her towards the small bedroom. "Come on, honey. Enough with the sodden memories. There's enough self-loathing in my family to last me a thousand lifetimes."

This time, as Jessie let Deuce do his thing, she found her mind drifting back to the old city that she, Rachel and Sandy had loved so well, with its age-old graceful wrought iron filigree, rows of majestic live oaks dripping with Spanish moss, and dolphins playfully cutting through the Cooper River. *Lovely old Charleston,* she thought. *Oh how I did love you, you poor old city with your old traditions and your old balls and all those people who just wanted to hang onto their olds a little longer. You brave old city,* she thought. *You fought bravely, and you could have perished. But there you are now, hanging on a little longer, growing anew, your old homespun Confederate uniforms disintegrating in dank dark attics.* She pondered how a war fought in part to save an antiquated agricultural system, in opposition to the industrial advances of the North, could still have such a damaging effect on a man today. For Deuce was a casualty of the war between the states as much as any man ever was, and Jessie was testament to that indisputable fact as she lay beneath him this night.

Yet, Charleston's troubled and storied history somehow revived her. She thought of the city now with renewed vigor, when once she feared to call it to mind at all. For she was fighting her own war that on some days seemed surely lost. But if the holy city could survive, if Charleston itself could survive and then thrive, then perhaps so could she. Perhaps Jessie Wheeler could live once again. Perhaps she, too, could thrive.

She thought about the pistol and wondered whether she could use it now on this man, someone she was starting to see as human and flawed as everyone else. Could she point it into his heart and fire? She wasn't sure. But summer was more than half over, and she was no closer to resolving the problem of her stalker than she'd ever been. Her friends were gone; Josh was gone. Perhaps it was already too late to win him back. She had to figure something out. But what? How? It was frustrating beyond belief, but Charleston's example was tangible, something she could hold on to. What was it she had once said to Josh? *There is always hope.* Perhaps Jessie should listen to her own advice.

She felt a little light come back into her soul as she recalled the pretty, colorful Charleston houses often referred to as Rainbow Row, or playing guitar with pensive Sandy and spritely Rachel on Folly Beach. She closed her eyes as an orgasm built inside her—contrary to her wishes but generally a necessary part of this exercise. Deuce wanted her well satisfied by his lovemaking. Despite all, he thought he loved Jessie, and he wanted desperately to please her.

He was more thrilled than usual when he turned his wary glance to her afterwards, and saw that Jessie Wheeler had a small smile on her face for once.

Ya done good, Deuce McCall, he conveyed to himself. He squeezed his eyes shut as the counterpoint to that also echoed in his brain, a disconcerting memory from his boyhood brought forth tonight by cheap wine, not to mention by encouragement from a quiet little audience. *Ya lousy failure, Booth McCall!*

Well. The good things in life were never really free. But his treasure here, well she came with a little thing called redemption—redemption for his family's past. Because Deuce-Booth-McCall was not a failure. He turned things around, undoing the wrongs of his family's collective history. His control of Jessie Wheeler, one of the world's biggest stars, put the McCalls back on top.

Literally, he chortled to himself as he grunted his way off Jessie so he could go take a piss. He laughed all the way to the filthy urine stained toilet, as Jessie stared after him in wonder.

Chapter Sixteen

The hazy sublime summer days grew shorter, calling boaters and hikers back to safe haven earlier and earlier each day before inevitable darkness overtook them. Jessie was scheduled to present a larger, more elaborate version of the fundraising show she toured the previous fall. This time she was booked into the Rogers Arena in Vancouver where ten thousand thrilled fans could attend a single performance. She had two creative, intensive spectacles planned, one Friday night and the other on Saturday afternoon. It was late August, a few weeks before she would be leaving the city to shoot a feature film in New York.

These shows were a sort of finale to the second fundraising series for the women's shelters. They were highly anticipated, but Jessie was dead tired, hurting from Deuce's increasingly rough aberrant ministrations, and low in spirit. She had yet to bring out her gun. She was terrified she would miss or that she would kill him and some invisible henchman would bounce into action like a yoyo on a string, scheduled to pounce the second Deuce reached his maximum impact. So she endured her aggressor, but barely.

Jessie had taken to self-medicating with liquor and weed more and more. It was the only way she knew how to deal with the deepening pain and loneliness, as well as Dee's constant frustration over Jessie's increasingly missed rehearsals and disregard for schedules. At the same time, she was more diligent than ever about not utilizing Matt and his security crew. She knew the tenacious Matt had followed her a few times and watched her sidle nervously into Deuce's building, but she lit into him angrily one rare evening at Charles' and Dee's home—she included the confused Keatings in her tirade—and he backed off.

She told them she was visiting a friend. Matt staked out the building and saw Deuce come and go, but McCall was smart enough to register his apartment in another name, to pay in cash and to wear a wig outdoors over his balding head. Matt didn't recognize him from the Charleston visit a year earlier. There were other tenants as well. Matt ran all of them through his computer. Apart from one sixty-year old with a forty-year old record for petty theft, and a grandmother whose sixteen-year old grandson had been arrested for vandalism, there was no indication of any serious shenanigans going on in the building. Still, it didn't sit right with Matt, or with Charlie and the Keatings. But Jessie had just turned twenty-nine in July, with a rather low-key birthday celebration, as was her custom. She was a grown woman with a mind of her own, and she asked them to leave her be. What choice did they have?

The night of the first big concert, Deuce had Jessie arrange a ticket and backstage pass for him. He dressed for it not as a businessman, but as a member of a motorcycle gang, complete with leather jacket and tight jeans. He also got her to dye his hair a deep black a few days before the show. His nerves were starting to fray. It was important not to be recognized by Matt and Charles, who had met him only briefly, but still…he was, after all, a good-looking man. Memorable, in his opinion. Jessie always got tickets for her Downtown Eastside friends, so adding one fictional "Mike Doucet" to the roster was a breeze.

The concert went well. Josh thought about not going but it was a chance to see Jessie, even if from a distance. He couldn't stay away. His friends stood around him and offered a sort of protection from whatever invisible wall he needed to hide inside. They were all quiet during the show. As much as they adored Jessie, even Maggie and Sue-Lyn felt betrayed by her for the way she dumped Josh as well as them. Still, they were mesmerized by her music.

Despite the difficult last few months, Jessie's music was better than ever. Songwriting and steadfast old Jim Beam were good places to hide. Many lonely nights over the hot summer were spent bent over her grand piano or the cherished Gibson, channeling the utter futility of Deuce's reappearance in her life out of Jessie's shattered spirit and into her music. Almost always her constant companion was a few shots of the dependable loyal Kentucky bourbon. After all, it was enduring. Since 1795, seven generations of the

Beam family produced the whiskey, and the company even survived the unrelenting and oftentimes dangerous darkness of prohibition. Her choice of deadening confidante was a survivor, just like Jessie.

She had some trouble with the dancing in the show, although only her own troupe was aware. Even mildly drunk, she was a consummate pro. Her balance was just a bit wonky on some moves. Lately, it took a lot of the hard stuff to even get her drunk. Sometimes she flung the empty bottle across the room in frustration and just that evening she'd narrowly missed Heidi, her hairdresser, when the long legged ebony-skinned woman entered Jessie's personal dressing room.

Josh had a hard time staying focused on the show until Jessie sang his ballad. There was no way the audience would let her go without singing it. The hopeful tune was still a Top Forty hit, hanging on to Number One for months. Sue-Lyn argued later that it was hypocritical of Jessie to sing it, for it was a tale of optimism and forgiveness and of moving on even when you don't think there is anything left of yourself worth loving. Jessie was forced to go somewhere really deep inside herself to get through it. Accompanied first by Christian's expert floating fingers on the piano, and then by an enchanting illuminated children's choir, the ballad was sung from a wooden stool in the center of the stage. All those small faces—Jessie prayed none of them were ever sexually abused during their lifetime. But the odds were against that. The choir numbered twenty strong. She ached for more Jim Beam during the singing of that song, which garnered her an immediate standing ovation. She didn't smile. She knew that the man she loved most as well as the man she absolutely and wholly despised but whose frailty was leaking and could be seen, ever so slightly, were both swallowed up in the darkness out there somewhere. Two ends of the love spectrum. And the song itself—well, it left an ache in her heart too big for words. A standing ovation was a simple Band-Aid on a soldier who'd been mercilessly torn apart by an IED.

Watching her, Josh shoved a fist into his mouth and bit his knuckles until they bled. He didn't dare look away. Somewhere in the far reaches of his mind, the sad girl on the stage was still his. He didn't want to miss a second of one of her songs. It disturbed him deeply to see her climb off the wooden stool after giving one of the most serenely beautiful, melancholic, spiritual performances of her life, then almost stumble and stand there so small and vulnerable as the entire arena of ten thousand adoring fans rose and shouted her name up to the rafters. She reminded him of the frightened boy singing *O Holy Night* that past Christmas, alone and afraid, trembling. He wished he had the guts to go up on that stage with her, pull her close, and strip away her fear and loneliness with touch and light.

Eventually Jessie rallied and finished the concert with a rousing encore that left both her and Josh in more hopeful spirits. The people of Vancouver were joyous that night. They were mighty proud of their Jessie, and the SkyTrain soon filled with jubilant fans travelling home with the gift of wings—music—overflowing from their hearts and souls.

After the concert, the usual gang gathered around the refreshment table in the backstage room set aside for meetings with the press, contest winners and wealthy patrons. Everyone from *Drifters* was invited to the after party, cast and crew. The western had quickly become the hottest drama on television, selling in sixty-four countries. There was something prestigious about having the team at Jessie's concert, according to Dee and her publicist.

Deuce sauntered in casually, attaching himself to the Downtown Eastside crowd. He would have been highly entertained to know that one of the people he spoke to was Arnie, the man who supplied Jessie with the gun she one day planned to pull on her tormentor. Yet, his disguise kept him under the radar of Charles and Matt, along with Charlie, who were all carefully watching the room. Although their vigilance had faded somewhat over the summer, none felt entirely secure with the notion that Jessie sank into what was obviously some deep depression simply because fans persecuted Josh.

In fact, all three men as well as Deuce kept a close eye on Josh. The actor was oblivious to the fact that he was being watched, though. He only had eyes for Jessie, and missed most of Maggie and Sue-Lyn's gossip as a result.

Deuce could feel a raging temper building within. Unbeknownst to Jessie, who kept her distance from him as she indulged in more and more Jim Beam, the little pulse at the side of his temple that generally alarmed her to his rising blood pressure was pounding away, and increasing in intensity. The closer she got to Josh, the worse the throbbing vein agonized him.

She hadn't intended to talk to her *Drifters* friends, but she knew she and

Josh were both safe in the company of not only Matt and his team, but also in the proximity of Arnie and the Downtown Eastside friends she'd invited. Besides, she'd been away for some of the summer and had been attentive to Deuce when they were both in the city together. And she was somewhat drunk. She longed to see her old friends and to hear the new storylines for the third season of *Drifters*. As the evening threatened to draw to a close, Jessie, her latest glass of the Kentucky bourbon gripped tightly in white knuckles, inched through crowds of well-wishers until she was near enough Maggie and Sue-Lyn to touch Maggie's arm and whisper a subdued *hello*. Her old friend whipped around and regarded Jessie carefully.

"You've gotten skinny," Maggie said, before warming Jessie's spirits with a cautious hug.

"Skinni-*er*," added Sue-Lyn, who was a little more ardent in her hugging.

Jessie smiled shyly back at them and focused on standing upright. A dark-skinned arm swooped her up in a big bear hug and she couldn't keep from squealing happily.

"Carter!" she protested cheekily, and then punched him in the arm. "Cute as ever. Got a girl these days? Where's Ashley?"

"Many," he replied, grinning. "One for each day of the week. Ashley's in the States for a while and we decided not to try the long distance thing."

"Well," she smiled. "One for every day. That's the way to do it, my friend." Out of the corner of her eye she saw Stephen step forward. Her eyes glistened when he held her and the subdued scent of goat's milk soap filled her nostrils. She breathed him in. "Ahhh. You smell like my old friend Stephen."

Holding her at arm's length, Steve frowned at her. "Maybe you should come around to ROAM once in a while. Then you wouldn't be calling me an *old* friend."

"And you can smell him all you want!" Sophie chuckled and shoved her man out of the way. "Jessie. It's good to see you." The women shared a gentle hug. They both had a wet sheen evident in their eyes, reflecting brightly in the overhead lights. Maggie, Sue-Lyn, Carter and Stephen also fought threatening heady emotions. The feelings were real. They all missed her, and she ached to be with them.

She could sense Josh's presence nearby but she fought the nerve to look at him. Now, Sophie took a deep breath and eyed her carefully, then gave her hands a gentle pressure as if to ask Jessie if she were ready. Then Sophie stepped aside.

He stood there nervously, leaning on one foot with his ankle turned up and his hands in his pockets, as he often did, shyly, and Jessie felt her world start to spin. He was so damned adorable—black jeans, camel fringed jacket, white button up shirt, black cowboy hat and—was it? Around his neck, the leather thong she'd given him for Christmas, the J pendant tickling the spot at the base of his neck that she once loved to kiss. The layered chestnut hair was longer, just brushing his collarbone, and she reached out and touched it with the fingertips of her left hand. Then she turned her hand over and, fueled by drink and a cocky adrenaline rush from the show, ran her fingers through his hair and let her fingertips touch his slightly bristly cheek. She looked up and forced a half-smile, and then she realized that as she touched him he'd reached out and nudged her elbow as if to guide her towards him. Jessie followed where the air took her, and before she knew it she was in his arms and was nuzzling his neck with her lips, whispering his name so that it tickled him. Josh rewarded her with a hesitant smile.

They stayed that way much longer than they should have, and it was as if the air was suddenly sucked out of the room, for it became hushed as people turned and stared. There were still rumors floating around about their break-up and, although most people sneered it off as a relationship based on lust, there were others who had genuinely thought they cared about each other. Then there were those from Dee's corner, who believed that it was Josh who'd left the nasty bruise on her cheek and lip earlier in the summer.

Watching them, Dee bristled; Charlie ached; Matt went on high alert; Charles tensed; Maggie, Sue-Lyn, Carter, Stephen and Sophie melted; Arnie wondered; and Deuce went-off-the-rails. He left the party and texted Jessie before he got to the little boys' room.

Fuckin bitch u have one hr

Jessie didn't get the message until she got back to her dressing room an hour later. By then she had laughed a little with her old friends, relaxing even more after noticing that Deuce was no longer present. She stood by Josh's side, leaning into him with her left hand on his belly, her baby finger hooked into his wide black leather belt, barely visible under his jacket. Her right hand was clasped firmly in his, and occasionally she allowed her head to rest against his shoulder. Partly her stance was because she was really quite drunk, but mostly she was so long gone from caring anymore about anything other than Josh that she couldn't bring herself to leave his side. She just kept telling herself it was only for a minute, that she'd behaved for Deuce, done what he asked of her. McCall was gone from the after party anyway so wasn't it okay to be with Josh just for a short time?

They stood there as a group and chatted together. Stephen held court as always, telling them jokes and stories while Josh tentatively placed his arm around Jessie's shoulders and then kept it there. Josh, Maggie and Sue-Lyn were hesitant around Jessie at first. After all, her departure from the show and seemingly from their lives was so sudden and cavalier. *Drifters'* ratings would drop dramatically without her presence as Kate. But underneath their concern for the show and their own hurts was an intuitive ever-present worry, too. So they warmed slowly to her and swapped tales and plans for the new shooting season, and cautiously asked her if she would consider doing a few guest appearances. Jessie tuned out a few times as the others chatted, and turned her nose into Josh's neck, quietly nestling into him and inhaling deeply. He turned towards her and whispered her name, ignoring the fact that it seemed the whole room was watching them. She giggled and reached up and took his hat off his head and placed it on her own.

"You are a vision," he murmured, his eyes alight for the first time in months.

"Vi-shun of what?" she asked saucily, slurring, tipping the hat forward so she had to look up in order to let him see her blue eyes.

He gazed appraisingly at Jessie's rather dangerously short silk strapless ivory dress with gold jewels edging the bust, and accompanying beige stiletto heels.

"Like in my dreams."

"I'm not your dream. I'm your nightmare," she pouted, her eyes clouding over as she snickered drunkenly and then clumsily placed the hat back on his head.

He adjusted the hat and then wrapped a second arm lightly around his old girl. Jessie stood there looking up at him and trying to smile, but then the

Jim Beam felt like it was wearing off and the effort was suddenly too much. But she had one last thing to murmur duskily to him before she would have to pumpkin.

"Run away with me."

He leaned his head back so as to see her better. His arms stayed where they were, so she couldn't get away.

This time it was barely a whisper, and a gentle graze of manicured fingertips accompanied it—on his chin, and then brushing across his inviting lips. Her eyes were desperate, pleading.

"Run—away—with—me."

Her curls were starting to droop and Jessie's eyes were bloodshot. She was too thin, although still muscular and fit, and there were bluish circles underneath her eyes, accented by smudged mascara. Josh thought she never looked more beautiful than she did that night, standing there leaning into him, staring up at him, entreating him. For that was what it seemed she was doing—begging, almost. In the year and then some to come, he would remember that moment, that look, every second of the day. It would be up there with her pleading with him to promise not to forget that she would love him always and forever, no matter what. At that moment in that room with the dim lighting and the crowd sounds floating around them yet not entering their secret bubble, Josh's knees almost gave way and he heard his heart screaming *yes yes yes* while his mind ruined the party with *no no no*.

"Jessie...," was all he could manage to utter, confused, and then Dee was there pulling her away from him, and he couldn't look away, nor could Jessie.

Then finally, sorrowfully, defeated again, Jessie dropped her gaze down to the high beige heels, and then up to her man one last time. And now the old mask was back and her eyes were dead again, and Josh found himself wishing he was a mind-reader, but he was only a mere mortal and so he let her go yet again. She walked away with her head down, weaving a little, the gorgeous dress emitting a soft floating shushing around her hips as she moved, and although Josh knew she was desperately inebriated, he didn't care. She was Jessie, and she had once again been his for just the last hour, and that was all that mattered.

Sue-Lyn hooked his arm in hers and the little group left right away, for once Jessie departed their company it seemed as if the lights had gone out, even though the party was ending and the arena staff had turned the overhead lights on so that indeed it was brighter than ever.

⌒⌒⌒⌒

In her dressing room Jessie threw on jeans, a blue v-neck T-shirt, and her favorite homey brown cowboy boots, and then she grabbed her phone. She almost fell onto the spacious couch when she spied Deuce's text.

Oh, shit.

It was already past the hour since the terse message made its way through cyberspace and landed angrily on her iPhone.

Fuck.

She was shaking before she had her bag packed, and she cursed at Matt when she ran into him outside in the hallway. He was expecting to drive her home.

Jessie pushed him aside with an angry arm. Charles and Dee had already said goodnight. Besides a few straggly dancers and some venue staff, they were alone.

He reached gently for her arm. "C'mon, girl," he said. "You can sleep in the car."

Shaking him off, Jessie stepped drunkenly back and glared at Matt.

"*Fuck you, Matt.* I'm taking the Mustang."

Matt was amazed. This was not the Jessie he knew and loved. He had spent time with her over the summer, mostly on the shows she did here and there, and this imposter broke his heart. She was often distant and quiet, yes, but rarely mean and spiteful. Yet, she was pretty drunk.

He put his foot down. "Jessie." His voice was raised. Firm. "I am driving you home. No question."

She would have let him but she was angry, late (and thus terrified) to meet Deuce, and she couldn't sneak out with her SUV when she got home, because Matt or one of his minions would be sticking around and guarding her building overnight. She tried to get away from Matt, but he grabbed her again.

"Jessie! You're not driving! Look, I'll get the Mustang to you so you have it for the morning, okay?"

"You're hurting me," she whined, stumbling as she tried to elude his grasp.

169

He let go and she started to back away.

"I have somewhere I have to be, Matt," she insisted, staggering. "I'll take the fucking SkyTrain, okay?"

"Jesus, Jessie, you just did a show for ten thousand fans. You're NOT taking the fucking SkyTrain." He reached for his cell.

"Who're you calling?"

"I'm calling Charles, who the hell do you think I'm calling?"

Wow, she thought in a detached sort of way. *I've never known Matt to be so angry. It's kind of cute.*

She threw up her hands. "Okay, I give! I give, Matt."

Deuce was going to skin her alive.

She was complacent after that, obedient and quiet. Incensed, speechless himself, Matt drove Jessie home in the Audi, and she let him watch her disappear into the elevator. She started to text Deuce, hoping he would let her off for that one night if she explained that she was being closely watched. As she stepped off the elevator into her private foyer, looking down to complete the text that was rather drunkenly misspelled, a shadow stepped in front, startling her. The phone clattered to the floor.

It was Deuce—rabid, pissed, volatile.

"H-how did you get up here?" she asked, her heart threatening to explode from fear.

He held up her keycard. "Your building's door crony is an idiot. I sent him on a wild goose chase for an old lady I paid off to be lost. And you shouldn't drink so much. You let your fucking spare door key fall out of your purse at my place."

Fall out, bullshit, she thought. She'd been looking for that spare keycard. He had obviously gone through her purse and taken it.

She growled, her eyes narrowing. "You shouldn't have come here, Deuce the fuck McCall. They're watching me like a hawk this weekend. One of these days they'll grab you and *sssuck* the life out of you the way you've *sssucked* the life out of me."

His hand came from nowhere, and the blunt force of it knocked her brutally to the floor. He'd hit her on the cheek again. She tasted blood on her lip, and put her hand over the sting to try to cool it.

"Fuck, Deuce!" she cried. "I have a show tomorrow."

"You should have thought of that before you mind-fucked me at the show *tonight*, girl."

She clamored to her feet and wobbled there. "What do you mean, Deuce, I didn't do anything wrong…"

He hit her again, and then grabbed Jessie by the hair and hauled her into the bedroom and threw her against the floor-to-ceiling window. Silently, she wished it would smash into a zillion pieces so she could hurl her aching body to the streets far below. She was now close enough to see the vein on Deuce's forehead throbbing.

She spied the pistol under her bed where she'd tucked it for safekeeping behind a spare pillow. It was time. In fact, it was way past time. With her left hand, she reached for it, but it lay just beyond her fingertips. She stretched and inched forward and almost had it, but then he kicked her and, with a cry, she instantly coiled up like a snake. She wanted to try again but the pain was overwhelming, and it took her a few minutes to attempt another reach. This time she fought the pain and like a lightning flash she whipped out and grabbed the weapon, but he stamped his booted foot down hard on her wrist before she could use it. She screamed in humiliation, frustration and pain as he twisted his foot around, and then she saw her last hope wither and die as McCall bent and retrieved the gun. He pocketed it.

"Was this to be used on me? Or on you?" he demanded too calmly, his breathing heavy and labored with the exertion of his temper and sudden high blood pressure.

Jessie laid her head on her good wrist and sobbed. This was too much. One golden hour with Josh was all the universe gave her. *One.* It provided enough fuel to briefly rekindle her fire, her desire to defeat this madman once and for all. The touch of Josh's skin on hers—the spicy, earthy scent of him—it was a heady cocktail. That's why she went for the gun, finally. She felt she had no recourse left. She might die here tonight under the misguided power of Deuce's fist. But she had failed miserably. She reached for the weapon, for him. Yes. She wanted to kill herself, to end this.

Deuce ignored her plea and then told her exactly how she'd pissed him off as he kicked Jessie and threw her around the room for the next fifteen minutes. Every second word was Josh. Deuce raged about the song, the way she stared into the audience—*you knew exactly where he was sitting, didn't you*—the way she navigated towards Josh at the after party. The way she touched him, hugged him, held him, whispered to him. And Deuce had left after only fifteen minutes of watching her with him. What happened afterwards? Did they fuck in a bathroom somewhere? Or in her dressing room, perhaps? The thought of what he saw and *imagined* incensed Deuce beyond all reason.

"I *will* kill him, Jessie," he screamed at her. "I *will* kill him!" And she could hear the knife again as it entered Sandy's chest—*thwunk, thwunk, thwunk, thwunk, thwunk, thwunk.*

Heartlessly, fired by a blinding white rage, Deuce dragged Jessie's broken body up and forced her belly down on the bed so that her legs hung off the side. In a few fluid motions he had her jeans down around her beloved boots. He ripped her underwear and left it shredded on the hardwood floor, then he unzipped his pants and forced himself inside her. It was only a few minutes, but it was painful and rough and was a message about whom she belonged to, about who called the shots for Jessie Wheeler.

By the time he kicked Jessie around a little more and then finished with her and left her bleeding and barely conscious on the floor, he had calmed down somewhat, yet he felt no remorse. As far as Deuce was concerned, Jessie was his property, plain and simple. He could do whatever he wanted with—or to—her.

Breathing hard from the exertion and adrenaline, Deuce took the long way down, via the emergency stairs. He veered out a back door, a hoodie over his face, avoiding security cameras. He knew Matt would be out there, slunk down hiding in the car. What he didn't know was that Josh was out there wandering around, too, and that Matt had an eye on the actor's empty pick-up.

Josh was feeling lonesome after time in Jessie's company. He just needed to be close to her. But he picked a bad time to park at her building in the middle of the night and wander around. He didn't see Deuce leave, nor did Matt. But Matt did see Josh climb into his pick-up at 3:11 a.m. Eyebrows raised, the Keatings' security chief noted the time and took some photos. Not much wonder Jessie didn't want Matt to drive her home earlier. She had a date with someone not many people approved of, someone they all hoped she had long forgotten about. *Hmmmm.*

Matt settled back into the Audi's roomy leather seat after Josh left, listened to some heavy metal station which he hated but which kept him awake and then, at four a.m. was relieved by Dan, a burly blonde Scandinavian in a Mercedes.

He went home to Julie and bed until nine, and then got up to shower, shave and make teddy bear shaped pancakes for his young daughter.

Later that morning, Matt kissed his wife and daughter and went back to work. Jessie had a matinee that afternoon.

It would be another long day.

Chapter Seventeen

Whenever possible, depending on Jessie's schedule, Saturdays were lazy mornings that commenced with strawberry rhubarb yogurt and French vanilla granola, highlighted by a quick trip to Rebel on a Mountain for a flat white or a latte. Sometimes Jessie even indulged in a mocha, depending on her mood. The barista, Chris, teased her relentlessly on mocha days. He was a diehard barista who believed in brewing the perfect cuppa joe. On mocha days he always asked Jessie if she wanted coffee with her chocolate, since he rightly thought the espresso was a complete loss when one drowned it in syrup. He would miss her this morning, but as Jessie stood in front of the mirror and inspected her battered body, she supposed the friendly barista would grant her this one absence based on the fact that she was between shows. But oh how she craved the comforting texture and taste of espresso on this crazy morning. She didn't know what made her feel worse, the nausea and headache from the Jim Beam, or the beating she'd suffered. She contemplated calling Matt and asking him to bring her a coffee. She knew he would, but she also had some foggy memory of screaming at him at the arena. No, it would not do to call Matt, for more reasons than one.

Fuck that Deuce, she screamed inwardly. *Fuck him.* Jessie felt like she was losing her mind, her tenacious grip on reality. She was slipping away.

Her wrist was likely broken. That would hurt when she danced. Guitar? Huh. Not a chance. For certain at least two ribs were cracked or broken as well. Her cheek was desperately bruised and sore. It hurt to breathe.

Jessie ran some warm bathwater and sat in the tub for a long while, ignoring her phone, which she could hear faintly beeping and ringing somewhere off in the distance. She sponged off the blood and seriously contemplated letting herself sink underneath the suds to a certain black eternity. Eventually she rallied and braced herself with her somewhat better (but still painfully bruised) hand on the side of the large soaking tub, arose agonizingly, and dried herself off carefully, patting softly the angry bruises and swollen wrist. She was thankful for the luxurious soft white towels Dee had given her for Christmas one year. As much as she was embarrassed by some of the luxuries her wealth provided, this was a day she was inordinately pleased for the presence of soft towels.

She limped out to the living room and gasped as she bent over to pick up the phone from the floor. Without bothering to check messages, she laid it on the coffee table. In a daze, Jessie wondered that she was alive. *Thank Heaven for small mercies*, she muttered to herself sarcastically as she laid her damaged arm on the kitchen island and wrapped a hand towel around her wrist, securing it with an elastic band.

Jessie sat on the couch and stared at the wall, pondering her options. She could not go to a doctor like this. She could not call the Keating physician to come to her place, either, at least not until after the show, or he would ask Dee to cancel it. But Jessie knew they were sold out. There were ten thousand fans waking up this morning excited to see the long awaited Jessie Wheeler concert. Many were coming in from out of town. She couldn't let them down.

She hobbled across the room to her silver MacBook. It was lying on the coffee table, where she'd left it the day before. Flipping open the lid, Jessie poked the power button. She navigated to Facebook and selected her fan page, and then sighed heavily. Although the comments and photos from the previous evening's concert were unanimously positive and inspiring, she pictured what the page would look like tonight. She was right about one thing— there would be passionate comments on the page that evening, but they were not anything close to what Jessie imagined they would say.

The first thought Jessie had when she got to Rogers Arena was that it was inordinately warm in there. She went early so that only a few people would see her on the way in. They were busy and just glanced at her briefly, from a distance. With a baseball hat pulled down over the hoodie on her head, she slipped by them easily. At any rate, they figured she was just hung over. The place was hopping with gossip about how wasted she'd been last night.

In her dressing room, she let out a sigh of relief. Her assistant had not yet arrived and the journey from her condo to the arena had been excruciating. How the hell could she do this show? Jessie spied a new bottle of Jim Beam on the craft table with some other snacks. She twisted the lid open and poured herself a hefty glass. *Sweet nectar of the Gods. Relief, as it washed through her body and cleansed the pain, the pain, the pain.* The searing pain.

The searing pain.

The searing pain.

Jessie perched on the closed toilet in the bathroom and drank great gulps of the bourbon, the broken wrist resting uncomfortably on her bruised lap. The warmth of the whiskey did nothing to calm her spirits or quell an intensifying throbbing pain. She sank to the floor and closed her eyes, leaning her pounding head on the welcoming cool porcelain of the toilet.

After a while Heidi arrived and called out to her.

"Jess? About an hour and a half before show time, they tell me. Want to get dressed? Jess?"

From the bathroom came a small voice. "Heidi? Can you come in here?" Jessie would need some help figuring this out. In her now feverish and drunken state, all she could see were clouds of lovely pink tinged cotton, like a Prince Edward Island sunset on an early November evening. All she could hear was music. She was in her *place* again, too numb to be frightened. She could trust Heidi, couldn't she?

Outside, Josh and Stephen arrived. They scooted past security on a guest pass to bring hot coffee to Kayla. It was Josh's excuse to see Jessie. He hoped he could sneak into her dressing room like in the old days, even just to give her a peck on the cheek and to tell her to break a leg. He was feeling like maybe she was trying to tell him something last night. Like any spurned lover, any positive actions were a sign of reinforcement, of hope. As they neared the dressing room his younger sister shared with the other female dancers across the hall, he peeked down at the second coffee in his hand. Was he just being hopeful? Would Jessie even see him?

He gave Kayla a hug and handed her the first compostable cup, then turned to saunter across to Jessie's space, where both Matt and Dan were now on guard, eyeing him curiously. He wondered if Matt had spotted his truck last night. *Oh, well, if he did, no biggie.* Jessie was with Josh at the after party. It made sense that they might have hooked up. He gulped. Matt could be rather terrifying, if he disapproved of you, but Josh always figured Matt was okay with him. *Whatever.* More the big blonde guy he should be wary around, anyway. The Scandinavian guy was a fucking mountain.

Josh was about to wander over, the nauseating smell of hot dogs and popcorn from concessions wafting down the hall, when the door to Jessie's dressing room flew open and Heidi hollered at Matt. The security chief disappeared inside, Dan hot on his tail, just as Dee, uncharacteristically in jeans and a summer top, was making her way down the hall with Charles. Josh saw her grab her husband's arm, and then the two of them picked up their paces and rushed into the dressing room, the door slamming behind them. Josh took two quick steps towards the offending door before Stephen managed to secure a vice-like grip on his arm. Josh swiftly turned towards him, his brown eyes flashing, but he knew before his friend shook his head that he, Josh Sawyer, was no longer invited to that party. Whatever was happening across the hall was not of his concern, at least it shouldn't be. He felt sick. Something was seriously wrong, he could feel it, and onlookers in the area were clueing in as well. Soon there were others crowding into the room and then, unbelievably, paramedics and a stretcher. Cops. There would be no concert this afternoon.

Kayla and the other dancers gathered together, watching, huddled in the horrifying fear of the unknown. She reached forward and grasped her brother's arm, then clutched his hand and crushed it tightly. He turned away, towards the wall, and leaned his forehead against it. *What the hell is going on in there?* They seemed to be taking forever.

Soon enough, the door opened and the next few minutes seemed like slow motion to Josh. Out came Dan and Charles, and then a paramedic pulling the stretcher on which lay Jessie, small and quiet, a cloth bandage over her cheek, a splint on one exposed wrist, and a white blanket pulled up to her chest covering the rest of her still body. Dee and Matt followed, and then Heidi was standing there in tears, watching.

Dee stopped in her tracks when she saw Josh, and then she ran for him. She was so quick that she was on him before he had time to think, to move, to react. She pounded him again and again. From the stretcher, Jessie discerned movement through a cloudy haze and looked up in time to see Dee wailing at Josh.

Dee was screaming, "You bastard, you bastard, you bastard, I knew you were no good, I knew you were a loser, I knew you'd hurt her, how could you do this? How?!" She was sobbing profusely. Josh let her hit him as he absorbed the shock, then he grabbed her arms and held her aloft until Stephen and Matt could grab Dee and pull her off him. He stood there, stunned, then turned to the stretcher where he could see Jessie trying to pull herself up.

"Jessie!" he cried, horrified, moving towards her with one eye on the frantic Dee. Dan grabbed him as he got close to Jessie, spilling the coffee Josh brought for her all over the arena hallway so that it puddled on the floor, an echo of lost hope and wasted dreams.

Agitated, Jessie was panicking. She was trying to tear her splint off. In the far reaches of his mind Josh could distinguish her screaming from the hysterics of the hyper Deirdre, whose husband was now frantically trying to calm.

"Get him away from me! Get him away from me!" is what Josh heard that day from the terror-stricken body on the white stretcher.

He thought he stood there for hours, disoriented and shocked at this sudden bizarre turn of events, but in reality it was only moments before Josh was roughly thrown to the ground and violently handcuffed. As he was hauled back up to his feet, dazed and confused, bruised, Dee broke loose and went at him again. Josh would never forget the anger in her eyes—fierce, utter hatred. He wondered what she would do to the real guy that had hurt Jessie.

And then he didn't care about himself anymore. He'd been right all along. Someone was hurting her, badly. He managed to turn and look imploringly, despairingly, at Stephen and Kayla before the cops dragged him down the hallway.

He expected to see anxiety, confusion, looks that read *it's okay Josh, we'll sort this out together.*

But all he saw, in the faces of those two people whom he loved dearly, was a disbelief born of *knowing.* Of knowing that if Jessie *implied* Josh did this to her, then clearly he had. Stephen and Kayla were looking at the man they loved in the manner you ponder someone who has cruelly deceived and wronged you.

They were looking at him with a mixture of disgust and pity.

He let the police carry him away, and hardly noticed how badly the handcuffs tore at his wrists. They'd be off soon enough. This he knew from experience.

Outside, Josh laid his head against the cool door of the police cruiser and closed his eyes.

Well. This day hasn't turned out at all the way I expected.

He whispered a silent prayer for Jessie as the cops pointed their cruiser towards the station. A long line of concertgoers watched it pass moments before they were told there would be no Jessie Wheeler extravaganza that day.

Deuce McCall sat nearby in his black car and watched the confusion. Fans were so angry they were spray painting sprawling graffiti messages on nearby walls and mailboxes. Rubbing his knuckles, Deuce was surprised that they hurt. He had almost forgotten why.

That was quite a workout last night at Jessie's place. The thing about Deuce McCall was that he was a man with a short fuse and a long reach. But he was also a smart man. He turned the key in the ignition and the Fusion roared to life. He'd better lay low in Charleston for a while. Someone might come looking for him.

What a laugh he had late that night in Charleston when he flicked on the news and saw all the hype about how Josh Sawyer had brutally beaten up Jessie Wheeler.

That was another thing about Deuce McCall. He always won.

Chapter Eighteen

At St. Paul's Hospital, Jessie underwent a rigorous physical examination. Charles engaged a female lawyer friend—in consultation with her as well as the police and medical staff, Jessie was asked whether she'd also been sexually assaulted. Turning her head the other way, she simply nodded. At that point a forensic medical exam was administered, and evidence collected for a rape kit.

She knew that such evidence would prove Josh was not her attacker and, given many people's thoughts about him, she wanted that on file. She was also aware that it would take a few days, if not longer, for the results to come back. That would at least buy Josh some time under the protection of the province. If he was behind bars, Deuce couldn't touch him. Soaking painfully in the bath that morning, Jessie had formulated a plan. It was the best she had. It wasn't foolproof, but it would have to do. In the meantime, she succumbed to the sweet saving grace of morphine.

Jessie had injuries to her face, neck, groin, back, legs, arms and chest as a result of blunt force trauma. Curved imprint bruising from Deuce's boots were found, as well as evidence of bruising by a swinging object such as a belt. She was lucky, in the greater scheme of things. Although examined and then monitored for internal organ damage, in particular her kidneys, which often caused serious issues after blunt trauma to the body, she escaped serious injury and would survive the dreadful beating. Her wrist was broken and would require surgery, and she had severe bruises on her left leg. She was torn and humiliated, but as far as she was concerned she was done with Deuce McCall. Unfortunately, that would also mean a harrowing time for Josh, who would be suffering his own personal agonies right now.

As she was wheeled off to surgery, Jessie groggily looked up and spotted Dee approaching, red-eyed and still somewhat hysterical. She grasped Jessie's hand, but Jessie turned away from her. She couldn't look at the woman who all along had been waiting "for the other shoe to drop" as far as Josh was concerned. Despite the fact that Jessie herself placed the blame for her battered body on him, Dee believed him capable of it all along. Jessie could not bring herself to look at Dee, or to talk to anyone, with the exception of a few whispers to the police, the lawyer or to her attending doctors and nurses. She just wanted to sink into oblivion and sleep the rest of the day away. She would deal with reality tomorrow.

When she awoke after surgery, the lighting in her room was muted. She could make out a murky outline slumped in the corner chair. Squinting in order to see better, Jessie saw that it was Charlie. Sensing a slight movement from the bed, he wearily made his way over to her. Bending over the rail on the right side of the bed, he looked sadly at his ex-fiancée.

"See? Told ya you should have married me."

Jessie whispered, "thirsty," prompting Charlie to reach for the call button by her right hand. Soon Jessie spotted pink scrubs emblazoned with teddy bears entering the room. She forced her tired eyes to look up, revealing that an attractive plus-size ponytailed nurse was wearing the scrubs.

"She's thirsty," Charlie pleaded, as if by making such a simple request on Jessie's behalf it would somehow solve this crisis. At the very least it gave him a purpose.

The nurse acknowledged both the request and his sense of futility with a glance at Jessie and a polite nod. She wheeled around and hurried out the door, professional but somewhat awed with the celebrities on her ward that evening. Moments later she returned with a small cupful of ice chips balanced in her left hand.

"How are you feeling, Jessie?" she asked as she helped her patient navigate the chips. Jessie sucked on some ice, relishing the cool comfort of something as simple as frozen water on her parched lips.

"Nauseous," she managed to mumble.

The nurse removed the little cup from between the star's lips and placed it on a nearby table. "It's likely from the anesthesia, honey. I'll see about getting you some Gravol." She checked a few vitals and then blushed at Charlie as she walked by him to exit the room. He didn't even notice her sideways glance. His eyes were on his ex-fiancée, lying in pain on a hospital bed before him.

Jessie couldn't look at him any more than she could stand to see Dee. They all blamed Josh before she even uttered a word. She was disgusted with all of them. Tears pricked her eyelids as she wondered where Josh was now, and what was happening to him.

Without looking at Charlie, she mumbled softly, "Are Charles and Dee here?"

He stepped forward again and brushed tiny wisps of hair off her sweaty forehead. "No," he replied quietly. "They were, though. They'll be back."

She shook her head. "I don't want to see them. Please. Just tell them to stay away."

His cool hand stopped moving. "Jessie. They want to see you. Dee will want to be sure you're living and breathing and…"

She looked up at Charlie, her eyes bottomless pools of grief. "Please. Just for tonight."

What she needed was some time to compose herself, to quell her anger and disappointment in Dee.

"Okay." He didn't understand, but Charlie would do anything to placate Jessie on this difficult day.

After a few moments, the nurse came back with the Gravol and some water. She tipped the tablets into the singer's mouth and then helped Jessie take a few sips of water. As she turned to leave, she gestured towards the door. "Someone here to see you, Jessie."

Framed in the doorway was a tall, slim silhouette with shoulder length hair. For a moment, in her groggy state Jessie thought it was Josh and her heart quickened. But then the nebulous shape stepped forward and she saw that it was Stephen. *Of course. They won't let Josh anywhere near me, now.*

Her friend glanced uncomfortably over at Charlie, whose stiff stance and angry glare were thinly disguising a brooding anxiety bubbling under the surface. Then Steve's eyes searched the bed and met Jessie's bruised baby blues; pale icy eyes that were almost swallowed up by frosty, sallow cheeks and a snowy pillow.

"Hey."

"Hey," she forced weakly in response.

Charlie acknowledged Steve with a slight nod and a frown, and then he moved back from the bed. "I'll go grab a tea. I'll be back, okay Jess?"

"Charlie." Her voice was small, detached. But the hardened tone was unmistakable. She had something firm to say that caused him to stop and turn back to her.

"Yeah."

"Tomorrow, okay? I'm not up for company tonight."

He was quiet, unsure. Charlie wanted to be there with her, to order ice chips and watch her breathe. To make sure she was, in fact, breathing. He fidgeted as he tried to call forth the words to tell her not to send him away, not to banish him as she had everyone else over the past few months.

Nodding towards the doorway where, just outside, a uniformed police officer stood talking to Matt, Jessie whispered, "I'm well protected."

Charlie's shoulders sank. "I'll be back tomorrow, then." He slumped away.

Jessie called upon some deeply hidden reserve of inner strength to give her the courage to look up at Steve, her dear friend. She was surprised to see that his eyes were ringed with a puffy red tinge. He had obviously been crying, which was unusual for the happy-go-lucky actor.

"Hey," she murmured again.

His lips moved soundlessly as he tried to find the words, any words, which would be appropriate in this horrible situation. Allowing his body to give in to the overwhelming emotions threatening to do him in, Steve rested his lanky elbows on the bedrail and avoided Jessie's searching eyes. Words wouldn't come, and so he hung his head in his arms and cried instead.

"Jessie," he choked. "I had no idea. None of us had any idea. Nobody suspected…"

She reached her right hand up to grasp his fingers, and he finally looked down at her through a mask of fear, fighting to regain control of his tattered emotions.

"It's okay," she said. She couldn't tell him the truth—not yet.

She was getting sleepy.

"Steve," Jessie asked in a draggy voice, her speech firing about thirty seconds behind her brain, "could you lie down with me for a little while? Do you think Sophie would mind?"

He was surprised by her request, but it helped him regain his equilibrium. "Yeah. Yeah, I guess I could. I'm sure she wouldn't mind." After a quick search for the buttons that lowered the rail, Steve carefully arranged himself on his side next to her, with his left arm crooked under his head. Jessie enclosed his right hand in hers and held it close to her, on her belly. She loved the feel of his fingers, and the way he smelled, like old times and cherished friendships.

"I'm really sorry," he intoned softly. "We all are. We should have seen this coming. We should have protected you."

"You couldn't have," she said, and that was the truth.

Silence.

"Steve?"

"Yeah kiddo?"

"Where's Josh right now? What's happening to him?" Under droopy eyelids, the badly beaten *Drifters* star was staring at the imposing sterile ceiling above.

Steve was stunned. But then again, he rationalized that she would, indeed, be curious.

"Besides burning in hell, you mean?" He immediately felt chastened for saying that as her body stiffened beside him. Burrowing his head in Jessie's neck, Steve whispered, "I'm sorry."

"It's okay. I get it."

"They arrested him. He's in jail over at the metro police station. Zach's been called. He's probably in the city by now." He groaned, as the weight of Josh's actions settled further into his brain, etching a permanent angry stain on Steve's psyche. "Just when everybody thought Josh had gotten his shit together, it all goes to hell."

Steve thought Jessie had drifted off to sleep, so it surprised him when she spoke.

"Will you be in touch with Zach? So we...so we know what's going on with...with Josh?" She could barely say his name. It *hurt* to say his name.

"Yeah. I'm sure Zach will be calling me."

Curious, but thinking Jessie would simply want to know Josh's where-abouts in the weeks to come, Steve resigned himself to the fact that he would likely be the conduit between Jessie and Josh, via Zach, for the next while. It was an awkward, uncomfortable place to find himself, with his best friend on one side—albeit not the guy he'd thought Josh was, all along—and his friend's ex on the other. But for Jessie's peace of mind, Steve would take the role.

He stayed with her for a long while, his left arm long asleep, Jessie's breathing even and controlled.

Occasionally the nurse peeked her head into the subdued room to check Jessie's vitals but mercifully the singer didn't wake, although Steve held his breath and tried not to move.

He watched her chest rise and fall, and a part of him wished she'd chosen him instead of Josh back during those first heady days of shooting *Drifters*. The shock was too much to bear—Steve couldn't believe Josh was capable of inflicting such wretched damage on the woman he so obviously deeply loved. Studying the bruises on Jessie's face and exposed arms, Steve wondered despairingly what the rest of her body looked like.

His body shook as he cried, yet, still, she did not wake.

Small mercies.

The Vancouver Police Department was located adjacent to the Provincial Courthouse at Main St. and East Cordova St. in the Metro Vancouver area. It was the second largest police force in the province after the RCMP, which patrols outside Metro Van in nearby municipalities. Earlier that day, while Jessie was in surgery, Zach parked outside the police station and summoned the courage to stumble inside. It took him a while to find and access his brother within the confines of the large building. Although what had happened to Jessie was a shock, particularly for its degree of violence, it was a busy day in Vancouver. Josh was a small part of the fabric of the city's crime that day.

Finally, in a small neutral washed-out room with a one-way viewing window, Zach Sawyer was able to sit down alone across from his baby brother at a scratched metal table. His chair screeched across the floor when he lowered his body ruthlessly into it. He didn't hold back, and Josh jumped when the sound of Zach's fist slamming into the heavy table startled him.

"Fuck, Josh," was how Zach started, at a loss for any other words. Frustrated, he lifted his palms upwards in resignation and loss.

His younger brother was agitated and scared. He dove in just as quickly. "Zach," he pleaded, his voice trembling. "It wasn't me. I didn't hurt Jessie. I could never hurt her! So what's really fucked up about this is that someone did. And whoever did it is still out there. Please, Zach."

He paused, afraid to voice the rest of the terror that had preoccupied his crazed mind since he'd seen his ex-fiancée on the stretcher earlier that day. "What if—what if he comes back to finish the job?"

Zach sat back and drummed his fingers on the metal table while he pondered his baby brother. Josh stared hard at the fingers as they moved rhythmically up and down. The persistent echo in the acoustically reflective room was going to drive him over the edge. He swallowed. Zach saw a man he hardly recognized in front of him, a man who he thought was—finally—successful, clean, and good. Josh had found and maintained solid friendships, reacquainted himself with his family, was working steady, and even managed to retain some sort of haphazard congenial relationship with his somewhat estranged father, of all things. Who'd have thought either of those two could manage to spend any time in a room together and be civil? Jessie was good for Josh, but she had removed herself from his life the last few months. Maybe she was the missing equation here—without her, the Josh they had all grown to love in the last few years existed no longer.

He shook his head as if to clear the unwelcome thoughts from the cobwebs of his mind. No. He'd known Josh his whole life, they were brothers, for God's sake. Sure, Josh struggled with some problems, but who didn't? In his heart he was a good man. He had always been a good man. Was he capable of this—of intentionally, in a fit of rage, hurting so badly the girl Zach knew he desperately loved, just because of her rejection of him? No. *No way.*

Zach wanted desperately to believe Josh. He wanted his kids to love their uncle unconditionally. He didn't want to be afraid to leave them in Josh's company. He lashed out at Hilary earlier that day for even mentioning it, but Josh was known to have a volatile temper, albeit a drug-fueled one. Zach groaned. Blood was thicker than water. Regardless of what Josh did or didn't do, he chose to take the high road. Zach was a good man, too, and their mother was long gone, although he could feel her presence in the room, coaching him and gently chiding him for doubting her beloved Josh. Their father? Well, he was off on safari somewhere in Africa with his girlfriend. Even if he was around, Zach doubted Wes would believe Josh, but then one never knew how the great and famous patriarch of the Sawyer clan would react, especially to something sinister such as this.

"Your truck was in her parking lot. Empty. Matt has photos, Josh. The few shots the security cam's building actually got show a guy with a hoodie that could easily be you." But his voice was quiet and subdued, not angry and accusing. Zach was giving Josh a chance to tell his side of the story.

Visibly relieved that Zach was at least being reasonable, Josh exhaled and sat back. "She was all over me at the after party, Zach. Jessie was drunk— yeah, I get that—but whatever. If I'd ever hurt her, would she be hanging onto me like that?"

"You can love someone and still be hurt by them. Maybe she was giving you a second chance."

"Aw, man, Zach," Josh responded in frustration. A second chance. Yes. He had hoped for that for months. He felt it in the air last night. She had asked him to run away with her. She nuzzled his neck. He could still feel her tender lips against his neck and see a faded hope in her eyes, an almost desperate pleading. He closed his own eyes as his throat contracted at the memory and his heart seized. He looked away and swallowed, trying to get a grip.

When he got it together, Josh forged ahead through the no man's land in which he and his brother found themselves, although the barbed wire was tearing him apart, inch by painful inch. "It was weird last night. I admit, after she left I was hoping that maybe—that maybe she was sending me some kind of message, that she was reconsidering our breakup. Maybe she missed me." He said it as if now, in the light of day or rather, in the light of the harsh fluorescents that buzzed above them, it was impossible to even comprehend. What was he thinking? He guessed now that the magic spell of the evening overpowered him. Watching her on stage again…there was so much love and affection in that arena, all aimed at Jessie. Why was she still so tormented? Well. That question was at least partially answered once and for all for Josh. Unfortunately, it was answered for Charles and Dee, Jonathon, Charlie, their friends…but grossly inadequately, as if the crime had led its all too willing followers down the wrong road.

"I went to her place, yes, I parked there, yes. I just wanted to be close to her. I wandered around a little. But mostly I sat on the concrete wall on the west side of the building and drank a coffee and thought about everything. About life. About the fucking muppets, whatever! I swear to God, Zach, it was just surreal, the way she hung on to me at the after party. I just wanted the feeling to last a little longer. If I had known…"

*If I had known…*the words hung there, on an invisible clothesline with no breeze, damp and stiff. Like soldiers who'd gone mad in their useless wars and no longer knew which way to run. Josh was there, just outside Jessie's building pondering life and love like some lovesick 1970's flower child while, upstairs, someone beat the shit out of the woman he loved. Tears stung his eyelids. The futility of the situation was killing him. All he had left was Zach. He doubted anyone else would come to see him. Jessie's word was respected and cherished, no one would doubt her truths. Thank God for Zach, who was sitting there pondering him like he did when they were children, after their dad hit Josh and hurled verbal assaults at him while Zach and Kayla received praise. Confused, wanting to help, unsure, disbelieving.

Zach filled in the silence with a dose of optimism. "Okay. So if you're telling the truth, and Josh I gotta tell you I want to believe you but at this point I just don't know…"

At the fear in his brother's eyes Zach paused, and then summoned the courage to continue. "Well, first things first. Jessie's safe. She's well guarded, but I'll ask Charles to up her security even more, maybe put someone at the entrances to the hospital and more on her floor, I don't know. Matt will take care of that. Second, I'll get them thinking about who is out there who might want to hurt Jessie."

He hesitated, looked up at his brother, squinted at him. Josh recognized from childhood that this was Zach's way of processing, of giving some kind of orderly thoughts to the chaos in his brain. "Josh. Do you know who might want to hurt her?"

Josh raked a hand through the layered hair Jessie loved. "That's the thing," he said. "I don't. I mean, the thing is, it could be anybody, couldn't it? A grip on *Drifters*, Charlie, frigging Carter for all I know. Or Christian, that doe-eyed piano player who's obviously head over heels in love with her. One of the dancers, stage crew at Rogers Arena. I have no idea, Zach. Although… she still won't talk about Charleston. Maybe it's someone from her past."

A thought he was afraid to voice bounced around in his brain like the rectangular cursor in an old Atari game. Dark eyes implored his older brother to tell him the truth. His tentative voice was a throaty, gravelly mess. "Was she raped? Zach?"

Zach fingered his cell phone, pushed the home button and watched as the screen lit up with texts from Hilary. His wife was with the kids at Kayla's place in Dunbar, and she was keeping a close eye on the Internet and television updates. But he already knew the answer. He didn't need to read one of Hil's texts to find out. Kayla's lawyer boyfriend Paul had called him earlier.

Staring at the phone, Zach nodded. "Yeah."

Somehow, intuitively, Josh knew the answer would be yes. He shoved his chair back and stumbled the few steps to the barren wall of the sparse little room. Leaning against the wall, his left arm above his head and his right on his hip, he pushed his forehead against the cool cream surface. He wanted to smash his head against the institutional wall, but that wouldn't help Jessie. He wheeled around and faced Zach.

"Well," he said without feeling. "You'll all know then that it wasn't me, won't you? I'm sure they're testing her…whatever the hell it is they do."

Zach sat, numb. This whole situation was unbelievable.

"Rape kit," he droned quietly.

After a minute to process what that entailed, Josh screeched his chair back a few feet and sat down before he fell down. He hung his head in his hands.

"Usually that takes a week or so but seeing as it's Jessie I expect they'll have an answer in a few days. Look, Josh. If you say you didn't do this to her, then I believe you. Okay?"

"Ha," Josh retorted. "I'm guessing you'll be the only one."

Zach reached out and rested a comforting hand on Josh's arm. "They'll come around."

He then decided it was time to get down to business. "I'll go see Charles right away, okay? Jessie's in surgery, so…" Josh looked up quickly. Zach added, "Her wrist. I think the left one, the opposite of you. In Seattle that time, you broke your right wrist, if I recall correctly."

His voice low, Josh managed, "Figures. Even in this, we complement each other."

Zach continued. "With Jessie in surgery, Charles and Dee have gone home for some privacy and to sort things out with their publicist. I'll hit North Van before I go back to Kayla's place. Tomorrow I'll be back here with a lawyer in tow. Maybe Paul too, as an advisor to us, although I know this isn't his specialty. I don't know. We'll get this sorted out."

He watched Josh balance on the edge of the metal chair trying in vain to stay in control of his emotions, and wished they were kids again with hope for the future still a fabric of their beings. Remembering the neighborhood rides they took on their bicycles with little Kayla following, her small legs furiously pedaling in order to keep up, Zach felt heartsick. The more he sat there with his brother, the more he believed Josh could not have intentionally beat Jessie to a pulp.

He rose. "I'll see you tomorrow. Keep the faith, baby bro."

Josh pushed back his chair and walked him to the door. "Promise me, Zach. Promise me you'll get Matt to put some extra protection on Jessie. Whoever did this…if he wants to finish the job…" Josh grabbed Zach just above his elbows, intent on getting him to listen, to take him seriously.

Zach patted him lightly on the cheek. He nodded. "No worries, Josh. Jessie will be safe. I promise." His gut clenched. *Geez, I hope that is a promise I can keep.*

As he walked away escorted by a uniformed officer, the sharp metal clinks and clangs of the jail unnerved him, but he felt somewhat relieved. You couldn't look into pained eyes like those of his brother and think he was in any way capable of such a heinous crime. Anyways, the forensic exam would be the proof they needed, that everyone needed, to ease their own minds. It was too bad human nature required such rock solid proof but it would be necessary, given Josh's occasionally unbalanced history, his violent battles with drugs and with his own father. It was just unfortunate such proof would likely be required by Josh's own friends and family, people who should be loyal and trusting no matter what twists and turns life decided to hand them.

On the way out, the officer gave Zach a quick rundown on Province of British Columbia law. In order to keep Josh in custody, three things would have to come into play. The investigating officer would have to prove occurrence—that the assault actually happened; identity, that the accused person was the one who made the attack; and consent—that the attack was not consensual sexual activity. Given Jessie's disturbing evidence—a battered and bruised body that depicted wounds typical of a physical and sexual assault—occurrence could be easily proven. It would be up to the rape kit to determine whether it was Josh who forced her to have sex. Because of the celebrity nature of the attack, and his own safety against upset fans, the police were keeping Josh in custody pending results. If those came out against his favor, he would be held pending a hearing before the judge, who then had the discretion to decide whether he still posed a threat to Jessie, or whether he could be safely released. If the forensics proved Josh's innocence at least in the rape, he would be immediately released.

Josh sat at the metal table and felt his panic rise once Zach left the room. He started on the inevitable *what ifs. What if* Zach wasn't welcome at the Keating house, *what if* they doubted him? Dee hated Josh anyway, there was no way she would be open to the idea that there was some other unbalanced soul out there taunting and hurting the girl she loved. *What if* they couldn't catch this maniac?

The cop grunted and told Josh to get his ass up. He led him out the door to a cold cell that stank of piss where he would spend the night on a rock hard mattress. The biggest question of all was rolling around in Josh's mind. *Why did Jessie place the blame on me?*

Josh's lonely footsteps echoed hollowly during that long walk to his overnight cell. Not once did he worry about himself or how all of this would damage his career, his reputation, regardless of the truths that would inevitably emerge.

He was a good man.

Zach thought about his conversation with Josh as he navigated the heavy traffic on the Lions Gate Bridge. He was nervous about facing the Keatings, but Zach had long been accustomed to fighting Josh's battles with—and for—him. He pulled into the curved driveway of the pretty yellow home and marveled that it could still look so lovely and fresh on such a dark day, the garden's invigorating lavender scent a welcome reminder that there was still beauty to behold even in the presence of evil.

There were a number of cars in the driveway. He recognized Charlie's infamous 911 Porsche. There were a few whose owners he speculated about. And there was Jonathon's BMW SUV, parked crookedly, as if the producer and loyal friend to Charles and Dee had needed to emerge from it in a hurry. Matt's Audi was also there, which surprised Zach until he rationalized that likely there were others from his security detail posted at St. Paul's, which meant that this rag-tag family was likely in the midst of a meeting about the day's events. He gulped, and fought down the nausea threatening to erupt in Deirdre Keating's pink roses.

Zach gave Hilary a quick call before entering the fray. He had to dial three times before he was calm enough to speak, and before his shaking hands would cooperate.

"Hey, Hilary."

"Zach. How is he? The media is crucifying him." She had the television volume on low so the kids couldn't hear. They were playing with Paul in the kitchen, laughing hysterically as they built boxy little houses with Lego and then destroyed them with tiny matchbox cars.

"He's holding it together. Barely. Hil—he insists it wasn't him."

She was silent for a moment. "Why would she imply it was Josh if it wasn't? What's the point in that?"

"I don't know. I'm working on that. But right now I'm at Charles and Dee's place. I'm hoping they'll let me in. I don't know, maybe this isn't such a good idea."

He was losing his nerve. He'd almost forgotten why he was there.

Hilary spoke up. "I've already had some calls, Zach. He's been pulled off the Susanne Bier film. She won an Oscar for that film on bullying, what's it called? *In a Better World*. She can't have a man who beats women in her next picture. I don't know what Jonathon will do. Cut him back or something. I don't know." She was close to tears. They'd tried so hard to get Josh back on the right path.

"It's okay, Hilary. There are more pressing issues right now anyway. If Josh didn't hurt Jessie, then there's someone out there who did."

He waited for the catch in her breath, which came instantly. "Zach." That was all she could manage until she processed what he'd said. Then, "I don't want it to be Josh, of course I don't, but that would mean there's someone still out there..."

"Yeah. Exactly." Zach looked up at La Casa, with its capacious curved entry flanked by Dee's exquisite talent for garden design. Her English roses were magnificent, strong and robust, like the woman herself. Zach sighed. "And on that lovely note, I guess I'd better go try to convince the lion lady to see beyond her closed mind. Wish me luck, Hil."

From the other end came a quiet, "Luck, Zach." And then, "Be safe, okay?"

"Yeah. Love you, Mrs. Sawyer."

"Love you back, Mr. Sawyer."

He held the phone in his hand for a minute and felt like he'd lost the one connection that was keeping him sane this day. Oh, well. An hour or so and he would be back with his wife and kids where he felt he belonged. Vaguely Zach wondered if Josh would ever experience such bliss.

Carlotta met Zach at the door with a look of trepidation and a handful of soaked Kleenex. She knew Zach from previous visits accompanying his wife Hilary, Josh's manager, who had met with Deirdre on "Josh and Jessie" business.

"Ah. I don't know, Mr. Sawyer, if this is a good time for you to be here. Everyone's pretty upset. They're just waiting to hear back from the hospital before heading back over."

He frowned. "I understand, Carlotta. To tell you the truth, I don't really want to be here either. But I have something to say that can't wait. I need to talk to Charles, at least."

The clinking of ice cubes dropping into a glass caught Zach's attention. Someone was fixing a drink in the nearby kitchen. It was Charlie, who needed a break from the heavy tension outside. He happened to glance through the doorway and see a very forlorn Zach standing in the opulent entryway. Charlie wandered over, holding his bourbon as if his life depended on it. Which, that day, it kind of did.

"Zach."

Zach watched as his brother's old friend from their early teen years took up a tired stance against the wall while Carlotta shoved the bundle of damp Kleenex deep in her apron pocket before marching back to the deck by the pool, where she needed to serve more drinks to keep sane the tense folks at this unscheduled gathering.

"He didn't do it."

Charlie shrugged. "She says he did."

"She wasn't exactly thinking straight at the time."

"The police talked to her. So did the doctors."

"What did she say to Charles and Dee?"

"She won't talk to them. She won't talk to any of us."

Obviously hurt by Jessie's choice to shut him out, Charlie's face was drawn and his eyes were swollen. Zach noticed that the shadows under the actor's eyes were even more pronounced by the unforgiving light of the overhead chandelier when Charlie lowered his chin. Which he did, in resignation.

"Except for Steve. For some inane reason." Charlie shrugged.

"Look, Charlie—Josh is terrified. And if he's telling the truth…"

Charlie clued in rather quickly, at that. Maybe because he'd seen how Jessie looked at Josh over the months they were together, maybe simply because he wanted to see her happy again…for whatever reason, Charlie also wanted to believe Josh was innocent. He straightened then, and turned and gestured Zach out the back door towards the others.

As expected, Zach received a frosty reception on the pool deck. But he steeled his nerves and spoke with courage and determination.

"I believe Jessie is still in danger."

Dee straightened; they all did, reacting to this turn of events.

"You've got some nerve," Dee spit at him, though rather hesitantly. Was it possible that he was right? Or was he just gas lighting them, trying to take the pressure off of Josh?

"Dee, I know you don't like Josh. I know you've never liked him, to be frank." He wanted to add *because you're a bitch lion lady*, but he managed to keep his cool simply because despite her obvious animosity towards his brother, Josh had not once spoken against her. And because Jessie loved her.

He continued. "It'll come out in a few days anyway. But maybe we don't have that long…" Everyone winced at the reference to the fact that Jessie was raped. A sob came from Carlotta at the bar. She had not been able to stop crying since receiving the awful news. Giselle got up and gave the maid a generous hug.

Charles glanced over at Matt. Should they take Zach seriously?

Matt stepped forward. If there was ever any kind of threat against his girl, he had the *responsibility* to take it seriously. "Zachary. Talk."

Swallowing nervously, Zach told them he'd just been to the jail, that Josh was beside himself with fear, insisting he hadn't hurt Jessie, and therefore someone else out there had. Immediately, without consulting Charles, Matt got on the phone to Dan. He stepped up Jessie's security at the hospital. Hell, Charles Keating could afford it. What he couldn't afford was to lose Jessie Wheeler.

Dee couldn't bite her tongue. She didn't have Josh to scream at now, but she had his brother, whom she really felt was just trying to cover up for Josh. Besides, she was on her way to becoming royally sloshed. "I always knew he was a loser, that brother of yours. From the moment I helped Jonathon cast him, I knew. I expect he's going to lose some jobs over this, including *Drifters*."

With a glance at Jonathon, Charles spoke sharply. "Deirdre. That's enough."

She continued from her comfortable recline on a big chaise lounge. "He just sucked his way into Jessie's life, like some gob sucking jellyfish sucker thing…" She emphasized the word sucker and, since she was drunk, it came out writhing and threatening.

"Deirdre! Enough!" That got her attention. Charles glanced sideways over at the despondent Jonathon again. Dee got the message.

Assessing the level of her inebriation, Jonathon stared hard at Dee, and then he looked uncomfortably back at Zach. He gripped his martini glass until his knuckles were white. He was sitting at a table with Charles, a nine o'clock to his friend's midnight. He asked Zach to sit, by gesturing to a chair he pulled out from the table near him. Charlie walked slowly over and took the opposite chair and sank into it with relief that something else could hold his aching body up for a while.

Jonathon spoke directly to Dee first. "Josh will not lose his job on *Drifters*, even if…if…even if it's proven that he did…that he's guilty."

"Jessie's not a liar, Jon." That was from Charles. Dee sat there across from them in her big chaise and looked smug. Zach noticed that she had her cell phone clenched tightly in one hand.

Uneasy, Jonathon peered over his reading glasses at Zach. "There's something you should know." He yanked the glasses off his head. He had been using them to read a text from Maggie, who had just informed her producer that Jessie was resting comfortably.

Zach frowned. He was intrigued by the fact that this snowy haired man who he knew Josh greatly admired, and who'd been around their house a lot when they were little kids, was planning to keep Josh on as cast even when all hell had broken loose around him. A tumbler of bourbon was set gently before him—Carlotta was heartsick, but still able to care for others. Accepting it gratefully, Zach shot an appreciative look up to the emotional maid, who squeezed his shoulder. Turning his attention to the producer, Zach then settled a little into his chair. What Jonathon had to say must be important. Everyone around them had suddenly become very quiet.

"Zach…I had my reasons for casting your brother. You see, I…when you were small…your father was away a lot, making films and bedding other women. Your mother, she was…lonely." He glanced up at Giselle, who knew, and who had long been telling him he should let Josh know the truth about his paternity, and who encouraged her husband now with a gentle smile. "I fell in love with her. And she with me."

As the lights came on and Zach's quizzical expression turned to wonder, Charlie slammed down his glass, making everyone jump. "Holy shit!" he hollered.

The others didn't react at all, including Carlotta, who managed to stand frozen and just take this all in as she stood at the bar preparing some hummus and vegetables for the downtrodden group.

Zach emptied a healthy swig of bourbon into his suddenly dry mouth.

He needed it, as he suddenly felt very woozy. "And Kayla?" he uttered, shocked.

Jonathon shook his head. "Your dad started working at home more, remember? He got the message loud and clear. He loved your mother too. Very much."

"But not Josh, obviously."

Wriggling in his seat, Jonathon decided not to leave anything to Zach's imagination. "Not so much, no. And your mother and I, well, we talked about her leaving the marriage but she was old fashioned, afraid of what people would think. And I think that in all honesty she really loved your father too. Although he made it pretty hard sometimes."

As he let the news sink in with Zach, Jonathon looked up at Charlie, who had a crazy smile on his pale face.

Charlie was succinct. "Somehow I don't think this news is going to help Josh much, seeing as the only job he's going to get to keep is going to be the mercy role."

Zach shifted uncomfortably as Charles came to his brother's rescue. "He's proven he's a damn good actor, Charlie. And maybe—just maybe…" He shook his head.

Finally off the phone, Matt spoke tersely and efficiently. He focused on Zach. "What evidence can Josh give us *today* to make us believe there is someone else out there who hurt Jessie? Also, if there is someone, who the hell is it? Who should we be looking for? Our friend from Charleston?"

He didn't wait for an answer. He glanced over at Charles. "We need to get Jessie to speak to us as soon as she's awake."

"She was with Stephen when I left," Charlie offered, still amazed and shocked—and somewhat amused—by Jonathon's announcement. "Maybe she said something to him."

Matt looked back at Zach, who in his current state of bewilderment could hardly put two thoughts together. But he tried. "He was a mess, Matt. Frantic. Terrified. He insisted he didn't know anything, about who it might be or anything like that…" He shivered, looking around the table, and all of a sudden everyone was uncomfortable. It could have been any of them. *Any of them could have attacked Jessie.*

"And the other thing is, he didn't have any marks on him. No scratches or bruises…" He let that thought trail away as he didn't like the images it conveyed. "Matt. Charles." He stared at Charlie, and then glanced over at Dee. "We *will* all know the truth in a few days. But until then, we need to take Josh at his word. Innocent until proven guilty. He was really scared," he added. "For Jessie."

Charles glowered at him. Mr. Keating could be an intimidating man. Zach tried to remain confident, but he really just wanted to go see his wife and little kids. He shrank against the older man's glare.

"Why did she put Josh in jail, then?"

Charlie had been pondering this. He knew Jessie better than any of them. He cleared his throat and they all looked at him.

"Because," he said. "She loves Josh enough to hurt him this way. To ruin his career, maybe to destroy his name forever. If this is true, if Josh is clean and there's some other asshole out there, then the rape kit will not point to Josh's DNA. She knows that. She knows they'll let Josh go once they find that out. But in the meantime…someone has a bone to pick with Jessie. And maybe with Josh, too. Remember the after party…she was all over Josh." He grimaced as his gut bit back at him, as he remembered the despondency he'd felt during that hour when his ex-fiancée had snuggled drunkenly up to Josh. "Hell, I was pretty pissed at the two of them last night, too."

Silence descended on the small group as they considered the possibility. *Shit*, they'd all just assumed Josh was the guilty party. Dee was mortified at her behavior, given the thought that Josh was in fact possibly innocent.

Charlie added, "If Josh is clean, then the only reason I can figure for Jessie blaming Josh when she knows for certain we'll all find out soon that he's innocent, is to keep him safe. He's in isolation in the prison, right Zach?"

"Yeah," Zach responded carefully. He liked where this conversation was going. But he—and Josh—were still on thin ice. "They're keeping him away from the rest of the prison population for his own safety. Apparently there are a lot of Jessie Wheeler fans in jail this weekend."

Carlotta spoke quietly from the corner. This was something she never did, spoke out of turn; after all, she was only the hired help. Her voice was small and tentative, but she loved the Keatings. Yes, the missus could be an old crank, but she was generally kind to Carlotta, and Jessie adored her. And Carlotta's boss was obviously in a lot of turmoil over this tragedy.

"Missus Keating," she said. "That might explain why Jessie doesn't want to talk to you right now." She shrugged, her confidence boosted by the fact that they all turned to look at her. They were listening. "She knows you never really accepted Josh, and that you would all blame him without question. That also explains why she only wants Steve. He's Josh's best friend. He's the closest thing she has to the man she loves."

There. She'd said it. Carlotta was a woman who understood love.

Raising herself off the chaise on shaking arms, her eyes misty, Dee sidled drunkenly over to her maid. Carlotta backed off, suddenly afraid she'd overstepped her boundaries, that she'd be slapped and maybe fired.

But instead Dee grabbed her and hugged her fondly. "Carlotta, my angel," she said. "That's why I love having you around. Because you have the wisest—and may I add kindest—heart of anyone I know."

"Jessie has the kindest heart," Carlotta said matter-of-factly, with determination and conviction.

And on that note, before they left Carlotta on the pool deck to clean up the barely eaten hummus and the drinks, the group agreed that this latest development—which may not even be true—must remain a secret between them if they ever hoped to catch the real madman. Jessie's tormentor might go deep underground if he knew they thought Josh was innocent and that they were seeking him instead. Matt would have to pull strings with the cops, too, to ensure the results of the rape kit, if it came out in Josh's favor, remained confidential.

As they climbed into their assorted vehicles and pointed their headlights towards the hospital in the dimming evening light, and Zach headed to Kayla's, they all prayed hope against hope that the dear sweet maid was right, and that their Jessie knew what she was doing, and that she would someday forgive them for their blind stupidity and quickness to judge.

When Zach got to Kayla's, he learned that she had gone to the hospital with Paul. He gathered his wife—his best friend—in his arms and she held him while his body shook.

It had been a helluva day.

Chapter Nineteen

Not surprisingly, by evening a large crowd was gathered in the waiting area of Jessie's ward. The security team had filtered through the names to ensure fans didn't sneak in but even so, when the Keatings returned around eight p.m., it was a full house. Most of the *Drifters* crew was sitting on the floor; two burly grips gave up their seats to the formidable Deirdre and Charles. Everyone had been patted down for weapons. After Zach's earlier visit to La Casa, Matt made the decision that no one was above suspicion.

The Vancouver entertainment biz patriarch and matriarch had tried to get in to see Jessie but she was asleep and, in the interest of breaking down barriers and being social, they chose to sit in the waiting room and chat quietly with Jessie's old friends. Maybe they would find out more about Jessie's relationship with Josh. Certainly they would discern whether the people he considered his friends believed in the possibility that he had—or hadn't—committed this horrific deed. Steve was still in with Jessie. Well, they would talk to him later.

When he had to take a leak so badly he kept jiggling, Steve finally got up from Jessie's side. He and the pony-tailed nurse raised the bar again to ensure Jessie didn't slip off the bed although he doubted that would be possible, given her deeply medicated sleep. He used the private bathroom and then watched Jessie sleep for another minute before forcing himself to turn and walk away.

Meandering from the semi-dark room out into the brightly lit hallway, blinking under the blazing glow of the hospital's white lights, Steve saw a number of people settled here, there and everywhere—a fiercely loyal army of supporters—Charles, Dee, Matt, Priya, Charlie, Jack and Lydia, Jonathon, dancers, and many of their friends from *Drifters*. Kayla and Paul were settled against a wall, sitting slightly apart from the others. Yawning, Steve acknowledged their presence by waving a sleepy hand towards the general group, and then he strolled definitively to the elevator and out the door towards home and Sophie. He needed a little normalcy on this strange day.

Steve was already desperately missing his good friend. When Matt called later, Steve admitted Jessie had told him nothing of consequence.

Little by little, the caring friends overflowing the hallway got up and said their good-byes. The crowd got smaller and Dee took up a second chair, then lay down and placed her head on her husband's lap.

Kayla got up for a stretch and decided she needed a walk. Paul, ever the observer, stayed and eavesdropped on people's conversations. As a lawyer and someone who genuinely had come to like Josh, he was devastated that even those people who worked with Josh for two seasons were condemning him without proof. Mob mentality had taken over. There was no doubt someone had to pay for this crime. But should that person be Josh?

The fluorescent lights were a harsh reminder of where she was as Kayla managed to put one foot in front of the other all the way down the long hall. At the end, near the entrance to an intimate chapel with a mystical stained glass window, she dropped some coins in a vending machine and selected a bag of rippled chips she and Paul could share. Her belly was growling and she remembered that they hadn't eaten. As she turned to wander back up the hall, Kayla marveled at the nurses with their normal careers out of the limelight. Engaged in curious little huddles, blushing nervously around Charlie and the *Drifters* cast, some of the nurses seemed somewhat awed at the unusual company on their ward that day. As much as they may have been curious about, or perhaps even envied, this group of celebrity entertainers, though, the mirror went both ways. *Why do people always think the grass is greener on the other side*, Kayla thought. Look where it got Josh and Jessie. One was in jail and the other was lying broken and damaged in a hospital bed. But then again domestic violence was a part of real life, too, unfortunately. It's just that these two had to share their dirty laundry so publicly with the whole world under another type of harsh lights, like those on television cameras and under the scrutiny of reporters and paparazzi looking for big paychecks.

Kayla stopped outside Jessie's door and, nervously, pulled her sweater down over her fingers, the chip bag rustling as she moved. She glanced over towards Charles and Dee. Good, they were dozing. She looked up at Dan, who was regarding her silently in his role as resident watchman next to a uniformed police officer. She noted that Matt was observing her from the waiting room. Geez, did these guys ever take a break? *No*, she answered herself with a little spasm. Jessie was more than a job to them. She was like a heartbeat everyone else circulated around, including Kayla herself. A magnet. The singer attracted people the way orange-red flames drew curious admirers who liked to watch their stirring splendor and mystery. Only in her case it seemed Jessie, at the center, wasn't immune to the heat. At any rate, she'd certainly been badly burned.

From the doorway, watching her sleeping friend, Josh's sister felt absolutely crushed, as pummeled as Jessie herself in the small bed. Childishly, wonderingly, Kayla observed the maze of IV tubes and blood pressure monitors and then she forced her eyes to look down at the cast on Jessie's arm. Then, the object of her detached observation moved. Startled, Kayla noticed that she herself was also the object of careful surveillance, albeit a sleepy, drugged-up one. Jessie raised her right arm and motioned the blonde dancer inside. Dan stepped warily aside after patting Kayla down again just to be doubly sure she didn't carry any concealed weapons. It was no secret that she was Josh's sister. He had watched her carefully all day. Sure, she was upset and teary-eyed, but then again these were all actors, this group. He wasn't taking any chances.

Kayla stepped hesitantly to the end of Jessie's bed, where the singer could watch her without having to shift her position. The dancer raised her head proudly. She would not allow herself to cry in front of Jessie.

"Kayla," Jessie began, but then Kayla raised her arm and stopped her short.

"It's okay," she said, staring over Jessie's head at the window, so as to avoid having to make eye contact. The tears were not far away. She didn't know how much control she really had after this long day. "I grew up with him. He is definitely capable of losing his temper. Especially after he was fifteen or so…he was always coming home with a black eye. It got to the point where our mom didn't bother bringing him to the ER unless he needed at least twelve stitches."

Jessie exhaled slowly. The pain in her body was excruciating. She was trying to avoid over-using the morphine pump the doctor provided. With the past summer's use of weed and alcohol, her medical staff was cautious as to the amount of morphine she was permitted, and had asked her to use discretion. They were monitoring her closely. She refrained from pumping, although her finger was on the button.

It pained her even more, though, to see her good friend and dancer standing there with big Dan standing guard over her, as if Kayla was capable of hurting her any more than Josh could. She saw a tear sneak out of the corner of Kayla's eye as the girl shifted and finally met Jessie's own tired eyes. *So much pain for so many people. Fucking Deuce the fuck McCall.*

"Honey," Jessie said, and she reached her right hand out to Kayla, who paused but then moved closer to Jessie and accepted her touch. She felt Jessie squeeze softly. "This will all be over soon. I promise you."

Kayla threw up her hands, forgetting that she had opened the bag of chips during the walk up the hall. A few flew out and landed on the floor. She would accidentally squish them later when she left, and the nurse would wonder what on earth had been spilled in this girl's room.

"*What* will be over soon, Jess? Josh's career? His life? He's already had death threats against him. People want to kill him. Hell, I think *I* want to kill him!" She put a thumb and forefinger up to the corners of her eyes and pushed hard. Anything to keep her emotions under control.

"No, look, Kayla. I won't let anything happen to him. Matt and Charles will watch him, I swear."

As that sank in, Kayla looked down at Jessie incredulously. Suspiciously. "And why, pray tell, would you want him protected, Jessie? Aren't you angry? Look what he's done to you!"

Fighting the pain and the urge to sleep, but wanting to put Kayla's mind at ease because Kayla was Josh's sister and she loved him as much as Jessie did, Jessie spoke as firmly as she could manage. "It's not what you think, Kayla. It's not. You'll see. Just give it some time, okay?"

Flustered, Kayla paused before she nodded. She cocked her head. "Is that somehow supposed to make me feel better?"

But Jessie's eyes were closed. Kayla pulled her friend's hand up and kissed the bruised knuckles, then gently laid her arm back down on the sheets. She turned to go, and a chip crackled underneath her foot. From the bed she heard her name, and she twisted around again.

"Kayla? Go see him. Please?"

The chip bag dropped to Kayla's side. "I don't know, Jessie."

"Please?" The voice was tiny and the eyes still closed. "Please."

After a moment, through a pain and drug induced midnight-purple haze, Jessie heard a response. "Okay," Kayla answered, her voice low-pitched and tender.

Jessie depressed the pump and a small allotment of morphine sent her over the edge into the blissful world of sleep.

Dan stepped aside, his big blonde bulk intimidating Kayla so that she side-stepped him as she left the room. His eyes followed her all the way to where she pulled Paul up by the wrist, and haunted the young couple as they walked hand in hand down the hall to the elevator. Kayla felt his stare even as she stepped inside; wow, he was kinda creepy. She shivered, and then the doors slid shut with a whoosh and she and Paul were momentarily free, until they exited a few floors below, and were the unwelcome subjects of a horde of flashes and hollers.

One of Matt's team, a tall serious sable-skinned man with a narrow chiseled chin, attractive high cheekbones, and a black tight fitting leather aviator jacket, escorted them to Paul's Honda CRV, and they slid inside, shaken. As it was occasionally wont to, life had changed in an instant.

Yup. She could kill Josh, all right. He wasn't the brother she thought he was. In fact, Kayla felt she didn't know him at all. She laid her head back against the headrest and let Paul navigate the streets of Vancouver while she tried to sort out the tangled mess in her head and heart.

The frenetic streets of historic Charleston were dusty and hot the next day. The costumed drivers of the Confederate Carriage tours constantly wiped sweat off their brows and wished for cooler October days in which to tell their intriguing exotic tales of a country that had, not so long ago, turned on itself. Their horses plodded over cobblestone streets and through trees dripping with Spanish moss. The tourists who nervously sat underneath the trees eyeing them for wayward snakes were so distracted by the oppressive heat they only heard about half of each interpretive story.

Deuce sat in his office at the bottom of Broad Street above one such horse drawn buggy and marveled that the city allowed the tour companies free rein in the streets. There were so many tours on the go all day long that each driver had to stop in front of a booth just off Anson Street and draw a bingo ball to see which route to take. He guffawed at the obvious discomfort of the passengers in the sweltering heat; then he sat back and sucked on a draught beer while cool air conditioning offered sweet relief. A walk in that over-heated inferno had just about done him in, although it provided the bene-fit of time to think. Deuce wanted to clear his head and coordinate his next move. He was also tired of the constant parade of staff at his door. All day long, there they were, anxious and upset because his businesses were left to their competent (and sometimes incompetent) charge all summer, while he attended to his own devices. They had questions only McCall himself had the answers to. But then again, Deuce was the keeper of many secrets that season. He laughed again, a deep-throated chortle clearly heard by Cindy in the hall outside. She was painting her nails and had to re-do one. Depending on his mood, she could be jumpy when her boss was around, although usu-ally she just chewed her gum and ignored him.

Deuce pondered his good and bad fortune. Stupid Josh, obviously still love-struck, had parked his truck in the lot of Jessie's building the night Deuce wreaked a severe punishment on her. *Score one for Deuce*. Josh was thrown in jail. *Minus one on the scoreboard*. But then again, he'd be out soon. Deuce was certain the medical and law enforcement staff would have used a rape kit on Jessie. Josh would be freed when the results came in unless for some strange reason Jessie would insist she had sex with someone else and then, perhaps, it was Josh that beat her, perhaps as punishment. But he doubted Jessie would go that far in hurting Josh. Deuce knew she had her lover boy thrown in jail because of Deuce's own venomous threats to kill her ex. She wanted Josh safe. *Minus another point. Jessie still loved the boy*. Deuce growled. Normally not cowed by her boss, Cindy shrank in her seat.

Well, no matter. Deuce doubted Jessie would turn *him* in out of fear that he'd do to Josh what he had done to Sandy. He'd get her back. He would be lying in wait for her when she got out of the hospital, maybe give her a few weeks to recover. They would not find Deuce's DNA in any sexual assault registry. Nor would they find a record of his fingerprints. He'd never had to beat and beg a girl before, they were always willing to be with him, in fact some begged him. Arrogantly, he reminded himself that he was wealthy, good looking, a respected Southern businessman whose family once owned a large plantation. He was descended from an aristocratic background, for Heaven's sake. People threw roses for him to walk on. He laughed as he imagined children with baskets of roses smiling and greeting him. He pounded his fist on the desk, rattling pens and pencils and overturning neatly stacked piles of notes, and flipped his chair around again to watch yet another horse and carriage tour make its way through the sweltering streets.

Why oh why can't Jessie see that I am good for her; that other people love and respect me? Why do I see hate and loathing in her eyes when she looks at me? Okay, so there is that little matter of killing her boyfriend after I raped her...

In his twisted mind, Deuce thought he'd done her a favor, that the rape taught Jessie about good sex, that Sandy was an anchor around her throat, a mere child with nothing to offer.

The next two weeks or so would be an exercise in patience. Oh, well, he ought to get these businesses back on track anyways. He had a lot of people coming in the door of the Renegade and now, since Jessie was so badly beaten "by her ex-boyfriend" they were coming in and holding fucking vigils! In Deuce's own fucking bar! They were setting up candles and cover bands were playing her tunes, and people were crying! It was a fucked up world.

Deuce touched the computer mouse, and the monitor in front of him hastened to life. Yes, he'd better get at those accounts. But first...he typed *Jessie Wheeler beaten* into Google. He ought to check on her condition, which he did every hour on the hour. After all, he had stake in the great Jessie Wheeler. She was his property. She was his light.

She was his *life*.

Chapter Twenty

$\mathcal{A}$s expected, the forensics came back negative for Josh's DNA. Jessie did not push the issue. She told the investigating officer she was angry with Josh after leaving him at the after party, and then the next day, well—she was drunk, she was hurt, and he was on her mind. The officer eyed her warily and then followed up with Deuce's theory, that she might still blame Josh for the beating. Perhaps he flew into a blinding white rage after finding her with someone else. She shook her head despondently. *No. Just let him go.*

Charles, Matt and Charlie dropped in for a visit just as Jessie was bitterly pushing some applesauce around with a spoon, contemplating whether it was worth tasting. She didn't have much of an appetite after the officer's visit.

Charlie started by presenting Zach's theory.

Jessie stared him straight in the eye. "Charlie," she said, laying down the spoon with a clink and pushing the applesauce aside. "I was drunk. And lonely. That's all. I flirted with him, but I shouldn't have. It was stupid. Afterwards I was just pissed at myself and angry with Josh for flirting back. If Josh was at my building after the concert, I didn't see him. He didn't touch me. I guess he was on my mind, that's all—I was kind of out of it on Saturday," she said, the sarcasm in her voice as thick as honey on a pantry shelf in winter. "I saw him in the hallway at the arena, I was confused, I was angry, so I guess I blamed him. I suppose it made more sense to my scattered brain at the time than admitting I had no clue who attacked me. Some nebulous shape in the dark…" She drifted off, remorseful.

In short, her version was not necessarily the same one Josh was telling. And she did not admit to throwing him in jail for his own protection.

SUSAN RODGERS

There were the death threats to deal with. Jessie admitted responsibility. That was the only time Charlie saw her eyes flicker with something akin to lying. He knew her well enough to note a subtle change come over her face when she said, "Matt, I screwed up. The least I can do is order some protection for Josh, at least until things settle down."

Frowning, Charlie leaned on the bed rail and tried to meet Jessie's eye but she kept her steady gaze glued to Matt. Watching her closely, Charlie saw that Jessie seemed to suddenly have trouble swallowing, and the fingers of her right hand grabbed the spoon again, clenching it so rigidly the knuckles turned white. She still wasn't telling the truth, as far as he was concerned. But why not?

Charles nodded at Matt's raised eyebrows. Dan and another of Matt's guys would shadow Josh until things cooled down, whether he wanted them around or not.

Eyes narrowing, Charles posed the next question. "So if it wasn't Josh who did this to you, who was it?"

Shrugging, embarrassed, Jessie stared at the sheets as she answered, twisting the top hem around and around a forefinger. "Like I said, some random guy whose face I couldn't see. Look, Charles, I was so drunk when I got home I could barely keep my eyes open. I passed out quickly." She dared an upward glance. The men were quiet, standing around her bed like statues. She continued, filling the silence with half-truths and lies. "He was strong, like an athlete, a football player's body type. Caucasian, I think. I remember him telling me he tricked the concierge somehow, that's how he got up the elevator into the foyer of my place. He was likely some sick fan from the concert."

There was a period of silence in the room as everyone pondered her testimony. There were holes that all three recognized as Jessie covering up for some reason. They weren't pleased.

Josh was released the same day. He was less than impressed with having personal security tailing him wherever he went, but he made it easy for them. He stayed home a lot. The *Drifters* season three shoot wouldn't be starting for a while, and he'd been canned from the Susanne Bier film. He had time on his hands to lie around and feel sorry for himself.

Before he left the safety of the jail, Josh met with a serious Zach, a subdued

208

but relieved Kayla, and the Sawyer clan's lawyer Mitchell Weldon, a grandfa-
therly sort who reminded Josh of a 1970's crime show star. Weldon sported
an older beige suit and comfortable tie-up shoes, a striped tie, thick gray hair
that stood up in unruly patches, a hefty paunch, and a kind, raspy voice. For
Kayla's sake, Paul tagged along to make sure the lawyer was doing his job to
the best of his ability. Just after Josh was informed that he was clear, at least
of the DNA rape test (they would continue to investigate the beating regardless of the fact that Jessie relented and said it wasn't Josh), the actor threw a
radical request into the mix.

"What if...would it maybe draw the real perpetrator out if the world still
thought it was me? Who attacked Jessie?" He was earnest. Josh had been
thinking about this as he tossed and turned on his bed of rocks last night.

Kayla cried out when she realized what Josh's silence would mean for
him. Zach groaned, despite the fact that the meeting at La Casa had already
put this on the table. The elder lawyer raised his eyebrows.

"Why would you want to do that to yourself, son?" Weldon's voice was
like comforting maple syrup on Saturday morning pancakes.

"Josh, there are death threats all over the Internet! You're already public enemy number one! Don't you want to clear your name?" Kayla moaned.

Zach just stared. Here they all thought Josh was some maniacal asshole
that beat up and brutally raped his ex-girlfriend when, in fact, he loved her
enough to further risk his reputation to try to trick some crazed fan into
revealing himself. All this to ensure Jessie's safety. He swallowed. He hated
himself for ever having doubted Josh, and he knew that Josh's friends would
too, once they realized the truth.

With great reluctance, Weldon agreed to talk to the Keating camp about
the possibility of employing such a ruse. Deftly flicking his twenty-year-old
briefcase open, he lifted out some paperwork he needed to finalize in order
to get the release process underway.

Kayla looked sadly at Josh. This was a roller coaster that was about to go
higher and fall faster. She was scared.

Later that day, Charles and Dee sat with Jessie at the hospital. Jessie was
still somewhat cold to Dee, although she did at least speak with her. The couple presented Josh's idea. Jessie closed her eyes.

"Dee," she said. "Why am I not surprised that you think it's a good idea that Josh's reputation stays tarnished?"

Dee took her hand. "We need to catch this guy, Jessie, unless…"

"Unless what, Dee?" Jessie was testing her.

Dee looked down, over at Charles, back at Jessie. "Unless for some reason you're still lying to us."

"In what way?" she spat back.

"Maybe Josh did find you with someone else. Maybe he did throw you around."

Jessie drew her hand away, disgusted. "Why are you always so quick to judge him, Dee? You've never liked Josh—from day one you hated him!"

Charles spoke up from his comfortable position in the big chair occupying the corner of the room. "That's not fair, Jessie. Josh came to you with a shaky background."

"That didn't mean you had to wait for him to erupt. He's not a fucking volcano!"

Dee was close to tears. "You're not seeing this thing from the outside, like we are, Jessie. You're broken and battered, and you're lying to us about it. You're protecting someone who does not deserve to be protected! Someone I'd like to strangle with my own hands for what he did to you!"

Painfully forcing herself higher on the raised bed, Jessie cried, "Yes, Deirdre Keating, I am protecting someone! But I am protecting someone who *does* deserve to be protected!"

She instantly regretted what she said. She had to be careful. Deuce had made very clear threats that horrible night only a few days ago. Jessie wanted to go back to sleep. She wanted everyone to leave her alone. Turning her head back towards the wall she wondered if this nightmare would ever end.

Dee grabbed her hand again. She was losing this battle. She did not want to lose this girl. "Jessie," she begged vehemently. "It is Josh, isn't it, who you're protecting? Please, please, just tell us that much! And if it is him, then I want to know why! Why can't you admit it? Why won't you ever talk to me?!"

Desperate to be alone because it was easier to keep her convoluted thoughts straight in her own head as opposed to trying to sort out Dee's, Jessie looked back over at her manager. She understood that the older woman thought of her as her daughter. She felt very much like Dee was her mother, as well. And that Charles was her father. But there were limits to what you could—or should—share with the people you thought of as your parents. There were limits as to how much hurt and pain you felt they could bear at your expense.

"Dee," she said forcefully. "I've got this under control, okay? You and Charles, you just get Matt to watch Josh so that every step he takes is monitored, so they always know where he is, at least for a few weeks. Otherwise you leave Josh the fuck alone, and you get Janet to tell the world it was Josh who hurt me, and that he has a court date, and you let him take the heat for something he didn't do and," her eyes narrowed, "why do I think you'll enjoy that?" She closed her eyes. "Leave me alone. I want to sleep." Jessie was suddenly very tired.

Frustrated at the girl's reticence, Dee wanted to say more but Charles eased himself out of the chair and clasped her hand. He led her out of the room past the handsome dark-skinned security guy whose name Jessie had discovered was Ulysses, and then he drove Dee to her favorite French restaurant and ordered her a bottle of wine to help cushion the sting of rejection.

Steve came in to see Jessie later, climbing on the bed beside her without asking. They didn't speak but there were certain truths in their eyes that begged for the omission of words that night—the night Josh was set free from a physical prison yet held hostage in a psychological one; the night Steve could not find the courage to go see the friend the world openly blamed for hurting one of their most beloved singer-songwriters; a girl whose music and lyrics had the power to elevate even the most downcast soul to a much higher, otherworldly plane.

They lay there in the dark and although he knew it was twisted, because Jessie was his friend, Steve found himself longing to make love to this girl, to erase the terrible wrong that had been done to her, to make her body right again. Delicately, he kissed her. She saw it coming so she let herself kiss him back, and that kiss from this man who had once been the closest thing to Josh—yet was now miles away—became the one light in her life during those dark days.

They lay there holding each other in such a tender way that when Zach dropped by later, he felt his heart sink for his baby brother, because he got tired of watching one soul hurt as much as Josh had been hurt in this life-time for no other reason than that the stars seemed aligned against him.

The word martyr crossed his mind as he thought of Josh, and he was angry with Jessie Wheeler that night. Little did he know that Stephen, to her, *was* Josh. He was the closest she could come to her man and, at that point, she was taking what the stars had to give.

Chapter Twenty-one

$\mathscr{A}$t was a week before Jessie was released from hospital. At the end of her care and supervision at St. Paul's, she was finally given the all clear from the very real risk of internal injuries such as potential kidney failure. Deuce's boots were hard and his temper out of control. The doctors reminded her she was lucky. That she barely escaped serious—potentially fatal—injury. A sarcastic laugh was their patient's immediate reaction. *Lucky? Me?* Jessie thought she survived because Deuce was so angry and blind drunk that he was off balance and lacked the power to really nail her good. She wondered if it was also because, as warped as it seemed, the Southerner loved Jessie and didn't want to kill her. She now understood that, for him, life would be unbearable without her in it. And that was what gave her all the power— the power to protect Josh. For, to her, life would be unbearable without Josh in it, regardless of the distance she had to keep him at for now.

Stephen hung out with Jessie a lot at the hospital and then, after her release, at the downtown condo. He could tell it was starting to wear on Sophie's nerves, partly because of the time he was physically away, and then because his mind was usually somewhere else when he and Sophie were in the same space. But he didn't have the energy to draw himself back to her. What had happened to Jessie left him damaged and shaken. As far as he and the rest of the world knew, Josh was still responsible. His best friend had committed this heinous assault. The only place Steve wanted to be was by Jessie's side, where he could keep an eye on her as if somehow it would erase the hurts his friend had caused.

Around two weeks after the assault, in the second week of September,

Jessie was supposed to sing at a house party in honor of Jonathon's birthday. The party was being held at his home not far down the beach from Josh's place. Everyone from *Drifters* was invited, cast and crew, as well as a myriad of business associates and friends. Dee dropped over to Jessie's condo a few days before. Over a glass of sparkling apple cider on the outdoor balcony, she casually dropped the fact that no one still expected Jessie to sing. She wasn't surprised when Jessie regarded her expectantly.

"I haven't forgotten about the party, Dee. I want to do it."

Dee sized her up. Jessie had changed over these last few weeks. She had evolved from happy-go-lucky to scared and unapproachable in June, to an alcoholic workaholic all summer, to the girl before Dee now—an angry Jessie. There was a fire in her eyes that hadn't been there all summer. The timid, frightened girl seemed somehow to have found some deeply buried pot of courage throughout this latest ordeal. She rarely, if ever, smiled, and she never talked about what happened to her. She kept Dee on topics of safe conversation, such as confirming her schedule for the fall and winter, although she seemed only half-heartedly interested. Generally when Dee dropped by, Jessie's mind was somewhere else. She was very unhappy, and would sit with her arms wrapped around her belly staring out at the Vancouver horizon, absent-mindedly watching massive cargo ships navigate their way to English Bay and on down Burrard Inlet, and listening to buzzing sea planes take off and land on the Inlet's watery runway. But then, wherever her mind would take her (Dee could only guess), a fire would light in her eyes, even if only temporarily. Charles told Dee he thought that was a good sign. It had been more than a few months since they'd seen any of Jessie's sparks.

Jessie spoke again. "Can you call Christian and ask him to come over on Saturday? I have a new song I'd like to work out with him. We can try it out at the party."

Relief washed over Dee. Her distant girl was still interested in singing. That was a good thing too, wasn't it? She nodded. "Sure. I'll see what he's up to Saturday. What's the best time for you?"

As they discussed a plan for the day, Dee found her own mind wandering. She was a super organizer and a multi-tasker. She told herself not to forget to ask Matt to tell his staff to leave the condo door open whenever any male visitor was in Jessie's place, whether it be Christian or Steve or Carter or any of her *Drifters* friends. That was another sad part of all of this. Since the attack, Dee didn't trust any men around Jessie. In her heart she still thought Josh was the culprit, that maybe he found Jessie with someone else that night, someone whose name Jessie wanted kept out of the papers, logically, since it could have been a married man or a celebrity or whomever, although Matt told them he had dropped Jessie off himself and that she was alone.

Jesus, Dee didn't even trust Matt. Maybe it was he who Jessie had sex with that night, she caught herself thinking at times. He was the last of their group to be seen with her after the concert. But then again, she reasoned, the doctors told them Jessie's sex that night was indeed non-consensual, and that the resulting tears and injuries were severe. Dee could not imagine Matt or anyone in Jessie's circle of male friends and co-workers hurting her that way. She would have still blamed Josh for the rape, though, had he not been officially cleared. There were others who did still blame him, regardless. Dee felt a little bad about that, but only a little. There were limits as to how far her tired brain and heart wanted to go to forgive Josh, until she knew the entire truth.

On Saturday, Steve scooped up his wallet and keys and informed Sophie he was going out. He couldn't look her in the eye. They'd had a nasty fight the other night after his return from visiting Jessie. Now the petite blonde stared miserably at him with remorse in her eyes, remorse that their relationship hadn't weathered this storm any better than HMS Bounty survived Hurricane Sandy. When Steve returned, it would be to an empty house. No girl could share her man with Jessie Wheeler. There was no coming back from loving Jessie Wheeler.

Steve found Jessie at the grand piano practicing the new song in preparation for her practice with Christian later that day. When she saw Steve at her door, though, she stopped playing and closed the lid. She looked up at him, and he felt her expression soften although she didn't smile. She had a faraway look in her eyes and wore the artist's mantle of creativity and expression, the one that, like the thin veil of All Hallow's Eve, was a perhaps penetrable barrier between this world and the next, a portent of brilliance perchance to come.

Pushing back the piano bench, Jessie lifted her healing body from her musical escape and met him halfway across the room. Smiling, Steve folded Jessie into his arms. She let him, returning the favor by placing her own arms around his waist and holding on tightly. She sighed. They stayed that way for a while, both grateful for the sanctuary each provided from the nasty reality neither wanted to think about, and then he kissed the top of her head and asked if she'd eaten. She hadn't. Steve made his way over to the fridge and, after a quizzical pause, started pulling out baby spinach, red and green peppers, a Spanish onion, a little bag of slivered almonds, and some leftover mandarin oranges in a small see-through container. He eyed the oranges suspiciously, holding them up at arm's length, peering through the sides of the receptacle.

Jessie plopped down on a stool by the kitchen island. "They're fine, I just opened them yesterday."

As he spread the ingredients out on the countertop and started opening and closing cupboard doors in search of a salad bowl, Jessie pointed her finger. "That one. Can I help?"

He retrieved a bowl and grabbed a knife out of a wooden block on the counter. He started with the onion while Jessie opened the spinach and clutched a handful to place in the bowl. She looked up at him a few times and, finally, paused with her hand in the air while she took in his shoulder length blonde hair, his laughing eyes, his ever-present grin. He caught her staring at him, but he mistook it for something it wasn't. He didn't know she was trying to memorize his features, that she was already feeling the impending loss of him and of them, of all of them, in fact.

They ate side by side while he regaled her with tales of Maggie, Sue-Lyn and Carter. He was careful to avoid any mention of Josh but, finally, when she couldn't stand it any longer, she brought up the name guaranteed to send confused signals to Steve's mind.

"Do you think Josh will be coming to the party tomorrow?"

Steve almost choked on his baby spinach. "I'm guessing he won't, Jessie." He looked intently at her. "He'd be crazy to show up there. It'd be like putting a chicken in with a pack of wolves."

Jessie thought for a second. She'd already told Charles to please make sure Josh would be there. She insisted Matt ensure he was well protected, although she knew it would have to be Josh's own thick skin that would have to keep the ignorant from pummeling him into the ground with their insensitive barbs and remarks. She only asked Steve as a test—a test to see how hard he would be on Josh. To gauge the level of undisguised disgust towards his old friend.

"Stephen," she said slowly. "Don't be too hard on him, okay?"

He frowned at her, incredulous.

"He's still the Josh you knew. Just…some things have gotten out of hand, out of control."

"I'll say." He set down his fork with a small twang. "Either you're the most forgiving person I know on this planet or perhaps even in this universe, or you're keeping something from me, Jessie."

Her expression was deadpan, a look she did not have to reach for in her bag of acting tricks. It was the way she actually felt—devoid of emotion, of energy. She shrugged. "It's just—Steve, he's still Josh."

"Not in my book he isn't." She could tell by his even tone that Steve was getting upset. But then, how could she expect him to understand? Maybe Steve should be let in on the small circle of people to whom she'd told a half-truth, whether any of them truly believed her or not. Josh would need his friends around him in the coming months. But there was a danger in letting too many people know. Secrets had a way of getting out. And so far, Deuce had not shown any signs of coming back into Jessie's life just yet. They all just needed more time. The trap was set and waiting, or so they thought. Little did they know that Jessie had her own plan.

In response, Jessie just nodded and faced her salad bowl. She forked up some spinach and mandarins and forced them into her mouth. She really wasn't very hungry but she knew she ought to eat something, both to please Steve who could report back to Dee that she ate, and to fuel her brain for this song she would finish writing later that day with Christian.

When the last sliver of almond was consumed, Steve gathered the dishes and washed while she dried. He took the dishtowel from her afterwards and wiped his hands on it. Then he reached out and touched the side of her cheek with the backs of his fingers. She closed her eyes and laid a hand gently over his. She swallowed.

He bent down and kissed her softly on the lips, and they stood that way for a while and held each other and just kissed. She cherished being so close to this man, who tasted of the honeyed mandarins he had prepared for her, even though Jessie selfishly knew she was with Steve for the wrong reasons. Love was all fucked up these days—love with romantic partners, love with family, love with crazed stalkers (on the receiving end, that is), love with ex-fiancés whom of course you still adored, and now this—love with a best, best friend. And it was that, indeed; it was love she was feeling for Steve, the real hard kind that hurt the worst because there were hidden truths in it, or lies, maybe, if you wanted to venture out on a limb and call Jessie's real feelings that. For whatever name you had in mind for what Jessie's heart knew when it came to Steve, it didn't matter, for no matter how society and the universe might disapprove, it was still a true and certain love that was being shared between them. It just happened to be the hurting, painful kind. But then, in Jessie's experience, so were they all.

She ached to go lie down with him on her big bed but since that awful night with Deuce, her bedroom was tainted. Besides, Josh had slept there many times. Jessie spent her nights there, usually not sleeping much, but instead hugging the pillow where Josh had laid his head, and rocking back and forth while she cried.

Now, she took Steve's hand and laid it on her breast, and then she pulled him towards the guest room, which wasn't lost on him—her choice of room—but he misunderstood that too, as easily as he had the faraway looks on her face earlier, at the piano and then over the salad bowl. They laid down together and held and kissed and touched, but that was as far as things got that day and that was okay, because it was beautiful again—this new kind of love with a friend that was going too far.

Jessie Wheeler was not a perfect soul, as much as the world had made her out to be. She was angry beyond reason about many things, these days mostly about who she had become—a rock star, a singer-songwriter, an Oscar winning actor. She first felt her life careening out of control the day of her twelfth birthday, the day her father died. She'd thought the universe was balancing her out again, after the hell of loving Josh while being engaged to Charlie. She had been with a man she loved beyond reason, her career was moving along well, and she and Dee were giving back in so many ways, not the least by opening women's shelters. But after having to let Josh go in exchange for his safety, at the mercy of a misguided man who thought he deeply loved her, Jessie had come to realize something. She hated who she had become—a woman who could not have what she wanted most because of the fame and success she had achieved. A woman who lived at the mercy of a deluded, deranged stalker.

She also realized one thing. She, as Deuce told her, was indeed in control. Maybe not fully, but partially. Enough to end this thing.

And so, as she knew an ending was upon her, she threw away her conscience and pushed the petite, pretty Sophie far from her mind for at least a little while. She loved every second of being with Stephen, and she was grateful to him for loving her that day, the day before the universe and her path in it would take another sharp turn the way a good script writer changes the beat of a film. She cherished her time with him, and it felt good to be touched for reciprocal, consensual love again. Yeah, she was selfish, Jessie Wheeler was. She was not perfect. She had a dark side. She told herself that day and the others before and beyond it that she no longer cared who she hurt. She was dead inside, and she took what she needed in order to keep herself alive.

Without having intercourse, Steve gave Jessie an exquisite orgasm. His fingers were experienced and delightful. She held him in turn, and then they slept in each other's arms until Christian's knock at the door awoke them. She called out to her accompanist that she'd be out in a second, and then she tenderly kissed her friend and told him to go home to Sophie. That was the worst of it, for him, that he couldn't stay with Jessie, that he would have to tell Sophie he had always loved Jessie. He didn't think he cared about hurting Josh. After all, the two had been apart for more than three months now, since *Drifters* wrapped. But on some intuitive level, deep down, Steve knew he'd be hurting him too.

He heard Jessie talking quietly to Christian in the living room, and then she was playing some chords for her pianist. As Christian picked up the appealing melody, Steve fastened the button on his jeans before wandering sleepily out to watch. He leaned against the hall door and listened for a moment as Jessie gazed at him, contemplating his presence in her messed up life. Then she lifted herself up off the bench, took him by the hand, and pulled him into a last intimate embrace. One final sweet, lingering kiss, and she whispered fervently one more time, "Go home to Sophie."

His heart ached and Steve decided that after the party tomorrow he would talk to her about having some kind of commitment between them. Then he would come clean to Sophie, even though he knew she likely already sensed that he and Jessie had become more than just friends. What he was about to find out, though, was that Sophie was one step ahead of him.

"Okay, okay," he murmured adoringly to Jessie. "Going now. Watch me go." He had his jacket, a soft brown blazer, hanging from his fingertips as he sleepily wandered across the room while looking back at her and grinning. She waved lightly, and Jessie felt her breath catch. She wanted to scream out to him not to go, but she had to let him go; they all had to go, *she* had to go.

Jessie's mood instantly sank, and so she threw herself into work mode. Tousled salt and pepper haired Christian made it easy on her. A laidback yoga fanatic, he wore Oxford shirts unbuttoned at the collar and wrists, lived in an overpriced loft in Vancouver's trendy Yaletown district, and knew Jessie well enough to discern that she needed to alleviate her stress through music. Within the hour, the two hardworking musicians had a full version of the new song ready for Jonathon's party.

Outside the door, in the foyer, Ulysses was on security duty. As he listened to the lyrics over and over again, he could feel his heart start to pound. Was this just any song, or was Jessie trying to say something specific to the people at the party? Oh well. What did he know about music? She was just a pop singer, albeit a greatly loved one, and this was just a pop song.

After playing through the piece one last time, Christian, well satisfied with their work, beamed through his Armani glasses at Jessie on the piano bench next to him, leaned an arm on her shoulder and asked her what the song was about.

"What I've learned about love these last few months. Rainbows," she said complacently.

That struck him funny since there were no rainbows mentioned in the song, or anything about color or rainclouds or anything that seemed to him to have any relevance at all when it came to rainbows.

She expanded on the notion of rainbows in her lyrics. "Think of rainbows as representing the different kinds of love. Each bow nests in the other, at least in a child's drawing it does, and if you want to look at it more scientifically, then rainbows maybe meld into each other, each color onto the other. I think one color is romantic love, one is family love, one is the love you have for your friends, that kind of thing. They're all there together, they fit into each other. At the top of the bow each is brighter in intensity, but on the way up they are usually lighter in color, as if they need to build up to the brightest kinds of love, and on the way down they are maybe losing steam, although you can still see them."

She shifted on the bench and hammered out a chord as she pondered her thoughts. Caressing the ivory keys, almost forgetting that she was talking to another human being, she said, "There is one kind of love that still belongs in the rainbow, although it's a dark, dark color, and that's the kind that is only one-sided. It can be just as intense as the others, so it's as brutal and unforgiving and painful and all those things for both the person who doesn't want to accept that love, and to the beholder. It's every bit as real as all the rest of the loves in the bow."

She plunked out a few more soft notes of her new melody and spoke so softly that Christian had to lean in to hear her. "It made it more bearable to be with bad love once I realized it was still love. I also realized that once it was reversed and I was the one painfully in love, whether it be for romantic love or family love or friend love or even future love—like having my own family, children—that I could understand the agony of the person from what I call the darkest color of the rainbow. Because I felt the same pain. I *feel* the same pain. Still."

She looked up at him intently. Christian seemed like a safe place right now. The countdown was on, and it was unlikely her accompanist was close enough to anyone to rat out any thoughts he might discern as dangerous or foreboding. Besides, he was an artist like Jessie. He would understand abstract thoughts.

"Christian," she said. "The other thing about rainbows is that they don't last. They are a sign, but they go away. They are sacrificed for the greater good, for sunny skies and happy days. They fade away into the sky..."

She had underestimated Christian. Sudden fear crossed his gentle face. He spoke carefully in response. "Rainbows are also a promise, Jessie. They are a covenant given by God. His way of saying He will not flood the world again."

"Yes, once given never forgotten, I understand that. His promise will always be there in spirit, floating on the wind. And the rainbows will be remembered. But they come and go, don't they? Some brighter than others, depending on the storm that preceded them."

Christian paused, serious now. He jumped up, sidled over to the coffee table with a frown thrown back over his shoulder at Jessie, and opened her MacBook. A minute later he lifted it, rested it on his forearm, faced her, and read, "A rainbow is an optical and meteorological phenomenon caused by reflection of light in water droplets in the Earth's atmosphere, Jessie."

"Yes," she said, swinging her legs around to the side of the piano bench so that she faced him as well. "It's that, too." And she remembered her father's prisms in the grass the day he died.

She looked earnestly up at Christian, begging him to understand. Inside she thought, *and oh rainbows are so much more.*

She went to sleep that night under her comforting cherry blossom duvet and dreamed of promises, of covenants made and broken by lovers and loves of all the different kinds. She hoped Deuce would be breaking the last one he'd made to her, the one where he swore he would kill Josh once and for all. But she was tired of the fear and the worry and she longed for tomorrow, but dreaded it just as equally.

As she woke with the first rays of a pink dawn, Jessie thought hard about the covenant she recently made unto herself. She knew it was one she absolutely had to keep, even though she also understood that it would tear her apart.

Chapter Twenty-two

*S*unday dawned bright and clear. On this perfect sunny September Vancouver day, the Fraser Valley was alight with promise, its populace expectant, optimistic, hopeful. Jessie joined Charles and Dee for church, and was happy when Charlie slid into the pew beside her, taking her hand and holding it for the entire service, occasionally whispering little jokes, trying to make her laugh but not quite succeeding. She glanced down at his fingers, intertwined with hers, and then she brought the fingers of her broken wrist over and ran them over his knuckles. *One more boy I must memorize*, she thought, at the same time he was thinking *maybe this is my chance to win her back.*

The four of them ordered hearty brunch entrees at Jethro's, causing quite a stir for the gossip rags as patrons indiscreetly filmed cell phone videos and uploaded them to YouTube before their omelets and gourmet pancakes even arrived. But Jessie no longer cared. As far as she was concerned, this crazy roller-coaster life as she'd come to know it would end today.

She asked Charlie to take her home to prepare for Jonathon's party. In the bathroom, she discreetly sent a text to Arnie. She had been down to see him earlier in the week on the pretense that she was simply visiting her old Downtown Eastside friends. Matt, with his high tech surveillance equipment, picked up the text and took a screen shot to send to Charles, but neither thought anything out of the ordinary. It read *happy Sunday off to a birthday party now.*

In the past she'd occasionally sent texts to old pals on the Eastside. Now, she needed all the friends she could gather around her, and it was not unusual for Charles and Matt to consider that she'd regressed to older friends from another time in her life, people who she would think of as safe. Still, Matt was tracking all of those texts and making notes of those friendships as well. The person who hurt Jessie was still out there.

Arnie texted back *have fun c u later.*

What Matt didn't know was that this was a signal, a sign, a secret code. If he was remotely aware of that, Matt would have driven to Arnie's and demanded the older man speak of what he and Jessie had discussed the last time they met. But instead, Matt set any queries aside for later and, in his own vehicle, followed Jessie and Charlie in the 911 as they drove to Jonathon's party in the house by the beach.

After checking in at the party, Charlie pulled gently on Jessie's good arm. He wanted her to himself for just a little while longer. She slipped off her sandals and he removed his canvas Vans, and they strolled slowly arm in arm down the beach. Jessie had to quell the butterflies in her belly. She was already mourning the loss of her friends and, regardless of the way she and Charlie had ended things romantically, she now counted him as someone she cared deeply about, in fact perhaps even more than when they were a couple. She understood now that some people were just not meant to be romantically intertwined, although their intimacies were every bit as significant.

They reached a pair of Algonquin deck chairs a few houses down from Jonathon and Giselle's large home. Obviously placed in the center of the beach to capitalize on ethereal ocean sunsets, they hoped the owners wouldn't mind a few stragglers seeking some time alone in their cozy down home comfort.

"How are you doing with all this, Jessie?" Charlie asked once they were settled. She seemed at peace sitting there next to him, peering out from under long dark eyelashes at lightly rolling whitecaps on the ocean, her curls gently buffeted by the breeze. He leaned forward, his elbows on his knees over the beige linen pants he rolled up at the cuffs, his white linen button-up shirt also rolled just above the wrists.

Jessie, exquisite but pale in a mid-thigh length sea-blue silk sundress that emphasized her ice-pearl eyes, a delicate crocheted beige shawl resting on her shoulders, smiled quietly up at him. She was so distant throughout church and lunch that he almost melted when she actually met his gaze.

"I'm okay," she said. And that was all.

He frowned. Why did he get the feeling that she had found some kind of surreal amity after the chaos of the summer? She was definitely different. He found himself thinking about a cousin who committed suicide in his late teens. The boy was very calm and relaxed after a time of relative chaos. Charlie remembered his aunts and uncles talking about him at the time. They said that suicidal people who made the ultimate decision—to end their lives—often found a sense of peace just before they did the deed because their torment was coming to a definite and irreversible end. He felt his heart quicken. Jessie had been through hell, apparently since June, if her behavior that summer was any indication. She'd distanced herself from everyone it seemed, except maybe Steve. They would have to keep an eye on her.

"Jess," he said, taking her good hand and holding it between his. "Will you tell me the truth about what's been happening to you?" There was something in the air that day that accompanied her quietude. For some reason, Charlie felt compelled to try to draw the truth out of Jessie. Maybe talking about it would make things better. Maybe that was the reason for the shift in the air around her—she was growing, ready to start healing.

Still, she took him aback when she whispered *yes.*

She looked over at some kids playing in the waves at the ocean's edge fifty feet away. They reminded her of another time, of innocence and apple trees and sand buckets and a beloved daddy, on Cavendish Beach in Prince Edward Island. Her mood mellowed even more and her shoulders relaxed slightly.

Inconspicuously, noticing that she had disappeared into some kind of reverie and aching to know what she was thinking, Charlie took a chance and pulled his iPhone out of his pants pocket. He glanced down and selected 'utilities' and then 'voice memos'. He hit the red record button just before she looked back, then he set the phone down on the seat next to him. He hoped it would pick up her voice. He prayed she would open up to him.

She had a demand for him. "You have to promise you will believe me, Charlie."

He paused, searched her liquid eyes.

"If you swear to tell me the truth, then I will, Jess." He glanced down at a shell lying peacefully in the sand between his bare toes, marveled at its simple existence, and wondered how many other lives to whom it had borne witness. Peering back up at Jessie, he prefaced his humble interrogation. "You've told some of us that Josh is innocent. I think you should know that some of the group does not believe you."

"The group being…?"

"Obviously Charles and Dee. Jonathon, and I think Giselle was there—at La Casa the day Zach told us Josh swore he didn't lay a finger on you. So obviously Zach. Maybe Hilary, then. Oh, Carlotta the maid was there. Matt, of course. I think that's it."

"Kayla?"

"Maybe Kayla. She went to the jail with Zach the day they released Josh."

"Okay. What about you, Charlie? What do you believe?"

"I was…hoping you would tell me what to believe, Jess."

"I want to know what you think *now*."

He exhaled slowly, and looked back down at the non-committal shell, wishing it would tell him what to say. "Then you'll tell me? The truth?"

"If you promise to believe me."

He straightened, and then raised his hand in a Boy Scout salute. "I will. Scout's Honor."

"So?"

"Okay. So…" He shrugged, and forced himself to relax a little. "I think that Josh did *not* hurt you. But I don't know for sure. I think you picked somebody up at the after party and arranged to meet him at your place—gave him a keycard. But he saw you with Josh at the party and got upset."

Their eyes met and it was at that moment Jessie realized she'd hurt Charlie too. *Why oh why is my presence on this planet so hurtful to so many people?* Her eyes revealed her sorrow. He recognized that she understood, and he nodded slightly before looking away for a second.

"You're close."

He glanced back. "You need to fill in the blanks."

"Ask me." He barely heard her. Charlie felt her reticence to offer the answers. He would have to question Jessie one query at a time.

"Wasn't Josh who beat you up, was it?" He said it firmly, with determination, as if he could believe it if he said it loudly and if her response was positive. Also, he wanted the iPhone to clearly pick up Jessie's response. He had others to convince.

"No."

"Not at all?"

"No."

"Why did you blame him? You know he went to jail. People want his head on a platter."

"To protect him. To keep him safe."

Charlie agonized over that response.

"From whom?" His voice was shaking. His conjecture at the Keating home that day was right on the mark.

She shook her head. "I can't tell you that."

"From the person who hurt you after the concert?"

"Yes."

"He wants to hurt Josh, too?"

She hesitated but didn't waver from his intense stare. Jessie was afraid that if she looked away she would lose her nerve. But she needed *someone* to know. "Yes. Now he does. Because of the concert and the after party…he made some real threats."

Now he does? Charlie felt sick. "Jess. Has this person harmed you before?"

She paused. "Yes." She looked down and buried her pink toes in the sand.

Charlie almost couldn't continue. It was a moment before he could pull himself together. He pinched his bottom lip painfully between his thumb and forefinger.

"How long has he been hurting you?" He stared out at the ocean, angry and sad. Overcome.

Quietly, he glanced backwards at her and narrowed his eyes, willing her to speak.

"Since June. Since *Drifters* wrapped."

Charlie heaved himself out of the low beach chair and paced in a circle, then exhaled deeply again. Eventually he found the wherewithal to sit down.

"Why are you telling me now?"

"Because it has to end."

"Why are you hiding Josh's innocence from the world?"

"To protect him. To keep him safe."

One last thought popped into Charlie's head.

"Does Josh know who's been hurting you?"

She shook her head. "No. He can't win against this guy. Nobody can."

"Is that why you never told anybody? He threatened you and you knew you couldn't win?"

She tilted her head sideways in that cute way of hers, her way of wordlessly acquiescing, and his heart leapt. Jessie gazed wretchedly at Charlie and implored him to understand so she wouldn't have to say it, and then *bam!* Like he'd been hit with a lightning bolt, suddenly most of the missing pieces fell into place.

"Jesus, Jess," he whispered.

And she knew he suddenly understood that it was Josh who had been at risk all along, that all of her actions that summer were motivated by the need to keep Josh safe. But she wasn't going to cry. It was all over now. Everything was over. Charlie would do the right thing—he would protect Josh. Charlie would take care of that for her because Charlie *loved* her.

One thing remained.

"Tell me who it is, Jess. Was it that second rate actor you were with last spring? Forester? This started after that, right?"

"No," she said, feeling her throat finally start to close up as tears threatened. "It started before. He gave me two weeks to end things with Josh. He said he wouldn't hurt him if I let him go. And I can't tell you who. He's extremely dangerous, Charlie. I think he's left the city now, at least for a little while. And as long as he, Josh and I choose to let the world believe Josh did this," she raised the wrist in its cast, "Josh is safe. I think," she added in a way that told him she wasn't really sure about that. "As long as he thinks the world believes Josh did this, then he has no reason to harm him because… because the world will punish Josh enough. All of you are already punishing him for something he didn't do."

Charlie winced.

"This *man* likes to hurt people and then watch them suffer. It's what he does. It's what he enjoys. He needs to be in control."

Charlie dropped his head in his hands and stared again at the shell. He wished he could crawl inside.

"You should have come to us for help. Any of us." A seed of anger was planted in Charlie then that would burn and grow for the rest of his life. They could have helped her. But no. She loved Josh too much to risk his life. Enough to set him free and to suffer for him. To sacrifice herself for him.

"Jessie. How much of this does Josh know?"

She shook her head. The tears slowly started to spill over. He touched one with a finger and it melded into his skin.

"None of it?" he asked, astounded.

"No. He would have tried to go after this guy. And he would not have won. He can't know, Charlie."

"Ah," Charlie groaned in frustration, not sure he could keep that big a secret. "And you won't tell me who it is. But I gather it is someone who is not from Vancouver. Jess. How can we catch and *destroy* this guy," he reached down and grabbed the harmless shell and crushed it on the arm of the deck chair, "if we don't know who he is?"

"It's better just to let him be, Charlie. I have a feeling he'll stay underground from now on. He won't go after Josh as long as everyone else is hurting him. As long as everyone believes Josh did this."

"That's a heavy burden to lay on Josh, Jessie. And for you to carry."

"It's better than being dead, Charlie," she said softly. He did not realize that she was only talking about Josh. She didn't care about being dead. She already felt dead.

"Let us try, Jess. Let us at least *try* to nail this guy."

She stared at him. "It's over, Charlie. Let it rest."

After a while he put an arm around her. "You can't let Steve and Maggie and Kayla go on believing that Josh did this to you. It's killing them."

"Then tell them the truth. But please, Charlie, just them. No one else."

"People are going to believe what they want to anyway, Jessie."

"They'll believe you," she said. "In their hearts they know he's innocent anyway."

Even after that terrible summer, Jessie still believed in the goodness of the human heart in the people she'd let into her own. Charlie was incredulous.

"Okay, little girl," he said after a while. "We better get back to the party."

It was only later that he realized she'd asked *him* to tell her *Drifters* friends the truth. Why couldn't she tell them herself?

As they approached the house they saw Josh standing outside on the deck, somber, hands shoved deep in his pants pockets. Not far away were Dan and Ulysses, keeping an eye on him. Matt and another security team member had tailed Jessie and Charlie, but were keeping a respectable distance behind them. Steve was with Maggie and Carter over at the outdoor bar. He had an eagle eye out for Jessie although he was in mid-conversation with Giselle, their hostess.

Josh was leaning against the wall of the house but he straightened as Jessie and Charlie drew near. He looked questioningly up at the couple and then took a few tentative steps forward, but Dan reached out and roughly grabbed his arm. Frustrated, Josh tried to throw him off.

"Jessie," he pleaded. "Just let me talk to you for a second. Please?" Then, to Dan, "Lay off, man!"

Dan retorted sharply, "You're not even supposed to be here, dude. You're court ordered to stay away from her."

Groaning because the last thing he really wanted to do was defend Josh, the man Jessie loved enough to let go, Charlie took the high road and jumped in.

"Dan, it was Jessie who asked that he be here. He's well guarded. Let him be for a sec. He's not going to do anything here." He could sense that Jessie, who had tensed beside him, needed a moment with Josh. She sure as hell deserved it, and so did Josh, for that matter. And Charlie would do anything for Jessie. He stepped aside to give them their privacy.

Jessie tiptoed closer to Josh as the entire realm of partygoers watched, spellbound, in awe of Jessie's courage to face the guy who they all thought beat the shit out of her. Maybe she'd spit on him...

He looked down at her, his searching eyes unable to hide any of his agonizingly mixed-up feelings. He eyed the cast, the bruised fingers, the healing yellow patches on her slender legs. Wordlessly, Jessie watched confusion and anger flutter underneath Josh's valiant attempt at control. Then, to the utter amazement of the curious onlookers, she drew him close and held him tight. His breath coming in gasps, he squeezed her back.

"Jessie," he whispered into her ear. "Why?" And then, "Who?"

She willed herself not to cry. She was an actor, dammit, a good one. One of the best.

Charlie looked away.

"I have to go," she said, pulling away, shaking her head and willing him to understand that this was not the time to talk. Her expression was no longer guarded. Her pink lips, flushed cheeks and the worry in her blue eyes all revealed that she was clearly pained.

He nodded, despite a desperate need to know everything. Josh was ready to go to battle for her, to end Jessie's solitary torment. But for now he thought she meant she had to go sing for Jonathon, for their—for her—friends. They would have time to talk again later, about the whys and the whos.

With her good hand, Jessie reached out and tucked the favorite piece of chestnut hair behind his ear, attempting to smile sincerely despite her angst for the first time in months. "So cute," she said forlornly, teasing him the way she used to. She rested her palm on Josh's cheek for a moment and he soaked up the warmth of it, of the way she was so calmly beholding him now with that little inner light he missed so desperately.

Watching with raised eyebrows, the other party guests felt sorry for Jessie. Such a sweet girl—but obviously not very smart, they thought. Why would she want anything to do with this guy who beat her up? Love was messed up sometimes. People were always going back to bad situations, for love, supposedly.

Josh's mouth curled up in a tiny smile and his breathing evened out.

Jessie looked deeply inside his soul. "Thank you," she murmured slowly, each word pronounced with extra care and weight, and he knew she meant for understanding something about the way this all had to go down; for bearing the weight of it all.

"I'm going to understand all of this one day. Won't I, Jessie?" His voice was low and dusky.

"Yeah," she breathed, in an opposite higher-pitched singsong voice. She ran a finger down his shirt, over the buttons, and then pressed her hand flat against his belly, memorizing the look and feel of him. He placed a strong hand over hers, willing her to meet his gaze just one more time.

As if she heard his voice once more inside her head, she looked up and smiled. "Yeah," she added more affirmatively. Then, in a serious tone, "Josh, you need to know that if you ever need anything, Jonathon will be there for you. Okay?"

He frowned. Sure, he and Jonathon had bonded over *Drifters* but now, with such dark accusations floating around...Josh taking the dive...he shook his head. "Not too likely anyone will be around for me for a while."

"Jonathon will," she said with certainty. "Trust me."

As he pondered the strangeness of that statement, and wondered when and how this torment would end, hurried hollow footsteps echoed on the flagstone walk. Dee was on her way over to them, almost tripping in her teetering Manolo Blahniks. Charles was right behind her.

"Matt! Dan! You asses!"

Jessie stepped back from Josh. As she swiveled coolly around towards the others, she felt her fingers slip from his grasp. She closed her eyes, and it was Charlie's gentle hold on her broken wrist that kept her standing.

Downcast, Josh lamented their parting fingers as she glided off to sing, an amorphous impervious fog in the sea-blue dress. Then Dan put a heavy hand on his shoulder, and he turned away.

Charlie led Jessie into the house via the back sliding doors on the deck. Jonathon's place was a modern multi-layered home not unlike Josh's, just a few miles down the beach. Designed by the same architect, the contemporary homes both featured pools on a lower level and small garages in the driveways, revealing that Josh's biological father and his son had much in common. Steve let his part in the conversation with Giselle lapse as Jessie walked by without acknowledging him. She was off somewhere distant again in her mind; he knew her well enough to recognize that. But it bothered him that she insisted Josh attend this party; it unnerved him that she hugged Josh, and it threw him completely that she didn't even bother to wave hello as she walked by less than six feet from where he stood. His intuition kicked in. Something was amiss this day.

Inside, Christian greeted Jessie warmly as Charlie attempted to calm down Dee. Matt and Charles raised their eyebrows at each other. To them, it made sense that Jessie was not afraid of Josh, if in fact both he and she were telling the truth. Dee still could not fully accept that. It was too hard on her head to imagine that someone they could not identify might be the maniac who'd hurt her girl. At least by blaming Josh she had somewhere to lash out.

The party was not marred by any further outbursts. It was a wonderful afternoon filled with jokes and friends and laughter, a pristine perfect day for Jessie to partake of from the perimeter, just watching it all go down. Steve made his way to her side as the cake was being cut, and although Sophie was quietly present with Maggie and Sue-Lyn, it was clear she and Steve were not together. Jessie was unconcerned with Steve's attention. He was affectionate, touching her fingers on occasion, whispering intimately to her when he could get away with it, but she was largely distant, only responding with the occasional subdued remark. She was there to watch, to observe, to sing.

When the time came, Jessie mounted the two steps to the small stage that the carpenters from *Drifters* had built for Jonathon's party. Jessie wasn't the only performer, but she was the last. By the time she stood at the microphone ready to sing, everyone had quieted and found seats or were standing by the walls. Jessie knew exactly where Josh was—once inside the expansive room, he didn't move from his place at the far left corner all day. Nobody spoke to him except Charlie, and Jessie found herself once again gratefully in Charlie's debt.

She sang a song for Jonathon first—a sweet, positive, upbeat tune about the passage of time that she wrote a year ago. The next song was *Promises*. It was the piece she and the carefree Christian fine-tuned just the day before, accompanied by a darkening Vancouver skyline and its associated burgeoning red and green nightlights outside her floor-to-ceiling window.

Christian's light melodic touch on the ivory keys of Jonathon's grand piano swept everyone away before Jessie sang her first note. Delicately touching the microphone as she started to sing, sharing her thoughts through lyrics, Jessie gained courage and found a spot on the far wall with which to commune. It was as if there was a spirit afloat there—perhaps a guardian angel to call the song home.

Entranced by how this girl could wrench the most beautiful music out of the worst kinds of pain, the guests at Jonathon's birthday party were awed.

There she was, a vision in sea-pearl blue, her hair in large curls caressing her shoulders, a cast on her wrist and faded bruises on her legs and arms telegraphing the ordeal she'd suffered a few weeks earlier; and she was singing loud and clear, as if her life depended on getting this song out for all to hear.

She sang of love the way she described it to Christian, a rainbow version of the different kinds of love, as if she were sending a message out to each— to Charles and Dee, to her friends, to Charlie, to Stephen. She did not sing to Deuce. The dark bow that she had indicated to Christian meant unreciprocated and dangerous love—remained buried within.

As Jessie started the final verses, her eyes shifted to the far left corner. There Josh stood, lost and confused—yet determined, courageous, and it was clear to everyone present that Jessie Wheeler also had a message for Josh Sawyer. As one, the crowd was immobilized as they wondered what she possibly had to say to him. Jessie and Josh's gazes did not waver from one another; his lips parted and he straightened as he, too, became aware that she had something to say directly to him.

> *Seek my heart in memories*
> *when we were lost in dust.*
> *My promise to you will always be,*
> *let tears fall if you must.*
>
> *Take the world as it wants to come,*
> *be true and real and wise,*
> *and let my heart remember you*
> *as if I'm by your side.*
>
> *You loved me once, I love you now,*
> *life got in the way.*
> *Don't let this good thing ever end,*
> *let tears fall if they may.*
>
> *A promise said, a promise true,*
> *A promise loud and clear.*

One thing remains forever real
*I hold you forever, **dear.***
I hold you forever dear.
I hold you-forever-dear.

The last three lines she sang with the emphasis on different words. The ballad was recorded on many cell phones in the room as the late afternoon sun silhouetted Jessie and Christian, a team who together had introduced many provocative numinous songs to the world. Everyone present was silent as Christian played the final notes, and then the room erupted as one, albeit confused as to what she had been trying to say to Josh. Was Jessie that real and amazing and true that she could so easily forgive him for what he'd done?

Stephen stood frozen. He watched her from the start as her husky voice hung above the guests; he could feel the blood drain from his body as he finally clued in to what she was saying to Josh. She still loved him, and always would, despite life; despite a clouded, complicated past few months. Steve felt his heart twist just as Sophie realized once and for all that her man could not win Jessie, and from one glass window to another that day echoed tender, sorrowful, acute reverberations of loss and hope.

Quietly observant, Josh had watched Steve with Jessie that afternoon. He leaned lower and lower against the wall as the tender touches his old friend let subtly play upon Jessie became evidence of deep affection and perhaps shared intimacies. It upset him to watch them together that way, and he and Sophie momentarily gazed upon each other in a wary but mutual sense of pity, until Sophie was afraid someone would see and she steered her eyes elsewhere. Charlie stepped over to Sophie then and tried to distract her with jokes and laughter, but the leaving was too real in her mind, the wound too raw. It wasn't until she heard and watched Jessie sing to Josh that she finally let herself breathe and relax; it wasn't until then that she knew her adversary, even if a real threat, would never love Sophie's man the way she herself did.

Josh slipped away after the song, gliding quietly into the shadows with Dan and Ulysses by his side, his heart weeping, yet in some ways jubilant. *She still loves me.* Like the night Jessie was so badly beaten, when she nuzzled his neck and asked him to run away with her and he sat there outside her building loving and missing her, believing there was still hope for them; he felt the same way now, buoyed, uplifted, ecstatic. Hadn't she said that to him once? *There is always hope, Josh. I will love you always and forever, no matter what happens.* And now, *I hold you forever dear.*

He would ponder in the months to come how odd it was that on that fateful horrific night, sitting on the concrete wall outside her building, as he remembered and cherished and missed and hoped for her the most—praying and wishing on the stars—that just above him, below the very same stars, the girl he loved was being so brutally kicked, beaten, raped. What were the stars trying to say? That there must be balance in love, in promises? A yin and a yang? A white and a black, a good and an evil? The more love you feel for each other, the more severe your punishment?

It didn't matter what the universe was thinking. It didn't matter what the people in Jonathon's house were thinking. He didn't care what the media thought, or what the world believed. As far as Josh was concerned, he had the knowledge he needed to carry on, to breathe in and out, to put one foot in front of the other each day. That was a start. The next step would be to find her true assailant, and to see that justice was served. If the universe wanted balance, he was a willing participant, even if it meant carrying out the worst crime in order to savor the most serene, beautiful and true love.

He slid into the back seat of Dan's Mercedes, and Josh Sawyer's protectors swifted him away.

～～～

Jessie accepted heartfelt congratulations from everyone with grace and charm. But she was done. She was *done*. She had nothing left to give these people, those who she once considered friends, parents, lovers. Her tank was empty. Carefully scrutinizing Jessie as she made the rounds, Charlie knew she was tapped out. Steve sat mournfully at a stool in the kitchen and helped himself to the spiked cranberry punch.

After sliding a piece of folded paper out of the small purse she had stashed in a cupboard upon her arrival at Jonathon's house, Jessie approached Maggie. Charlie observed as the women hugged each other affectionately, and he saw a quizzical glint pass over Maggie's kind eyes as Jessie handed her *Drifters* co-star the paper. As Maggie tucked it into her own purse for later, Charlie watched Jessie turn and hug Dee tightly before swinging around to make her way down the hall, probably to the ladies' room. *Ah*, he figured. *She likely needs some time alone.*

Behind her, he noticed Matt discreetly following about ten feet away. The other security guy stayed at the entrance to the hall. Nobody went outside—Matt didn't see the need. As long as someone eyeballed Jessie at all times, he felt she was adequately covered. Oddly though, Jessie turned back once. Curious, Charlie watched as she gazed distantly, detached, around the large room. Walking slowly backwards, her eyes rested on people here and there. Charles, Dee, Maggie, Sue-Lyn, Carter…Jonathon…Stephen, whom she had to crane her neck to see…when she met Charlie's eyes, she held his gaze for a bit, slowing, before turning back around and continuing down the hall. *Huh*, Charlie thought, wrinkling his brow.

In the bathroom, Jessie pulled open the single window and silently slipped through, her exquisite sundress tangling up around her waist. *Whatever.* She heard it rip on a coarse brick but she could have cared less. No more expensive silk sundresses for her. No more expectations. No more *friends* and *family* who were false when it came down to a tough, tough choice. No more performing monkey. *And no more Josh.*

She ran to the hedge and slipped through, her sandals in one hand. There at the corner waited the trustworthy kind-hearted Arnie, an angel from another time, with a friend's old silver Pontiac Sunfire. Arnie leaned over from the driver's seat and shoved open the passenger door of the two-door car. It was heavy, awkward, but she grasped it and then on her friend's instructions pulled down a button behind the front seat to allow herself room to slide into the back seat. Arnie yanked the door shut, and they were off well before anyone suspected Jessie of taking a little too long in the ladies' room.

They all felt she was likely emotional. Everyone was so excited over the second song that they were all talking amongst themselves. In the end it was Charlie who felt his interior thermometer rising. It was Charlie who finally vaulted forward past the first security guy and then past Matt. It was Charlie who had to bear the burden of discovering that their beloved Jessie was gone.

She hadn't even bothered to lock the door.

Chapter Twenty-three

"On the average, every day in Vancouver ten people go missing. That's like, what, 3,650 people a year?" Sue-Lyn told the group gathered around a large table on the patio at ROAM on a misty, rainy day. She was astonished. They all were. She looked back at her smartphone where she'd pulled up a website about missing people in the Fraser Valley. "Oh. But they usually find most of them. There are only about two that still have not been accounted for. Some are murdered," she swallowed, and then continued, "some kill themselves," her voice got smaller, "some have accidents hiking or out in the woods or mountains, and," her voice rose hopefully, "some move away and create new identities for themselves." She set the phone down triumphantly next to her cinnamon sprinkled mocha.

Around her, the assembled group was quiet. Maggie looked at her impassively, fingering her latte mug but not drinking. Stephen was subdued, Carter angry, Sue-Lyn forlorn and red-eyed. Christian, sipping his chai latte with reluctance and an air of despondency, also joined Jessie's friends on this strange day. There had been no sign of Jessie since she went missing three days earlier. And there was no communication whatsoever.

From his peripheral vision, Charlie spied an Audi pulling up to the curb beyond the coffee house. It was now or never.

"All right, guys," he started. "Listen closely. We are here to figure this thing out, and I've got something to say. I am asking all of you to be patient, to have open minds about this." He added, "To trust Jessie."

He opened his laptop and double-clicked a file.

And suddenly it was like she was speaking to them from beyond their reality, from the unknown, mysterious cosmos into which she disappeared.

Their conversation on the beach—his voice and Jessie's—was being played for all of them to hear. So enraptured were they at hearing her voice and the clues and truths held up as an offering that no one noticed Josh, flanked by Matt and Dan, walking quietly up behind them. The latecomers stood back and watched and listened, but they'd all heard this before. Charlie had played the file for them at Josh's place a day earlier.

Several intakes of breath were heard as the voices continued, disembodied and surreal. The little group on the ROAM patio on that foggy day was at once shocked, angry, disgusted with themselves, and genuinely relieved. Their friend was innocent, if one could find it in his or herself to believe this conversation. But *they* were not innocent. They had been judgmental, vicious, unkind. But they had also been lied to. Victimized.

Collectively they sat in silence, hoping for more even after Charlie closed the laptop. They saw his eyes move beyond them, and the friends turned too, almost in slow motion. There stood Josh, impassive through their new knowing like a ghost of a war battled without prejudice and malice, but one that had to be fought just the same. It was as if they were suddenly being born again, those old friends of his, as if they'd come through the birth canal anew, wrinkled and red and now alight with a new hope. They were utterly and unmistakably relieved and chastened.

Sue-Lyn, who was on the verge of tears for the last three days anyway, jumped up and threw her arms around Josh, uncertain as to what his response would be but willing to go the distance anyway. He didn't falter. He held her close and breathed her in. Josh was having a hard enough time of it. He needed the solace of friends, regardless of what state of repair the rekindled friendships would require. Maggie was next, openly sobbing, her sorrow as fresh as the soft day. Carter slapped Josh on the back and gave him a man hug, obviously openly pleased. Stephen stood and took Josh's hand and gave his arm a squeeze. He wasn't up for hugs just yet. Christian shook Josh's hand with vigor and a quiet understanding.

Amidst the girls' tears, Charlie gestured for Josh to sit. They had some things to figure out. First, he explained the situation—that Josh was willing to publicly go along with the charade that he harmed Jessie in order to try to suss out the real tormentor and also, as per Jessie's wishes, to try to keep him safe. Suddenly the friends had a new worry—no longer was Josh the hunter. He had, in a few short minutes, become the hunted.

The question at hand then became who was the hunter and what were his tools of the trade? They now knew why Jessie had been so terrified to involve her friends, Matt, the police…but they were angry about it. They wanted—needed—to know more. And they were angry with her, for not trusting their confidences.

The group sat around the table and, despite the tension and strangeness of having Josh with them, he made it easy on them. He wasn't sure he would have treated any of them any differently, given the circumstances. The only real downside to the day involved Steve's hesitancy to openly welcome Josh. He was still hurt over Jessie's public display of affection for Josh at Jon's party, over the realization that she loved him and only him. He was curt and dismissive of Josh, the rigidity in his posture like a tiger about to strike. Josh was careful around him that afternoon. He didn't want to cause any more problems than the large one they were already dealing with.

Charlie brought them to the task at hand by asking for contributions of odd behavior, or clues Jessie may have inadvertently provided. Josh texted Kayla and asked her to join them. She showed up twenty minutes later with Paul, amazed and relieved to see her brother at the table with his friends. Kayla was a key, as far as Charlie was concerned, as she had spent a great deal of time with Jessie over the summer, travelling on and off with her dance company for various shows.

"All I can really tell you is that Jessie was really distant all summer. She was sad, she drank a lot, she smoked weed, even." Kayla sipped on a vanilla latte as she talked, her left hand resting comfortably on Paul's thigh.

"In her room? Or did she go out? With others or alone?" Charlie demanded.

Matt was on duty with Jessie for the summer shows as well. He jumped in. "Jessie is a free spirit, you all know that. She often went out alone. She refused security more times than she accepted it. We tried tailing her a few times but she learned a long time ago how to evade us. She got pretty angry when she discovered we were following her, too. It pissed me off, but technically she's my boss, right?"

Kayla shrugged. "She stayed in her room a lot too, though. I remember thinking she was acting like a hermit. Sometimes she came to dinner with us, but she was usually jumpy, never relaxed. We'd talk about it, the other dancers and me, because she'd changed so much…but we attributed it to the shows, you know—late nights, not always able to eat right, and then of course," she glanced at Josh, "the breakup with Josh. She was miserable. All summer. Not mean, just sad and quiet."

"She never talked to anyone? Became friends with anyone? Or dated anyone?" Maggie asked. She wasn't the type to beat around the bush. And she was filled with sorrow that Jessie suffered alone all summer.

Kayla shook her head. "No. Not that I could see. She sat with Dee most of the time when we were travelling or at meals. If anyone knows anything, it's likely Dee."

"All right," Charlie said. "We know this all started in early June anyway. Before *Drifters* wrapped. Let's talk about those last few weeks."

They discussed life on set and didn't find anything unusual there. Every grip and electric was thoroughly talked about; everybody was a suspect. But no crew had changed, everyone was well liked…there wasn't anyone on set they felt could possibly be someone Jessie was afraid of, who'd hurt her so badly. It wasn't lost on Josh or anyone at the table that they'd all readily believed he was capable of doing what they thought others could not.

Stephen spoke up. "We spent a lot of time together on weekends, too."

Charlie looked pained for a moment. So much time lost with Jessie… time that the others had shared with her. "Doing what?"

"Having coffee here…" Sue-Lyn offered.

Carter added, "Going out to eat."

"Cooking meals at someone's place, going to shows, theater, ballet… hanging out at your club," Maggie reminded him. "Whatever was on the go. We went out a lot, all of us."

Charlie looked at Josh. "What about the two of you? Doesn't sound like you spent much time alone together."

Josh shifted uncomfortably in his chair. "Not nearly enough."

They were silent.

Then, from Stephen, "We did a lot of Motocross in the spring. Just taking the bikes out to Agassiz, taking some lessons, riding around, practicing. Most of the time the whole gang went. Depended on Jessie's rehearsal schedules with the dance company and that, but she was often with us."

Matt interjected again. "Did she ever talk to anyone unusual? Anyone who struck you as strange or who didn't fit in wherever you were? Or maybe someone who did fit in but who seemed to always show up?"

They all stopped and thought for a moment. Nobody came to mind. They were just a happy-go-lucky group, an ensemble cast from a hit television drama that enjoyed each other's company. They hadn't really ever taken the time to study their surroundings, or the people in them, in any great detail.

"What about pictures? Photographs? Are any of you into taking snap-shots?"

Everyone looked at Maggie. She was the one who always insisted on snap-ping pics. She held up her iPhone. "Just on this little thing," she said. "Not like they're professional shots or anything."

"Go back to the time when you think all of this started, when this stalker may have first approached Jessie. She said it started around the time *Drifters* wrapped. Where might you have been and what kind of shots might you have taken?"

Maggie nodded and started thumbing through her pictures.

Charlie looked at Josh. "Think about when her behavior changed. You said it was sudden. What clues did she give you? What might she have said that was unusual, that might have conveyed what was suddenly happening?"

Thoughtfully, Josh leaned forward, rested his elbows on his thighs and clasped his hands, and then looked at Steve. His friend's eyes were on fire. He was hurt. But, thanks mostly to Jonathon's recent birthday party, the boys both thought the same thing at the same time.

Steve stared intently at Josh. "She spoke through songs."

Nodding in affirmation, Josh sat back, still looking at his friend. *So, Steve got the message loud and clear too, on Sunday.* He was glad someone else under-stood, even if it resulted in an estranged friendship. He tensed at the way Steve was glowering at him. Josh was getting tired of being the recipient of angry stares.

"What the fuck, Steve?" he said quietly, one arm now on the back of his chair.

Steve shrugged, but his glare didn't waver from Josh's eyes. "You haven't been with her in months."

"What the hell's that supposed to mean?"

"It means whatever you want it to mean. To me it means Jessie's single and available."

Josh's eyebrows rose quizzically but at the risk of keeping some semblance of peace he didn't say what immediately came to mind, which was *and you were single and available?* He thought of the sweet Sophie, and his heart cracked a little further.

"Lonely, you mean," he finally said, dismissing the urge to crack a knuckle on Steve's forehead.

"Hell, yeah! Someone's been terrorizing her. She almost died. I guess lonely could enter into it." A loud screech echoed across the patio stones as Steve stood and towered above the rest, his hands fisted at his sides. Slowly, Josh rose as well, as did Carter and Matt. Charlie sat back, amused.

"Look, Steve, I don't know what the hell happened between you and Jessie, and to tell you the truth I don't think I want to know. But if you were there for her, then I'm grateful. If you fell for her, then that sucks because she's got some kind of wall built up between her and the rest of the world these days. She's not letting anybody in. Least of all me, so you can stop looking at me like you want to tear my eyes out."

Steve's voice got deathly quiet. "For all I know she's still running from you, you bastard."

Josh put his hands up in front of him, palms facing Steve, and shook his head. "Look, just chill, man. Let's just sit down and sort this thing out. Jessie could be in a lot of trouble, and us fighting over her isn't going to help her. And I don't want to fight you, Steve. Not today."

Maggie reached up and took Steve's hand. She was witness to how close he and Jessie became during the singer's hospitalization. She was pissed at Jessie for pulling him in, in fact. They all liked Sophie and were sorry to see that relationship end for someone whose behavior was as erratic and tenuous as Jessie's, lately. Maggie gestured for Steve to sit but he had one last thing to say.

He pointed a finger at Josh. "I get that you loved her, man. That you still do."

Josh felt tears prick the corners of his eyes. Well, that wasn't news. He held his ground.

"But just so you know, when she comes back to us you're going to have a fight on your hands. Because you don't have the only all access pass to Jessie Wheeler, Sawyer. Yeah, so she sang you a fucking song. What the hell is that? She's a singer, a poet. She sings about love. She's sorry that you got messed up in this thing. I get that. But just so you know, you're not the only one who has loved her all this time. Maybe I loved her too."

With a lightning quick movement, he shoved Josh backwards so hard that Jessie's ex almost lost his balance and fell. Matt grabbed Josh and steadied him.

Josh was cool in his response. He knew Jessie's power better than anyone. He waited a few moments while he composed his thoughts. Then he said evenly, "Name one man at this table who hasn't loved her, Steve."

Steve took this in, and then looked down at Charlie. He'd almost forgotten he was there. Subdued by that thought, Charlie stood and took Stephen's hand, pumping it profusely. "Welcome to the club, mate."

Carter raised his hand. "Okay, so she's pretty hot, but she's not everyone's cup of tea, Sawyer. She's too, y'know, artsy and flighty for me. Too fuckin' deep, man. Artists are cursed."

Christian and Paul looked at each other.

"She's amazing, but not for me either, bro," said Christian, grinning as he thought about what Jessie would think of this weird conversation. "Just a music partner, that's all."

Kayla raised her eyebrows at Paul. He bowed to her and then squeezed her hand. "I'm happy with my girl."

Matt didn't respond, and instead gestured to Josh to sit. He adored Jessie, but not in the way Steve was referring to. But he would jump in front of a truck for her. He figured rightly that all of the men assembled there would do the same.

Soon after, the tension eased when Steve sat, too. But for some unfathomable reason, Josh felt this wouldn't be the end of the discussion.

Matt brought them back to the table. "So, we know she communicates through her songs. What has she written over the summer that's new?"

Everyone looked at Josh. But it was Christian who spoke up.

"Saturday, after we worked out the new song, I asked her what it meant."

He explained it as best he could, trying to remember what Jessie had said. "I can't remember all of the lyrics," he said. "But it sounded to me like a goodbye song."

As they reflected on that, Maggie suddenly remembered the paper Jessie gave her just before she slipped away. It was lyrics from the song currently under discussion. Maggie had thrust it into her purse at the time, vaguely wondering why Jessie made the gesture. It was the first time she was aware of that Jessie ever gave the lyrics to a new song to anyone. She dug in her purse and triumphantly held it up.

"The song," she said. "Lyrics, I mean."

She spread it out on the table and read the words. She raised her eyebrows and looked up at Josh. "There's more," she said. "She's added a quote she says is something of John Lennon's. "Love is a promise, love is a souvenir. Once given, never forgotten, never let it disappear."

When she was done, they pondered the words. Steve tried to stay calm and force his mind on the task at hand, but it was hard. Clearly she loved Josh. Clearly. But he would fight for her. Josh just hung his head, disconsolate. Why couldn't he have been there all along? To love her and to help her through the hell of the past few months? Would they ever be together again? Why send him these cryptic messages and then disappear? Her words, the message of a ghost, only served to drive the dagger in deeper.

It was Sue-Lyn who raised the question about the *lost in dust* part of the lyrics. "Lost in dust? Like…being dead? Ashes to ashes, that sort of thing? Like…the end of a relationship?" She flicked a sideways glance at Josh and mouthed *sorry* before adding, "Or is she talking about dust in the literal sense…?"

Carter fingered a phrase on the paper and then wrapped his arm around Sue-Lyn. "It says memories before that. Memories are in the past, not the future, you dolt." She elbowed him.

"When would we have been lost in dust, then?" Maggie asked. "Or Josh and Jessie. Did you guys take weird spa treatments the rest of us weren't aware of?"

Josh stared hard at her, and then looked suddenly over at Steve, his eyes widening. It only took Steve a second to catch on. He straightened.

At the same time, the boys said, "Agassiz."

"That last time we were there, that's definitely the night the shit started," Josh said. "Remember? At the restaurant. She was in the restroom forever, then she and I left early. I took her home because all of a sudden she wasn't feeling well. I asked her about it more than once, about what the hell happened that day, did she get some weird text or something? But...nothing. She wouldn't talk." He didn't add *and after we made love that night she told me she would love me always and forever, no matter what happened. She held my face in her hands and told me to always remember that.*

"But nothing happened at Agassiz," Steve said, reflecting on the day. "She was fine the whole day, and on the ride back into the city."

"She was fine at the restaurant until just before the food came," Sue-Lyn chimed in.

Carter was staring at Maggie's iPhone. She'd stopped looking at photos and had set it down next to her empty coffee mug. He looked up at Charlie, who was leaning thoughtfully on one elbow as he took in the discussion.

"We were looking at photos then, of Steve and Josh learning the free-style stuff, mostly, and of Sue-Lyn and Maggie horsing around by the bear sign. Remember?"

Maggie's hand shot out. She grabbed the iPhone and scrolled through the pictures from that particular dusty day at the motocross park. "There are lots of the boys on the bikes, a few of us girls messing around, in the stands and stuff...a couple of group shots we got one of the locals to take just before we left. A sweet one of Josh and Jessie holding hands..." She glanced at Steve and then Josh. "Sorry."

As she handed the phone around, everyone shook his or her head. Nothing untoward jumped out at any of them.

"What about these background people?" Charlie asked.

Steve shrugged. "Just locals. They were friendly, for the most part. Jessie wasn't scared of any of them, I don't think."

Matt had the phone now. He scrolled through the pictures slowly, pausing at each to carefully look deeply both inside and outside the frames. What might be on the perimeter of each shot? Who was in each shot? He was careful to look past the main subjects of each. At the group photo, his sharp intake of breath stopped all conversation.

He stared at the worried faces around the table, and then held up the phone with a look of utter consternation.

"Here's one guy who is definitely *not* a local," he said with dismay. He handed the phone to Charlie. "Behind Josh. The guy waving at the photographer."

Maggie spoke up. "Locals were always trying to get in our pics. We thought it was cute."

"This guy was trying to make a point, Maggie," Matt said.

"You recognize him," determined Charlie.

Steve and Josh eyed each other warily. Maybe once and for all Josh's innocence would become accepted fact.

Matt sat back and pulled his own cell phone out of the breast pocket of his blazer. He had to call Charles right away.

"A year ago in June, the day Jessie left for the East Coast, Charles and I took a trip to Charleston to look into the man Jessie used to work for, a guy by the name of Deuce McCall." He nodded at Josh. "She'd asked Josh to get Charles to check into a man in a blue trench coat. It seemed she suspected that this McCall might be that man. The one who dropped Terri off at the crack house the night she died."

A cold chill swept across the patio. Everyone shivered. Paul drew Kayla closer, and Sue-Lyn snuggled into Carter.

He continued. "She told Charles one night when they were recording that nobody could stop McCall, that it was impossible. He'd finally told her we went there, to McCall's restaurant and lounge in Charleston, the Renegade, the one Jessie made famous because she played there as a teen. I checked him out. He was clean, a respected businessman."

Charlie passed the phone around.

Matt went on, "We checked him out again over the summer, and took another look at him after Jessie got hurt. It was like we couldn't let him go. But there was nothing on him. He has alibis up the yin-yang. The guy is squeaky clean."

SUSAN RODGERS

He got up to go call Charles. "But there he is, in living color, a few feet behind Josh, at Agassiz. Showing Jessie how close he can get to him. Waving to the camera, cocky bastard. We've long thought he might have something to do with Jessie's messed up summer. I think we have our stalker."

He walked away, signaling to Dan a few tables away to be extra vigilant, to keep a good eye on the group sharing a table on the café's patio.

"Maybe we'll finally find out what happened in Charleston," Josh said quietly. "Although, for the second time today, let me just add that I'm not sure I want to know."

Kayla reached out and wrapped her big brother's hand in hers. Charlie concentrated on putting the laptop away as the others gathered empty mugs and shoved back their chairs.

It was a subdued group that left Rebel on a Mountain Coffee that day. Yet, finally, *finally*, they had a place to start looking.

Chapter Twenty-four

$\mathcal{T}$wo weeks later, on a morning which broke as misty and grey as the muzzled feelings of the close circle of people Jessie left behind, Josh tensed at the muffled purring engine of a sports car as it drew to a halt nearby. He was working on his Harley in the garage as Dan patiently monitored the immediate environment from his own indigo blue Mercedes at the end of the driveway. Outside, Stephen slipped out of his Audi TT and waved casually to Dan before walking over to the security guy's driver's side window and offering him a take-out drip coffee.

Dan punched a finger on the window control button and fresh cool air breezed in as it opened, reigniting his senses and awakening him from an overwhelming desire to nod off.

"Geez, man, don't you get bored?"

"If you mean do I want this to end, yes, I do," Dan growled, the tedium leaking through his generally calm demeanor. "I'm sure Josh does, too. But it's my job, Steve. It's what I do. I keep people safe."

He was also trying to express confidence. He knew the *Drifters* cast was badly shaken up when Jessie ended up in the hospital. After figuring out just who was the source of Jessie's fear all summer, they were doubly terrified. *Is he working alone? Maybe not, if he has alibis. Is Jessie alive or dead? Will McCall strike at Josh? At us?* No wonder they were scared. They were living on a thin wire stretched tautly across their lives like a guitar string that could snap with the wrong note. Deuce McCall was likely a psychopath. If indeed it was he that was terrorizing Jessie, then he was a man who could not be reasoned with, and that was the worst kind of aggressor.

SUSAN RODGERS

Steve sauntered up the driveway, a second take-out cup in his hand. Inside the garage there was a warm slight orange glow that bled into the driveway. It lent a surreal luminosity to the mist surrounding the building, as if Josh were encased in more than just Dan's protection that day, as if it were the radiance of spirits that entombed him within, daring any foe to step closer, to take to task the supernatural universe and its power to caress and to save. Perhaps Jessie was there, in spirit, among the legions of the immortal ones. They didn't know if she was alive or dead, although there was no evidence of Deuce McCall or any other uninvited guest in the washroom from where she'd silently disappeared that strange Sunday. All they found was a tiny sliver of silk on a brick on the exterior wall of Jonathon's house, a sea-blue reminder that she was once there, and that she drifted away without saying goodbye, except in song.

Calmer today, feeling not so much a foe as a united warrior, Steve pushed open the side door to the garage. The main door was down, an attempt on Josh's part to both keep out the cold mist as well as the stares of the man who watched over him.

Steve held out the hot cup. "Peace offering," he said.

Josh was crouched next to the Harley, wiping its chrome for the seventeenth time in a few days. He needed to be busy. He needed to make things shine again. Upon Steve's entrance into his lonely sanctuary, he stood.

Warily he took the coffee, eyed Steve with suspicion, and then bent over the cup for a tentative sip. "You poison it?"

Steve tried a half-hearted grin. But for all they knew, Jessie had been drugged and hauled away. His attempt at good humor failed him and the grin faded away. "Nah," he retorted. "I need all the friends I can get right now."

Josh took that as a good sign. Steve was referring to him as a friend. He gestured to a nearby lawn chair and, as Steve slumped into the seat, Josh leaned against the sturdy wooden workbench he had constructed a few years earlier.

"What's up? Are you here to fight about Jessie some more?"

Forlorn, Steve leaned his face into his right hand, his elbow resting on the arm of the lawn chair. Around them were the comfortable tools of any man's workspace—hammers and wrenches and screwdrivers and nails, lots

250

of nails, enough to secure any man's coffin closed. Everywhere these days Steve saw death. Not knowing where Jessie had gone, or how she left, was killing him. He wondered how people were supposed to get past the loss of a person when only mystery remained. There was no body to bury. There was no Jessie at all.

Straining, he twisted his neck around and peered behind him at the Honda Motocross bike. It was dirty, dusty. Josh hadn't cleaned it the way he was spit-shining his Harley. Steve turned back and narrowed his eyes at Josh.

"Why aren't you spit shining that bike?"

Josh held the coffee in both hands, to warm his chilled fingers. "You know why."

Steve nodded. "Yeah. I suppose I do." Silently, he gratefully acknowledged that Josh somehow seemed to have accepted the fact that he, too, had feelings for their missing girl. The bike was a reminder of better times. It would remain as is, for it was too painful to endure wiping those memories away just yet.

"Where do you think she is?"

And then Josh understood exactly why Steve showed up in his garage that day. He was there for the same reason Jessie had clung to Steve those last few weeks. He needed to be near the person she loved the most. One stop away from Jessie herself, as Steve, to Jessie, had been one stop removed from Josh. He was humbled.

Steve tried again, but the words were faint, a reflection of his faded state of being. "Do you think she's dead?"

"If you're asking do I think she killed herself, I say no. She wouldn't do that to Charles and Dee. If you're asking do I think someone else, maybe this McCall, killed her, then I also say no. For reasons she's already given us. So no, I don't think she's dead. Besides," he added, playing with the tab on the lid of his cup, "I think I'd know if she were dead."

He looked over at Steve, sitting there all hunched over as if his belly hurt, pale and wan in a faded old beach chair.

Steve dove in a little further. "Do you think she left of her own accord, or do you think McCall has her?"

"I think she said her goodbyes and then she left. Of her own accord."

"You seem pretty certain."

Josh frowned. "I didn't help her leave, Steve. I don't know where she is. I'm not hiding her somewhere. And in that conversation with Charlie on the beach, she said that it had to end. So I think maybe she's hiding from McCall."

"Do you think we'll ever trust each other again? You and me?"

"No. Probably not."

"Where do you think she went? Prince Edward Island?"

"Maybe. Her mother is there, in a seniors' home. I doubt she'd stay there, though. She knows we'd look there first."

"You can't find someone who doesn't want to be found."

Josh paused.

"No." Then, "She took her dad's guitar, Steve. Her old teddy bear. There were large withdrawals from her bank accounts. She planned this. And she would not have gone away with McCall."

"Not of her own volition, she wouldn't have. *You* don't think."

"No."

"So what's to say she didn't go with him just to please him? To get him off your case? Or to try to destroy him herself?"

Pondering this, Josh replied soberly, "I don't have the answers, Steve. I wish I did. But I'm guessing she'll take another week or two, or maybe a month, and then we'll hear from her. She wouldn't just disappear forever, and I think she's already learned, the hard way, that this McCall guy is a damned defiant foe. I can't see her choosing to be near him, not now, anyway. She needs a break from his messed up brain. And as for running away for any length of time, well, there are too many people here who care about her, who she cares about…as I said, she wouldn't do that to Charles and Dee. Besides, she's supposed to be starting on that film in New York. They've already delayed production in the hope she'll be back." He gave the shiny Harley another swipe, as if the action would affirm his thoughts and make them real, set in stone.

"Charles and Dee," Steve muttered, eyeing a greasy hole in the wooden floor. "What about us?" Challenging, he regarded Josh, daring him to dispute his own feelings for Jessie.

Taking the high road, Josh accepted that his friend was as hurt over

Jessie's actions as he himself was. He exhaled and a low whistle escaped through his teeth. Biting his bottom lip, he shifted uncomfortably and tapped a finger against the single light bulb so that it swung back and forth on an eerie sweeping arc.

"Don't go there, man. Jessie's not exactly typical. And she's been through hell. Don't start questioning how she feels about *us*." He emphasized the last word so that Steve could interpret it however he saw fit.

"Look, it just pisses me off that she left the way she did. We can question all we want what her motives were and we can justify that she needs some time, but I can't help but think she could still be in trouble out there, locked up in McCall's basement or something. It's a fucking cruel thing for her to do. And I don't know about you, Josh, but if she took off because she needs a break, as you say, then I'm fucking pissed that she didn't tell somebody. Or leave a note or something."

As he said that, he realized that Jessie had indeed left some kind of note— in her song at Jonathon's party. But it wasn't enough for him. Steve needed more closure than a song that nailed down Jessie's feelings for Josh.

"She said her goodbyes, Steve, and you know it."

Standing and facing his co-star, Steve bristled. "Half-assed goodbyes, you mean."

"Yeah, well, whatever."

"Your cracks are showing, bro."

"What the hell, Steve? What do you want from me? You want me to start throwing things around, to get really angry? Maybe destroy this place so everyone knows how I really feel?" For emphasis, he slammed his fist against a metal can filled with finishing nails, which splattered all over the floor with a startling crash that jarred Dan out of a quiet reverie outside. With a hollow ring, the empty can laid itself to rest against the neglected motocross bike.

"Jesus, Josh," Steve jumped, and then complained feebly. "Was that really necessary?"

"Isn't that what you want? For me to lose my mind over her? Did you ever stop to think that maybe, just maybe, she's not worth the worry?"

After a lengthy pause during which he studied his friend and adversary, Steve responded with, "Huh. As if." He knew damn well that Jessie was worth the worry. And he could see in Josh's hurt, concerned eyes that he was more upset than he was letting on.

Rubbing his forehead, Josh spoke in a pained voice. "Look, Steve. I *am* angry with Jessie. For a lot of things, the least of which is why the hell she wouldn't open up to me when this all started. Or if not to me, then to Matt, or Charles or Dee, or to Charlie, I don't know…" He looked over at Steve, who seemed desperate for any kind of consolation, for anything to ease his troubled mind. "You. She should have talked to you, even. But she didn't. So yeah, I'm pissed at her. So maybe it's good that she went away for a bit, to let *us* cool off. Maybe Matt will find this McCall asshole and hang him by his balls, and then Jessie will come back and we can all go on with our happy little perfect lives. But in the meantime, it's not going to do us any good to dwell on last June, or what happened to Jessie all summer, or what Deuce did to her that put her in the hospital." He grimaced. "We just need to let her go for a while so we can deal with the shit she's left us to pick up. Including our own fucked up feelings about this whole mess."

Steve considered this last tidbit from Josh, and then started towards the door. Once there, he turned and looked back at his old friend.

"I just hope she's okay, man," he said simply. "And that she reaches out to us if things get crazy for her. That she comes back. Soon."

Spent, his emotions tattered, Josh's shoulders slumped. He had nothing left to say. The thought of Jessie never coming back was too great to bear.

With one hand on the garage door, Steve looked back. When he met Josh's grief-stricken eyes, he was crushed. He got past himself enough to remember that his good friend's burden was likely ten times ten thousand times worse than his own.

"See you on set, old man." Steve pushed open the door.

Slowly, Josh raised his coffee cup in salute, and then Steve was gone, lost to the ethereal abyss of mist and spirits.

Later, Josh closed up the garage, popped inside the house for a quick cleanup, and then climbed into the sedan with Dan. They drove to North Van, to the Keatings' pretty yellow house Jessie loved so much.

Carlotta met them at the front door. "Come in," she welcomed them. She leaned forward and gathered Josh in her friendly arms. "You are always welcome here as long as I am the maid," she said. She held him at arm's length. "My family says I have the power of second sight. I know your heart. I know Jessie's heart. I know love when I see it."

He smiled sadly at her. "Carlotta," Josh said. "Just so you know, I know love, too. And I know Jessie loves you dearly."

She moved away with a guffaw and a wave, "pshaw," but she was genuinely moved. No wonder Jessie loved this man. No one else had stopped to consider how much Jessie's disappearance affected Carlotta. No one at all.

Josh made his way into the front room, where Deirdre Keating sat quietly waiting for him. She didn't move with the exception of a wave of one arm offering him a seat on the chaise across from her. She watched him settle uncomfortably on the edge and straighten the blue linen blazer he chose for this visit. Deirdre herself was adorned in a beige Jackie Kennedy sleeveless dress with a cream cashmere sweater, pearls, and beige heels. Ever the sophisticate, Dee had her ankles crossed as good manners decreed, but her mascaraed eyes were strained and grey.

They studied each other carefully.

"Josh, I don't know why Jessie left or where she went, but I have the feeling she'd want me to apologize to you for all the wrongs I've done you."

He exhaled slowly, pondering the right choice of words. He figured Charlie would have no problem with this woman, but—he wasn't Charlie. He struggled.

"Mrs. Keating," he started.

She put up a hand. "Please. Call me Dee."

Josh hesitated. "Dee. You have your reasons for feeling the way you do about me. I get th—um, I understand that. Let's just leave it at that."

"The world is going to be hard on you, Josh Sawyer." With the exception of speaking, the elegant Deirdre didn't move a muscle.

"I know. But eventually they'll forget. Someone will take our place."

"No one will ever take Jessie's place." Her eyes teared as her shoulders sank.

"I know that, too."

"Do you think she will come back?"

He found it interesting that she, like him, refused to consider that their girl might be dead.

"Yes," he said, in a whisper. "I do. The great loves endure. All of the great loves."

She knew he was referring to the last song Jessie sang, the one they all now referred to as her goodbye song. Like Jessie's message to Josh, the verse meant for Charles and Dee was also heard loud and clear.

"We'll be her magnets, Dee. We'll pull her back."

She was struggling to remain composed now, sitting there silhouetted against the window, amorphous in the grey light so that he had to strain to see her eyes.

"You have to let us protect you, Josh. And you have to promise me that you won't go looking for McCall. Because…"

She couldn't finish, but he knew where she was going with that. If something happened to him…then Jessie would have no real reason to come back. Despite Jessie's love for Deirdre and Charles, there was no doubt that Josh was the biggest magnet of all.

He moved forward and grasped her manicured hand between his rough fingers. He was amazed at how small and fragile they looked; somehow Josh figured a woman like Dee would have strong, powerful hands. She was diminished here today. Lost without Jessie.

"Dee," he said. "Jessie has more reasons than just me to come back. And she will, when she's ready. When she's had some time."

Dee smiled through the mist of tears. "Thank you, Josh," she whispered.

Suddenly they were bound, these two strange and unlikely companions. Unexpectedly, they were on the same path in the proverbial yellow wood, trodding on blackened leaves and tiny white pebbles towards a resplendent silver spark beyond the forest's edge, to a place where love in all its wondrous and mighty splendor would reign again.

They shared a cup of chamomile tea with Carlotta, who sat amicably by Josh on the chaise she had long vacuumed and dusted for Deirdre Keating.

And then they parted friends.

Had Jessie been watching from the window, she would have been mighty pleased.

Chapter Twenty-five

$\mathscr{T}$he day after Jonathon's party, they'd leaned on the hood of the borrowed Sunfire before Jessie said goodbye. Arnie pulled out a flask of rum, two of his wife's chipped mugs, and some Coca Cola he picked up at a convenience store in the sanguine tree-lined streets of the Dunbar neighborhood in Vancouver. Grinning at Jessie's nerve, he toasted her.

"To the red headed wonder from P.E.I."

"There's only one red headed wonder from P.E.I., Arnie, and it sure as hell ain't me," she retorted.

He laughed and reached out to touch her shortened red locks. "Looks good on you, girl."

After he scooped her up from Jonathon's party, Arnie drove like a mad man to his small apartment on East Hastings. He escorted Jessie in the back entrance, ensuring they were unseen, although he brought a hoodie to place over her head anyway. Inside, they colored her hair an unnatural bright punk red and then, sworn to secrecy, his gal gave her a short bobbed haircut, which changed Jessie's appearance dramatically.

They drove until the dawn, and before he toasted her Arnie gave Jessie a passport for a redhead named Annie Hayden. She had stashed other items at his apartment earlier that week—cash, Tedsy the teddy bear, her dad's Gibson, some clothing and personal items, and credit and debit cards for a bank account Arnie helped her arrange for Annie Hayden, containing limited funds shuffled over from some of her own accounts. She didn't bring any Jessie Wheeler identification. She would make her way on her own if and when the money ran out, as she had before, in what seemed like another lifetime. She also had the magnificent Tiffany & Co. engagement ring from Josh, secured on a tiny leather thong and placed around her neck, under her clothing.

As a pinkish-orange streak lit the edge of the earth and a new cobalt blue sky created dusky outlines of barns and houses, Arnie and Jessie toasted the end of one life and the beginning of another.

Then the man who promised never to ask questions had his say.

"You don't have to do this, girl."

"Yes. I do."

"Why?" He took a swig of the rum and watched the colorful dawn slowly rise to a lofty height in the sky as he felt himself shrink and become insignificant, despite the grand role he was playing in the universe that day.

She turned to him. "Are you happy, Arnie?"

"Yes. Very much so."

"Why?"

"Because I live with a woman I love, who loves me back. We have shelter, food. Friends. All the things that you have." He turned to look at her.

"All of you are safe." She raised her glass to him. "May you stay that way."

"We are," he said. "As safe as one can be living on the Downtown Eastside, that is. And so could you be, if you'd let me in on what's been going on with you. I have friends in high places."

"It's not just that, Arnie. Life has suddenly become complicated, that's all."

She took a drink.

"Whoever said love was *not* complicated, my dear?" he probed gently.

She stared sadly at the expansive world laid out in front of them. "All of this," she said, "the barns, the houses, the families. That's what I want. A normal life. That's what I've always wanted. I never chose this life I've been living. Somehow it seems to have chosen me."

"Do you think Prince William chose to be born into a family where he will be king some day? Not much freedom of choice there! Do you think Gandhi or, or—Nelson Mandela or Martin Luther King chose the difficult journeys they were on, that they endured?"

He reached out and let his fingers slip through her red hair. "For whatever reason, there seem to be people placed on this earth to help move it along, to help change things."

"Ah, Arnie," she responded, frustrated. "I'm a singer. I'm not a politician or an activist."

"Girl, you just don't get it, do you?"

She glanced sideways at him, her friend, sitting there on an old Sunfire, content as could be with his life of relative poverty and a constant struggle to make ends meet, yet helping the downtrodden—and her—find what they needed for their own survival.

"What don't I get?"

"Your songs move people, Jessie. Even before, when you just played for me and my friends on Hastings, when you slept under the stars in cardboard boxes and never spoke, you had the power to inspire, to give people a glimpse into a world where there is light. Where there is *hope*. You give people the power to find it within themselves to continue on in this tough old world. Don't take that away from us. We need you."

"You're sweet, Arnie," she said, blushing. "But maybe I'm at the point where I've given so much of myself away that I have nothing left to give."

"Then, dear girl, go recharge your batteries for a while. And then come back. Y'hear?"

"I dunno, Arnie. I just don't know."

She thought of Charles and Dee, Carlotta, Jonathon and Giselle, Zach and Hilary, Kayla and Paul...Christian...Matt and his cronies...Sue-Lyn and Carter and Maggie...Charlie and *Stephen*, and *Josh*...

She knew it was cruel to leave them this way. But she also knew that it was the *only* way she would have the courage to go.

Was she going to find Deuce? No. She needed a break from Deuce McCall. She felt certain he would leave Josh alone, if she weren't there as a bargaining piece. For if he killed Josh, she would most certainly never return. What scared her was that a part of her wanted to return to Josh one day. If she did, Deuce would likely reappear. After all, he waited more than ten years to re-enter her life after she left Charleston. He could likely wait another ten—if he had to.

Deuce McCall was a man obsessed. Yet, she reminded herself that she

SUSAN RODGERS

had also come to understand that he was a man in love. And she now knew from first-hand experience that truly loving someone was the most excruciatingly painful experience life had to offer. Parents, friends, lovers…longed-for children yet to be…no matter whom, love was a delicate, fragile thing.

A white butterfly scooted out in front of the car. Its wings glistened pink in the emergent sunshine of the cool fall day. Jessie reached out her hand as it floated by and wondered what life would be like as a butterfly, anonymous and free, floating on the gentle breezes brought forth each day. A tremor of excitement coursed through her veins.

An hour later, Arnie watched her go as she disappeared into a crowd of travelers seeking adventure, reunions with loved ones, business meetings. She turned and waved goodbye and smiled at him, mouthing *thank you*. Jessie touched a bruised finger to her eye, then laid a hand over her heart—the cast hidden under a denim jacket—and then pointed a finger back towards him.

The last he saw of her was the newly bobbed bright red hair swinging from side to side as she carried the Gibson towards a nebulous future. And he thought, *dear sweet girl, you are loved, too.*

And then, with a flick of the short hair she was still getting used to, Jessie Wheeler was gone, as mysterious and free as the butterfly; from within her soul, her unseen wings a soft silver-orange glow.

The End.

Hello!

Like what you read? I hope you are enjoying the Drifters series as much as I am enjoying writing it. I am hopelessly in love with Josh, Jessie, Jacob, and the rest of the gang. If you have a moment, please go to Amazon or Goodreads and leave a rating and/or review. Us Indie authors depend on those for our survival in the eBook world.

Thank you!
Happy reading!

Susan

www.susanrodgersauthor.com

Facebook: search **Susan Rodgers, Writer**

Twitter: **@srbluemountain**

www.bublish.com

email: **fatcat@pei.sympatico.ca**

About the Author

Susan Rodgers' first novel *A Certain Kind of Freedom* was a Finalist in the Writers' Federation of Nova Scotia Atlantic Writing Awards for unpublished manuscripts. Her short story from the novel of the same name, published in two anthologies, has received rave reviews, as have the Drifters novels, Susan's all-time favourite books to write.

Owner/Operator of Bluemountain Entertainment, Susan is a 'Diploma With Honours' graduate of Vancouver Film School. She produces mostly documentary style client films and short dramas with plans to one day shoot a Feature Drama based on the novel Atlantic Blue.

Formerly a Museum Curator, in winter Susan lives with her partner Steve and her striped cat Oliver (Lucy Maud Montgomery once said the only good cat is a striped cat) in Summerside, Prince Edward Island, Canada. In summer, she hides in a small trailer in Darnley, P.E.I., where she writes novels, paddles kayaks, and crafts sandcastles on the beach. She makes frequent trips to Vancouver to visit her son Christopher, where she enjoys life in the hippie city while listening to great music and sipping on good espresso.

Books by Susan Rodgers

Drifters series:
A Song For Josh
Promises
No Greater Love
Riptide
Whispers of Home
And Then There Was Silence
Let the Music Cry
If I Could Sing You Home

Other:
A Certain Kind of Freedom
Seasmoke
Atlantic Blue

Feature Screenplays:
The Story of Jack & Emma
Atlantic Blue
Beautiful Jane
They Were Dreamers (adapted)

Short Stories:
S12
A Certain Kind of Freedom
A Gentle Peace

www.ingramcontent.com/pod-product-compliance
Lightning Source LLC
Chambersburg PA
CBHW021958050726
47498CB00006BA/1744